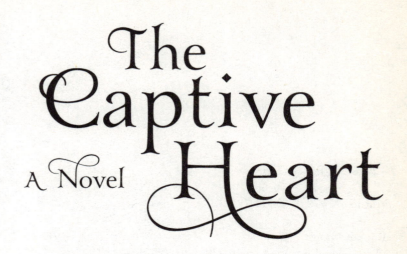

The Captive Heart

A Novel

MICHELLE GRIEP

SHILOH RUN  PRESS

An Imprint of Barbour Publishing, Inc.

© 2016 by Michelle Griep

Print ISBN 978-1-63409-783-3

eBook Editions:
Adobe Digital Edition (.epub) 978-1-63409-785-7
Kindle and MobiPocket Edition (.prc) 978-1-63409-784-0

All scripture quotations are taken from the King James Version of the Bible.

This book is a work of fiction. Names, characters, places, and incidents are either products of the author's imagination or used fictitiously. Any similarity to actual people, organizations, and/or events is purely coincidental.

Cover design: Kirk DouPonce, DogEared Design

Published by Shiloh Run Press, an imprint of Barbour Publishing, Inc., P.O. Box 719, Uhrichsville, Ohio 44683, www.shilohrunpress.com

Our mission is to publish and distribute inspirational products offering exceptional value and biblical encouragement to the masses.

Member of the
Evangelical Christian
Publishers Association

Printed in the United States of America.

Praise for *The Captive Heart*

The Captive Heart is filled with heart-tripping action and romantic tension between a half-Cherokee frontiersman and a proper English governess. Quickly engaging, fast-paced, and set on the American frontier, the novel reminded me of *The Last of the Mohicans* in all the right ways. Well done, Michelle Griep!

—Julie Klassen, bestselling author

Bold and captivatingly beautiful, *The Captive Heart* is a book destined for accolades. Fans of the movies *The Patriot* and *The Last of the Mohicans* have found new characters to love in Samuel and Eleanor. A masterpiece, from first page to last.

—Elizabeth Ludwig, author of *Tide and Tempest*

Reminiscent of the wildness, adventure, and romance of *The Last of the Mohicans*, *The Captive Heart* sizzles on every page. This is Michelle Griep's best book yet and one that played out before my eyes like an epic movie I kept wanting to watch over and over.

—MaryLu Tyndall, author of the award-winning
Legacy of the King's Pirates series

I am adding Michelle Griep to my list of favorite authors!

—Laura Frantz, author of *The Mistress of Tall Acre*

This is my first Michelle Griep novel, but it will not be my last. From the opening scene to the final words, Griep kept me spellbound with her lyrical prose and her masterfully drawn characters. Who can resist a pair of misfits who each think they are unworthy of the other? I promise you'll be thinking about Samuel and Eleanor long after you've turned the last page of *The Captive Heart*!

—Kathleen Y'Barbo, bestselling author of the contemporary Pies,
Books & Jesus Book Club series
and the historical Secret Lives of Will Tucker series

Michelle Griep has managed to combine all my favorite story elements into one gorgeous book—*The Captive Heart* is utterly captivating!

—Roseanna M. White, author of the Ladies of the Manor series

Oh, wow! Not enough praise can be given to Michelle Griep's *The Captive Heart*. This riveting, action-packed adventure set on the American frontier will leave you breathless with its beauty and power. By far, my favorite book of the year.

—Margaret Brownley, author of *Left at the Altar*

Dedication

To the ones who hold my heart captive:
the Savior of my soul,
and the frontiersman who shares my life, Mark.

Chapter 1

London
February 1770

My precious Lord;
My only hope;
My Saviour, how I need You now.

Eleanor Morgan repeated the words, over and over, scrubbing her fingernails more vigorously with each repetition. Prayer was always better than blood. Perhaps if she focused on the simple child's verse she taught her charges, she wouldn't feel like heaving. She bit her lip, trapping a scream behind her teeth. A merciless idea. Better had she cried out at the unfairness of it all, for now blood wasn't merely under her nails. Saltiness warmed the tip of her tongue.

A rap on her chamber door stopped her scrubbing. The nailbrush clattered into the basin, her heart into her stomach. Before she could think, she turned and snatched one of the brass candlesticks off the bureau. Hot wax spilled onto her skin, the pain barely registering. Duke or not, this time she'd do more than scratch the man's face. Lecher. Beast. She raised the makeshift weapon, the flame extinguishing as the door swung open.

A tiny woman in a lace wrap entered. Eleanor choked. The candlestick slipped from her hand and crashed to the floor.

My precious Lord;
My only hope. . .

Duchess Brougham's gaze darted to the rolling candlestick, then back to Eleanor's face. One of her brows lifted.

Eleanor rushed forward and sank to her knees in front of the woman, not caring to grab a dressing gown to cover her shift. Why bother? Humiliation was cloak enough. "Your Grace, I swear I did not encourage your husband's advances. Please, you must believe me. I would never—"

"Rise, Miss Morgan." The lady waited, a single furrow marring her forehead, until Eleanor stood on shaky legs. Was that compassion on her face. . .or resentment?

Duchess Brougham sighed, long and loud, as if she might expel whatever demon anguished her soul.

Eleanor knew she ought say something, but all her words dried up and blew away like the last leaf of autumn.

Slowly, the lady's mouth curved into a fragile smile. "Did you not wonder, Miss Morgan, why we have had four governesses in the space of a year?"

Eleanor grimaced. She would have inquired had not pride muddled her thinking. The position of governess in a duke's household didn't seem nearly as prestigious anymore. La, what a foolish dolt she'd become.

"You'll never aspire to anything higher than a trollop, girl."

The sting of her father's prophecy slapped her with more brutal force than she'd dealt her employer. She lifted fingertips to her own cheek, coaxing out a whispered confession. "I assumed lack on the part of the other women, Your Grace, and for that I am woefully repentant."

Duchess Brougham's eyes glinted with an odd intensity. "The *lack* is in my husband. I had hoped that this time. . .for you see, the children dearly love you. . ." Her voice cracked, and she shook her head. "It is a sorry business, but there is nothing to be done for it. For your sake, Miss Morgan, you should leave. Now. Walk out the door and do not come back."

Leave? The word made as little sense as finding the undressed duke in her bedchamber earlier. Eleanor wrapped her arms around herself, gaining what comfort might be found in the action. If nothing else, perhaps it would hold together her grip on reality. "But it is the middle of the night, Your Grace. Where am I to go? I have no relations, no one to—"

"You do not understand the severity of the duke's anger." Though a head shorter than Eleanor, the lady grew in stature as she lifted her chin. "You have done more than rebuke him. He shall have to account for the scratches on his face at the club tomorrow. The passions grafted onto wounded pride are the most inveterate, and my husband's appearance *is* his pride. At best, the duke will see you never again work in England. At worst. . ."

She didn't finish the sentence. She didn't need to. Just last week, Eleanor had heard the downstairs help gossiping about the fate of young Joe. For naught but a cross look at the duke, the lad now resided in a holding cell at Newgate on a trumped-up charge of thievery.

Eleanor retreated to the side of her bed and sank onto the counterpane, grateful to the mattress for holding her up. All her dreams of becoming London's finest governess had just been yanked from beneath her, the unfairness of it staggering. Fresh tears burned tracks down her cheeks.

"There, there, Miss Morgan." The duchess took a step toward her, then stopped and clasped her hands. Though Eleanor longed for a comforting touch, the woman would approach no closer. She had already breached propriety by coming to Eleanor's chamber.

Drawing in a ragged breath, Eleanor gave in to a moment of self-pity, hating how weak she was in light of the lady's strength and dignity.

"Do not despair so." The duchess's words were quiet. Intimate. As if she were speaking as much to herself as to her governess.

Eleanor looked up, surprised to see the lady's eyes glistening with unshed tears. Indeed, the woman's face was a portrait of misery, and why not? How awful it must be to live with an unfaithful husband.

"Now then." The duchess sniffed, her shoulders straightening with the movement. "I have a cousin in Charles Towne, Mr. William Taggerton. I shall send him a missive, posthaste, recommending you. Lord knows his children could use a proper education in that uncivilized land. Book yourself passage, and I shall have him meet you with the fare once you land. The Colonies are the best I can manage on such short notice."

The Colonies? Eleanor swallowed back a sour taste. The tales she'd heard! The sideshows she'd glimpsed of savages and ruffians and wild animals. This was where she would spend the rest of her days? A shiver charged across her shoulders, leaving uncertainty in its wake. But besides a beggar's cup—or debtor's prison—what choice did she have?

None. For a moment she nearly gave in to opening the cage door to a wild hysteria. But truly, what would that accomplish other than possibly attracting the duke back to this chamber?

Sucking in a breath, she stood. So be it, then. If that were her fate, she'd do her best to not only embrace it but to conquer it. Mayhap across a sea, in a land of foreigners and anonymity, she'd finally be successful at blotting out her father's words. Indeed. She would be a success or die in the trying.

"I thank you for your kindness, but. . ." She paused and angled her head for a clear view of the lady's face. "Why? Why do this for me?"

The duchess smiled. "You are a rare one, Miss Morgan. I have appreciated your candor, spoken with such grace and humility. An exceptional trait in a servant. You, I shall remember."

Blinking, Eleanor fought another round of tears. Had anyone ever been so kind? "Thank you, Your Grace. Neither shall I forget you."

"Pack up your things and ready yourself to leave. I will return shortly with a note of reference."

The duchess departed before Eleanor could think how to reply. In truth, though, what more was there to say? She relit the candle and tucked her two spare gowns into her traveling bag. By the time the lady returned, Eleanor had dressed haphazardly, slipped into her mantle, and tied her hat ribbon tightly beneath her chin.

"Here is the note, and also some money." The duchess stood in the doorway, holding out her hand. Creased and folded, a single banknote rested atop her palm along with a small parchment. "I grant 'tis not a large amount, but it should at least keep you fed on your journey."

Eleanor hesitated. She wasn't owed any wages for several more months. It didn't seem right, taking money from this lady. Still, her own paltry coins would get her nowhere.

Duchess Brougham stepped into the room only so far as to set her offering down upon the bureau. Before she turned to leave, she reached toward Eleanor, then slowly let her hand drop. "Godspeed, my dear."

With the closing of the door, the candle sputtered, fighting for life in the shadows left by the lady's departure. Eleanor stood, dazed, knowing she should move, should breathe, should. . .something. How had her life come to this? And worse, what did the future hold? Gooseflesh rose on her forearms, and she fought the urge to whirl about and dive beneath the bedstead. She hadn't realized that allowing self-pity to enter her thoughts also invited fear to tag along, hand-in-hand.

Bear up. Bear up!

Despite her inner rallying cry, her heart skipped a beat. Too bad the silly thing didn't quit altogether, sparing her the horrors of traveling alone, unprotected. Bowing her head, she closed her eyes.

My precious Lord;

My only hope;

My Saviour, how I need You now.

Chapter 2

Two months later

Clutching the ship's railing with white knuckles, Eleanor closed her eyes and inhaled deeply. The salty tang of sea air did little to remove the stench clinging to her skirts and skin. Would she ever escape it? After seven weeks of sharing a coffin-sized pallet with two other women, it would take a miracle to scrub away the reek that soured her body, mind, and spirit.

Water purled against the hull, and she sighed, thoroughly sick of the sea. If land weren't sighted soon, she just might pitch herself into the black waters below and be done with it. For a moment, she held her breath, calculating just how long it would take before abandoning life to a cold, cold grave—then shivered from the horror of her twisted thoughts.

"Frightened, miss?"

The question pulled her safely back to the topside of the *Charming Lucy*, where she stood with one of her bunkmates. "No more than you, Molly. No more than any of us."

"Aye. . .I suppose."

Eleanor glanced at the woman beside her, surprised once again at the courage contained in such a small frame. She herself could barely endure the voyage with the loss of comfort, her dignity, her dreams—and even her small valise, which had been stolen before she boarded. But Molly had lost so much more.

She laid her fingers atop Molly's arm, hoping to impart some measure of compassion. "Forgive me. I am a poor companion today, I think. I cannot imagine what you must be feeling. I am so sorry your husband. . .that he. . ."

"La, miss, don't fret." Molly patted her hand, then pulled back. "'Tis a sorry lot the fever took him. Dreadful way for Freddy to go, but his suffering's ended now. And truth be told. . .I hardly knew him."

Eleanor gasped. "But you were his wife!"

MICHELLE GRIEP

Molly cast her a sideways glance.

Heat rushed to her cheeks. Would she never learn to keep her thoughts to herself? Why did the very same qualities she'd abhorred in her father flourish in her like so many weeds? "Oh, Molly, I have no right to voice such an astonishment. Please forgive—"

"No offense taken, miss. Why, you've been the gentlest soul I've encountered on this whole journey. The thing is"—she peeked farther down the railing where the finer ladies gathered, then inched closer to Eleanor—"Freddy and I were wed naught but two days afore we set sail, and even then I'd known him scarcely a fortnight. He was a charmer, but a stranger, nonetheless. Why, I feel I know you and Biz better than I ever did Freddy."

Eleanor frowned. Overhead, the sun ducked behind a cloud, as elusive as Molly's words. Though the woman's sentiment was common, Eleanor could barely understand it. Marriage for a governess was out of the question, but it didn't mean she hadn't considered what it might be like to be wed. If the opportunity were ever offered her—which it never would—she'd marry for love alone. Nothing less. On that she would not be moved.

Apparently Molly held other convictions. From the corner of her eye, Eleanor studied the woman's profile. Long lashes, surprisingly smooth skin, hair the rich color of dried tea leaves fresh from the Indies, though it'd not been washed in two months, or more. Yet even garbed in a filthy gown, there was no denying Molly's beauty. Surely many men had vied for her attention.

The ship canted, and Eleanor grabbed the railing. "Why, Molly? Why marry a man you did not know? The gentry do it out of necessity, but surely you were not forced into such a union."

A small smile curved her lips. "Nah, weren't nothing like that. Freddy, he...well, he had this dream. It were like a faerie tale, miss. Freddy said after our five-year service, we'd have a little house on a little plot of land, with little ones runnin' around everywhere—all bright eyed and full bellied."

Her smile grew, lighting Molly's whole face and nearly pulling Eleanor headlong into Freddy's dream.

"Freddy's words filled me clear up with hope, miss. First time I ever felt so light. Like I were floating. You ever felt that way?"

A shadowed memory fought to surface. Light, love, promise...despair. Even after all these years, the hurt was too deep, too raw. She blew out a sigh, dispelling the smallest whispers of remembrance, refusing to examine them. "Not often enough, I am afraid."

"Fear? Pah!" The words barged in from behind, accompanied by the clink of chain and drag of a cannonball across wooden planking.

A wad of chewed tobacco hit the deck beside Eleanor's skirt. A wiry woman, all bones and bluster, stared at her with eyes so blue and intense, it was a dare to simply meet her gaze. Eleanor couldn't help but smile. There was nothing subtle about Biz Hunter. The woman was inappropriate from the tip of her cursing tongue to the bottom hem of the man's waistcoat and jacket she wore over her filthy skirt. Even so, Eleanor admired her spunk and daring, though she claimed to be a year junior to Eleanor.

"Fear's for cowards!" Biz's voice rose to rival the flapping of the sails. "You won't last a day if you give in to such weak-kneed rot."

"We can't all be as brave as you, Biz." Molly's quiet tone couldn't have contrasted more.

"Aye." Biz cocked a brow. "That's a truth now, ain't it?"

In light of the sun, which had finally decided to break free from the clouds, a smirk slanted a defiant streak across Biz's face. Was the woman truly so fearless? Eleanor brushed an errant strand of hair from her eyes to gain a better view. "Do you not have a care who your new master will be?"

"Hah! I know who my master is." She thumped her thumb against her chest. "Me!"

"I own I'm a bit nervous." Molly smoothed her palms along her skirt, again and again, further wearing the threadbare fabric. Any more of that and she'd need to patch her patches. "Starvation in a familiar alley seems a mite more comforting than perishing on a foreign street."

Biz snorted. "The way I heared it, we're going to a land o' milk an' honey. And the way I sees it, the law did me a favor by packing me off on this tub o' boards. Good riddance to London town." She flourished her hand in the air, as one might flick off a horsefly.

Eleanor bit her lip instead of rolling her eyes at the woman's dramatics. No sense refuting Biz's embellishments. She lifted a smile to Molly instead. "I am sure Biz is correct. Whoever puts down money for you would not willingly see you perish. That would be a bad investment."

"La, miss." Molly quit smoothing her skirt. "Yer so smart."

"Not smart enough to travel with the real ladies, though, are you?" Biz nodded toward the upper-class passengers clustered near the bow. "I wonder why."

The challenge hung heavy on the air, like a squall about to break. As much as she liked Biz, she also wouldn't mind slapping the smirk off the woman's lips. "Curiosity is a dangerous virtue at times."

"And other times it pays off." Biz's eyes gleamed. Was she provoking on purpose, or did she really know something?

"All right, me beauties." One of Captain Fraser's men sauntered along the bulwark and joined them at the railing. The smell of hemp and hard work accompanied him. This was a change, for other than lewd comments, the sailors mostly kept their distance. Eleanor had thought it strange at first, until she realized were she in their shoes, she'd stay an arm's length away from death and disease as well.

The man lifted a finger, indicating the stairwell to the hold. "Time to take it below."

Eleanor squinted over her shoulder, calculating the sun's height. "Our time is not yet finished. We are allotted an hour at the rail."

"I says it is." He folded his arms, his stance ending further discussion.

Biz planted her fists on her hips. "Well I'm not goin'. Not now. Took all my strength to lug this ball up the bleedin' ladder, and if you think—"

A whistle from high up in the ratlines cut off her words, followed by, "Land ho!"

Shading her eyes, Eleanor scanned the horizon, expecting to see a thin line of green or darkness or. . .something other than sunlight sparkling off waves.

"Please, mayn't we stay?" Molly asked. "We won't get in the way. It's so stifling below."

The sailor shook his head. "Captain's orders. He's had one too many blighters jump ship, short-changing him on the fare. Ye're all confined to quarters 'til he holds a fistful o' coins from a buyer. So as I said, off ye go, my pretties."

With a last look past the railing, Molly turned to leave. Not Biz. She spit out curses as deftly as she had the tobacco, denigrating the sailor's appearance, character, and finally, his mother.

He drew back his arm, fist raised.

Eleanor raced between them, holding out her hands. "Please, sir! Surely you will not strike a lady."

He sneered past her at Biz. "A poxy strumpet is no lady."

"Ahh, blow it out yer—"

"Biz!" Eleanor warned.

"Bah!" Biz ran her fingers through her tangled hair, scowling. "Yer right, I suppose. I'm a-goin'. I'd rather swelter below with that vomiting lot than stand here sharin' breath with the likes o' this one." She hefted her cannonball with a grunt, then hobble-walked to the stairs, crouched from the weight and the shortness of her shackle.

Once the sailor finished spewing his own string of curses, he turned to Eleanor. "Off with ye, too."

"Sir, please." For the moment, all her hope was packaged in this scruffy seaman. Lifting her chin, she sent up a quick prayer. "Allow me to remain. I give you my word I will not run off. Once I find my employer, my debt shall be paid. I am to contact a Mr. Taggerton, who has no idea as to what ship I am on or the day I am to arrive. He merely knows that I am coming. He will, however, pay in full once he discovers that I am here, for he is related to my former employer, Duchess Brougham. So you see, it is imperative I find him."

"Duchess, eh?" He scratched the stubble on his chin.

Good. Obviously her words had some effect. The tension in her shoulders loosened.

Until he reached over and grabbed the fleshy part of her arm. "No time for prattlin' now, missy, but if you like," he leaned closer, his breath hot on her cheek, "I'll stop by after me duties, and we can talk then."

She wrenched away, rubbing the spot on her sleeve his fingers had wrinkled. "Please, time is of the essence. I can pay you, if need be."

A smile spread across his face, exposing teeth the color of mouse fur. "Now there's a switch. A lady payin' me. Hah! That's a good one, that is. Usually I'm the one leavin' behind a coin, but if that's the way ye want to play it, I'm game."

Eleanor frowned. Men. All alike. "The only payment you shall receive is if you allow me to slip away to contact Mr. Taggerton. A few pence ought to close your eyes long enough for that. Your captain shall be paid, none the wiser for my short absence, and you shall have enough money in your pocket to 'leave behind a coin' several times over."

"All righty, then." His grin flattened into a straight line. "But if you double-cross me, I'll make it so's no one with eyes will even look at you twice."

He glanced over his shoulder to the foredeck, then held out his tar-stained palm. "Let's have it."

"Give me a moment." She turned her back to him and faced the open sea. Hiking her skirt was bad enough. Giving him an eyeful would

15

be worse. Carefully, she lifted the outer fabric of her gown to reveal the petticoat beneath, where she'd sewn the banknote from Lady Brougham into a seam. She patted the area. Nothing but loose threads met her touch.

Her stomach sank.

The sailor's voice grazed over her shoulder. "There a problem, missy?"

A thousand pinpricks traveled from scalp to toe. Without that money—and more importantly the note of recommendation—her only hope was that Lady Brougham's letter had reached Mr. Taggerton ahead of this ship and that he was looking for her. For if he weren't, this was more than a problem. It was slavery.

She'd be sold off to the highest bidder to pay for her passage.

Chapter 3

Trapped. Desperate. Eleanor tried in vain to ignore the strangling emotions as she tipped her face toward the only light intrepid enough to slip through the grate in the ceiling. She'd never longed for fresh air as much as now. With the temperature in the hog pen rising, so did the stench—and it was especially ripe today, with two more bodies yet to be removed. At first, she'd spurned Biz's slang for the hold. Not anymore. If anything, the term was too generous. Even swine would have a hard time breathing down here. A pox on Lord Brougham and the captain for assigning her such a fate.

"I'm not stayin' a day more, I'll tell ye that." Behind her, Biz's voice filtered through the stench. "I'm leavin' with the next buyer what comes down those stairs, and I don't care a figgity nigglet if it's a one-legged snake charmer a-wearin' an eyepatch."

With a last inhale, Eleanor turned. It took a moment for her vision to adjust to the darkness and focus on Biz, though the woman stood hardly ten paces away. Lanterns hung from the bulkhead, stretching the length of the narrow compartment. None were lit, their candle stubs long since melted into memories of light.

Eleanor tugged her bodice, lifting the damp fabric from her skin. "Are you really going to be able to still your tongue long enough to keep from frightening off another prospect?"

Biz raised her chin. "Aye."

"No matter what?"

The woman rolled her eyes. "I said aye, din't I?"

A worthy try, but Eleanor would not be put off. "I believe I have heard that before."

"Well, this time I mean it. Let 'em look at my teeth, my hair, my feet." She flashed a defiant smile. "Why, I've half a mind to lift my skirt if it'll do any good."

"Biz!"

Her smile vanished. "And don't pretend you won't, too. Yer as close to crackin' as the rest of us, standing below that grate from sunup to evenin', staring like a blind woman after a lover long gone."

Eleanor frowned. Biz was more right than anyone knew. Desperation courted her with all the determination of a relentless suitor. If Mr. Taggerton didn't come for her soon, well. . . Despite the heat, she shuddered. With the exception of harlotry, there wasn't much she wouldn't consider.

Biz paced three steps forward, three back—as far as her ball and chain allowed. "It ain't right, cooping us up like animals. No light. No air. Food ain't fit fer Newgate bait, and I know that for a fact." Curses sprinkled her tirade like a steady rainfall. "Even my worst days on the streets, I could catch a whiff o' breeze or snatch a bucket o' water to wash in."

Two pallets over, straddling the border where light gave up its ghost and darkness began, Molly moaned—then twisted and emptied her stomach off the side of the cot.

Biz took a step nearer to Eleanor and lowered her voice. "How's she doin'?"

Eleanor bit her lip. Would that Molly's body might not be counted among those carried out in a sailcloth. "She needs to get out of here."

Bootsteps pounded overhead, followed by a rattle of keys—the sweet, sweet sound of freedom.

Biz's eyes shot to Eleanor's. "What if it's not yer Mr. Taggerton this time?"

The question circled like a vulture over a carcass, each pass one more peck at her faith. Why did God not answer? Why did the man not come? She was nearly the last left aboard, other than Biz and a few others who were sicker than Molly. Surely Lady Brougham had sent the missive directly. Surely those were Mr. Taggerton's footsteps above. She forced a confidence she didn't feel into her voice. "I shall hope you are wrong."

"For what it's worth"—Biz angled her face—"I hope so, too."

"Thank you, Biz. I believe your heart is bigger than you let on."

The woman's blue eyes widened, then she turned and dragged her shackles to the hull, leaving behind a trail of profanities that could drop a sailor to his knees.

Eleanor fanned herself, hiding a grin. At first she'd suspected Biz of stealing her money while she slept, but the more she got to know the woman, the less plausible she thought the idea. Biz's rough exterior was as thick as the layer of grime that coated them all, but her heart was pure through and through.

"Miss?" Molly wobbled where she sat on the edge of the pallet, her face thinner than a beggar's. "Could I trouble you for water?"

"No trouble, Molly." In truth, it would give her something to think about rather than wondering what was taking Captain Fraser so long. Retrieving the dipper from a bucket hanging on a beam, she filled it and carried it to Molly. The woman drank without spilling a drop—and still the captain hadn't appeared.

"Come on, Moll." Eleanor set the dipper on the pallet and offered the woman her arm. "Might do you some good to walk around a bit."

Her lips stretched, and then she gave up, as if even smiling were too much effort. "I think I'll just sit here, if you don't mind."

"Of course I do not mind." With a sweep of her fingers, Eleanor brushed back the hair tumbling over Molly's brow. Cool skin met her touch, thanks to God. "Your fever is gone. You feeling better?"

"Aye, a little."

"Good. Perhaps today, you shall—"

Door hinges creaked, and boots thudded down the ladder. Eleanor straightened and whirled, words of encouragement dying on her lips.

Captain Fraser carried a lantern, and for a moment, Eleanor recanted her wish for light. Lifeless eyes—more than she'd accounted for—glinted back a glassy sheen from the pallets around her.

"Swales! The smell! What kind o' ship you runnin'?" The words did not belong to a family member of a duchess.

Nor did the fellow look like a family member. Traipsing beside the captain, a short man with a crooked back scowled. One eye was slanted shut, not quite puckery, but indented nonetheless. So...Biz hadn't been too far off in her eyepatch prediction. The man's nose was a doorknocker, large, long, and thick enough to grab hold of. Atop his head, a patch of white hair stuck out as sparse and prickly as that on his jawline. Deep lines creased his brow, matching those etched into his chin. Eleanor got the distinct impression that should the fellow flip upside down, his face would look exactly the same. Handsprings wouldn't be likely, though. He had a good fifty—possibly sixty—years' worth of cares bowing his shoulders.

As though the man hadn't spoken, the captain stalked across the hold. "These are the three I recommend, Mr. Beebright, though yer welcome to take a looksee at the others if you like." He swept the lantern in an arc.

After a glance into the hold's recesses, leastwise as far as the light dared to venture, Beebright huddled closer to the captain. He lifted a finger and pointed at Molly. "That one don't look too good." His finger and his gaze swung over to Biz, his eyes hardening as he stared at her shackles. "And that one will be a pack o' trouble from the get-go."

Biz glowered, but for once her lips pressed into a thin line instead of spouting contempt.

"But this one," Beebright's finger came full circle, aiming right at Eleanor. "I'm lookin' for a house maid, a nursemaid, and some kind of uppity lady's companion—whole lot of nonsense, if you ask me. You qualified for any of those?"

Better prospects than remaining with the dead and dying, but still...this might be—*Oh God, please let it be*—the day Mr. Taggerton came calling. She straightened her shoulders and tried not to look at Mr. Beebright's slant-eye. "I do have experience with children, sir, but I am sorry. I already have an employer."

Beebright squinted up at the captain. "I thought you said—"

"Miss Morgan," Captain Fraser cut him off. "We've been moored for nigh a week and a half. If your Mr. Taggerton were coming, he'd have arrived by now. I know of a brothel on the north side of town that'll pay me a percentage of your earnings until your passage is paid in full, but if that's not to your liking, then Mr. Beebright here is the best option"—his gaze slid to Molly and Biz—"for each of you."

Beebright hitched his thumb toward Biz. "I won't be taking that one."

Biz shoved off from where she leaned against the hull, chains rattling.

Eleanor cleared her throat, several times over, until Biz took the hint and halted.

"Suit yourself, man,"—the captain shrugged—"but you've seen what I've got. You should've been here days ago if shopping the market was what you were about."

"Weren't for lack of trying. Newcastle's not just a spit and a holler down the road, you know."

"Take 'em or leave 'em, but the next load of servants isn't due for another fortnight." Fraser cocked his head. "Can your patrons wait that long?"

Beebright rubbed a hand over his prickly head, again and again. Was it really that much effort to think? "Patrons. Mighty fine name for those what paid me hardly enough to cover my travel." His jaw worked, and a sour look developed before he finally answered. "All right, Captain, I'll take 'em, but can we do the paperwork up where's we can breathe?"

"Landlubbers. All the same." Fraser sneered. "Makes no nevermind to me. Come along. All of you." The captain turned on his heel. Beebright followed like a large moth hovering after the lantern.

"What about these chains?" Biz hollered after them.

"Lug 'em up the ladder one more time, missy," the captain called over his shoulder. "Soon as you make your mark and I've the coin in my pocket, I'll take 'em off."

Curses rolled off Biz's tongue, but the men's boots already pounded up the ladder.

Molly tugged on Eleanor's skirt. "I'm not sure if I can do this, miss."

"Neither am I, Molly." She glanced down at the woman, the last of her hope plummeting with the movement. Frightened eyes stared up at her, and she forced a pleasantness to her voice she didn't feel. "But I am convinced God shall be with us, even in Newcastle."

Wherever that was.

Chapter 4

One false move. A careless breath. Samuel Heath would shut down even his heartbeat if it meant he'd remain undetected. He stood still as a corpse, a move he'd perfected. Life lived in the shadows was not without its benefits.

Five paces to his left, half-hidden in a stand of young sugar maples, his blood brother drew his bowstring taut, the weapon as much a part of him as his soul. The slightest movement of his finger would mean an arrow through the lungs.

Forest sounds contracted into a cacophony of birdsong and insects. Air whooshed into Samuel's nostrils and he held it, savoring the tightness in his chest. The thin space between life and death never failed to exhilarate.

Ahead, a white-tailed buck lifted its head in their direction, shying to the right. His friend's focus shifted, as did one of his feet.

Snap!

The break of a twig beneath the man's moccasin prodded the deer into flight.

Samuel sighed. There went supper, and breakfast, and dinner for a good many days. Though scoping out a new trapping route was his primary objective, bagging a deer along the way would've been a blessing.

His brother lowered his bow and returned the arrow to the quiver strapped across his back. He did not make eye contact.

Shaking his head, Samuel snorted. "Blasted dry spell. It's not right, sticks cracking like the bones of late autumn though it be barely June."

Inoli lifted a dark gaze. "The error was mine, Brother, and well you know it."

"Still, we need rain." He tipped his head toward the flattened trail left by the deer and set off that direction.

Inoli joined his side. "*Adewehi* sees dark clouds. None heavy with water."

Samuel cut him a sideways glance. "Sounds ominous."

"Such is the spirit of a tempest."

He paused, studying a disturbed bed of trillium. The buck doubled back here, putting them at the forefront of the faint breeze. Wily animal. Gazing upward, he calculated the sun's cast against the wilt-leafed canopy. Might as well press on and—by luck or providence—hopefully find the does, sure to be nearby. He turned toward the west, taking care that his own moccasins would not misstep.

"The elders have spoken to me." Inoli's words traveled quiet and low, matching the cadence of their pace.

"That sounds ominous too, my friend."

Inoli kept his face forward, making it hard for Samuel to read. As much as he respected this man, sometimes the urge to chokehold him was irresistible.

"They say it is time for you to take a woman."

He bit back a laugh. "Let me guess. They have one picked out for me. Or more like Running Doe has convinced them she's the one."

Mockingbirds answered. Inoli did not. His long legs covered much ground before he spoke. "Running Doe is a strong woman. Hard worker. Good teeth." He angled his head, his dark eyes shining. "Her wide hips are fertile as freshly turned earth."

"Oh, no." Samuel shook his head, suppressing the growl in his throat that would surely scare away any chance of finding a deer. "No more babes for me. I can barely manage the one."

"Exactly. As the elders have said, you need a woman."

"True, which is why I've got one on order."

"On order?" Inoli's lips flattened, the closest he ever came to frowning. He stopped and faced him. "I do not understand you, Ya'nu."

"Sometimes I don't understand myself." He scrubbed a hand over his face. How to explain? "Grace means the world to me, and I love her more than my life, but she needs a mother. So. . .I bought one."

"But Running Doe—"

Samuel shot up his hand. "I appreciate the offer. Tell the elders as much. You, above all men, know your peoples' hearts beat with mine. But if Grace is to have the best that this land offers, she must be raised with white manners."

A fine line creased Inoli's brow. "And the *un'ega* will not frown upon your purchase of a woman?"

Half a smile slid across his mouth. "You make it sound as if I've bought a harlot."

Black eyes bore into his. His smile faded. Inoli was right. That's exactly what people would think. Grace would be shunned in proper company. Samuel sighed. "As always, you give me much to think about."

Inoli tilted his chin. A superior angle, one most often seen when he'd scored a point at stickball—and one that opened the door wide for opportunity.

Guilt and shame nipped at Samuel's conscience. He was no preacher—but a rogue urge compelled him to try. Again. "And you, Brother? Have you thought much on our last conversation?"

The tilt didn't go away, but Inoli's eyes glittered cold. A nerve had been struck. Good.

"You know I do not listen when you speak of the White Christ. Why do you waste your breath?"

Samuel chuckled.

Inoli grunted. "You laugh? At me?"

"Peace, man." He shook his head. "I laugh because you remind me of someone."

The glitter softened. "Yourself," Inoli breathed out.

Suddenly the man's gaze settled beyond Samuel's shoulder, and he lifted a finger to his lips.

Instinct squeezed Samuel's gut. Slowly, he removed his bow, accepting the arrow Inoli held outstretched. He nocked it and pivoted in silence. Twenty-five yards off, a small patch of tawny hide stood out against the dull green of a woods in desperate need of rain. In one fluid movement, he raised the bow, pulling the string. He narrowed his eyes, aiming just above chest cavity, and—

A squalling cry rent the forest air. He threw down the bow, unsure what irritated him most—his daughter's wail or Inoli's laughter.

"You need a woman, no matter what color skin."

Unlacing the sling he'd created to tote around little Grace, Samuel slipped out his arms one at a time and shifted her to his front instead of her usual perch on his back. Tears sprouted at the corners of her eyes. Her mouth opened wider. Hunting was definitely over for the day.

"We'll camp here." Cradling Grace in one arm, he pulled out a salted piece of jerky for her to chew on. Her chubby fingers grabbed the chunk and popped it into her mouth, quieting her screams. "Guess she was hungry."

"As will we all be if hunting continues at this rate." Inoli began stomping down a flattened area.

Pressing a kiss to Grace's head, Samuel ignored his friend's warning, focusing instead on his daughter's downy curls—the only softness in his life.

The wagon lurched around a corner. Eleanor jerked with the movement, jostling Molly, whose head rested in her lap. Molly's lips parted, but no sound came out—or maybe it did. Hard to tell with the grind of wheels against gravel, the shouts of hawkers selling their wares, and Biz, who gave a running dialogue of the wonderful, wide streets of Charles Towne.

"Another redcoat!" She wiggled her eyebrows at Eleanor. "Wonder if I knows him. Din't think to see so many of that vermin over here."

Another bump jolted the cart, and Eleanor flung out her hand, grabbing the side. "Perhaps you ought sit down, Biz. Have you not had your fill of attention from the law?"

"I got nothin' to be afeard of. I ain't done nothin' wrong." A slow smile spread across her face. "Mostly."

Biz's hand disappeared inside the ridiculous waistcoat she refused to take off. When it reappeared, two peppermint balls sat in her palm. "Like one?"

Eleanor shook her head. "How did you manage those?"

Her grin grew. "Snagged 'em off one of the officers we passed down at the docks."

"You do know that stealing is wrong, don't you?"

"Oh, it weren't stealing. He lent 'em to me." Her face tipped to a provocative angle. How often did the girl get in trouble with that look? "I asked him real nice like."

Eleanor narrowed her eyes. "We hardly had time to catch our breath between the ship and this wagon."

"I din't say it were a lengthy conversation."

"I suppose you merely whispered it under your breath as your fingers slipped into his pocket?"

Biz's eyes sparkled. "You're a smart one, you are."

A gust of hot air whipped a piece of hair across Eleanor's lips, but by the time she swiped it away, Biz had turned, precluding further comments. The afternoon sun beat down, relentless despite the breeze. She'd heard of the browned skin of Colonial women. Now she understood why as she dared nudge her sleeves up a little farther.

"Din't think to see that." Biz's voice was tight, strained in a way incongruous to her devil-may-care exterior.

"What?" Taking care not to disturb Molly overmuch, Eleanor leaned sideways, craning her neck.

"Over there."

Her gaze followed the length of Biz's outstretched arm. Ten, maybe fifteen paces off the side of the wagon, a young boy lay in the mouth of an alley, red trickling from his nose. Another lad, held by the throat, kicked his feet in the air. The man holding him shouted in his face. All wore nothing but rags.

Eleanor stared, unable to pull her gaze away though desperately wanting to. The little boy's legs slowed, and as the wagon rolled past the horrid scene, they quit moving altogether. His body hit the dirt, next to the other.

"No!" Did that raspy cry belong to her? Eleanor slapped her hand to her mouth.

Biz sank to the wagon's bed. "I thought. . . . Well, I hoped. . . ." She lifted glassy eyes to Eleanor. "I can see it ain't to be no better here."

The dullness in Biz's gaze choked Eleanor as tangibly as the brute had squeezed the little boy's neck. Yet how to impart encouragement from an empty well? She sucked in a breath, praying for wisdom on the exhale. "You do not have to be a victim of circumstance, Biz. This is your opportunity to change the course of your life. You are a housemaid now. There is dignity in such a position."

"A new life, eh? There's a thought." Drawing her knees up, Biz wrapped her arms around her legs and lowered her head.

Molly groaned, twisting on Eleanor's lap. Though her hair clung to her temples, it was hard to tell if the fever returned. Eleanor's own shift stuck to her skin beneath the Charles Towne sun.

Balling up her shawl, she eased Molly's head to the bundled fabric, then scooted to the front of the wagon, where Mr. Beebright held the reins.

"Mr. Beebright, it would be to Molly's benefit if we spent a night or two at an inn. I feel sure she would regain her strength and—"

"Pig's teeth, woman!" Beebright scowled at her over his shoulder. "This t'aint a pleasure ride. I'm on a schedule, and erring on the hide-tanning side of being late. Greeley will see to that."

"And how will Greeley feel when you pull into town with only two women instead of three and discovers he paid for nothing?" She lifted her chin, though the bumping of the wagon made her teeth grind.

Beebright's good eye squinted. "She that bad off?"

"I fear so."

For a moment, he rubbed his lower lip with the pad of his thumb. Oh, how lovely it would be if they all might rest their heads on a pillow—or even a simple cot—beneath the roof of an inn this night.

Beebright leaned to the side and spit off the edge of the wagon. "See to it she lives, then. I'm holdin' you responsible, missy."

He faced forward, apparently finished with the conversation.

But she wasn't. "I am no nursemaid, sir."

"You are now. You just signed a contract for it."

"You can hardly expect me to—"

The wagon jerked to a stop. Beebright turned. If he'd possessed two good eyes, she'd have been dead on the spot from the rage darkening his gaze. "If you don't learn to keep yer trap shut and do as yer told, ye'll have a far worse time of it with Samuel Heath than I ever will with Greeley. Yer not in England anymore."

She swallowed, the truth of his words an ugly reminder of her situation. It was easy to tell Biz she didn't have to be a victim of circumstance—but quite another thing to live out those words in her own life.

Chapter 5

Breaking the cadence of stone shushing against metal, Samuel set down his tomahawk and whetstone, then reached to work out a knot in his shoulder. Even after his trek with Inoli last week and several days of hunting on his own, all he had to show for it were sore muscles and a skinny rabbit sizzling outside on the spit. Next to him, Grace slept soundly in her crib, and why not? She'd had the ride of her life strapped against his back, bouncing up and down, scaring away prey with her happy squeals.

He peeked over at her, dark eyelashes fanning against her pink cheeks, a wet thumb hanging half out of her mouth. In spite of himself, half a grin tugged his lips. Though he'd wanted a son, he wouldn't trade his sweet girl for all the lads in the whole blasted South Carolina colony.

A late afternoon cross-breeze sallied in the open door. He shot to his feet, sniffing. There, almost imperceptible, hiding amid the waft of fat and smoke from his supper, he inhaled something musky. Maybe even a little tangy. He cocked his head. A blend of earth, sweetness—

And danger.

He strode to the door, schooling the urge to utter a curse as he would have in the past. Next time he saw Inoli, his friend would have ringing ears by the time he finished with him. The man meddled more than Grandmother.

Leaning against the porch timber, he waited. The hare sizzled over coals in the clearing that ran along the front of the house. Beyond the yard, a maze of hickory and pine painted a background of greens. His gaze slid to the east, where the creek lumbered downhill.

The beginnings of a magnificent headache rapped at his temples as he sighted a graceful figure cresting the embankment. Rays of sunlight reached through the canopy, highlighting the woman's every step. She wore her black hair long and loose, like a queen's mantle, the determination of her stride regal as she drew closer, adding to her imperial aura.

He folded his arms. "What are you doing here, Running Doe?"

"It is said Ya'nu needs a woman." She ascended the few steps and stopped a breath in front of him, lifting her face to his.

Out of habit, he shook his head, letting a swath of hair cover the scarred side of his cheek. "I told Inoli that's been taken care of."

She shrugged one shapely shoulder, then shimmied past him and stepped into his house uninvited.

He pushed off from the timber and followed, his gut clenching. This would not end well.

Inside, Running Doe's dark eyes darted from his bed to Grace's crib, then on to the stacks of pelts against one wall and crates against the other. Finally she turned in a circle, arms spread wide. "I see no woman."

Her tone challenged, as did the flash in her eyes. He knew that look, the one a woman gave just before her heels dug in. Once again he folded his arms, remaining in the safety of the open door. Sometimes flight was the better option.

So was silence. He said nothing.

"What I see"—her eyes narrowed—"is a *sa'gwali digu 'lanahi'ta*, too stubborn to accept what the elders have spoken."

He sucked in a breath. He'd maimed men for lesser insults. Inwardly, he counted to ten in English, then again in Cherokee before he spoke. "Go home, Running Doe. I am not the man for you."

Like one of the mountain lions that roamed the Blue Ridge, she put one foot in front of the other, her gaze fastened on his as she neared. She pulled his hands loose and set them squarely on her wide hips, locking them in place with her hands atop. "But I am the woman for you. Why do you fight it?"

Her body flamed beneath her buckskin sheath, he could feel it, as relentless as an August afternoon. Ahh, but she was a beauty, all soft and warm. It'd been a year since he'd lain with his wife. A year of cold need and loneliness.

Running Doe rose to her toes, her breath brushing against his lips. She leaned closer, and—

He pulled away, horrified at how easy it was to teeter on the thin line between saint and sinner. She followed his move, but he held out a hand, staving her off. "You are a fine woman, Running Doe, but I will not have you."

A tempest brewed in the black of her eyes. "Yet you will take a white wife." She aimed the words like a musket ball, straight at his heart.

He grabbed her arms, subduing the urge to squeeze lest he leave behind angry bruises. "Do not think to question me, woman. You know what I've done for the *Ani'yunwiya*. What the English have taken from me. This isn't about skin."

"Then what is it?"

Her question cut—deep. Too deep.

He growled and released her, stalking over to where Grace yet slept, her chest rising in an even rhythm. His fingers itched to brush back her hair, touch the silky tresses, and root himself to the reason for his decision. He'd faced bears, Shawnee bent on a killing spree, famine, and disease. Not one of them had cornered him so thoroughly as this innocent one. To give her the best life—one he'd never known—it was either let her go for another to raise, or marry a woman acceptable in the world's eyes.

Both of which tasted like blood in his mouth. He'd never felt so trapped in all his life.

He turned back to Running Doe, putting his whole life into three simple words. "It's about Grace."

For a moment, she looked like a fish out of water, her mouth working open and shut. "You choose to favor a white woman you don't know when you could have me, all for the sake of a child?"

He clenched his jaw, barely able to force words past the anger closing his throat. "I'd give my life for her."

Running Doe laughed, without humor or mercy. "And so you shall, foolish one, for no English will give herself to a man without he first giving himself to her." She sashayed over to him, her voice deepening to a husky tone. "I make no demands, Ya'nu."

"Maybe not, but I do." He strode away, thundering stomps shaking the floorboards, and pointed toward the door. "Go, Running Doe. *Ha!*"

She strutted up to him, poking a sharp finger into his chest. "You will regret this day." Then she turned and quitted him, as silently as she'd come.

Samuel watched the forest eat her up. True, there were many days he regretted, yet this wouldn't be one.

But what of the day he married again, to a woman he'd never met?

Twelve days. Twelve never-ending days. Two hundred eighty-eight hours and—honestly—occasionally Eleanor had counted the minutes as well. She swiped the moisture from her brow with the back of her hand as the wagon jolted up yet another hill. Though early evening, the heat seemed to increase with the humidity, as did the gnats. In fact, the entire journey from Charles Towne had been a sun-scorched, bug-swatting eternity. Thank God that today the nightmare would end. No more sleeping in a wagon bed. No more blood-sucking insects. And—grace and mercy—no more of Mr. Beebright's incessant whistling.

"There she is, ladies. Yer new home sweet home," Mr. Beebright called from his perch on the driver's seat.

Biz scrambled to grasp Beebright's seat back as the wagon crested the hill. Truly, the woman was as agile as a cat. "Sweet rat meat! Don't tell me that's Newcastle."

"What? Too much for you?" Beebright chuckled. "Beauty of an out-post, eh?"

Unsure what to make of the conversation, Eleanor glanced at Molly, who sat next to her. "Are you ready to face our future?"

A small smile curved her lips. "Aye, miss. Why, if it weren't for you, I doubt I'd have a future. Thanks again for your care."

"Think nothing of it. If anything, caring for you gave me experience to nurse a sick little one should the need arise."

"Speaking of little ones, I suppose now is as good a time as any to tell you. . . ." Molly's hand slid to her belly.

Eleanor's eyes widened. "You are. . .with child?"

A blush to shame the sunrise bloomed on Molly's cheeks, and she nodded. "Near as I can tell."

"Oh, Molly! I am so happy you *and* the babe are well." She pulled the woman into an embrace.

"Aww! Quit yer jib-jabbering." Biz's voice cut into the tender moment. "Don't ye want to see the slap-shacked hamlet tha's to be our new home? Why, we'd a been better off stayin' in the hold o' that ship."

Eleanor pulled back and quirked a brow at Molly. "It can't be all that bad. Shall we?"

Molly scooted to one side of the wagon, Eleanor to the other, each bracing themselves from tumbling overboard as the wagon descended one more rolling hill.

Eleanor's chest tightened. Not that she hadn't seen ramshackle villages back home, but this? No. Absolutely not. This was little more than a collection of cut logs nailed together, huddled along each side of a dirt trail that ended at a river—or what should have been a river. Even the body of water had the good sense to pack up and move on from this pathetic settlement, leaving nothing but a trickle over rocks as a farewell wave.

For once, even Biz was speechless.

"Oh, my," Eleanor breathed out.

Except for the bumpity-bump of the wagon wheels and creak of an axle that by now needed a good greasing, they rode the rest of the way in silence. A smithy stood near a building on the outskirts, watching their advance. He hailed Mr. Beebright with a "Hallo!" and the lift of a sooty hand. Dark smoke belched into the air behind him from a shed that leaned like an old woman with a cane.

"Hallo, Zeke," Beebright returned. "I see the town's still standin'."

Fiddle music poured out the next open door, off-key, and with all the rhythm of a drunken sailor walking a plank. A beast of a man stood in the threshold, looking out. He wore deerskin breeches and a stained linen shirt, cinched at the waist with a wide belt. He cradled a rifle across one arm, and when his dark eyes met hers, she sucked in a breath. Bold. Dangerous. Determined. She'd read of frontiersmen, wild men who lived months at a time in the wild—but words on paper weren't nearly as frightening as this man's real-life dark gaze.

Maneuvering over crates and sacks toward Molly, she put as much distance as possible between herself and the man's suggestive stare. The scramble added another tear to the hem of her skirt, but the damage was worth it.

A legal agency came next, maybe a gaol. Hard to tell. Next to that, judging by the pelts stacked high on the porch, was a fur trader. And at the end of the row, a charred lot.

Eleanor shivered as she stared at the timbers, ash-whitened tips punctuating the scarred earth, like bones laid out to warn of the dangers of fire. Something bad had happened here. She could feel it. Not too far in, broken pieces of porcelain poked up from the rubble, looking for all the world like fangs about to snap shut. In one corner, an upturned cooking pot blossomed like a fat, black fungus. Ragweed crept inward from the edges in a valiant effort to choke out the dark tragedy with green. She frowned. Why had no one thought to clean this up?

Mr. Beebright pulled the wagon to a stop, the sudden lack of movement bumping her into Molly's shoulder.

"Miss Molly gets out here." Mr. Beebright clambered down from his seat, rounded the wagon, and swung open the back gate. The wood lined up even with a dock, making for a solid walkway, and he held out his hand.

"You other two climb up front. I'll send out young Sutton to unload."

Eleanor might almost feel sorry for Molly to live across from the blackened plot of ground, but her new home looked cheerful enough. The building stood two-stories tall, and though it bore no paint, was constructed of actual boards, sawn flat, not logs. Based on the hand-painted placard reading GREELEY'S MERCANTILE above the door, the place appeared to be a regular shop of commerce. It was certainly the finest building in town—if not a bit pretentious for this settlement in the middle of a wilderness.

Molly took Mr. Beebright's hand, allowing him to help her transfer from wagon to docket, then faced them. "Good-bye, Eleanor. Good-bye, Biz. I'm certain I'll see you around, and be glad for it."

"I am sure of it, Molly." Eleanor smiled, for she'd make a point to visit her new friend. Maybe even daily, if she packed up her new charge for a stroll. "All the best to you." She waved.

Biz just shook her head. "Off with you. I'm tired of your pretty face."

"Oh, Biz." Eleanor sighed. "Can you not be more pleasant?"

"What?" Biz bunched her nose as if she smelled something rotten. "I just said she were pretty, din't I?"

Mr. Beebright and Molly disappeared inside Greeley's, but before the screen door slapped shut, a man's voice raged inside. Poor Molly. What a greeting. Hopefully Biz and she would fare better than that.

A strapping fellow emerged next. He greeted them with a tip of his cap and a "Good day, ladies," before he bent to retrieve the first burlap bag nearest the wagon gate.

His accent shot straight from Eleanor's ears to her heart, the twinge of homesickness hitting her hard. "Good day, er, Mr. Sutton, is it? You are a Bristol man, if I do not miss my mark."

"Aye." He straightened, hefting the bag over his shoulder, his green eyes wide and bright in the last of the day's sun. "That I am. Have you kinfolk in the area?"

A smile curved her lips. "No, none. But it does my ears good to hear something other than a Colonial drawl."

"Aye, and that be the truth of it, eh?" He pivoted and disappeared into the half of the building that looked like a warehouse.

Eleanor stood, debating if she should swing her leg over the seatback like Biz had done in order to gain the front seat or if she should climb over the rest of the wagon's crates and barrels and have at it from the side. Either way was an unladylike proposition, but quicker if she just gave in to impropriety and hurdled the seat. She landed with a thud on her bottom and a new tear in her skirt.

Ignoring Biz's laugh, she pressed out what wrinkles she could from her gown, glad she'd managed the feat before Mr. Sutton returned. "I wonder why Mr. Beebright did not drop us off first, unless he's planning on turning the wagon around for another sweep through Newcastle."

"Who knows? Maybe he wanted to unload first. Makes no nevermind to me, long as I don't have to sleep one more night in the open. Not that I've never shared a bed with vermin before, but the bugs 'round here have steel chompers." Biz shaded her eyes from the lowering sun, eyeing her with a smirk. "Why, you'll prob'ly scare the little hem-chaser you're to look after, what with all them welts on your face."

Reprimanding the woman would do no good, for it was likely true. What a sight she must look. She smoothed back her hair, coaxing loose ends into the knot she'd fashioned with what remained of her hairpins. She could at least do that much. Hopefully, with cold chamomile compresses and time, the bumps on her skin would go away. And until then, oughtn't a friendly smile put a child—and a master—at ease?

Master. The thought stung, and she lowered her hands to her lap, clenching them. Oh, she'd felt trapped by employers before, but she could always walk away if the situation merited. Or run, as in the case of her last position. But this time, God help her, she'd signed a legal document. If she left before the seven-year mark, she'd not only be a promise breaker but a criminal.

"Quit yer sighing." Biz elbowed her.

"Was I?" She straightened, hoping good posture might lift her spirits as well. "Sorry."

Biz spit out a curse. "And quit yer blessed apologizing, too. Look around. Yer in America now, not pandering to lords and ladies. Yer proper ways will do you no good out here."

Eleanor pressed her lips together. Manners and order, not chaos and erratic behaviour, just might be the salvation of this wild and rugged land.

Mr. Beebright's whistle exited the building before he did. Apparently he'd not taken to heart whatever tongue-lashing had occurred inside. He paused his tune to thank Mr. Sutton and secure the back gate.

"Off we go, ladies. Might as well stay where you are, for we haven't far to go." He climbed up next to them and, with a slap of the reins, urged the cart forward. He turned right at the end of the building. The road followed along the riverbed and ended in a graveyard.

A graveyard? Why would he bring them here?

But he turned right again, passing beneath a bower of pine, and there the ground opened into a sweet little patch of land, a surprisingly large house nearest the road, and a crop of green mounds dotted with purple flowers behind.

Eleanor's heart swelled. For the first time since that horrid night nearly three months ago, she smiled in full. Not that she'd choose to live in the middle of a backcountry with wild men and a woeful lack of necessities, but to reside in such pastoral scenery might almost make her feel at home.

Mr. Beebright set the brake and hopped down. "This be the reverend's house."

Biz belted out a bawdy laugh. "Ha! Looks like you better be a-watchin' yer manners here, under God's eyes and all, aye, Elle Bell?"

Eleanor subdued a flinch at the nickname, determined not to let it ruin her happy moment. "I can only say that I hope you shall have yourself as merry a home as—"

"Out you go, Miss Biz."

"What?" Their voices rose together, followed by a string of foul curses from Biz.

Biz scrambled over the top of Eleanor, putting distance between herself and the house. "No! You can't make me stay here. Why, I oughtta—"

"Greetings, Mr. Beebright. Happy you've finally made it back." God himself spoke, or rather what looked to be a god in human form striding out the front door. His hair was the color of October acorns, pulled back and tied into a neat queue. His eyes were so violet blue, they would shame a garden of periwinkles into wilting a bow. And when he smiled—Lord have mercy. Eleanor was tempted to fan herself. Next to her, Biz did.

"And glad I am to be back, Reverend," Beebright answered. "It were a dogged-hard trip. I'm gettin' too old for this."

The reverend patted him on the back, then lifted his face to her and Biz. "Welcome to America, ladies. I'd offer you refreshment, but, well. . . God knows I lack in my house-tending skills, which is why I'm happy you are here. Which one of you—"

"I am! Tha's me! I'm your girl." Biz crawled over her and jumped to the ground, landing so close to the reverend, she grabbed his arm to balance. She leaned toward him with a sway of her hips. "Point me in the right direction, and I'll tend whatever ye'd like."

Eleanor gasped.

Red crept up the reverend's ears, and he retreated a step, escaping from Biz's hold. "Oh, er. . ." He shot a glance at Beebright. "Mr. Beebright, are you sure—"

"Back it off there, missy." Beebright poked her in the shoulder, wedging himself between the two. "That there is the Reverend Jonah Parker, so keep your distance."

Beebright paused to spit out the wad of tobacco he'd been chewing since their last stop, the juice of it sending up a puff of dirt as it hit the ground. Swiping his mouth, he turned to the reverend. "And this here is Miss Elizabeth Hunter—Biz, as she calls herself. Keep an eye on that one, though. Sorry to be doin' this to ye, but she were the best I could buy."

Jonah Parker's throat bobbed, but then he recovered and straightened his shoulders. "Very well. Not like I haven't had to deal with a difficult woman before, hmm?"

"Well said, man." Beebright snorted. "I'd best be off, then. Not much light left. As is, I'll have to sport my Bessie and a lantern. Truth be told, though, I'm looking even less forward to spending a night under Heath's roof than with the wildcats in the woods."

"Oh, that reminds me." The reverend held up a hand, halting Beebright's stride. "I meant to tell you that both ladies should remain here for now."

With a cleared shot to the reverend, Biz sidled over to him, aiming her finger at Eleanor. "We don't need Miss Prim and Proper. I'm plenty enough for you."

The man's jaw clenched as he once again looked to Mr. Beebright, the narrowing of his eyes censuring him for his choice of housekeepers.

Eleanor frowned. Why would the man want two of them? "Am I not to care for a young child, then?"

"Yes, ma'am, you will, but I am instructed to let Mr. Beebright know he is to inform Mr. Heath of your arrival. Mr. Heath himself asked for you to wait for him to pick you up instead of Mr. Beebright delivering you."

Odd. Why could they have simply not stopped by whatever building housed him? She shook her head. "I am a bit confused."

"Actually. . ." The reverend glanced heavenward. Was he praying? Here? Now? Then he directed his gaze at her. "It might be best that way."

What was that supposed to mean? Clearly the man was retaining information, for truth hid behind his forced smile. Surely a reverend wouldn't willfully deceive. . .would he?

Nibbling her lower lip, she laid out her precious few puzzle pieces of information and tried to make some sort of picture. She'd had cryptic conversations before, even excelled in creating codes to keep her charges inquisitive and sharp, but now that the technique was turned back upon her, she wasn't so sure she liked it.

Why did her master, Mr. Heath, not trust Mr. Beebright to deliver her?

Chapter 6

Eleanor lay on the sharp edge of slumber, half-awake, half-dead with fatigue. It had been a fitful night. Biz's snoring jolted her from sleep more than once. But now, with dawn's grey just beginning to lighten the sky outside the window, she'd found a comfortable niche in the straw mattress, just out of reach of her bedmate's sharp elbows, and she sank into oblivion—until the door burst open with a crash.

Eleanor shot up, clutching the counterpane to her chest, adding to what little modesty her shift allowed. Next to her, Biz cursed the noise, the hour, and for some odd reason, St. Patrick, then dove under the pillow, stopping up her ears.

"Which one?" A deep voice filled the room, belonging to a man who stood a few paces inside the small chamber. Yet even at such close range, his face was shadowed beneath the brim of a black hat. He was a silhouette, really. Darkness upon dark. Like the grim reaper paying a sudden visit without benefit of a calling card.

And he wore a tomahawk hanging off his belt.

Eleanor's heart beat hard in her chest, a caged bird frantic to break loose. The man looked to be a savage.

"Really, Mr. Heath." The reverend followed, out of breath and apparently out of charity as well, for his voice strained. "This is not in any way acceptable. You cannot enter a woman's bedchamber!"

The big man turned to him, all but blocking Eleanor's view of the reverend, and she gasped. A golden-haired child with snarls that needed a good brushing peeked out from a deerskin wrap tied to Mr. Heath. Craning her neck, the girl twisted to look at her with huge brown eyes. For a moment, the little one squirmed, planting her feet on the man's back and arching up for a better view. Then, evidently satisfied she and Biz were not monsters, the girl popped a thumb in her mouth and settled down, resting her cheek against her father's broad shoulder.

"Which one, Parker?" Mr. Heath's tone demanded nothing short of complete obedience. "The sooner I get out of town, the better. But I reckon you know that."

Tension throbbed in the room, quite the contrast with the way the small girl rested so contentedly on the man's back. The reverend huffed like a horse. Eleanor wasn't sure what to make of the exchange, but one thing she did know—despite the sweet little cherub he carried, Mr. Heath was not a master she wished to serve. She huddled closer to Biz, who clutched her pillow all the tighter.

Sidestepping Heath, the reverend approached the bed, his mouth drawn into a straight line. "My apologies, Miss Morgan, Miss Hunter. Mr. Heath seems to be in quite a hurry this morn, as he generally is when he comes to town. If you wouldn't mind Miss Morgan—"

"And if you wouldn't mind." Heath wheeled about so fast, the little girl squealed with the movement. "Miss Morgan, is it? Let's go. Now."

His dark gaze pierced her against the pillow, so sharp were his eyes. His long hair—deep brown—crashed against his shoulders like a wave ravaging a Cornish cliff, all jagged and wild, hiding half his face with the thickness. The half she could see sported a shadow of stubble, riding just below the sharp angles of his cheekbones. Was everything about the man stormy blackness?

"Mr. Heath." The reverend's jaw clenched. "I insist you employ milder manners in this household."

Biz bolted upward, throwing her pillow at the both of them. "Take yer quarrel downstairs! I've had more peace sleeping in a Shoreditch gutter."

The reverend's jaw dropped. Mr. Heath merely turned a steely glower upon Biz as her pillow bounced off his chest. Lightning flashed in his eyes, yet he said nothing—which made it worse.

Eleanor clutched the counterpane to her neck, using it as a shield. Highly illogical and pathetic, yes, but it was all she had. The realization struck her dumb for a moment. All that remained to her in this world was her fading sense of dignity—and the debt this man had paid for her passage from England.

"I shall be ready within ten minutes, Mr. Heath." It was a lie, of course. She'd never be ready to leave with this wild man. It took all the effort she owned to force out the rest, her voice nothing more than a peeping sparrow. "Please wait for me downstairs."

Mr. Heath stiffened. A muscle stood out on his neck as he slid his gaze to the reverend. "She's English."

The words were an indictment, one in which she was found guilty as charged—and left to swing from a rope.

"What did you expect, Mr. Heath? It was the best Mr. Beebright could manage."

Something guttural rumbled in the big man's throat. He pulled out a pocket watch and flipped it open, then looked at her. "I'll give you five minutes, no more."

He turned and stalked out, the little fair-haired head bobbing behind him. Eleanor blinked at the incongruous sight, frozen in place.

The Reverend Parker sighed with a shake of his head. "I am so sorry, Miss Morgan. Had I known he'd stomp up here, I'd never have let him in the house."

"I am sure you could not have known, could you?"

The reverend shrugged and headed toward the door. "He is a troubled man, much acquainted with grief. There's a good heart somewhere in there, beneath the anger." He paused on the threshold with a nod toward her. "It's up to you and God to find it."

When the door shut, Biz let out a long, low whistle. "Looks like yer gettin' the worst of it, Elle Bell."

"Do not address me so!" Eleanor launched from bed, cross at herself for snapping at Biz. Cross that she was to live with a barbarian for the next seven years. Cross that it appeared her father's prediction would come true. She sniffled, and though she pressed the heels of her hands to her eyes, tears escaped anyway.

"No. No weeping. Don't ever let a man make you cry. They ain't worth it." Biz came up behind her, turning her with a gentle touch on her shoulders. "Come on, Ellie. You like that better? Splash yer face with some water, and I'll help you into yer stays and gown. Better you should make a grand entrance than have that Heath fellow tromping back up here and dragging you down the stairs like the brute he is."

She drew in a shaky breath. Of course Biz was right, but for a moment, moving was out of the question. Fear weighed her down as if she were a paralytic. How could she force herself to leave this place of safety?

Biz did the moving for her, cinching her into her stays, helping her on with her gown. No time remained to style her hair, so Biz simply wound it up and stuck in the last of her pins.

"Off you go. Give him what for. I surely would." Biz winked.

Suddenly emotional, Eleanor wrapped the bony woman in an embrace.

"You are a good friend."

Biz shoved her away with a curse. "Get on with ye." She dove back beneath the covers, leaving Eleanor to face her fate alone.

A fate that rapped on the door. "Miss Morgan?" The reverend's voice leached through the wood. "Mr. Heath and I are waiting for the ceremony to begin in the big room."

The reverend's summons made as much sense as Biz's mumbled gripes. She opened the door, wondering at the strange colonial customs. Had Molly endured such a ritual yesterday? Was there to be shouting involved here as well? No doubt, if Mr. Heath were involved.

"What ceremony, sir?" she asked, feeling foolish for her ignorance.

"Er. . .did you not know, Miss Morgan?" His gaze darted everywhere except to her.

She tensed at the familiar tactic. She'd seen it hundreds of times from charges who'd stolen sweets from cook or short-sheeted her bed. Something was up. She'd wager on it, were she a rascal like Biz.

"Know what?"

The reverend gazed at her like a beggarly tot to be pitied. "You are to be wed."

Wed? The word buzzed in her ears. Somewhere behind her eyes, white rage exploded, blinding and hot. She gaped, sucking in a sharp breath. The agreement she'd signed aboard ship had said nothing of vows or marriage. She'd read it. Carefully. If Mr. Heath thought to bully an illiterate woman who didn't know any better into lifelong drudgery—no, *slavery*—then she'd teach him a thing or two about intimidation right now. Convention be hanged. She brushed past the reverend.

"Miss Morgan, are you all right?"

The man's question nipped at her back like a horsefly biting off bits of flesh. No. She was most certainly not.

Samuel gripped the mantle, facing a large, rough-hewn cross hung above the hearth. One of Grace's shoes kicked against his back. He'd gladly take spikes through his hands and feet rather than bind himself to an Englishwoman.

English! He stifled a roar. Couldn't Beebright tell the difference between an Irish, a Scot, or a murdering, thieving *gilisi*?

"Why God? Why?" He kept his voice low, but it shook. He yanked off his hat and ran a hand through his hair. Too many memories, too much tragedy, flashed through his mind. Redcoats and blood. His mother's last breaths. His father's shouts.

The reason he'd left his wife and child alone.

Closing his eyes, he bowed his head. "I can't do this. I can't. Give me one reason why."

"Mr. Heath! Marriage is for the purpose of relationship and sanctification, a living picture of God's union to the church, not a convenient way to meet your needs of housekeeper, nursemaid, and who knows what else."

His head jerked up, and he wheeled about. A whirlwind in a dark grey skirt blew through the door.

Miss Morgan halted in front of him, hands fisted on her hips, blue fire in her eyes. "The contract I signed is a legal attachment, yes, but for seven years. Not life. I will *not* marry you, sir."

Grace pulled a hank of his hair, as stinging as the sudden insight that this feisty woman felt as trapped as he did. Two foxes in a snare, both willing to chew off their foot to escape. But reality tugged his hair harder, then buried a soft face against his neck, giggling. For Grace's sake, he was the one who would have to give.

This time, anyway.

"Miss Morgan." He lowered his tone, keeping an even tempo, a negotiation trait that'd saved his life many times. "I allow that nothing in the document stated anything about marriage. I thought Grace needed a nursemaid, but I've since revised that opinion. She needs a mother."

Her pert chin lifted. "And if I refuse?"

She had pluck, he'd give her that—and up the ante himself. "Then return the redemption fee I paid for you and walk out that door a free woman."

He nodded past her, to where Parker strode through the opening.

"I. . .I cannot." The woman deflated, studying the tips of her shoes, head bowed as if in prayer.

Parker stepped beside her, and she turned to him. "What happens if I do not reimburse what is owed to Mr. Heath?"

A fearsome scowl raged on the reverend's face. "Mr. Heath can press charges, Miss Morgan. Gaol time, most likely, until the full amount is reimbursed."

"Gaol or marriage?" She choked on a bitter laugh. "Sounds the same to me."

Samuel snorted. "Aye, that it does."

Her gaze shot to his. A spray of freckles darkened across the bridge of her nose. She said nothing as she stared, and he got the distinct impression that she might as well be gawking at a wagon wreck, so distastefully did her lips pinch.

Finally, she spoke. "I counter your proposal, sir."

"Do you, now?" He grunted. This one could go nose to nose with Running Doe—and possibly come out the victor. "I would hear it."

She stepped up to him, offering her hand. "I agree to marry you and care for little Grace on one condition."

His gaze slid to her fingers. Except for a slight tremor, she held it true. "Name it," he said.

"We are husband and wife in title only, and that is as far as it goes. My body remains my own, as does yours." The burst of flame on her cheeks rivaled the red streaks in her hair.

A bold move. One he might make. And definitely one he could live with.

"Agreed." He took the woman's small hand in his own and faced the reverend.

Parker shook his head. "I do not think this is a good idea."

Heaven and earth! Neither did he—nor did the woman, judging by the clamminess of her grasp.

He set his jaw. "Even so, Parker, marry us, before the eyes of God and man."

Next to him the woman stiffened. Grace squirmed, trying to climb over his shoulder. Steeling his spine, he reached behind and loosened the sling ties. He would enter this union for the sake of his child's future, nothing more. Did God understand how much He was asking him to sacrifice by sending him an Englishwoman? With a swoop belying the heaviness of his heart, he pulled Grace around and cradled her in one arm.

He reached for the woman's hand once more, catching a glimpse of the cross above the mantle. Sacrifice indeed.

God help him. God help them all.

Chapter 7

arried! And only an hour ago?"

Molly's exclamation made Eleanor flinch, along with attracting the eyes of two other women who lingered over bolts of fabric. After a glance to see that Grace yet played with a ball of string on the floor where she'd left her, Eleanor pulled on Molly's sleeve, leading her closer to the front door of the mercantile. From this angle, she could keep an eye on Grace, see Mr. Heath and Mr. Sutton loading supplies into the wagon outside, and hopefully keep from serving fodder to the town's gossips.

"I can hardly believe it myself." Her hands shook, and she smoothed them along her skirt, trying to brush away the feel of the man's rough calluses imprinted into her palms. He'd gripped her fingers until the reverend pronounced them man and wife, then he'd splayed his own and stalked off. Not that she was a romantic, but at the very least, an encouraging half-smile from him would've done much to calm her heart—a heart that even now rampaged against her ribs like a frenzied stallion.

A sob welled in her throat. "I had no choice, Molly. It was either that or gaol."

Molly's grey eyes peered into her own, then turned and looked out the glass. "He's a fearsome sight, that one. Bigger than a dockhand a-heftin' crates off a merchantman. Hair wild as a gypsy's. And those eyes, piercing enough to see what's in a body's soul and beyond. Why, I'd shake beneath my skirts if I had to face him alone. I think I'd rather be a prisoner."

Molly whirled, slapping a hand against her chest. "Sorry. I had no right—"

"No, you *are* right. For that is truly what I am, a hostage to this land, and now to that man." The words coated her tongue with despair, and she swallowed them down, where they lodged like bricks in the pit of her stomach. She wrapped her arms around herself, squeezing.

"What have I done?" she whispered.

"Poor thing. And here I thought I had it bad with Mrs. Greeley."

Molly lifted her hands and held them out. "But I suppose this is naught compared to what you'll suffer."

Eleanor snatched the girl's hands into her own and studied the red welts atop the backs. "What is this?"

"When I make a mistake, Mrs. Greeley whacks me with a switch, miss."

She frowned. "I am not a miss anymore, and please, call me Eleanor." For she couldn't bear to be called by her married name. Not yet—and maybe not ever.

Releasing Molly's fingers, she checked on Grace one more time. The little girl—mayhap a year and a half or nearly two—alternately dropped the yarn ball then scooped it up again, laughing. How could the little one be so happy with a savage for a father?

Not willing to ponder that question too deeply, she turned back to Molly. "What kind of mistakes could you possibly be making? You have hardly been here a day."

"Oh, everything. Anything, really." A weak smile played on her lips. "What do I know of laying out garments or dressing hair or beauty treatments and such? I'm a tavern wench. What Mrs. Greeley wants is a proper lady's maid. Can you imagine? Out here? The airs that woman puts on would make the king feel a pauper."

"I might be able to help you, at least a little." She cut a glance to where the other ladies stood, their gazes still pinned to them like falcons to a scampering rodent. At least Mrs. Greeley hadn't swept in from the back rooms—a small mercy, that.

Eleanor lowered her voice. "I have lived in grand houses and know some tricks. Serve the lady her breakfast in bed. Not a large meal, mind you, maybe some toast and tea. . .or whatever it is they drink around here. Keep her gowns hung and brushed out, not folded in a trunk or left on a peg. And before bed each night, offer to comb the tangles from her hair, then braid it. She will sleep the better for it, and you will have a much easier task come morning."

Molly beamed. "Thank you, miss—er. . .Eleanor."

"Oh, and one more thing, ask her—no—require that she change into her best gown for dinner, put on earbobs, and a necklace. Above all, use confidence in your tone, and for heaven's sake, keep your hands out of reach of her switch. You might even find a new storage place for it, hmm?"

Molly pulled her into a hug. This close to the window, the movement caught the eye of Mr. Heath, who angled his head at her. Between his untamed swath of hair and the way his hat rode so low, half his face hid in shadow, but his meaning was unmistakable.

"I must be off." She broke free, missing the woman's camaraderie before her fingertips left her sleeves.

She scooped up Grace, and the little girl wrapped her arms around her neck with a babbling sing-song.

Molly bent, retrieving the yarn ball. "At least you've got the wee one to console you."

"True. She is the best part of this situation." She nuzzled her chin against the top of the child's head, amazed once again at the tot's peaceful spirit.

She walked the few steps to the door, then turned back to Molly. "I'll stop in for a visit as soon as I may."

"God bless you. . .Eleanor."

She grinned. "You as well."

With a deep breath for courage, she crossed the threshold, wishing someone could give her advice for how to deal with the glowering brute outside.

Samuel swiped the sweat from his brow, then pulled his hat down low. Not yet noon and already the sun beat down with a heavy hand. But the longer he stood, staring across the road at the ruined corpse of a burnt house, the slicker his skin grew. Ahh, but what a liar he was. The sun had nothing to do with the perspiration coating him.

It was shame.

He flexed his fingers, trying to let go. Sure, he was a different man now. Fire had a way of forging one's spirit, purifying, cleansing, making way for new growth.

But it also killed.

Pinching the bridge of his nose, he breathed out for the hundredth time, "Forgive me, Mariah."

Just like always, no answer came from her lips—and never would.

He turned his back on the charred patch of earth and stamped across the loading dock to where Ben Sutton hefted another crate to his shoulder. The sooner he left behind this heat, this town, the wicked ugly memories, the better.

Squatting, he heaved upward, lifting the box of long-overdue supplies. With a new wife, he'd likely have to make this trip more often.

Wife. He clenched his jaw so hard it crackled. The word stuck in his craw like a hunk of unchewed meat. Yet it was done now. No going back.

He pivoted and hauled the crate to the back of the wagon, setting it next to the one Sutton set down.

Ben rubbed his hands together. "That ought to do it."

Coppery-red flashed at the corner of his sight, and he turned. Inside the storefront window, the woman—what would he call her?—looked out at him with pale blue eyes. He gave a sharp nod for her to finish up and come out.

"Whoa." A man's voice called from behind—so high-pitched, it sounded as if he'd taken a good kick to the groin.

Unbidden, the sinful thought crossed Samuel's mind that he'd like to be the one to give that kick. *Ahh, Lord, forgive me,* he prayed silently as he turned. Ignoring Angus McDivitt was an option, but it was always better to face an enemy head-on than take a stab in the back.

"Hallo, Heath." McDivitt touched his forefinger to the brim of his hat in a half-hearted greeting. "Heard you married again."

Samuel rolled his shoulders, working out the stiffness. This—*this*—was exactly what he hated about town. Everyone knowing everyone else's business, or leastwise thinking they did. He skewered Angus with a scowl. "You heard right."

Yellowed teeth peeked out from the man's beard. "Hope this one knows how to tend a fire."

Next to him, Sutton drew in a sharp breath.

Samuel clamped down on every muscle to keep from launching off the dock and pummeling the smirk from the man's face.

Angus turned his head to the scorched plot across the road. A stream of tobacco juice shot out of his mouth, desecrating the ground, before he slipped his hooded eyes back to Samuel. "Oh, that's right. Wasn't her fault, was it?"

Samuel's hands curled into fists, clenching so tight his knuckles might pop through the skin.

"He's baitin' ye, Heath," Sutton said low and slow. "Leave it be."

Samuel cocked his head at the young man. Sutton backed away, hands up. Smart fellow.

He swiveled that same killing stare to Angus. "You might fancy yourself a gentleman, McDivitt, but that beard, your manners, and the stench I'm catching downwind of you say otherwise. If you got words for me, then out with it. Otherwise, I'll thank you to be on your way."

Footsteps tapped across wood, lightly, accompanied by the swish of thin wool and linen. He didn't have to turn around to see the woman draw near—he watched her approach by the widening of Angus's eyes and the lust that grew in them with each of her steps.

Samuel may hardly know the woman, but she was his wife now. He sidestepped, blocking Angus's view.

Angus glowered at him. "Does she know?"

He froze, breathing hard.

"Do I know what, Mr. Heath?" The woman's voice drifted over his shoulder—

And stabbed him in the heart.

A shrewd leer twitched McDivitt's beard, and he kicked his horse, trotting away.

"Mr. Heath?" the woman repeated. "Is there something I should know?"

He turned, then hesitated, taken aback for a moment. Grace curled one chubby arm around the woman's neck, and with the other, ran her thumb over her cheek. Nothing astonishing, really, for his daughter was ever the most accepting of souls. The woman's response, however, stymied him. Why would a prim-and-proper Englishwoman allow such an intimate touch from a child she barely knew? Nay, not merely allow, but lean into it? It looked as if they belonged to one another—and for some odd reason, that rankled him.

"We've a ride ahead of us." His voice came out gruffer than he intended, and he worked to soften the rest. "Time we be going."

He pulled Grace from the woman's arms and trotted down the few steps, waiting for her at the front of the wagon. He offered his free hand to aid her up to the seat, and when she took it, she paused halfway up, staring hard at his exposed wrist and failing at stifling a gasp.

Thunder and earth! Had the woman never seen scars before? He shook his head. He had so many marks on his body, he'd lost count. If a little disfigurement gave her such pause, how would she react when she caught full sight of his face?

Depositing Grace in her open arms, he tugged his hat lower and rounded the front of the wagon. The big horse stamped his hoof at the movement. "Peace, *Wohali*," Samuel breathed out, speaking as much to himself as to the horse.

Swinging up to the seat, he grabbed the reins and snapped the leather. Wohali whinnied a complaint at the added weight but turned onto the road. Samuel made straight for the creek, and as the horse descended the small embankment, the wagon bumped and jostled to one side, tipping the seat at an angle. Grace laughed, but the woman grabbed his arm and didn't let go, even as the wheels splashed through the water.

Samuel hid a smile. Was the proper Englishwoman too dainty for a spray of creek water?

She yanked back her hand and glanced over her shoulder as Wohali led them up onto even ground. "Where are we going?"

He stood, scanning for the two tracks of grass flattened by his earlier ride, and guided Wohali toward them before he sat again. "Home."

"But. . .the road, the town. . .they are behind us."

Transferring the reins to one hand, he scratched the stubble on his chin. "Whatever gave you the impression I live in Newcastle?"

A martin's song kept time with the roll of the wheels. Grace babbled nonsense mixed with Cherokee and a few English words thrown in until finally, after a big yawn, she settled on the woman's lap and closed her eyes. The woman said nothing. For miles. Not even when the thick of forest ate them alive.

Reaching into a pouch at his side, he pulled out a piece of jerky, took a bite, then handed the rest to her.

Her eyes went wide, and for the briefest of moments, the freckles on her nose darkened, but then she set the jerky to her mouth and nibbled.

At last, she spoke. "Mr. Heath, may I ask how much farther it is to your home?"

"Woman, you can ask anything you like. You're not in England anymore. And you can drop the mister. Call me Heath, or Samuel, if you prefer. Mister's for a gentleman, which I'm not." He wiped his mouth with the back of his hand. "To answer your question, though, we ought to make it by sundown."

Grace shifted on her lap, the smell of jerky pulling her from her dreams. The woman looked to him with a question in her eyes, but none on her lips.

"She can have some," he answered. He studied her face, what he could see of it from such an angle, anyway. The sun burnt her cheeks to a rosy red and washed out some of the color from the wisps of hair escaping her straw hat. She chewed quietly, while Grace smacked her lips.

"You know, most women would've jawed my ear off by now."

She quirked a brow. "Sorry. . .jawed?"

"Talked. Spoken. *Gawonisgv*." Her face twisted as the Cherokee slipped from his tongue, clearly confusing her. "Look, if you've a mind to say something, then say it. I don't hold with pretense."

"Very well." She shifted herself and Grace so that she faced him. "Am I correct in thinking you would like me to teach your daughter proper English?"

He nodded. "You are."

"Then I suggest you start by speaking it yourself, sir."

Somewhere deep, in a long-forgotten storeroom in his chest, laughter rose and rumbled out. He threw back his head and howled until moisture dampened the skin beneath his eyes. He'd opened some kind of floodgate, but what? And where?

In her. . .or in him?

Chapter 8

Eleanor's head bobbed as she fought the urge to give in to fatigue. A wicked temptation to lean sideways, rest her head against the arm of the wild man beside her, and pass out almost nudged her that direction—until the next hard bump lifted her off the seat and crashed her backside against the unforgiving wood. She grimaced. Surely that part of her would be nothing but purple on the morrow.

At first the big horse pulling the wagon frightened her for it seemed as wild as its owner, but now, as they ascended yet another steep stretch of road, she was glad for the powerful muscles that strained against the harness. She gripped the seat's edge as they wound through more trees. She'd seen better goat trails on the Devonshire moors.

They lurched over one more rise, the ground evened, and Mr. Heath called out, "Whoa." His thick arm flexed, pulling the horse to a stop in a small clearing.

To one side, down an embankment, a small creek cut into the earth like a vein. La, what a thought! Clearly the shadowy forest colored her attitude to a gloomy hue. She cast her gaze to the other side. Here, a few outbuildings huddled near one another for safety, the towering pine behind hemming in the area. A tremor shivered across her shoulders. This foreboding place looked like a wicked wood from a Gaelic faerie tale.

Mr. Heath set the brake and hopped down.

Grace bounced in her lap, reaching her arms out for her father.

Eleanor bit her lip. They'd already eaten. No foliage blocked them from continuing. So why did he swing Grace around and set her on the ground? Was this some kind of traveler's shelter to duck in for an evening?

She laid her hand atop his, using his strength to ease her rattled bones to the earth. "Why are we stopping here?"

He cut her a glance, half his face hidden in the growing dusk. "This is home."

Peering one way, then another, she looked for the house. Was it beyond, in a trail through the woods? Impossible to say, for greens and blacks choked out the view. The only buildings she saw were the two in front of her. One was larger, but not by much. Both were made of crude logs, stacked atop each other. Pine needles and moss littered the roofs. On one, stairs led to a porch—maybe—so much stacked wood made it hard to tell. The other was clearly a byre, straw and hay strewn on the ground in front of a shut door, a pen of rough-hewn timbers circling behind. Surely Mr. Heath would lead her and little Grace beyond these coarse structures to his home.

But his long legs loped up the stairs and disappeared between the stacks of wood. Grace pulled herself up behind him, one chubby leg at a time.

Eleanor stood, gaping. Alone. In the middle of a wilderness. The last of day's light fled, and darkness crept toward her on silent feet. She wrapped her arms around herself, squeezing, trying desperately to remember that God was in control, that this was His creation every bit as much as an English dell or holly hedgerow.

A growl rumbled out from somewhere in the maze of tree trunks. Low. Throaty. She clutched her skirts and scampered up the stairs, suddenly preferring the wild man with the tomahawk at his side and the knife that peeked out his boot top.

She stopped just inside the threshold. Throbbing started at her temple, spreading outward, and she pressed her fingers against it. The hold of the *Charming Lucy* had been bigger than this room. Her gaze darted from a primitive hearth, to piles of pelts stacked against a wall, skipped over a chair and a crib, and finally landed on the bedstead—the only bed in the room. Her heart quit beating as she stared, horrified.

"You'll never aspire to anything higher than a trollop, girl."

Oh, she was married all right, but did the words "I do" make her any less a trollop than what her father had prophesied? She licked her lips, refusing to look at Mr. Heath.

He lit a grease lamp, and as the flame grew in strength, light spread from corner to corner. Truly, there wasn't much more to see other than a few pots in a heap and some crates on end.

"I'll see to the horse and freight."

She jumped at the man's voice and stepped aside, giving him a wide berth as he passed. The door clattered shut, and then patting footsteps flew across the room. Arms wrapped around her legs and squeezed. She could hardly see Grace's little face through a blur of tears as she swung her up. A yawn stretched the girl's mouth, and she popped a thumb into her mouth.

Eleanor yawned as well. "Tired little one? So am I." Her voice lowered to a whisper. "Weary of this day, this wretched land. . .my life."

She set Grace down in the crib, then rummaged through one of the crates, pulling out a tiny nightdress for the girl. By the time she crossed back to the little one's side, Grace curled into a ball, eyes shut.

She couldn't help but smile. "I do not blame you."

The jingle of harness from outside stole the smile from her face. Mr. Heath would be back soon. In here. With her.

Turning in a circle, she surveyed the room once again, looking for. . . what? A secret passage leading to a chamber fit for a princess? Bitterness pinched her throat tight. Yes, that's exactly what she wished for.

With a sigh, she plopped down into the chair, avoiding the bed altogether. What was the point? There was no possible way she could undo her stays by herself—nor would she lie with her husband.

Hopefully, Mr. Heath would remember what he'd agreed to.

Samuel shoved the stable door shut, putting an end to a very long day. Halfway to the house, he stopped, letting the night air soak into his skin, damp and cool. Closing his eyes, he filled his lungs with the tanginess of pine. Here, in the midst of shushing breeze and cricket song, he knew God lived.

And grace upon grace, God knew him right back.

"Lord, have mercy," he prayed as he stalked to the house. How did one suddenly live with a woman again?

Using the same footing as if hunting a panther, he stepped over the threshold quietly, not willing to wake Grace or startle the woman. The grease lamp burned as bright as he'd left it. The bed lay untouched. And there, reclining on the chair, head turned aside and eyes closed, the woman breathed evenly. He pressed the door shut behind him with a silent hand. She must've been so tired that she collapsed without thought.

He removed his tomahawk, then loosened his belt and slipped that off as well. The woman shifted at his movement, but did not waken. At that angle, all bent and draped on the hickory chair, she'd surely be stiff come morning. Ought he lift her as he would Grace and carry her to bed? He raked a hand through his hair. No, that would surely scare the breath from her and stir up Grace in the process. He crossed over to her and halted—then frowned. If she opened her eyes now, with him towering like a bear on hind legs, the result would be no better. So he squatted, arms resting on his thighs.

For the first time, he studied her unguarded. Fair skin, roughened in patches by wind and reddened by the sun, curved over high cheekbones that were quite fine, almost sparrow-like in delicacy. Without the harshness of daylight, her hair took on a burnished sheen, like the ridgeline of an autumn sky, when reds and oranges flared as the sun set. Her lips, somewhat chapped, were surprisingly full, almost overlarge compared to the oval of her face—but not alarmingly so. No, he rocked forward, leaning for a closer look. On the contrary, the only thing alarming about the woman was the way she kept herself all buttoned up tight, as if she'd never known the freedom of laughter in a meadow or running her toes along the soft silt of a creek bed. What kind of life had she known, living among his enemies?

Repentance never came easy, but he'd learned that when it did come calling, to open the door wide with a hearty welcome. He never should have treated this woman so harshly in town this morning. The rude awakening. The heartless marriage vows. His silence on the drive home. All because he was too consumed with ignoring his own pain to be mindful of her feelings. He hung his head. *Oh God, forgive me. Again.*

Weary to the bone, he lifted his face and nudged her leg with the backs of his fingers. "Woman, go to bed."

White knuckles gripped the chair arms, and she shot forward—which only widened her eyes farther when she nearly touched him, nose for nose.

He stifled a laugh as she shrank back, one hand flattened against her chest, the other choking life from the chair's arm.

"It's been a fair long day for you." He kept his voice even, using the same low tone as when he tamed a horse or stopped Grace's tears. "This is your home now. You needn't sleep in a chair."

Her blue eyes took on a grey color, like the first billows of a spring storm, then she turned her head aside. "Clearly I am able to."

"You're able to what?"

"Sleep in a chair."

"It won't do for you to walk with a hobble come morning. Grace is. . . well, she can be a handful, sweet as she is." He rose and swept out a hand toward the bedstead. "Go ahead and stretch yourself out. Get some rest."

She snapped her face back to his, her cheeks flushing as if he'd bruised her. "Thank you." She snipped out the words. "But I prefer to remain as I am."

Interesting. Something he'd said or done had perturbed her, but what? He rubbed his jaw, going over the past few minutes, and came up empty-handed. "Listen, woman—"

She shot to her feet. "I have a name, sir!"

"So do I, and it's not sir."

Her eyes glittered with unspoken terror. This was about more than a name. He stepped toward her, and she retreated, bumping against the chair.

"Mr. Heath, I believe I made it plain that I will not. . ." She pinched her lips and looked at the bed.

Ahh. . .of course. He should've thought. Her conditions for marriage, the way she recoiled whenever he drew too near, the measuring and weighing of every glance all made sense. She'd never been with a man, and he chided himself for not thinking of it sooner.

"*Tatsu'hwa*." The name rolled off his tongue, clear and true, feeling as fitting as if she'd been called so from her first breath—and far less dangerous than calling her wife.

She whirled, the hem of her skirt swishing in a whirl above her feet. "Pardon me?"

"You're stubborn as a mule, determined as an oxen, but anxious as a wild bird." With each word, he took a step closer, until he reached out and snagged the loose piece of hair off her shoulder and held it up for her to see. "A red bird. And so I'll call you Tatsu'hwa."

"Tot-soo-wah?" She jerked away, brows weighted with a fierce glower. "I do not understand you. If you so disdain the English language, then why take on an English wife?"

The question cut, and the answer drew blood. None of the other women in town would have a murderer.

Shoving down a growl, he stalked over to the pile of pelts and worked one loose. The accusation fit him like a well-worn moccasin. He clutched a fur and strode to the door.

"Where are you going?" she asked.

The question followed him outside, unanswered. The day had been hard enough as is, but his gut told him the night would surely prove to be a devil.

Chapter 9

Eleanor woke with a start. She shot up from the chair, then grabbed the side of her neck where a wicked muscle stabbed pain clear into her shoulder. The sting was nothing, though, compared to the torment of her dreams. . . .

A beast of a bear had been chasing her, pawing the hem of her skirt until she fell face-first into the dirt. Even now she could feel the grit in her teeth, the scrape of her chin against gravel, so real had it been. When the bear roared, she'd turned, only to stare into the dark depths of a worse nightmare—the all-consuming gaze of her new husband. He pulled her to him, wrapping his arms around her, but she could only see half his face—the half she'd yet to see.

Claw marks ran the length of it, leaving trails of pooling blood. . . .

She shivered and rubbed her hands along her arms. When she worked up enough courage, she dared a glance at the bed. No bear. No man. The tightness in her shoulders loosened. Would that the unmerciful squeeze of her stays might slacken as well. She tugged at the boning. She'd have to figure out some way to remove the stays laced at her back—and soon.

But for now, Grace peered at her with big brown eyes, gnawing the edge of her crib with tiny, white teeth.

"Poor thing!" She rushed over and scooped up the child. "You must be hungry. Shall we see about some porridge then, hmm?"

Grace giggled and tugged at Eleanor's hair, pulling loose the few strands yet moored by pins. Eleanor frowned. She'd have to figure something out about that unruly mess, too.

The girl fidgeted, and she set her down. Grace took off like a musket ball, and Eleanor watched, wondering at the child's speed. The girl raced over to a pot in the corner and hiked her little shift.

Eleanor turned with a smile as liquid tinkled against earthenware. Managing Mr. Heath might be bothersome, but Grace was a continual delight.

After a thorough search of the cabin, which uncovered more jerky, dried corn, a jar of mashed berries, and a mixture of who-knew-what, she abandoned any hope of finding a sack of oats for porridge. Maybe he'd purchased some yesterday?

She held the front door open for Grace. "Come along, little one. We have a hunt ahead of us."

Eleanor paused on the porch while Grace worked her way down the few stairs. Cool air whispered through the pine boughs, lifting a wisp of hair across her face. She batted it back, taking strange delight in the way morning sunshine dappled patterns of contrasting greens on the cleared plot of land. England had its woods and forests, but not planted on rising slopes such as this.

Grace scampered toward the stable, falling once with arms outstretched, but even as she surely must have felt the burn of gravel on the heels of her little hands, she never quit singing. *"Edoda, Edoda."*

Lifting her skirt above her shoe tops, Eleanor descended from the porch and crossed the yard. As soon as she pulled the stable door wide enough for Grace to slip through, the fair-headed pixie darted inside.

"Edoda!" Whatever the girl babbled about, she emphasized with a shriek.

By the time Eleanor stepped inside and her eyes adjusted to the dim light, Grace's happiness folded into a fat-lipped frown. She sat on a brown-furred pelt next to a stack of crates, clearly as rankled as the woolen blanket twisted into a ball near her feet. One stall over, the big horse stamped her hoof and whickered.

A guilty stain spread over Eleanor's heart. Clearly this was where Mr. Heath had spent the night. She'd driven the man—her *husband*—from his own house to sleep in a stable. What kind of woman did that?

Instantly the shame evaporated, leaving behind a hard set to her jaw. The kind that didn't want to be married in the first place.

She snatched a metal bar from the bench near the door and stalked over to the crates, determined to pry the lid off each one until she uncovered some oats. Whether she liked it or not, this was her lot now. She'd make this place the best possible proper-English-home in this backcountry wilderness—or die in the trying. With each wedge of the bar and accompanying lift, wood splintered, but wouldn't budge.

"You'll never aspire to anything higher than a trollop, girl."

"Yes, I will. Yes. I. Will!" She hadn't realized she'd cried the words aloud until little hands wrapped around her legs from behind. She froze, staring at ruined wood. The lid would never be used again, for she'd battered it into nothing more fit than kindling.

Spent, she let the rod slip from her fingers to the dirt floor, then turned and picked up Grace. "Come on, wee one. I think I know where there is some jerky."

She stepped out into the light—and nearly rammed into the broad chest of Mr. Heath. The top of his blue trade shirt was loosely laced. This close, she could see the curve of his collarbone, the hard planes of tanned skin sporting the same dark hair that flew wild from beneath his hat. The morning coolness remained, but why was she so hot?

She retreated a step. "Good morning, Mr. Heath."

Grace twisted in her arms, reaching for the man. "Edoda!"

He grabbed the girl and swung her high, his long hair rippling with the movement, like a curtain blown back from a glass.

Curious for a peek at his whole face, Eleanor stretched her neck.

He bowed his head so quickly, his swath of hair plummeted back into place before she could sneak a glance.

Settling the girl in one arm, he rested his gaze on Eleanor.

La! She ought not be so inquisitive about his appearance when she must look every bit the savage herself. She grabbed her hair and pulled it back, holding it at the nape of her neck.

He smiled. "Looks like you had a rough night, Tatsu'hwa."

She licked her lips, stalling. The foreign name chafed, sounding so strange. It was like the wiping of a slate, erasing who she was and forcing her into a creation of his own making. Ought she say something? But what was the alternative? The thought of her Christian name on his lips or worse—*wife*—was far too intimate. No, better he use his silly, made-up title than that.

She met his gaze, noting a few stray bits of straw in his hair from his own rough night. "As did you."

"Trust me, I've had worse." He winked. "Are you hungry?"

"Famished." She spoke loudly to cover the agreeing growl of her stomach.

"Good. I've brought you something." He set down Grace and unloosed a strap crossing over his chest.

Oh, no. She would not be drawn into looking at his muscles again. Eleanor shot her gaze to her feet, not wishing a repeat view of his flesh. Two mounds of dun-colored fur landed near her shoes, sending up a puff of dirt where they hit.

She lifted her face to his, brow crumpling. "What is this?"

"Rabbit."

Her mouth dropped, horrified. Apparently he wanted more than a nursemaid and wife—but she was no cook.

"Don't tell me. . .ahh." He nodded, and for a moment a wisp of breeze pulled his long hair to the side. He dropped, snatching up the rabbits and giving Grace a bucking ride that made her giggle. When he straightened, he turned slightly, the swath of hair once again hanging like a veil on his left cheek. Was everything about the man secrets and questions?

"Why don't you go fetch water, and I'll skin these for you. This time, anyway."

She gaped, trying to gather his words and lay them out in a sensible fashion. Clearly he expected her to do something with the rabbits once the fur had been removed, and worse—she'd be the one doing the skinning in the future. "I am sorry, sir, but porridge is the extent of my culinary skills. I was a governess back in England, not a cook."

"Woman, need I remind you that you are not in England anymore?" He nodded toward a large metal bucket sitting next to the stable. "You'll find water, what there is of it in this drought, at the creek. Think you can manage that?"

She whirled, unwilling to let him see the flare of insult burning on her cheeks. Beast! He was more an animal than anything roaming these woods.

Or was he?

Suddenly the bucket weighed heavy in her hand, and she turned, forcing a light tone to her voice. "There are not any, em, wild animals around here, are there? I mean, this close to the house and all."

"You're in the middle of the backcountry." He chuckled, shaking his head like a shaggy dog. "Of course there are. . .bear, wildcats, wolves. But it's the rogue Shawnee or Creek sneaking up on you with a knife that are the most dangerous."

Her heart pounded hard in her chest, yet she stifled any outward sign of fear until she stalked past him. Then she bit her lip, stiffened her shoulders, and swept her gaze from side to side, trying hard not to imagine advancing savages.

No, indeed. This was not England.

Samuel laid the rabbit skins out flat in the stable. He grabbed a stretching rack and tied off the first pelt, did the same with the other, then hung them to dry from the rafters.

Stretching out a kink in his lower back, he eyed the bearskin on the ground. Maybe he ought to grab another one and double it over if this was to be his new bedchamber. He bit back a grin. What would the little governess do if he demanded to sleep under his own roof? In his own bed? The skittish filly would no doubt bolt and run—much as she'd almost done when he'd slapped the rabbit meat on the table. He could yet see the image of her wide eyes, whites as large as a summer moon.

The shrill cry of a mockingbird shot through the open door. Nothing unusual—except for the repeated seven-note staccato at the end. Inoli's call. He scrubbed his jaw. Should he invite the man in and introduce him to Red Bird? He snorted at that thought. If a mere rabbit set her skirts akilter, what would meeting a Cherokee warrior do for her constitution? Mayhap better to put that off a day or two.

But if he joined Inoli for a day in the woods, would the woman be able to manage on her own, her first day here? And should he really neglect once again the smokehouse he ought be building? Put off clearing some farmland? What about the fence? The new pen? All the chores he'd saved for fine weather? No. He really should not run wild instead of tending to business.

The call came again.

Hang it.

Snatching his quiver of arrows from a peg near the door, he strapped it on, then grabbed his bow and slung it over a shoulder. He raced outside and sprinted into the woods, legs stretched at full run, breeze fresh on his face. Ahh. He belonged here. Without Grace tied to his back, he ran like a stag, bounding through ravines and leaping over logs.

Ahead, in a small clearing of mountain fern, stood his brother, black hair pulled tight and falling down his back like a horsetail. Inoli turned at his approach, raising his arm in greeting.

Samuel shrugged off his bow, threw down the quiver, then launched his full weight atop his brother. Air rushed out of Inoli's lungs as they hit the ground. They wrestled like lads of twelve, one gaining the upper hand, only to be taken out at the knees with the next strike.

Finally, breathing hard, Samuel pinned Inoli to the dirt. "Enough?"

His brother turned aside and spit out blood from a split lip. *"Eligwu!"*

Samuel pulled back and half stood, resting his hands on his thighs as he drank in air.

Inoli rolled over and swiped his hand across his mouth, then speared him with a black stare. "Why does Ya'nu strike?"

"Why does my brother send women to my door? And don't bother denying it. I know you had a hand in telling Running Doe about me taking a wife." He strode to where he'd cast off his weapons.

By the time he returned, Inoli stood with folded arms. "Running Doe is not happy."

He cuffed his brother on the back. "Then maybe you should be the one to bring her happiness, my brother."

"Pah! She will have none but you—and well you know it."

"Then she will have none." He shrugged. "I am a married man now."

They turned in unison and headed into the woods, their moccasins silent on the deer path. Samuel narrowed his eyes. Overgrown fern fronds brushed against his shins. Ash and hickory volunteers flattened beneath his step. Though squirrels chattered and insects buzzed a low drone, no large animals had traversed this trail for quite some time.

When the path widened, Inoli gained his side, creeping up like a shadow. "How goes it?"

He cocked a brow at his brother. "I slept in the stable last night."

Inoli's shoulders shook with held-in laughter. "White women know nothing of passion."

"Maybe not." *Or maybe. . .* He batted away a persistent mosquito diving for his brow. Something flared in the Englishwoman's cheeks whenever he stood too near. Fear, most likely, but she held it in check—and that took strength. "Grace will benefit from her, I think. The woman is intelligent and learned."

Inoli grunted. "At least you are free to hunt unhindered again."

The woods thinned, and they paused at the edge of a narrow-throated meadow. Inoli squatted and pulled out a pouch of pemmican. He took a bite, then handed some over.

Samuel crouched beside him, chewing. He savored the salty sweetness, for his next words would leave a bitter taste. "I spoke with Ben Sutton in town yesterday."

His brother's eyes shot to his.

"He gave me this." He reached into a pouch at his side and pulled out a small deerskin scrap with a crude map drawn in black. "Lifted it off a trader come from Keowee, making for Charles Towne."

Inoli traced the painted strokes with his finger, his lips forming the names of nearby rivers and landmarks, yet no sound came out. Eventually, lines hardened at the sides of his mouth, and his neck stiffened. "This is our land."

Samuel nodded. "That is right, my brother. It is as we suspected. Attakullakulla is making plans—plans of which the Sons must be told. Yet I daren't leave Grace and Red Bird—"

"Red Bird?" A furrow plowed across Inoli's brow.

He'd laugh at the sight, if the gravity of the future of their lands weren't drawn out for sale on a piece of animal skin.

"My wife," he said simply.

Inoli stared off into the meadow, as if reason might be found in the sway of the grasses. "You do not use her *un'ega* name?"

"I will not. I tried civilized life with Mariah, and look how that turned out." He rubbed the tightness in his neck, a vain attempt to smooth memories too knotted to ever be undone. "As I said, I daren't leave the woman and Grace alone to make the trek to Charles Towne. Red Bird can hardly fetch water without fainting from fear. Before I venture away for days on end, I need to teach her some defense skills. Wouldn't hurt to teach her to cook something other than porridge, either."

Inoli watched him, his sharp ears hearing the unspoken. They were two sides of the same blade—for he'd have done the same.

"What are you asking, Ya'nu?"

He scrubbed the last bits of pemmican from his lips. "I need you to make the run this time."

The caw of an overhead crow rode the crest of Inoli's rumble of dissent. "I do not have enough English words."

"No need." With one more reach inside the pouch, he pulled out another scrap, this one of rag paper, smaller, rolled into a tight coil, and sealed in wax. He held it out in an open palm. "I never meet my contact face-to-face anyway. Just slip into Circular's Graveyard, off Meeting Street. In the third to last row, closest to the hedges, there's a skull engraved on the fifth headstone, a space carved out in the mouth. Name on the stone is Simmons, though I doubt that information will do you any good. Tuck these inside the hole—but watch your back."

Inoli's lips straightened into a line, unreadable in every sense, yet he reached for the note and the map.

A movement on the far side of the lea drew both their faces aside. The smallest flash of fawn rustled in the undergrowth, maybe twenty-five yards off. They stood together, the quick jut of Inoli's chin handing him the privilege.

He frowned, but shrugged off his bow and reached for an arrow. It was certainly no privilege that he'd just handed his brother—it was a death sentence should Inoli be caught by the English.

And his own life if they tortured his name from his brother's mouth.

Chapter 10

Cool night air crept across the floor and wrapped around Eleanor's ankles, working its way up her legs beneath her skirt. If the front door had blown open, she sure hadn't heard the gust of wind. She turned from the table she'd fashioned out of planks, then froze in place. Her husband had not only entered, but had already shut the front door and hung his hat on a peg. How could a man that big move with such silence? His gaze darted from the newly made table, to a mug of wildflowers she'd picked with Grace, then swept the perimeter, taking in the straightened crates, the pots hung on a wall instead of heaped in a pile, and the folded pile of Grace's clothing set sweetly in a basket.

His lips parted, but it took awhile before sound came out. "What have you done?"

Clasping her hands in front of her, she lifted her chin. "This place was in need of some tidying up, Mister—"

His dark eyes shot to hers, and she clamped her mouth. Though he'd told her to call him otherwise, his name stuck in her throat, scraping it raw. It was too intimate to call the man Samuel, yet Heath seemed so harsh, something the likes of a pirate might catcall.

And husband was out of the question.

So she stood there, biting her lower lip, saying nothing.

"Well." He kept his voice even, the half of his face she could see as stoic as a rune stone and about as impossible to read. "Looks like you had quite the busy time of it."

Was he pleased? Angry? What? The longer she stood there trying to decipher the curve of his shoulders and set of his jaw, the larger her uncertainty grew—until it nearly squashed her beneath the weight.

Oh, bother! Why care what the man thought? He'd been gone all day, leaving her to fend for herself and Grace. Desperate for her hands to do something other than twist into knots, she swept her arm toward the table. "Would you like some dinner?"

His brow disappeared into the dark swath of hair covering his forehead.

"I already ate dinner at noon. Around here we call the evening meal *supper*. But in answer to your question, aye. . .I've a fair appetite."

In six long strides, he crossed the floor and straddled the barrel she'd hauled in.

She stood near her own barrel, opposite his, waiting for the brute to rise until she sat.

He merely picked up his knife.

She cleared her throat, several times over.

Finally, he cocked his head, suspending his speared piece of meat over the pot at center. "I suspect you've got something to say."

A retort sat on the edge of her tongue, prickly and condemning. She swallowed it back. Why should she presume a wild man to know anything about manners?

"A gentleman waits for a lady to take her seat first," she explained.

"That so?" He grunted like the animal he was. But to his credit, he set the meat back in the pot and rose, towering over her. "That better?"

"Much." She awarded him a half smile, then spread her skirt over the barrel as she sat. The movement cut her stays into the bruises on her ribs, and she stifled a moan. Before he could load up his plate, she held out hers. "And a gentleman always serves a lady first, as well."

His barrel groaned as he shifted—or had the noise come from his throat? No matter, for he skewered a piece of the rabbit she'd boiled all day and scraped it onto her plate, using the rim to lever it off.

A horrid odor wafted up from the grey chunk of meat in front of her, similar to the way leather shoes smelled when they'd been worn one too many times. She pressed down her knife—for knives were the only utensils she'd found—yet the meat in no way gave to the pressure. So she employed a sawing action, only to have the rabbit skate from one edge of the plate to the other. She dared a peek across the table, where he fared no better.

"The meat may be a little overcooked, I think." Oh, that was brilliant. Her conversational skills suffered as much as she in this godforsaken country.

He wrapped his big fingers like a fist around the knife handle, then stabbed the point into his meal, pausing before popping the piece into his mouth. "I hauled home some venison today. Maybe you'll fare better with that."

He chewed, and chewed—then chewed some more. His jaw worked overtime, the muscles on the side of his neck standing out against his long sweep of hair. His throat bobbed, and she averted her eyes, not wishing to watch the big lump travel the length of his throat.

He snatched the mug off the table, guzzled a big drink, then spewed liquid all over the floor. "What is this?"

She frowned up at him, then took a sip of the tea she'd brewed nearly as long as she'd cooked the rabbit. A sour taste lodged at the back of her throat. No, not sour. The liquid tasted like death. Maybe those hadn't been tea leaves in the pouch she'd found. She coughed her mouthful back into her cup, mortified, then seized the scrap of cloth she'd fashioned into a napkin and wiped her lips, tempted to dry off her tongue, too.

His eyes widened. "And what on God's green earth is that?"

An angry whimper from Grace's crib chided his volume.

"A napkin." She forced her voice to remain calm, hoping the effect would bring peace.

He stood so quickly, the barrel wobbled. "Woman, didn't I tell you you're not in England anymore?"

She shot upward as well, anger shaking the fabric of her skirt. The nerve of the man! Everything about this severe and rugged place screamed at her, accusing her of her foreign status, reminding her she didn't fit in—would *never* fit in. Nor did she want to, despite her pathetic attempts otherwise.

The crib rattled side to side as Grace rolled fitfully.

Eleanor tucked a loose piece of hair behind her ear, unsure how to navigate the waters of roiling emotions churning in her empty belly. She frowned at her husband—then scowled inwardly at herself for thinking of him as such. "Manners are not bound by geographical locations, sir. If you want Grace to have a proper upbringing, then you will use a napkin when you dine."

"I'm not hungry anymore." He strode to the door.

"Wait!"

He wheeled about, a question written in the curve of his shoulders.

A sigh drained the rest of her anger, and she tugged at the stays digging into her ribs. This wasn't how it was supposed to be. Indeed, nothing about this encounter was going as expected. He should've been pleased with her cleaning efforts, sated and relaxed after eating his fill of dinner, or supper, or whatever he wanted to call it, so much that he'd grant her request of going in to town on the morrow.

But the tainted taste of meat in her mouth and unused napkin staring up at her from the table trapped the appeal in her throat. She couldn't ask him now, not when he bristled like a cornered porcupine.

Defeated, she simply nodded toward the pallet of pelts she'd made for him in the corner farthest from the bed. "You do not have to sleep in the stable."

His head reared back, and he looked at her down his nose. "What are you saying, woman?"

Her mouth dried to ashes, and she licked her lips. Surely he didn't think she'd just invited him into her bed? "I made up a pallet for you. This is your home, after all."

For a moment, something flashed deep in his brown eyes, then disappeared as fast as it came. "No, it's *our* home. And I thank you."

He strode to the pallet and sank, pulling off one boot and then the other, though she wondered if they could be called such. Tall as Hessians, crafted of soft leather, sporting fringes at top and laces up front, these were nothing like she'd ever seen—and neither was the man. Oh, she'd spied many a brawny redcoat back in London, but Mr. Heath was more than height and muscle. Something about him filled the entire space of a room when he entered. Why? Was it the determined tilt of his jaw? The air of mystery he hid behind that swath of dark hair? Or maybe. . . .

His gaze flicked up to hers, catching her in the act of studying him. She blustered into action, scraping the dinner remains back into the iron pot and covering all her humiliation with a lid. He chuckled.

She ignored him. Removing the glass chimney from the lamp, she blew out the flame. Darkness settled over the room, as even as Grace's breathing. Eleanor padded to the bed and lay down on top of it, unwilling to commit to slipping beneath the blanket. Had she done the right thing by allowing him to remain in the same room all night? She turned to her side, slipping her hand beneath the pillow, and rested her fingers atop the cold metal of the knife she'd hidden.

"I'm facing the wall, Tatsu'hwa." The man's voice blended with the shadows, wending its way across the room. "I will not turn around. Be at peace and do what you need to ready yourself for bed."

"I am in bed." The words came out before she thought. Heat blazed from head to toe for saying such a thing to a man, even if the man was her husband.

His sigh rose, drifting somewhere up near the rafters. "You can't sleep in your gown forever, woman. It will rot right off your bones. I give you my word I will not look."

Her throat closed. If only it were that easy.

"Have I given you cause not to trust me?" His question came out low, husky, almost as if it might never have come out at all if he'd not forced it.

She shifted her head, sifting through the layers of what he asked, sensing her answer held some kind of strange power. The man knew tragedy—deeply, bitterly—as evidenced by the lack of a mother for Grace. Had his first wife not trusted him? What had happened to her? Was that the root of his brusque ways?

"No," she said at last. "It is not that."

"Then what is it?"

She bit the inside of her cheek so hard, a metallic taste spread on her tongue. How to answer? Invent a story? Concoct a logical answer that might satisfy? Embellish or outright lie?

She smoothed a hand along her tummy, and her stays took a bite. If she didn't answer honestly, she might be buried in this bodice—soon. "It is my stays."

The noise started low, kind of a rumble, really. She lifted her head, listening hard, and a great belly laugh slapped her in the face.

She rose to her elbows. "I find no humor in the situation, Mr. Heath!"

The laughter faded, and as soon as it disappeared, she missed the happy sound, for what came next chilled her to the marrow.

Rustling sounded on the pelts. Feet hit the floor.

"Get up," he said.

She froze. "Pardon?" The black silhouette of the man stood at the foot of her bed. What little light crawled in through the cracks of burlap hung on the windows brushed moonfire along his profile, tracing half his face, the cut of his cheekbones, the square angles of his jaw, and the lines of his full mouth.

"I said get up, Tatsu'hwa."

There was no disobeying that voice. She'd heard it before in the summons of a duke or instructions from a countess.

Rolling over, she slid the knife beneath her sleeve, concealing the weapon should she need it, then rose on legs as shaky as a newborn foal. What did he intend?

But he did not advance. He merely folded his arms. "Take the gown off."

"Mr. Heath!" She backed up until the log wall slammed into her back.

He widened his stance, broad as a mountain and every bit as unmovable. "Take the gown off, and I'll get you out of your stays."

"And how do you propose to do that? For I shall not allow you to touch me." She sucked in air, mind whirring. Instinct told her that simple scratches on this man's face would not deter him as it had the duke. The knife pressed against her skin, cold and hard inside her sleeve. Would she be forced to use it against him?

Could she?

"No touching involved." Moonlight slid along the sharp edge of his own raised blade, hers nothing but a child's toy in comparison.

"No!" Her eyes widened. "Absolutely not. Come no closer."

"How long have you been in that gown?"

Her cheeks scorched. This was worse than mortifying. This type of discussion would never happen in England.

Slowly, her head sank. As he had so aptly reminded her, England was far, far away. "Two days," she whispered.

"Well, then I figure it's like this." He stepped toward her, stopping an arm's length away. "There's not another woman around for miles to assist you. Either you let me help, or you'll develop such a rash as to take the hide off your bones. I suspect even now your ribs are bruised and you're chafing something fierce."

She jerked up her face, scowling. How would he know?

"So, Red Bird," his voice softened. "Shall I cut the blessed thing off or unlace it?"

Her gaze shot from his face to his knife, then back again. Searching inwardly, desperately, she mustered every scrap of courage she could find to say what she must to this stranger. "Unlace it, please. But turn around, first."

Staring at her like a great black panther, he tucked the blade into the waistband of his breeches—thank the Lord he'd taken to his pallet without removing them—and turned his broad shoulders to her.

She slid out the knife from her sleeve and returned it to her hiding spot beneath the pillow. Her fingers trembled as she unpinned her bodice. As she peeled off her gown and slipped out of her petticoats, lying all on the bed, she shivered. In naught but her stays and shift, she felt as stripped bare and vulnerable as the many times her father thrashed her with a switch.

No. She would *not* think of him. Not now. Stiffening, she turned, so that they stood back to back. "All right. I am ready."

He moved without sound, but move he did, for she could feel the burn of his gaze against her skin. She clenched every muscle, her fingernails digging crescent-moons into the palms of her hands.

His fingers skimmed over the fabric, warm as an August breeze tasting every leaf, then worked the knot set between her shoulder blades. Had Biz purposely tied such a tangle?

The dark world turned watery. This was silly. Hadn't Biz said never to cry because of a man? Even so, this was not the way she'd envisioned marriage, the way of a husband with a wife. Unbidden, a single tear slipped quietly down her cheek, landing on her lip.

His breath moistened the nape of her neck. The heat of his fingers traveled down to the small of her back as he loosened the binding. The warmth of his body reached across the thin space between them and rippled across her shoulders, along her arms, and settled in her fingers, all shaky and moist. He smelled of earth and pine, like a beast of the forest in human form, all salty and woodsy.

A summer sun couldn't have scorched her more thoroughly. She crossed her arms over her chest, a vain attempt to still the pounding against her ribs.

"I can almost hear your heartbeat, Tatsu'hwa," he whispered, bending close, his words caressing the naked curve of her ear lobe. "Be at peace. I am not your enemy."

She froze, standing there long after he retreated to his pallet across the room, concentrating on nothing but breathing for the longest time. If she let her thoughts roam free, she knew exactly from what cliff they'd plummet.

Allowing the man to remove her stays in the dark of night was one thing—but how would she get the wretched garment back on in the light of morning?

Samuel rolled off the pallet before daylight even thought of rising from its bed. Across the room, the woman breathed easy, as did Grace from the crib. Innocents always slept. He'd tried, well into the witching hours, but who could sleep when memories taunted without mercy? His body remembered all too well what it was like to touch a woman. His mind was assaulted by the civilizing ways of Red Bird, striking too close to the habits of his first wife, all fine porcelain and linens. And his heart? Well, other than God Almighty, who could plumb the depths of that capricious organ? He shoved his feet into his moccasins. Not a man such as himself.

He grabbed his coat, rifle, and hat on his way out the door. Pre-dawn air stung his face, and he sucked in a big draught, letting it go deep. He should've thought to ask the woman if she'd needed anything before leaving Newcastle the other day. Now there was no choice but to go back.

Wohali snorted a greeting as he flung open the stable door. After rummaging through a stack of his finest pelts, he pulled out and lashed together enough to purchase a firearm for Red Bird and anything else she'd need. Half a smile tugged his mouth as he readied his mount for the journey. Women's garments and a firearm—both deadly.

By the time he rode off, grey light slivered across the horizon. And by the time he reined in Wohali at Greeley's Mercantile, the sun beat hot against his shoulders. He tied his mount, keeping his back toward the charred lot across the road. Hard to tell which of the two—sun or nightmare—trickled sweat between his shoulder blades. He'd have to do something with that piece of dirt and blood.

But not yet.

He took the stairs in two strides and blew through the door like a summer storm.

Jonathan Greeley looked up from behind the counter. Though Samuel stood at least ten paces away, he smelled the man's hair powder, something akin to toadstools after a fresh rain, though if asked, Greeley would swear it was the latest fragrance sent from France. The shopkeeper's face was clean-shaven, and trim nails prettied his hands. Not a stain or wrinkle marred his work apron or suit beneath. He was a dandy, all right. A strutting peacock of a fellow. Or maybe he was just afraid of his wife's wrath should he present himself any less formal.

"Morning, Heath." Greeley shut his ledger and set down his pen. "Didn't expect to see you twice in one week."

Samuel tipped his hat brim forward a notch in greeting. "I need a few things."

"Such as?"

He scanned the shop, wall to wall, pausing at the corner near the window. A fabric table was heaped with bolts of cloth, most sturdy but a few too flimsy to be of any use on the frontier. Shelves of ribbons and all manner of sewing things lined the wall behind it. Everything a woman might want—but no women in sight. Good.

He swung back to Greeley. "Ladies' things."

Greeley rolled to his toes, leaning forward. "Such as?"

74

He gritted his teeth. It'd been bad enough removing the woman's stays last night under cover of darkness. Now he must speak aloud of the lacy bits of nothing? No. He stepped up to the counter and planted his feet. "Whatever it is that a backcountry woman might require."

Greeley's lips twitched. Clearly the man enjoyed this conversation far too much. "Such as?" he repeated.

"Blast it, man!" He threw his arms wide. "My wife needs clothes."

A slow smile stretched across the shopkeeper's mouth.

Reaching across the counter, he grasped Greeley's collar and pulled him forward. "So help me, Greeley, if you say 'such as' one more time, I'll march right out to that warehouse and upend every box and crate until I find what my wife might need."

He splayed his fingers.

Greeley stumbled against the counter, coughing. "Really, Mr. Heath!" He tugged at his collar. "You are in town, sir, where such rough-and-tumble ways are frowned upon."

He snorted. "A scuffle does a man good now and then."

Greeley ignored the challenge, smoothing back his hair instead—though it only served to knock the greased strands more askew. Why he and his wife had set up shop in Newcastle, the dividing line between Cherokee country and civilization, had always been a wonder. They belonged in a city.

"Come back in a few hours." Greeley sniffed. "I'll have my wife's new maid put something together for her. Being she's from England as well, she might have a better idea than I what provisions your wife may need."

"Good. Oh, and Greeley?"

"Yes?"

"You might want to. . ." Ought he tell the man a hank of his hair had broken free in the tussle and now stood at attention, like an Indian feather straight and tall on top of his head? Samuel ran a hand across his chin, debating.

"Go look in a mirror, man," he called over his shoulder on his way out.

Wohali nuzzled him as he loosed the reins from the post. He walked the mount down the road, shying to the edge of the rutted dirt. A few horses clomped past, but he didn't look up. He didn't need to. The sneers were always the same. Not that they bothered him in the least. It was the occasional drawn lines of pity weighting a person's brow that he couldn't abide.

He crossed over to the trading post and hitched up Wohali, then unleashed and hefted the pack of pelts onto his shoulder. He mounted the few stairs and strode through the open door into dim light and an odor so powerful it could knock a grown man flat. Greeley might smell of hair powder and grease, but he'd take that any day over Renner—a man who'd not seen a comb, a bar of soap, or any sort of cleanliness in over a decade.

"Heath." Renner's words were as sparse as his teeth.

"Renner." Samuel thwunked the pile of pelts to the floorboards, then stepped back.

Renner shot out from behind the counter. He crouched in front of the furs, running his fingers along the softness, then whipped out a knife and cut the binding. He sorted one after the other, rubbing them against his filthy cheek. When each fur had been measured and examined, he rocked back on his heels, then pushed up and resumed his perch on a barrel behind the counter. "What you trading for?"

Samuel sidestepped the pile of fur. "I need a firearm."

Renner craned his neck, eyeballs hunting for the weapon strapped on Samuel's back. "What's wrong with yours?"

"Nothing."

"What you looking for?"

"Something small. It's for my wife."

The man hopped off his barrel, then flipped it on its side. Beneath sat a pistol, a little rusty on the barrel, but a firearm nonetheless. He stood, holding it out on an open palm.

Samuel hefted the pistol in his own palm, weighing merit against detriment. The eight-inch barrel might need to be traded out, but would hold for now. He ran a finger along the lockplate, breech, and trigger. Solid. He squinted. No hairline fractures. Cocking the trigger, he listened hard. The flintlock mechanism clicked with ease. The bottom of the handle was broken off, though he could fashion a new one, or at the very least, mend it. Old scrollwork faded into nothing toward the edge of the muzzle, but cosmetics be hanged. The size and lightness of the weapon were perfect for Red Bird.

"I'll take it. And I'll need more lead for shot." He slid his gaze from the pistol to Renner. "Be back for it in an hour."

Behind him, boot steps thudded up the stairs and crossed the threshold.

"Thought I heard you rode into town." Tobacco splatted against wooden planks, less offensive than the high-pitched voice. "Your new wife giving you trouble already?"

Turning, Samuel raised the pistol, sighting McDivitt's chest with the muzzle. The man's nostrils flared. Good. Let him think the thing was loaded.

"Good morning to you as well, McDivitt."

Rage simmered beneath McDivitt's glower, more satisfying than a plate of mutton hash. Samuel lowered the pistol and handed it back to Renner, making sure to keep Angus in a straight line of sight. One never knew when a snake would strike.

Renner collected the pistol, wafting a fresh stench of sweat as he moved. "You trading today, McDivitt?"

"Mmm-hmm." Angus nodded. "For information."

McDivitt stepped closer. "Seems that Indian friend of yours was spotted heading south, Heath. So I'm wondering. . .why would an Indian willingly leave the safety of Keowee and run headlong into white territory?"

The muscles of his neck and shoulders tightened. If McDivitt had Inoli followed all the way to Charles Towne. . .but no. His brother surely would not fall prey to such a scheme. He shifted his stance, one foot in front of the other, his back to Renner, ready for anything. "Since you're of a mind to trade, what are you giving for the answer?"

Angus whipped a skinning knife from inside his coat and dropped to a crouch, the sharp edge of the blade ready to strike. "Your ability to walk out of that door still breathing."

Behind Samuel, a hammer cocked. "Take it outside, McDivitt!"

Samuel smiled. After the past few days, a good fight was exactly what he needed. "Don't fret, Renner. I got this."

McDivitt growled. "Pride goes before a fall, Heath."

"You ought to know." Samuel slashed the man with a cutting sneer. "Since Mariah chose me over you."

The blade scythed toward his throat.

Samuel flung up his right hand, catching McDivitt's wrist and twisting his arm. He locked the man's elbow in place and slammed the heel of his other hand against bone. A sickening crack sliced the air, followed by the clatter of metal against wood.

McDivitt roared, landing a left hook onto Samuel's jaw.

He spun with the movement, lest his own bone give way, then slammed McDivitt's body onto the planks next to his knife. Lungs heaving, he spit out a mouthful of blood and pinned McDivitt with a knee between his shoulder blades. "What Inoli does or doesn't do is not your concern."

Then he stood and stalked toward the door.

McDivitt's voice, strained to a fine point, stabbed him in the back.

"Everything about the backcountry is a regulator's concern. I'm the law around here, and I've got my eye on you, Heath. On you, your Indian friend—and your new wife. You'll pay for this. You hear me? You'll pay!"

Chapter 11

Eleanor waited until the front door shut, then bolted upright in bed, drawing the counterpane to her throat. Thick darkness filled the small cabin, but the sun would be up soon. She knew. She'd counted each minute of the never-ending night, all of Grace's sleepy murmurs—and every slight movement of her husband on the pallet across the room. Ever since he'd unloosened her stays, a different kind of constriction squeezed her chest.

Fear.

Which was silly, of course. If he'd wanted to take advantage of her, he'd surely have acted upon the urge by now. Even so, she knotted the blanket in her fingers. Lying in the same room with a man, clothed only in her linen shift, was atrocious behaviour. No, worse.

Her father had been right.

She pressed the back of her hand against her mouth, concealing a cry. To what further depths could her life possibly plummet? A tremble shivered across her shoulders.

Oh God, protect me.

Outside, horse's hooves dug up dirt, fading as she listened. She sat there a long time, wondering if they'd pound back, until eventually, robins and blackbirds sang the morning into being. Grey light slid into the room through the spaces between burlap and window frame.

And still the man did not return.

She dropped the blanket and swung her legs over the mattress. Snatching up her stays from the floor, she raced to the table, where the remains of the horrid dinner accused her from the pot. A frown pulled her brow. She'd have to deal with that later. Grabbing a knife, she took care to wipe it well on the man's unused napkin, then sat without sound and worked steady and sure before Grace awakened.

It took a fair amount of effort, prayer, and a few grumbles to cut the stays down the front and remove enough of the boning to leave supple fabric to work with. But that was only half the battle. How to bore lace holes? What to use for laces? And how in the world to sew without a needle and thread? This could be an all-day project. Would that Mr. Heath might remain away for that long.

And if he didn't?

Her heart raced. So did she. The entire morning and half the afternoon flew by as she cared for Grace, hunted for needed materials, and worked on fashioning front-opening stays. Her ears hurt from straining to hear approaching hooves, but still Mr. Heath did not return.

At last, she held the fabric up for inspection. A little raggedy. Definitely not proper, but. . . She squinted, apprising her tailoring skills. Not spectacular but entirely workable.

She handed Grace a wooden spoon to play with. "Here you are, little one. It's not much, I grant you, but I will find something more suitable for you in just a moment."

Dashing to the side of the bed, where her gown and petticoats lay in wait, she turned her back to the child and slipped on the new stays. A little puckery where she'd made the holes too wide apart, but good enough. She tied on her petticoat and skirt, and coaxed her gown into place with a few well-placed pins. Glory be! Decency restored.

She smiled. A small victory, but all wars were won a single battle at a time. Next skirmish, a toy for Grace.

"Now then, shall we see about a new toy for you?" She whirled, then slapped a hand against her chest. The front door gaped wide open. The wooden spoon lay forgotten on the floor near the threshold.

"Grace!"

Eleanor took off at a dead run. Any number of terrifying dangers lurked outside the cabin walls. How could such a small child move so quietly—as silently as her father?

Kicking aside the spoon, she dashed outside. "Grace!"

She raced down the stairs.

Then skidded to a stop before she tumbled over the child.

Grace sat in the dirt, hardly five paces from the house, laughing up at her. Folding toward the ground, she grabbed two handfuls of soil and bobbed up, raining earth atop her head. The whites of her eyes and flash of her tiny teeth were the only clean spots left.

A reprimand quivered on Eleanor's lips, but gave way to a grin when the little girl laughed. Who could be cross with such a cherub—dirty or not? "Well, I suppose this is as good a time as any for you to have a proper bath, hmm?"

Bath? Ahh. Just saying the word washed over Eleanor from head to toe. Had Biz and Molly been able to scrub away the months of travel at their new homes? The thought stole her grin. Would that she'd been able to live in Newcastle. With no means to bathe out here in the backcountry, would she ever be fully clean again? Swiping back a filthy strand of hair, she set her jaw. Yes. She would—and now was the time to do it with Mr. Heath still gone who-knew-where.

"Come along, Grace." She reached out her hand, and filthy fingers wrapped around hers. "We shall have an adventure in the stable, you and I. Perhaps we will find a tub in there, and if not, then we shall suffer the creek, hmm?"

Grace's little steps patted double-time with hers, and with the jaunty movement, streamers of dust trailed in the air behind. The girl started a nonsense song—or maybe it was Cherokee—as Eleanor flung open the stable door.

It felt strange entering the man's work area, as if at any moment she might turn around to his scowl or questioning gaze. His bedding remained where he'd left it, in a heap to one corner. Overhead hung rabbit skins, stretched on frames. She ducked aside them and delved deeper inside, Grace batting at her skirt from behind.

The whole stable took all of five minutes to dissect. She and Grace discovered many items, but no tubs, no large barrel, nothing but more blessed crates and long-handled tools. Annoyed, she kicked a bucket filled with cobwebs, hardly large enough in which to soak her feet, and—hold on.

She bent, narrowing her eyes, her vision now adjusted to the dim light. Why would the dirt be so disturbed beneath a bucket that looked as if it hadn't been used in months?

Grabbing a shovel, she scraped the ground. The metal edge thudded against wood. Scraping a bit more, she discovered a lid, less than a hand-span in length. Ought she uncover the secret that lay below? Mr. Heath had obviously taken lengths to hide whatever it was. Did she really want to know the man's business?

Grace shot forward and dug her little fingers into the ground, lifting up the lid with a shriek. A cascade of loosened dirt fell inside. Grace tumbled backward on her bottom.

Eleanor squatted, holding out an open palm. "Give it to me, please."

Grace rose up on chubby legs, leaned forward, then turned and ran the other way.

"Little imp!" Eleanor chased after her, grabbing her before she escaped out the door. She swung the girl into her arms, Grace laughing all the while. Eleanor couldn't help but soften her tight lips—then immediately pursed them and cocked her head.

Her heart skipped a beat. Pounding hooves grew louder the longer she stood there.

She raced back to the hole in the dirt, Grace in one hand, the wooden lid in the other. Dropping to her knees, she lined up the lid with the edges of the buried box—and her gaze landed on the contents.

King George II stared up at her. A bust of him, embossed on a bronze medal. She blinked, trying to see the sense of it. Why would a man hide an award instead of displaying it?

Why keep a medal of distinction buried like a dead man's bones?

Samuel slid from the saddle and walked his mount. His gaze darted from the wide open house door, to the patch of earth scratched by little fingers, to the woman standing in the stable's doorway. Pink spread over her cheeks, and for some odd reason, she appeared out of breath. He led Wohali closer. Indeed, her chest rose and fell as if she'd just finished a rousing game of *Anesta*—and the state of her dust-covered skirts declared her the loser.

"What have you been doing, Tatsu'hwa?"

"I was simply. . ." Her eyes widened, and she ventured past the door, her gaze locked on his jaw. "You are hurt."

He brushed his knuckles along the ache where McDivitt's fist had connected with bone. Sure enough, matted stubble met his touch.

Grace charged out from behind Red Bird and plowed into him, shrieking all the way. The girl could scare a mountain lion back to his lair. He bent and swept her up. Dirt rained down, her teeth a flash of brilliance against a canvas of earth. Her light hair wore a layer of soil. So. . .this little urchin was the reason for his wife's sorry appearance.

His lips twitched into a half smile—a full one might split the gash on his jaw. "Looks like we could all use a dip in the creek."

Red Bird gasped.

He held up a hand. "Peace, woman. I meant separately."

Setting down Grace, he edged to Wohali's flank and unstrapped the package wrapped by Greeley. "I picked up a few things in town for you."

Her mouth dropped as he handed her the bundle. "For me?" Eyes the color of an endless August sky searched his. "But why?"

For the space of a heartbeat, he allowed the unhindered connection, then turned aside and tugged down his hat, making sure the scarred half of his face remained in shadow. "You act as if no one ever bought you anything."

"It is. . .unusual."

Samuel watched her, looking for a hint of the woman inside. What kind of life had she led? A laced-up, prim and proper beauty on the outside, but what sorrows lurked in the corners of her past?

"I don't know what you're used to," he said slowly. "But if you need something, I will provide. I take care of my own."

Grace wrapped her arms around his leg and tried climbing up. He smiled down at her. That was some statement he'd made. His own daughter looked as if he'd abandoned her to a pig wallow.

"How? I mean. . ." A ray of sunlight reached through the canopy, casting a rosy halo around Red Bird's head. The way she worked her lower lip, clearly thoughts tussled one another, much as he and Inoli had wrestled on the ground.

"If I may be so bold," she finally said, "what is it that you do? As an occupation, I mean."

He laughed and slapped Wohali on the flank, freeing the horse to amble down to the creek for a drink. "You married a trapper and a scout."

"A trapper?" The word rolled off her tongue as foreign as when he'd handed her some jerky.

"I got you something else, too." Reaching behind, he pulled the pistol from his belt. He set it on top of the pack she hugged to her chest, as if he might snatch it away at any moment.

Color drained from her face. "I know nothing of firearms, sir."

"Well, I reckon you'll learn right quick. You'll need to." He sidestepped her and strode to the house, the thought of jerky rumbling in his gut.

Grace's footsteps scampered behind.

As did the woman's swishing skirt. "Is it so dangerous here?"

He rummaged through one of the stacked crates, easily retrieving a hunk of dried meat. Though he would not admit it out loud, it was easier to find things since she'd straightened up the cabin. He took a big bite, checking on Wohali out the open front door as he chewed. The mount had returned from the creek and now nibbled on the wild grass among the ferns at the yard's edge.

Turning back to Red Bird, he leaned against the door frame. "That friend of yours, the one who came over with you on the ship, why do you think she crossed?"

For a moment, Red Bird's nose crinkled, then cleared as she set the bundle on the table. "Oh, you must mean Biz. She was sent here because of. . .umm. . .indiscretions."

A smirk pulled his lips. Lord have mercy. As if the woman's English stays hadn't been tight enough, must her speech be just as constricted? "I'd wager that the woman's 'indiscretions' are nothing compared to the rest of the criminals shipped over here every day, and that's one of the reasons why I bought you that firearm."

He pushed away from the door and sat in the chair, allowing Grace to climb up his legs and onto his lap.

"What are you saying, Mister—" Red Bird pressed her fingers against her mouth, retreating a step.

He frowned at the movement. The woman was more skittish than an unbroken colt. He'd handed her no cause to react as if he might strike her at any moment. Why such a response?

"The colonies are a dumping ground for rogues and scoundrels. For those wily enough to flee from their masters, the backcountry provides safe hiding." He nodded toward her pistol. "I'll teach you to shoot tomorrow."

Her brow twisted into a question mark. "But surely there is some kind of law even out here?"

"There is. And it's sitting right on that table where you left it."

Her gaze traveled to the pistol, then cut back to him. "What of magistrates and courts? The British Empire was founded on such principles as order and legality. Oh, I know, I am not in England anymore, but King George is sovereign in this land, as well. Justice must be meted out in a suitable fashion."

"Must it?" He set Grace down and shot to his feet. The woman could have no idea the blow she'd struck. A punch to the kidneys would've been kinder. He strode to the door. "I've seen better justice carried out by a pack of wolves."

"You speak as if—"

He turned on her. "As if what?"

She blinked, the blue of her eyes deepening with realization. "You are not entirely happy with the crown."

He bit back a curse, swallowing the bitter aftertaste. "Would you be happy to have your hard-earned coins line the pockets of some dandy in a wig? One who knows nothing of sweat or hunger?"

"It is the same across the ocean." Red Bird bent, handing Grace a wooden spoon, then once the child began dragging it around in some kind of imaginary game, she straightened and faced him. "There is want and need in London as well, yet taxes are paid without such vehement protest."

He stifled a snort, tempted to pinch himself to see if this was a dream. A political conversation with a woman? And an English one at that? What kind of woman had he married?

"No." He shook his head. "It is not the same. Those people are under direct representation. There is a name and face to petition for their grievances."

"And there is none here, is that it?" Her head bowed for a moment, and when she looked up, one shapely brow lifted. "But what of virtual representation?"

He widened his stance to keep from staggering. The woman's intellect stunned like a morning sunrise stretched brilliant across the horizon. He could admire such a mind—were it not so dangerous. "And what would you know of that?"

She clasped her hands in front of her, the picture of innocence. "A governess living in a peer's home overhears many conversations."

He couldn't help but smile. Men would die to gain the information stored in that pretty head. "Clearly you were not employed for the Earl of Chatham, for he claims virtual representation is the most contemptible idea that ever entered into the head of a man."

Her jaw dropped. "How would you know that?"

"We're not as ignorant out here in the backcountry as you may think."

Red crept over her cheeks. So. . .that's exactly what she'd thought.

He shoved off from the door frame. "To be fair, there is probably someone to address my grievances to, but they've changed the parish lines so many times, one hardly knows which district we live in today, let alone who to appeal to."

She pursed her lips. "That does not seem right."

"Because it isn't."

She closed the distance between them, stopping but an arm's length away. Curiosity lapped at the shores of those sea-blue eyes. "Are you, or are you not, loyal to the Crown?"

His breath caught in his throat. Men had given their lives for answering such a question. Did she hold her breath as well?

He gazed down at her. Behind her long lashes, blue sparkled. He could drift in that ocean—and lose his soul in the depths if he weren't careful. She smelled of dirt and toil, but something more. Distant horizons, foreign and exotic. He reached a hand toward her, then coiled it back before his fingers could brush against the hair at her brow.

"I am a man who's loyal to God alone, Tatsu'hwa. Leave it at that."

He turned and stalked across the porch and down the stairs. He'd have to watch his step around this woman. She was nothing like his first wife, and he wasn't entirely sure why the realization sank low in his gut—and stayed there.

Chapter 12

A lion roared. The growl rumbled inside Eleanor's chest, clawing to get out. A screech rent the air, frantic. Panicked. Sounding as if at any moment the beast might strike and rip flesh from bone.

Eleanor's eyelids popped open. White light flashed, transforming the ceiling rafters into long blades, like larger-than-life knife edges suspended overhead. She lay frozen, trying to sift dreams and nightmares from reality.

Another rumble. Another cry.

Her breathing steadied, and she rolled over, reaching for her wrap. Grace wailed. Poor thing. Of course the resounding thunder frightened her. She'd tuck the wee one inside her own blanket and hum away the frightening noise. Sometimes a good cuddle was all one needed to right the world—that and a good soak. She felt so much better after her early evening dip in the creek, having scrubbed away grime and a few of her anxieties about Samuel. He'd not only honored his word to keep his distance while she bathed, but he'd also looked after Grace the entire time.

She swung her feet off the bed, then stilled when light flashed again. The black silhouette of a bear leaned over Grace's crib and scooped her up.

Eleanor pressed her knuckles to her mouth, stifling her own cry.

The next flicker of lightning etched along the broad lines of Mr. Heath's shoulders as he neared the door, moving without so much as a whisper of sound.

La! What a dolt. She watched as he and the crying girl disappeared outside.

Tying her wrap tight, Eleanor followed. Why would he take his daughter from the cabin? Why would he take her at all? She paused just inside the open doorway, unable to see him, but unwilling to break whatever magic spell he'd woven around Grace, for her cries faded to shaky sniffles.

Samuel's voice rumbled in the dark, low as the thunder and every bit as forbidding, yet not terrifying in the least. "Face your fears, little one. You're safe in my arms."

Eleanor stiffened. A sob burned in her throat. His words both broke and mended her heart in one fierce slash. What would it be like to have strong arms wrap around her and murmur such words? How would it feel to be loved so intensely?

The mad thought hit her hard, and she balanced a hand against the log frame for support. What was happening to her? She barely knew the man, questioned his loyalties even, and. . . . Her grip loosened, fingers sliding off the hewn piece of wood. Whatever the man's political leanings, he was clearly loyal to those in his care. As rugged as this wild land was, perhaps she ought be thankful he provided for her.

"I know you're in the shadows, Tatsu'hwa." His voice carried in, catching her in the act. "You might as well come out."

Suddenly she was four years old again, hiding behind drapery, unaware the tips of her shoes peeked out beneath the hem. The same humiliation twisted her twenty-five-year-old stomach.

Shoving down the memory, she stepped onto the porch. Lightning backlit tree branches bent in a macabre dance. Thunder rolled a bass drone. But. . .wait a minute. She strode to the edge of the wooden decking and reached out a hand, palm up. Not a drop of moisture dampened her skin.

She turned back to Mr. Heath. "Why is there no rain?"

He shifted the little girl in his arms, and Grace lolled her head against his great chest. "There is." His voice lowered, an angry edge sharpening it. "Six or seven miles off."

"You do not sound pleased." She peered at him, a dark mountain looming against more darkness. Reading his face was impossible. "Will not some rain help the drought?"

"Does one kind word heal months of hurt?"

Her lips parted, breath trapped in her throat. How could one predict what this man might say? She drew a step nearer, waiting—praying— for another flash of lightning to read his face. Were all Colonial men so unguarded, so piercingly direct?

The whites of his eyes flashed, pinning her in place. "You study me as if tracking a wildcat."

Fire burned over her ears and settled in her cheeks. She clutched her wrap against her collarbone, twisting the fabric, holding on to any dignity she could find. "Even so, I would think every bit of rain helps."

"True, but for now, it's the lightning that concerns me most."

Her brow crumpled. "But you said it is at least six miles off."

"How long do you think it would take a fire to eat up that much ground?"

Fire? She licked her lips. Wild animals, a husband as changeable as a spring tempest, wilderness and Indians, and now she must add fire to her list of fears in this strange land? She whirled and searched the woods, straining to see any spark or flicker of red or orange.

"Don't fret. I'll keep watch." Samuel's breath ruffled the loose hair atop her head.

She turned. He stood so close, she felt the heat of his body rolling off him in waves. He smelled of leather and gunpowder and a warm autumn day, all crushed leaves and dried grass.

He leaned, transferring Grace into her arms. "Go to sleep, both of you."

The little girl nestled her face into the crook of Eleanor's neck. Samuel stepped aside. As she crossed the porch and entered the tiny cabin, she searched the queer feeling tingling low in her heart, nearly out of reach. Maybe, perhaps, it was an inkling of what it felt like to be loved.

She quickened her pace and pulled Grace into bed with her, lifting the covers over her head. More than fire or storm or threat of beast, the foreign feeling alarmed her most of all.

Creek water hit the back of Samuel's calves, barely above his ankles even after last night's storm. He squatted and dipped his hands into the cool liquid, bringing a scoopful up to his face and washing away another night of fitful sleep. Then he shook off the excess and leapt to the bank where he'd left his boots. The woman ought to be up and dressed by now.

Grace's sing-song carried out to mingle with the high-pitched chirps of cardinals. He shook his head as he bounded up the stairs and into the cabin. The girl was as boisterous as her mother had been.

Speedy little feet dashed over to him. "Edoda!"

He lifted the child, eye-level. Nary a hair was out of place. "My, my. . . aren't you a little lady? Next thing I know you'll be wanting lacy dresses and ribbons and such."

Red Bird turned from the hearth, a kettle in one hand. She poured amber-colored liquid into two mugs, then brought him one. "You took me on as Grace's caregiver. I intend to do my best."

Setting Grace down, he sniffed the steam, which mostly smelled like a September day. He took a sip. Aye. It tasted of fallen leaves as well. Swallowing back a gag, he eyed her over the rim. "What is this?"

"Tea."

He massaged the back of his neck, thinking on all the supplies he'd stored in crates. "Woman, I don't have any tea."

"You do now. I improvised." Half a smile quirked her prim lips. "I also did not have a chance to thank you for the bundle of provisions you brought from town yesterday. Molly must have had something to do with it, I suspect, for it all suits me. I am grateful. Thank you."

Her freckles darkened, and she turned away.

With her back to him, he leaned out the door and dumped the contents onto the porch. Inoli would surely split open his side were he to see him drinking *tea*—or more like boiled nettle and mulberry leaves. He returned the mug to the table and snatched up the pistol, where the woman had left it untouched. "Come outside, Red Bird. But see that Grace is occupied first."

He strode out to the front stairs and sat. Resting the pistol on his thigh, he retrieved a small piece of whittled hardwood from a pouch. Fabric swished behind him.

"What can I do for you, Mister—"

He cut her off with a scowl over his shoulder. He'd played the part of a gentleman once. Never again. "Look, if you refuse to call me Samuel or Heath, then call me nothing at all. Have a seat."

He scooted sideways, making room for her skirt.

She sat without a word, but her mouth dropped when he reached for her hand and wrapped her fingers around the pistol.

"Oh! I really do not think I should—"

"I told you I aimed to teach you to shoot. I mean what I say."

Her throat bobbed, but glory be, she did not drop the weapon.

"We'll start small. See this?" He held up the piece of wood. "You'll use this in place of flint. We won't even load the barrel. There will be no big noises and no shots. We'll work up to full charges gradually, so as not to spook you any more than you apparently are."

Her lips puckered, and she refused to make eye contact.

He smirked, then using his index finger, pointed out the appropriate mechanisms. "This is your frizzen, frizzen spring, pan, cock, jaws, and jaw screw. Can you repeat that?"

She shot him a sideways glance, sharp as a dagger fresh off a grindstone.

"I am no imbecile, sir."

He lifted a brow.

She pointed to each part in turn, using the correct names.

"Good. Here." He held out the wood shaving. "You'll use this in place of flint for now. Put this piece into the jaw and tighten the screw moderately. When the cock is released, the flint strikes the frizzen, flush across the face of it. Adjust the flint—or in this case, the piece of wood—if you need to, then fasten it snug. Give it a go."

She hesitated, then her fingers flew to work, and she lifted the pistol for his inspection.

He squinted, eyeing the job. Sweet mercy! The woman was a natural. He set the cock full open and gave it back. "Aim and fire."

Her brow crumpled.

"Just pull the trigger. It's not really going to fire."

She stood, gripping the pistol in surprisingly steady hands, and pulled the trigger. The resulting snap of metal against wood made her flinch.

He rose beside her. "Good job, Red Bird. Practice that same routine throughout today. We'll prime the pan and load the barrel when I get back."

"Where are you going?" The pistol lowered to her side, and she fluttered her free hand to her chest, looking away from him. "I mean, not that I question your right to come and go, I was simply. . .curious, is all. Forgive me for asking."

"I've a mind for something other than jerky, and thought I'd hunt some fresh meat." He swiped some hair from his eyes, and she jerked back from his sudden movement. Curious. He narrowed his eyes. Why was she so twitchy? Red crept up her neck, and she shrank farther away. Strange reaction—and he doubted very much it was from the mention of meat.

"I should check on Grace." She whirled and flew up the stairs and across the porch.

He beat her to the door and held out an arm, barring her entrance. "I don't know what you're used to, but I will never lift a hand against you, despite what anyone may say."

For a moment she met his gaze, then bowed her head. "Let me pass, please."

With one knuckle, he lifted her chin. "What kind of home do you come from?"

Pride angled her head, away from his touch. "The finest in England."

He frowned. What kind of fine home turned out a woman like this, leaving her to fend for herself in a foreign country? "Then why do you cower like a whipped hound when I make a sudden move or you chance to speak your mind?"

Retreating a step, she straightened her shoulders and met his stare. "I was a governess. Employers frown upon a candid tongue."

"To the point of a whipping?"

"Of course not." She shrugged. "Letting me go without a reference would have been punishment enough."

Ahh. That was it, then. The woman must have spoken her mind in the wrong company. "Is that why you're here?"

She bit her lower lip, a trait he was learning to decipher as stubborn determination.

He stepped closer. "What happened to you, Red Bird?"

She retreated a pace, an insane dance, one that would lead her to the edge of the porch in no time. "A powerful man made advances that I did not welcome. I responded in a way that ruined any chance of me ever working again in England."

"You. . .responded?" As she stood there, pistol in hand, fire in her gaze, he wondered what on earth the woman might have done. A grin split his face, large enough that it pulled at the tender skin left behind by McDivitt's uppercut. "Thunder and turf, woman. Maybe I ought not be teaching you to operate a firearm. God help the man that crosses you."

She stood silent, staring, a picture of sweetness and lightning with the way her fingers yet curled around the handle of the pistol.

He laughed and stalked from the porch, toward the stable. He might have to rename the woman Red Tail Hawk with her fierce gaze and tense focus. He grinned at the thought and shook his head. He wasn't aware that he was whistling until he heard it himself.

And he hadn't whistled in years.

Chapter 13

Eleanor retied her apron while Grace did her best to jump up and pull the strings from her hands. She spun and scooped the little imp off her feet, inhaling the child's ever-present smell of sunshine and dirt.

"So much naughtiness in you today, little one." She pressed a kiss to the crown of Grace's head. "We shall put that energy to good use, hmm?"

Grace bobbed and wriggled, all the while repeating, "Hmm? Hmm?"

Bending, she released the girl, then straightened and surveyed the cabin. She'd already swept the floor and cleaned the breakfast dishes—easy to do when she'd taken to serving hardtack and jam. Samuel, as usual, left them alone immediately after eating, striding off into the woods to do whatever it was that trappers did.

Over the past two weeks, she'd developed a routine—of sorts. Not that anything about this land could be regulated into the daily schedule of the fine homes she'd served in. Still, she'd found a small way to fit in by teaching Grace the value and educational benefits of productivity. Together they'd cleaned, organized, and beautified the space between these log walls. The trouble was, though she'd tidied the cabin, she'd nearly worked herself out of a job.

"Come along, Grace. Maybe it is time we expand our endeavors." She strode to the front door, flinging it open to a sunny June day, leastwise what rays could travel into the tunnel-like entrance on the porch. Heaps of wood on either side, stacked from decking to roof, blocked most of the view.

A slow smile tugged her lips. Who'd have thought her next opportunity was right outside the door?

She stooped to Grace's level. "How would you like to help me clear this off? We shall make it a fun game, shall we not?"

Grace reached up her hands, planting a palm on each of Eleanor's cheeks. "Edoda?"

"No, sweetie. This game is just for you and me, not your father, though it shall be a grand surprise for him when he returns." She stood, eyeing the stacks through narrowed eyes. Indeed. Clearing the porch would be a welcome surprise, especially if she dragged out a few barrels for sitting on, and perhaps fashioned a small table from a crate. Why, if she potted a few plants, it might even pass for a poor replica of an English garden sitting cove.

They worked well past dinner, until perspiration stuck her shift to her skin and Grace hunkered down by the front door, sucking her thumb. After a meager meal of porridge, she laid Grace in her crib, then heaved herself up and dove back into work.

Eventually, all the wood lay in one of two piles on the ground at each side of the porch. Swiping the dampness from the back of her forehead, she retrieved a broom from inside and swept off the bits of bark left behind, concentrating so hard, she jumped when a question hit her from behind.

"What do you think you're doing!"

Samuel strode across the lot, his step so determined, his deerskin leggings clung tight against his thighs. On one hip, a knife tied to a buckskin tether swung at his belt. On the other, his ever-present tomahawk. He wore no coat, just a trade-cloth shirt with laces hanging loose at the neck, his thick leather belt cinching in at the waist.

She set the broom aside, keeping it within reach. The man looked like a wolf on the hunt.

He took the stairs in a long-legged leap, surveying the empty deck from one end to the other. "What have you done?"

A raven screeched from the top of a tall tree, adding to the forbidding vision Samuel drew. He was a fearsome sight, all wild-haired and cagey, his fingers curled tight at his sides.

Eleanor clasped her own hands in front of her, fighting the urge to wring the life from them. Why would the man not be pleased with her industry?

"I thought," she spoke slowly, as though explaining a point of grammar or mathematical concept to one of her charges, "if the wood were cleared away, the porch might provide extra living space. Perhaps we might sit out here in the cool of the evening."

He turned on her, a storm brewing in his dark eyes. If a bolt of lightning shot out, she would not have been surprised. His swath of dark hair covered half his face, but she didn't need to see it to read his emotions. The tight lines of his mouth and the strained muscles on his neck revealed enough.

"House not big enough for you?" His voice was a growl.

"No. . .I mean. . .of course it is." The words slipped from her mouth like a broken necklace, the beads rolling in every direction. She clenched her fingers tighter, hoping the action might squeeze out some courage. "It is a very sturdy home. I simply thought—"

"You thought?"

She swallowed, retreating a step. She much preferred his glower to this unnerving grin.

In three long strides, he closed the distance between them, towering over her. If she looked up, she'd face that disturbing smile, so she kept her gaze fixed on the leather strap crossing his chest, the one holding his rifle against his back, and tried hard not to notice the tanned skin stretched tight over muscle where his shirt hung open.

"And while you were thinking, did you stop to think why I might've hauled all that wood to the porch in the first place?" His shirt strained against the strap as he sucked in a breath.

She stood mute. What was there to say? That the thought never crossed her mind? That she hadn't a clue there'd been some purpose in it other than his laziness to retrieve wood from farther than the front door? That she thought him untidy and unorganized and altogether intriguing?

Intriguing?

Jerking up her chin, she met his piercing gaze head-on instead of dwelling on such a rogue notion. "I did not. I am sorry."

And she was. Sorry to be in South Carolina. Sorry to fail at yet another position. Sorry to breathe.

He stilled, and for a long while, said nothing. But something stirred inside him, for his shoulders slowly slackened.

"Fine," he said at length. "But stick to caring for Grace instead of turning this place into some high and mighty English manor. You're living in the backcountry, woman. Get used to it."

He wheeled about and stalked off on silent feet, nothing but the shush of the breeze left by his movement ruffling against her cheek.

Her eyes burned. She blinked, refusing to let one tear fall. She'd been wrong. Horribly wrong. Despite her best efforts, she didn't fit in here.

And never would.

A staccato birdcall pecked against Samuel's ear, adding to the tension thick between him and the woman. He didn't have time for this. Not now. But her eyes swam blue, the hurt caused by his harsh words hot and liquid. Her chin trembled, barely perceptible, but enough to catch his eye. He ought say something more, soften the blow from his tongue lashing, reach out and wipe those tears away before they brimmed over and washed her whole face, maybe even pull her to him and let her cry away the pain.

The soft feeling punched him in the gut.

Seven more notes struck. He pivoted and stamped into the woods. He should have known adding a woman would change things, but the blasted lady wasn't just changing Grace and the house. He shoved down a growl. How could a snip of an Englishwoman get under his skin in a fortnight? She wasn't much to look at, all red-haired and scrawny. Yet he saw her face as he lay on his pallet in the dark of night, night after night. Her soft breathing a strange kind of incense, and if he sniffed, he just might scent her here and now, for he remembered everything about her.

He cut off the path and dove through the underbrush, relishing the scrape of thorns against his forearms and roots to snag his step. Better to think on green wildness than a red-headed woman.

Ahead, a brown shape emerged from a tree trunk. Inoli was shirtless except for a quiver and bow strapped to his back. His brother's deerskin leggings matched his own, as did the knife and tomahawk at his waist, but he also wore a traditional breechclout and short moccasins.

Samuel narrowed his eyes and drew up close, circling the man. Faded purple splotches and a few knuckle-split cuts colored his skin. "Looks like McDivitt's men caught up to you."

Inoli's dark gaze searched his face. "Looks like Red Bird leaves a mark on you also, my brother. You charge from your home like a man bent on battle. All you need is war paint."

He clasped his brother's forearm with a smile. "Not a bad idea. Let's walk."

They turned onto a deer path, broadleaf plantains crushing beneath their feet.

"Are you wishing you'd taken Running Doe instead?"

He chewed on the question like a tough bite of venison. Running Doe might have been ready and willing to welcome him into her arms, but she'd never have taken to Grace the way Red Bird had. He shook his head. "No, Red Bird's already taught Grace new words and how to sit proper at the table."

"You have a table?" Humor rippled at the edges of Inoli's voice.

He turned, shrugging. "She's changed everything."

"Even you?"

A scowl waged war on his face, and he wheeled about.

Inoli laughed, the rumbling sound scaring a squirrel up a tree. "So she does not share her bed with you yet."

He broke into a sprint, preferring flight to fight. One could never win a war of words with Inoli. He'd learned not to try. By the time he passed pine ridge and reached the big rock nestled at the bottom of the next ravine, his shirt clung to his back and sweat trickled down his temples. He climbed up, and his lungs slowed their heaving by the time Inoli scrambled to sit at his side. He may not win at word games, but he could always best his brother at a footrace.

Pulling out a pouch of pemmican, Samuel handed some over. "Tell me of your journey."

Inoli caught his breath, then chewed good and long before he answered. "Three men tracked me."

"How far?"

Inoli glanced at him without so much as twitching his face. "As far as I let them."

Samuel reared back, studying the man's quiver. Sure enough, three new red beads, thread fresh and white, added to the design sewn into the leather. He sat forward, resting his elbows on his thighs. The taking of life, especially that of the unredeemed, sank a rock into his gut. "McDivitt won't be happy about the loss of his men."

"It could not be helped."

He let out a long breath. "No doubt."

Insects, birds, and small game all chattered, yet for a while, they sat in peace. In an odd way, connection and understanding thrived on the non-words. The forest spoke like God's voice, alive and real, leaving healing and hope in the wake of silence.

Shadows stretched longer, and finally Samuel spoke. "You delivered the message?"

Inoli grunted. "I will go to Charles Towne no more. Nor should you. Even by night Redcoats roam the streets like rats in a storage hut." He fumbled with a pouch at the side of his waist and pulled out a scrap of rag paper.

Samuel unfolded the note, his gut tightening. Getting information to and from the Sons of Liberty had always been difficult, but with more Redcoats prowling the city, it would soon become downright impossible. Shoving the thought aside, he focused on the note, black ink now faded to grey, scrawled dead center.

neg. K.A. attend

"Blast it!" He wadded up the piece and pitched it far into the undergrowth.

Inoli's dark gaze followed the arc, then turned to him. "What does it mean?"

Lifting his hat, he ran his hands through his hair, then tugged the rim down low. "Seems there's a negotiator coming to Keowee to speak with Attakullakulla about swearing allegiance to the British. I'm to be present and report back the conversation."

Inoli's head cocked like a raven, keen interest shining in his eyes. "How will you know when this man comes?"

"Well, either I'll have to trust Sutton to get me word, or I'll have to make more frequent trips into town." He jumped down from the rock, the jolt of hitting solid ground juddering up his legs. "Come home with me and meet Red Bird. I think she's fair enough ready to meet you by now. More than enough. She's got spunk, I'll give her that."

Inoli joined him on the ground, resting a hand on Samuel's shoulder. "No, my brother. Another time. I am off to Keowee."

"Oh?" Samuel studied his friend's eyes, but he might as well gaze at a blackened sky. Inoli allowed no hint of what hid behind his placid stare, but something was up.

"Would it not be prudent to see if Attakullakulla is there?"

"Aye. As always, you think one step ahead—which is why I no longer game with you." He lifted a brow, humor lifting his lips. "There will be time for you to meet Red Bird when you return."

"*Doh-nah-dah-goh-hun-i.*" Inoli turned to stalk off.

His brother's parting words—*until we meet again*—were custom, but something in his tone made Samuel reach out and grab the man's arm. "You have another reason for going, don't you." It was a statement, giving no quarter to dodge left or right.

Inoli's dark eyes glittered. Then he pulled away and stalked off.

Chapter 14

Heat sweltered through the front door, waves of it keeping time with the chopping of Samuel's axe outside. Eleanor fanned herself as she peeked into Grace's crib. The girl lay in a mess of blond hair that stuck to her cheeks and shoulders, yet her eyelids finally closed. Grace had been cranky and naughty and not just a little teary-eyed all morning. If the last of June were such an inferno, what would July and August bring? How would she even stand it?

Eleanor fluttered her skirts, hoping to create a draft. Oh for a steady London rain.

She rose and edged her sleeves up farther, desperate for air against her skin instead of fabric. Yes, indeed. A little air would be just the thing. She strode toward the door, scooping up an empty bucket on the way. Some water on her feet wouldn't hurt, either.

Outside, the steady *chuck-chuck* of the axe grew louder. Earlier this morn the noise had chafed, but now the pattern soothed in an odd sort of way. Instead of tromping off into the woods, Mr. Heath had been working at something since after breakfast. What was he doing?

She padded to the edge of the porch and peeked around the corner. The heat of a thousand blazing suns hit her hard, and she reached out a hand to the support beam.

Mr. Heath wore nothing but buckskin breeches.

Eleanor bit her lip, mortified, yet unable to turn away.

Tanned muscles rippled on a back as naked as the day he was born. Sweat glistened on his bronzed skin, kissed by the sun. Four long lines, reddish, puckered, reached from backbone to rib along one side. The same dark hair that grew wild on his head also curled on the plane of his chest.

Her knees weakened. This wasn't right. She ought not be looking. She knew it in her head, and in her heart, and by all that was right and holy—but her eyes paid no mind. She went right on staring, heart racing. Guilty. And completely enthralled.

With each swing of the axe, his biceps swelled. The strength in one swipe could kill a man. He drove the blade into the wood, and a snowstorm of splinters flew out. Her husband was a work of art in motion. A beautiful, frightening force of nature. Part animal, part divine.

Without warning, he straightened. His body stiffened, and he jerked his head. Dark eyes locked onto hers, asking questions she did not want to answer or even consider.

Ever.

The bucket fell from her fingers. Sweet, merciful heavens! She *was* a strumpet.

She ran from the porch, tore down the stairs, and dashed across the yard, sprinting into the woods. Her skirt caught on underbrush, slowing her, but she didn't stop. She plowed down the small embankment and right into the stream, stopping smack in the middle, letting the bite of water wash over her feet, shoes and all. What had gotten into her?

A cry of frustration welled in her throat. This land, this wildness, had clearly taken effect, stripping her of dignity and decorum. What kind of woman watched a man without a shirt in broad daylight?

And how had her father known she'd become such a woman?

Wading to the bank, she deflated onto a rock and closed her eyes, trying to think. Trying to pray. But too much anger, disappointment, humiliation—too many emotions even to name—pelted her like kicked gravel. So she sat, a statue. A hard piece of granite, one with the rock.

Eventually, she folded forward. Cool water wicked up her skirt, plastering her shift from knees to toes. She bent forward, trailing her hands in the water, letting her fingertips run along pebbles worn smooth by years of gentle yet persistent pressure. She grabbed a handful and squeezed. Muck oozed between her fingers. Why couldn't the pressures in her life feel as gentle?

On the far bank, a twig snapped. Ferns rustled. Something moved.

She opened her eyes and sat upright. For the space of a breath, she blinked. Surely she was seeing things.

She shot to her feet before everything shut down. Her breath. Her muscles. Time.

Directly across the creek, a bear lifted its great nose and sniffed. The beast lowered its head, swinging it like a scythe. Black eyes stared into hers, sucking the marrow from her bones. The mouth stretched wide. White teeth chomped, clacking like a hammer.

Lightning charged through her veins, pooling in her hands and feet, all sharp needles and white fire. She should turn. Run. Something. But her feet would not move. Even her heart stopped.

The bear rose up on hind legs. A monster of matted fur, except for a scarred section of naked, grey skin puckered at its throat. Rank muskiness wafted across the water. Like meat left raw on a counter. Like death.

A scream started in the pit of her stomach. Rising upward. Gaining momentum. Stalling in her throat from the enormity of it.

Courage. Take courage!

La, who was she kidding? She opened her mouth to release the squall that could no longer be contained.

And hot, calloused fingers covered her lips, pulling her back against a rock-hard chest.

Keeping an eye on the bear, Samuel bent and whispered into Red Bird's ear. "Face your fear, Tatsu'hwa. I've got you."

She pressed back into him, her body aquiver from wet skirt to mussed hair.

He widened his stance to keep them both from stumbling.

The bear, still alert on two legs, sniffed and snorted. Good. Curiosity was always better than aggression—and a perfect opportunity to teach the woman what to do should this happen again without him nearby. "I'll remove my hand, but keep watch." He willed strength and calmness into his voice, casting it like a lifeline for her to grab hold of. "And do not scream. Am I clear?"

Her head moved up and down beneath his hand.

He slipped his fingers a breath away from her mouth, testing if she'd honor her word. One never knew how a woman given to terror might react.

She didn't make a sound.

He guided Red Bird behind him with one arm while he stepped forward, placing himself between her and the bear.

The animal dropped to all fours, slapping the ground with a forepaw—the smack of it blazing along the scars on Samuel's back.

Averting his gaze, he stared at the beast but not in the eyes. He pulled himself to full height and squared his shoulders. There was a fine line between dominance and aggression. He spoke with a firm but soothing tone. "Flee, brother bear. There is no threat here."

The animal snorted, blowing a fine spray of droplets into the air.

Samuel retreated a step, pushing the woman along with him.

Black lips lifted. White teeth clacked together.

He took another step back.

The bear wheeled about and tore off into the woods, smashing and crashing through the brush.

He smirked. "Safe travels, my friend."

A strangled cry gurgled behind him, pulling him around.

Red Bird wobbled on her feet, her face drained of color. He grabbed her before she fell. Sweeping her into his arms, he stomped up the bank. For a moment, she tucked her head into his shoulder, a huge shudder rumbling through her slight body. Six strides later, he set her down, her skirts tangling in a heap of fabric around her.

"You all right?" He peered at her. Splotches of color brightened her cheeks now—a little over-bright, but color, nonetheless.

"I hardly know." Her chest fluttered.

He gave her space and time, two gifts often overlooked but worth more than gold.

Finally, her breathing evened. She turned her face to his, brow crumpling. "Why did you not simply shoot the beast?"

He spread his arms wide. Warm June air wrapped around his bare skin like a lover's caress. "Do I look like I'm wearing my rifle?"

Her face paled again, and she scooted away, mumbling all the while. "But he, that bear, what if. . .you might have been killed." Her eyes widened. "Because of me!"

"No danger of that." Bending, he slid his knife out from the sheath on his boot and held it up. "I may not have my rifle, but I am never unarmed."

A curl of red hair stuck to her forehead. A rogue urge to reach out and brush it away tingled in his fingers.

He shoved the knife back into his boot, giving his hands something else to do.

"Should I be armed?" Her voice rose, as twittery sharp as the cardinal chirping from a pine bough. "Is that why you have taught me to shoot?"

He chuckled. Her? Hunt? The woman paled at cooking a dead animal. She'd never be able to take the life from one. "Don't fret, Red Bird. If you come upon a bear, it is easier to stand and take charge like I did. Tell it to go away. More often than not, it will."

Her gaze shot to the scars running from his back to his ribcage, burning along each twelve-year-old line.

He frowned. She was too perceptive—was that a virtue or a detriment? A fly buzzed near his eye, as bothersome as the thought, and he swatted it away. "Aye. I learned that lesson the hard way."

"I do not understand." She shook her head. Sunlight glinted a fire on the loosened strands of her hair.

Blast it! He forced his face forward, better to not notice such a forbidden fruit.

"Why teach me to shoot at all?" she asked.

McDivitt's threat reared in his mind, as potentially deadly as the bear. He shoved down a curse and blew out a long breath. "It's the two-legged animals that are most treacherous of all."

"Mr. Heath!" She spit out his name like a shot of tobacco, splattering against his ear. "I would never kill a man, if that is what you are thinking."

"You don't have to kill a man to stop him. Go for the thigh, then run the other way."

Recoiling, she slapped her hands to her chest. "Why tell me that? What kind of place is this?"

Frustration punctuated her voice—the kind that crawled like ants beneath his skin. He sat back, gazing upward. The overhead canopy shivered with a hot wind on high. "One that's getting more dangerous every day."

Chapter 15

The trail wove a maze through a particularly thick stand of trees. Samuel pressed on, undaunted. He could hike this stretch with his eyes closed. It's what lay beyond, past South Ridge Creek, that held possibility. Last year's trapping had been good, but expanding his route, setting more steel jaws and taking in a greater amount of pelts, that would be better—especially now that he had a wife to feed besides a daughter and himself.

He clicked his tongue and tugged on Wohali's lead, guiding the horse. Inoli and his mount following behind. He'd waited a full two weeks since his last meeting with Inoli, and now he'd been waiting the better part of the morning for his friend to finally tell him what he hid inside, but no amount of prodding would cause the man to speak before he was ready—a lesson learned long ago.

Each plod of Wohali's hooves dug deep into the pine needles, adding to the spicy, sweet scent of the woods. Samuel inhaled until his lungs burned. Indeed, this must surely be what heaven smelled like.

The trees thinned, and Inoli caught up to him. "Have you heard from Sutton yet?"

"No." He angled his head at his brother. "And though you told me Attakullakulla is at Keowee, you have yet to tell me what the elders have said."

"There is division." Inoli kicked a rock, tracking the skittering path with his gaze. "Some follow the Beloved Man in joining with the English. They think it is the only way to keep the whites from taking more land. Others still swear revenge against Montgomerie and Grant. Agreement will come at a cost."

Samuel grunted. Of course it would cost. So many Cherokee lives had been needlessly spent by Montgomerie and Grant, so much suffering and destruction, he doubted agreement would come at all. "And you?"

Inoli's black eyes shot to his. "You question my allegiance?"

"Just wondering if it's changed. I question everything nowadays." A

107

sour taste rained at the back of his throat, and he turned aside to spit it out. It wasn't right that he must ask his most trusted friend, but betrayal stabbed hardest when unexpected—and by a loved one. He knew that better than most.

"We are one, my brother. In life—and after death."

And there it was. The clue, the opening, the split in the rock for inner waters to spill out. He arched a brow at Inoli. "Then you have changed. Tell me. For we both know you are hiding something."

A small smile erased the fearsome lines carved at the sides of his brother's mouth. "When we last spoke, I told you some of what took place in Charles Towne. I did not tell you all."

Samuel shook his head. "That is no surprise."

The path turned to follow the creek. Wohali's tail switched back and forth, flicking at a persistent blackfly.

Inoli waved off a cloud of gnats. "I was seen in the cemetery."

The words made as much sense to him as when he'd tried to explain to Red Bird how to load her pistol. "You? Who moves as a shadow of night?"

"One cannot hide from the eyes of God."

Samuel yanked Wohali's lead, stopping the animal dead in her tracks. A resulting complaint whinnied out of the mount's raised lips. No matter. Silence signified on a hunt, not on scoping out a new trapping run.

He turned to his brother and folded his arms. "I would hear this. All of it."

The thin line of tiny blue dots tattooed in a curving pattern on his brother's cheeks lifted. "A Black Robe rose from one of the tombstones."

Samuel's brows shot upward. Why would a priest haunt a graveyard? "From the dead?"

"Now who is the superstitious one?" Inoli's dark eyes danced. "No. The man said he was told to lie in wait. He did, then fell asleep."

The information sank in his gut, like one of Red Bird's meals and every bit as indigestible. "Lie in wait for who?"

"Me."

"Blast it!" Samuel roared. The echo rifled out along the creek and into the woods. "You were compromised. McDivitt's men must have—"

Inoli shook his head, his braid swishing like spilled ink against his shoulders. "No, my brother. Those men had already been dealt with. The Black Robe said it was God Himself who told him to go to the stone and wait for a fox. I startled him, for he expected an animal, but even more, his words startled me. The man spoke the first people's language."

"Odd, indeed." Why would a Charles Towne priest speak Cherokee? Unless the man had been a missionary, which could be plausible. Still. . .the tale shivered down his spine. "And the man's reaction when you told him your name, Black Fox?"

"As surprised as mine when he spoke of the White Christ."

Samuel rolled his eyes. "I have told you the Gospel time and again." "Yes." Inoli grinned in full, his teeth a white burst of sunlight on his tanned face. "But this time I heard it."

Stunned, he searched his brother's shuttered eyes. The man was a master of hiding his true self. Could it be? Since his own conversion a year ago, he'd spoken of nothing but the grace that saved his life, and all to no result. But there, in the depths of Inoli's gaze, there was no compromise. No guile. Only truth and light and. . .what?

He looked deeper. The restlessness, the haunted hurt was gone, replaced with a serenity he chided himself for not noticing when they'd last met. He reached out and clapped Inoli on the back. "My heart is full, my brother."

"As is mine." Inoli pulled away and lifted his chin, proud as ever but in a completely different way.

Samuel clicked his tongue and started them on the move, following the bank. "Why did you not tell me this before?"

"Does one shout of his wedding night the morning after, or does he lie sated with his lover? I needed time with God alone."

A chuckle rumbled in his chest. The man was as blunt as a dulled axe blade. "Indeed."

He stopped before a bend in the creek, near a mound of limbs and dried undergrowth. Leaving Wohali to drink her fill, he ambled up the bank to relieve himself of the skin full of water he'd drunk not too long ago, then stopped suddenly before going any farther. Near the base of a tree lay a dead beaver. Some flies landed, but not many. Newly killed, then. Strange. So far from the water? Grabbing a stick, he turned the thing over. The animal's guts spilled onto the ground, uneaten, split wide by the slash of a claw.

Narrowing his eyes, he surveyed the immediate woodland. Squirrels scurried from brush to trunks. The rattle of cicada's whipped into a whirring. He massaged the back of his neck as he called for Inoli. "Something's not right."

His brother scrambled up and squatted next to the carcass. "It's a fresh swipe. Bear."

"Then why not finish eating the kill?" He turned to his brother. "And why kill at all? Berries are abundant."

"Maybe it got scared off mid-meal. Maybe by us."

"No. We would have heard it." Samuel scoured the nearby landscape, then strode to a disturbed piece of ground and squatted. A massive bear paw scarred the dirt. He measured the depth of the indentation with his forefinger. "Looks to be a three-hundred pounder."

Standing, he exchanged a glance with Inoli.

His brother rose, lifting the remains of the beaver by its hind legs. "Will you keep this?"

Unease crept across his shoulders. Unlike man, bears didn't kill for the thrill of it. "Aye, but bag it and let's move on. I don't feel right staying here."

Retrieving the horse, he and Inoli tromped through the woods, stepping on twigs, kicking through glossy rhododendron and hemlock shoots. Creating enough noise to frighten away any wild animal.

Not much farther, four ravens swooped and dove. Inoli sucked in a breath.

Samuel released Wohali's lead and ran, scaring off the scavengers and dropping to his knees next to a dead deer. Once again, a mighty slash gaped from ribs to flank.

Air whistled through Inoli's teeth as his feet stopped next to him. "Four ravens. It is an omen, my brother."

"Omens and faith do not mix." Samuel stood, looking out at the endless wildness. He didn't need omens to tell him something evil lurked in this stand of pine. The churning in his gut was enough.

But he did need faith to conquer the fear crawling up his throat. "We may have a hunt on our hands for a rogue bear. Let's hope not."

Eleanor dipped the rag into the bucket, wrung it out, then bent to scour the wooden planks. Who'd have thought that signing on as a nursemaid would also include the work of a below-stairs servant? She smirked and scrubbed a little harder.

Behind her, the bucket crashed. She shot to her feet, lest her skirt take the brunt of the dirty water.

"Uh-oh!" Standing in the puddle, Grace lifted a chubby finger to her mouth and surveyed the spreading flood.

Eleanor sighed. Who could be angry with that?

"Well, little one,"—She snatched up the bucket—"I suppose I needed fresh water. A trip to the creek for us then, hmm?"

"Creeeeeeek!" Grace squealed, clapping her hands.

Eleanor grabbed her pistol and powder horn off the table, tucking both into her pocket on their way outside. No matter what Samuel said about bears, she'd feel better using a firearm instead of only her bravado. Days of practice whenever Grace chanced a nap increased her confidence. Why, a few more weeks, and she just might give Mr. Heath a challenge at marksmanship.

Clouds ambled across the early July sky, dragging shadows along the ground. Grace darted from shady patch to shady patch, stopping in each one and twirling. Oh, to be so joyful, so pleased with the simple gifts slipping from God's fingers.

"Why not?"

She spun, expecting Samuel to be standing behind her whispering the words. But no one was there. The space between her and the house was empty.

Grace's giggle turned her back around. The little girl held out her hand, clearly inviting her to join the game.

Eleanor nibbled her lip, the *"why not"* flitting across her mind like the shadows on the ground. She darted a glance around the edges of the yard. No Samuel. No one. So why the queer feeling eyes watched her every move?

"Etsi!" Grace squealed, flailing her fingers toward her.

Who knew what the word meant, but it didn't matter. The girl's bright eyes said enough. Clutching the bucket in one hand, Eleanor dashed forward and entwined her fingers with Grace's. They raced from shadow to shadow, Grace squealing happy, her smiling big.

Until they entered the woods—the dividing line between safety and wilderness. She'd seen maps of the Americas before, and where the cartographers had left off between explored land and that which no one had yet set eyes upon, they printed the words *here be dragons*. Her smile faded. Perhaps they ought change that to *here be bears*.

Nearing the bank, she stamped a small area of ferns, creating a flattened play area for Grace. She gathered a few rocks and some sticks, then set them in a pile. "Sit here, Grace. I shall be back in a thrice."

She waited until the girl whomped onto her bottom and started stacking the rocks into a tower. The gravel path, worn from daily use, crunched beneath her shoes. She paused several yards before finishing the descent, eyeing the far bank. The ferns rustled, but only by a slight breeze. No sticks cracked. No gamey odor. Nothing to indicate a threat by black fur and white fangs.

Eleanor shifted her gaze side to side. A shiver skittered across her shoulders even though God's creation appeared to be all greens and browns and placid beauty.

La, what a flappable ninny she'd become. She padded down to the water's edge, the creek shrinking smaller every day without rain. Bending, she kept one eye on the spot where the bear had reared a week ago and dipped in her bucket.

A child's scream tore through the woods.

Grace!

Eleanor dropped the bucket and pulled out her pistol, all at a dead run up the embankment. Could she shoot a great beast? What if the thing had the girl in its jaws? She sprinted faster, leaping up the last of the ridge.

Ten paces ahead, Grace stood pointing at the ground. Another screech ripped out her mouth.

Heart racing, Eleanor scanned from trunk to trunk, shrub to shrub, past fern and hemlock and spindly-limbed oaks. No bear. No wildcat. No danger.

Grace screamed again.

Eleanor pocketed the pistol while closing the distance between them. Her gaze followed the child's index finger, aimed like a rifle barrel at the greenery. A large, hairy spider crept over her pile of rocks.

As much as Eleanor hated spiders—and this one was enormous—the tension in her jaw loosened. She swept up Grace, who clamped her arms around her neck in a chokehold, and rescued the child back to the gravel path.

"Well, that was frightening, was it not?" She kissed the crown of the girl's head. "All is well now, my sweet."

She bent to set her down—then immediately straightened, clutching Grace as tightly as the girl rewrapped her body against hers. To their right, underbrush crashed. Sticks cracked. Something big. Something fast.

Something getting louder with each heave of her labored lungs.

Her throat closed, and not from Grace's clutches. Fear sprouted on her brow, her spine, the soft, tender skin just behind her knees. This time there would be no Samuel to save her.

Oh, God. Her mouth dried to bleached bones.

Whatever it was came at great speed—trapping her and the girl between house and stream. Easy prey.

Grace squirmed, her foot kicking the pistol in Eleanor's pocket and driving it into her thigh, shattering the horrible trance.

Eleanor whisked the girl to the ground and yanked out the pistol, so quickly the powder horn fell to the dirt in the process. No matter. She'd make the first shot count. Opening the hammer wide, she fingered the trigger and squinted through the trees. Ten yards away, a flash of white blurred between black trunks. A great snort filled the air—and hooves pounded a rumble against the earth.

Hooves? Bears didn't have hooves.

"Thank You, God," she whispered. Though it was but a runaway horse, her legs still shook and her fingers jittered as she tucked away her firearm. She spun to pick up Grace.

But the girl squatted with the powder horn, cap off and upturned, raining black granules over the fingers of one chubby hand.

"Grace! Very naughty. Give that to me, now."

The girl blinked up at her, but thankfully complied. Samuel would surely not be pleased to discover such a waste. Why could she not seem to manage one small child?

She grabbed Grace's hand and wiped it on her own petticoat, then entwined her fingers with the girl's. The short amount of time it took for Grace to get into trouble was staggering. Perhaps a nap would do them both good. She sped down the path then paused at the edge of the woods.

Near the stable, a rawboned horse pawed the dirt. What on earth? Why had the thing halted here?

Eleanor ushered Grace across the lot to the porch and pulled out a small ball of twine from her other pocket—a lifesaver she'd learned kept the child occupied. String, of all things. The charges in the rich houses she'd served in weren't even satisfied with a porcelain doll or illuminated picture book, yet Grace could play for hours with string.

"Stay put, Grace," she ordered, then left the girl behind with the improvised toy to see about the stray horse.

The white mount, all bones and whinnies, nudged the stable door with its nose.

"Go home, boy." She waved her arms, taking care to keep enough space to escape a wild kick. "Good horse. Off with you now."

Lips lifted over browned teeth, releasing a great whicker. The horse trotted in a circle, resuming its head bobbing at the stable door.

Eleanor frowned. What was so enticing in the stable? Wohali roamed the woods with Samuel, so the mare couldn't be the draw. Or was it maybe the mare's scent left behind that attracted?

The horse snorted, its chest contracting, flesh riding the swell and dip of its ribcage.

"Ahh," she breathed out. Not the mare, but Wohali's provender, no doubt. Giving the horse a wide berth, she circled the animal and swung the stable door open, all the while speaking in an even tone. "Are you hungry, poor fellow?"

The horse trotted over to Wohali's stall and blew out a snort—which surely must be a yes in horsey language.

Eleanor rummaged for a pail, then found the crate housing the sack of oats. Samuel kept the food far from Wohali's reach. He was particular about how much and what his mount ate, and had been sure to impart that knowledge to her. Something about gorging or foundering or some sort. It hadn't mattered much to her at the time, so she'd only half-listened, but at least she remembered where he kept the extra feed. She filled the pail partially and returned to Wohali's stall—then hesitated. Ought she be feeding someone else's horse in here? What would Samuel say?

Pivoting, she strode from the stable and set the pail outside. Maybe the horse would eat its fill and move on to return to its home.

Another scream rent the air. Grace stood on the porch, pointing like a French Spaniel at the woods.

Eleanor huffed. This was turning into quite the trend today. She followed the line of Grace's outstretched arm, expecting to see another of the horse's companions drawn by the smell of oats.

Sunlight dappled from leaf to leaf, nothing more. No other horses. No bears. No. . .anything, really—except for the finest hairs at the nape of her neck rising up like pricking needles.

She grabbed the bucket and returned it to the stable, then shut the door. Let the thin horse eat in peace. Samuel could deal with it when he returned. She kept her gaze on the trees as she scurried toward the house. Nerves, most likely, but maybe she and Grace should spend the rest of the day in the cabin. An eerie foreboding wrapped around her chest and squeezed, and she upped her pace. She suspected what Samuel had said last week held even truer now.

This place was getting more dangerous every day.

Chapter 16

Samuel traveled the rest of the trail home alone, leaving Inoli to check on his own land—or more like the woman he was interested in—before coming to meet Red Bird. Probably a good thing. It would take his brother a good three weeks to trek to the overhill town of Chota and back, giving Eleanor more than enough time to acclimate not only to the wilds but also to an even wilder-looking man such as Inoli.

Wohali whickered and sidestepped. Not that he blamed the animal. He and his brother had tensed a time or two as well since finding the mangled deer and beaver, but they'd never discovered any more clues as to what had gutted them. Either the bear was more ghost than rogue—or something unknown roamed these woods.

He and Wohali splashed across the creek and up the bank, where he paused. His gut hitched—a sense that'd saved his life many a time. He scanned from tree to familiar tree. Nothing different. So why the unease skittering along every nerve? He slipped from the saddle, sniffing, separating the fragrance of loamy earth from a metallic, almost sulphuric taint. He padded forward a few more steps, and his gaze shot to the ground. Gunpowder sprinkled the earth like a dusting of fear.

Clicking his tongue, he led Wohali to the edge of the trees. Could be nothing. Could be Red Bird tried her hand at target practice in the woods today and dropped her powder horn. Or maybe Grace had stolen the thing and made a game of chase out of it.

Or else. . .he narrowed his eyes. Had trouble paid a visit in his absence?

The last of the day's light slanted through the trees, ringing the yard in a murderous glow. Both stable and house doors were shut. Grace's laughter wafted out the open window. The new lean-to still remained unfinished on the east side. All appeared to be well.

"Come, Wohali." He tugged the horse onward. "We are old women, you and I."

But when his boots hit the clearing, he slowed. Hoofprints, smaller, shallower than Wohali's disturbed the ground, leading to the stable. What the devil?

He tethered his horse, then swung the door wide. Inside, an unfamiliar nicker cut through the growing shadows. A white head bobbed out from Wohali's stall. His gaze cut to the cabin. Was someone in the house with Red Bird and Grace?

Wheeling about, he stalked halfway across the yard, when a thunder of hooves pounded up the road. He slung the rifle off his back and cocked the hammer by the time McDivitt and two other men—Rafe O'Donnell and Charlie Stane—fanned the yard in front of him.

Samuel cradled the rifle, fighting the urge to point it at McDivitt's heart, yet keeping it handy. "What you doing on my land, McDivitt?"

Angus tipped his hat. "Good evening to you too, Heath."

Samuel slid his gaze to Rafe, who turned his head aside, then on to Stane, whose intentions hid behind eyes so grey and lifeless, one wondered if any soul resided within.

He turned back to McDivitt. "I don't believe you rode all the way out here for a social call."

"Rafe here's lookin' for justice, and I aim to give it to him." McDivitt nodded toward the man on his left. "Says his horse was stolen. You know anything about that?"

Samuel's jaw hardened, a muscle twitching up near his ear. He'd spent the past decade trapping animals of all kinds in this wood and beyond in Cherokee country. This snare was ready to bite into his throat.

He glowered at McDivitt. "Why would I?"

A piercing whistle trilled past Rafe's lips. Hooves trotted out from the stable. The three men slid from their mounts, Rafe jogging over to snag the white horse.

"Well, well." Yellowed teeth peeked from McDivitt's beard, and he speared Samuel with a sneer. "Looks like we found our horse thief."

The spikes of the trap snapped shut. So. . .trouble *had* paid a visit in his absence today. Lifting the rifle, he clicked the hammer wide open and aimed at McDivitt's legs. For now. "We both know it wasn't me. I been out all day."

"What I know is that you're not going to shoot me in front of two witnesses, so you might as well put that firearm down." Angus turned to the thin man with the thinner horse. "Rafe?"

"Yes, sir."

"That your horse?"

The man nodded. "Yes, sir."

McDivitt hitched a thumb over his shoulder. "That your stable?"

Rafe shook his head. "No, sir."

Angus pivoted and stalked over to the other man. Samuel followed the movement with his barrel. Charlie Stane eyed Angus with a face as blank—and dangerous—as a snake.

"Stane," said Angus, "whose horse is that?"

"Rafe O'Donnell's." Stane's voice was as cold as his gaze.

"And who's stable is that?" Once again, McDivitt pointed.

Samuel blew out a breath, long and low. It was either that or start shooting to end such dramatics.

"Samuel Heath's," Stane answered.

"So. . ." McDivitt paced in front of the men, the tails of his riding coat swinging with each step.

Samuel lowered his rifle—but kept it at full cock.

"Mr. Stane," Angus drawled, "are you swearing as a witness to the recovery of Rafe O'Donnell's horse, found inside Mr. Heath's stable?"

Samuel clamped his teeth so tight his jaw ached. He'd never had a run-in with Stane, but it appeared that was about to change. How much had McDivitt paid him?

Stane swiveled his head, training his vacant eyes on Samuel. "I swear."

"So be it, then." McDivitt strode to the side of his horse and untied a leather-braided whip hanging from his saddle. "Penalty for horse thieving is a whipping, Heath."

White hot anger blazed a trail from his gut to his throat. "Quit hiding behind your own version of the law, McDivitt. If all you want is revenge, then say so, and take me on alone. . .unless you're afraid. Is that it?"

Angus's shoulders stiffened as if an arrow pinned him to a wall.

Samuel snorted. Pathetic excuse of a man.

Behind him, the cabin door flew open and little feet beat double-time on wood. He flipped the hammer to half-set and lowered the muzzle to the dirt before he turned.

"Edoda!" Grace scrambled down the porch steps, racing toward him. Her little fair head bobbed—and could just as easily be split wide open if she were caught in this fray. McDivitt might even consider it a score against him.

He held out his hand. "Stop!"

The harsh roar of his voice halted Grace in her tracks. Her face twisted, and huge tears pooled in her widened eyes. "Dada?"

Red Bird dashed out the cabin door, her skirts rippling. "I am so sorry. She got away from me."

Samuel grimaced. The woman and the girl could have no idea what they were running headlong into. He pivoted, putting his body between the men and his family. "Rafe's got his horse back. Now ride on out of here. All of you."

McDivitt advanced, uncoiling the whip. "As a regulator, I'm to uphold the peace. A crime's been committed. Justice must be served."

"What crime?" Red Bird's voice shivered at his back.

McDivitt jutted his jaw. "You might want to step inside, madam."

A rat couldn't have been more cornered. If Samuel shot now, he could take out one man, but the others would be on top of him before he could reload. His tomahawk could stop one more, but not before Rafe or Stane struck—and with Grace and Red Bird possibly caught in the crossfire. He worked his jaw, pivoted, angling to keep the men in sight yet also make eye contact with Red Bird. "Do it. Take Grace in the house."

The lowering sun lit a thousand questions in her gaze. Even so, she grabbed the girl's hand without giving any voice.

In one swift movement, he swung around and lifted the rifle, pulling the hammer wide and fingering the trigger. "I'm going to give you one more chance, McDivitt. Get off my land—now—before someone gets hurt."

McDivitt cracked the whip, the report sharp and echoing. "That horse was in your stable. You took it. And as a representative of the law—"

"No, he did not." Red Bird's voice breezed past him like an ill wind, prickling along his backbone. Samuel whirled, urging her to silence with his stare.

She ignored him. "I did."

McDivitt turned toward her. "Did you, now? Hmm. That changes things a bit."

Samuel's gut tightened into a knot. Rage simmered, ready to blow.

McDivitt bared his teeth in a grin. "Going to be a shame to mark up that pretty back of yours, Mrs. Heath. Still, the law must be upheld."

Angus nodded toward Rafe and Stane. "Take her, men."

Sweat dampened Eleanor's palms, her grip on Grace's hand slick. The man with the whip looked down his nose at her—a nose that'd been broken and healed wrong, leaving a crooked hump on the ridge. He wore a beard, labeling him wilder than her husband—or any other man she'd encountered.

The other two men, halfway across the yard, started toward her, their boots scraping along the ground, shaving off layers of her courage with each step. A rope dangled from the hand of one. What had she just confessed to?

She swept Grace behind her and faced the man with the whip, unsure if her voice would work. "I fed and housed a horse. That is all. Is that such a crime?"

The bearded man smiled. "Is the horse yours?"

"No."

"Then you broke the law, Mrs. Heath. Any and all persons, and I quote"—his gaze drifted upward, as if he read some great tome in the skies—"who shall be indicted and found guilty of stealing any horse, mare, gelding, colt or filly, for the first offense will be punished with the loss of an ear and/or be publicly whipped, not exceeding thirty-nine lashes on the bare back."

"But I did not steal that horse!" She whirled to Samuel, fighting the desire to run into his arms and bury her head against his shirt, allow him to chase away the fear as he had the bear. "I—I had no idea. I only meant to give it some food and trusted you would know what to do with it when you arrived home."

"You didn't do anything wrong. I'll take care of this." His dark eyes flashed at the advancing men. "Stop right there."

They didn't—until he pulled out his tomahawk. "I'm not going to let you touch her. We all know this is a false charge."

The bushy-bearded man laughed. "You ain't gonna be swinging that blade around. Think of the blood, the mess, the nightmares your pretty wife there will have for years to come. . .and yer child. She'll be scarred for life, I imagine."

Samuel's shoulders stretched tight. The tomahawk hit the ground as he turned to her. "Take Grace inside. Now!"

The harshness of his tone settled in the hollow of her bones, adding to her fear, and starting a wail from Grace. Eleanor swept up the child, happy to leave this macabre scene.

"Put the girl down, Mrs. Heath." The man cracked the whip.

The tail of it whiffed near her ear.

Grace screeched.

She froze.

Samuel roared. "McDivitt! So help me, if you touch my wife—"

"Justice must be served, Heath." The man closed in on her. "Rafe, Stane, tie her up."

His words smeared across the coming darkness, ugly, black, and sinister. She swayed, her breathing shallow. Her knees shivery. No! Everything in her screamed a bloody absolutely not.

Samuel slid between her and the man with the whip, the breadth of his shoulders blocking her view.

"Then whip me. It's my privilege as a husband to take on my wife's sentence."

Her mouth dropped. Was this real—or a nightmare?

Grace's tears soaked into Eleanor's bodice. "Etsi!"

Eleanor retreated. Oh that she may gain the safety of the cabin before anyone noticed.

Her view widened as she backed away.

The man jerked his head toward Samuel, the whites of his eyes huge. "You'll serve her debt?"

"I will."

Her step hitched, as did her breath. A jolt hit every nerve, leaving behind a jittery unease. Had he really just agreed to a lashing? Because of her?

As if he'd read her mind, Samuel's dark gaze bore straight into her heart. He nodded toward the house.

She turned and ran.

Once inside, she slammed the door shut and leaned against it, glad for the support. Grace choked her, squirming in her arms. What to do? She slid to the floor in a daze.

My precious Lord;

My only hope;

My Saviour, how I need You now.

The prayer circled back and slammed into her, as shocking as the crack of the whip outside. She flinched. Of course she needed help—but Samuel needed it more.

Rising, she dashed over to her bed and unwrapped Grace as she might a wet cape, so unyielding did the girl cling to her. The snap of the whip violated the coming evening.

"Here, sweet." She grabbed a rag doll off the pillow where Grace had last played and thrust it into her hands. Then she looked deep into the child's blue eyes, swollen with tears. "Stay put. You hear me? Do not move!"

Grace's lip quivered.

Eleanor softened her tone. "I shall be back straightaway. I promise."

The child let out a shaky breath, then dove under the pillow.

Eleanor snatched her pistol off a shelf and darted for the front door, hesitating with her palm on the latch. Could she do this?

Crack!

Indeed. If Samuel hadn't stepped in, that would be her back bearing the lash. He wouldn't have left her alone with nothing but angry men and pain.

She slipped out the door, strode to the edge of the porch, and stopped. Going farther was not an option. Her feet wouldn't move.

Across the yard, two of the men stood with arms folded, watching the brutality. They'd tied Samuel to a tree, arms above his head. His shirt lay in a blue heap on the dirt. The fabric was probably still warm from his body, still smelling of a day spent in the woods, of pine and smoke and strength.

The bearded man reared back. His arm snapped forward. The whip uncoiled, slicing through the air faster than her eyes could follow. By the time the leather thong returned to a standstill, a spray of red droplets had arced through the air and violated Samuel's shirt—and another jagged line opened on his back, flesh split wide open.

Samuel took it silently. Letting the man rip long gashes into his skin. Draining his blood in weeping drips that soaked into his breeches.

Crack!

His body recoiled with each strike, yet he made no noise. Not a moan. No groans. Not even a cry. Was he breathing?

Hot tears ran down Eleanor's cheeks. For an instant, she stood helpless, great sobs roaming in her chest, flinching with each sickening blow.

Then she cocked the hammer and pulled the trigger. Gunpowder exploded.

The shot fell short, yards from where the men stood. One of them smiled. The other stalked toward her.

But the one she really wanted to stop whaled another wicked blow onto Samuel's back, more brutal than any of the previous strikes. The whip fell to the ground like a black snake.

"Leave the woman be. I'm done," the bearded man ordered. "Untie him."

Eleanor pressed a knuckle to her mouth. Hard. Pinching the tender skin between bone and teeth, unable to move away but unwilling to move any closer. Yet.

Once the rope was loosened, Samuel dropped to his knees and tipped forward, his shoulder catching against the tree. The bearded man laughed as he coiled up the rope. One of the others stomped on Samuel's shirt as he headed for his horse.

Eleanor's heart lurched, and she dashed down the stairs.

The bushy-bearded man wheeled about, and when his gaze snagged on her, he stalked forward, coiling up the whip as he came. Odd twitches jerked the sides of his mouth. He reached out a hand. "Don't cry, Mariah. Come home with me."

She backed up a step, her blood turning cold. She'd visited Bedlam once, forced to accompany a countess and her charge. This was the same glassy stare she'd witnessed there, pupils pinpoints on a white canvas.

"I am not Mariah." The calmness she forced into her voice mixed with her own mad cry, and the words came out ragged.

A wave rippled across his face, starting at the jaw and working its way upward, until his brow lifted in understanding. "No, you aren't, are you? But that don't mean you can't leave with me. My offer stands."

Was this country made up of nothing but lunatics and ruffians? She clutched her skirt, prepared to run back to the cabin and lock the door. "No thank you."

"We're done here, McDivitt." The largest of the men dug his heels into his horse's flanks and tore off down the road, twilight's shadows swallowing him. The other man followed, the white horse tied to his mount and trotting behind.

The bearded man's gaze swept over her from head to toe.

She held her breath. Why hadn't she thought to grab more shots?

But then he turned and loped to his horse. He swung up into the saddle, the whip crossing at an angle over his chest like Samuel wore his rifle strap.

She waited until his horse pounded down the road; then she darted over to Samuel and sank to her knees beside him. "Samuel?"

Blood dripped down his back. His chest heaved. His voice was a whisper. "Help—" He sucked in a breath. "Help me inside."

His big arm landed on her shoulder, and she hefted upward with all her strength. He rose to his feet with a grunt, leaning on her.

"I am so, so sorry."

"Don't. . .take in. . .stray animals." Every word cost him, his voice growing thinner. Tighter. Heat poured off him, and her gown stuck to the sweat and blood on his skin.

The last flare of sunlight dazzled between the trees, painting his face in orange light. His usual swath of hair was plastered against his damp skin, revealing ruined flesh from temple to jaw, puckery, as if it'd been melted and reshaped on his cheekbone by a rough hand.

She sucked in her own breath. How much suffering could one man take?

Chapter 17

Life always came down to a choice between dark and light. Blackness promised oblivion and relief, but oh, Lord. . .that was a lie. Samuel had learned that a long time ago. So he forced open his eyes to brightness and blinked from the shocking contrast.

"You are awake!"

Fabric rustled. A whiff of wood-fire and sunshine, sweet and surprisingly musky, feathered over half his face—the half not mashed against a pillow.

"Aye." His voice rasped, and he cleared his throat.

He blinked again. This time, the world shifted into focus like the turn of a great kaleidoscope. Worried blue eyes, flecked with golden sparkles, stared into his. Afternoon sun—ever brightest in the west-facing cabin—set Red Bird's hair aflame. He should've been up hours ago.

He shifted his head on the pillow. "Must've been a rough night."

"It has been two."

"Two?" Lord, have mercy. What kind of man lolled about in bed for days? He shoved up—then cried out as fire sliced from his shoulders to the small of his back. He dropped onto the straw tick with a groan. Blast that McDivitt! The good-for-nothing. . .hold on.

Straw tick?

He pushed to his elbows, slowly this time, like Ezekiel's dry bones coming to life. Sure enough, he lay on the bed usually occupied by Red Bird. She knelt next to the frame, close enough that he could count the pale freckles romping over the bridge of her nose. Any closer and she'd be lying next to him.

Despite the searing pain raging in his muscles, laughter begged to be released, and he chuckled until he winced. What a tale this would make for Inoli. With a little embellishment, he could stop the teasing from his friend.

"Mr. Heath! Please, do not overtax yourself." A nattering wren couldn't have scolded any better. "You have suffered a severe beating.

There is nothing humorous about this."

"Ahh. . ." Again with the *Mr. Heath*? He was certain she'd called him otherwise earlier. Sweat beaded on his forehead as he struggled to sit and swing his legs over the side of the bed. Fresh agony burned along each gash. He waited until the room stopped spinning and he saw only one red-headed woman—not two—eyeing him as if he were a lunatic.

"But you see, Tatsu'hwa, I got to sleep in your bed." He winked at her, followed by a grunt. Sweet white-clouded heavens! Even his face hurt.

The woman's cheeks turned scarlet as she rose to her feet. "The bed is not mine, sir. It was yours to begin with."

He'd snort—if the movement wouldn't hurt so much. "Life needn't be so serious."

"But this is serious!" Her hands clasped together in front of her, her fingers laced so that her knuckles were white islands in a sea of red. "You almost died because of me, and I am so, *so* sorry. About everything. I had no idea feeding a stray horse was against the law."

This time the snort would not be denied—and he paid for it with a stabbing slice across his shoulder blades. Once he caught his breath, he lifted his face to hers. "This wasn't about the law, the horse, or even you, so stop blaming yourself."

Fine, white teeth worked her lower lip as she digested his words. "Then. . .it is about that man, McDivitt, is it not? There is a quarrel between the two of you, I think. Why?"

"McDivitt is a greedy bloodsucker who'll stop at nothing to get what he wants—and what he wants is anything I've got." Had he spoken this of anyone else, a twinge of guilt would've spiked his gut, for it would've been slander. But in McDivitt's case, he spoke true. The man was as wily as a creek gorge during the spring melt.

"He is not right in the head, is he?" A slight ripple worked its way down to the hem of Red Bird's skirt as if her knees shook.

He frowned. "Why do you ask?"

"He mistook me for someone else, but it seemed more than a simple mistake." A shadow crossed her face, though the afternoon sun blazed unhindered through the window. "It was like. . .like he really thought I was her."

He gripped the edge of the bedframe. Would this never end? "Let me guess. He thought you were Mariah?"

"Yes." Her gaze snapped to his. "Who is she?"

The question ripped into him like the tip of the whip. How to answer that? She'd been his bane, his sorrow, his mistake—

His wife.

He shot to his feet. Night fell hard. So did he.

"Samuel!"

Chest heaving, he fought once again to stay in the light. A groan scraped out his throat, and he clung to the bedframe with shaky arms, forcing himself to remain upright.

Red Bird dropped to her knees before him, resting a light touch on his knee with her fingertips. "Are you all right? Is there anything I can do?"

The waves of pain eventually ebbed, and he met her gaze. "Lend me a hand."

"Surely you are not thinking of standing?"

"The sooner I move, woman, the sooner I heal." He lifted a brow at her. "And the sooner you'll get your bed back."

She set her jaw.

He stared her down.

"Very well." She sat next to him, her sigh a reproach. "Put your arm on my shoulder, and we shall both stand on the count of three. Ready?"

"Aye."

"One. Two. Three."

His head floated, and he wobbled, but at least the room didn't spin. Red Bird's small frame pressed against his, shoring him up. He took a step, then another. Soon, the worst of his pain stemmed from the woman's arm digging into the small of his back where she supported him. He unwound his arm from her shoulder.

But she didn't let go.

"I'm fine, Tatsu'hwa," he ground out. "Let go."

She hesitated. "Are you certain?"

"Have you ever heard me say anything I wasn't sure of?"

Her brow creased—but she stepped aside.

He hobbled to the door, his steps slowing as he passed Grace's crib. She slept with her feet hitting one end and her head the other. He'd have to build the girl her own bed soon.

Outside, the fragrance of tangy pine floated warm on the afternoon breeze. He leaned against the porch post, filling his lungs with the sweetness, but his lips twisted into a sour pucker. Across the yard, a few gashes marred a pine where the whip had missed its mark. McDivitt had planned that ambush with the skill of a wildcat. He must've been prowling about, just waiting to spring when the time was right. Dirty son of a jackanapes.

The scuff of wood on wood pulled him from his thoughts. He turned. Red Bird hauled a barrel across the porch to his side.

"You ought to sit." Her tone brooked no argument, and he wasn't sure how to feel about that. Thankful for her compassion? Or irritated she told him what to do?

He grunted—but eased himself down.

She swooped in front of him. "Shall I get you a drink? Are you hungry? Maybe you ought to—"

Irritation won out. "Stop flapping about like a mother hen. And for heaven's sake quit looking at me as if I'm about to break. I've seen worse."

"I—I only meant to help." Her shoulders slumped as if he'd been the one to brandish a whip against her. She spun toward the door, her skirts a'twirl around her legs. "I should see to supper."

He stifled a groan—but not from his pain. That he'd hurt her was evident. That it bothered him was a surprise. Crossroads were a notorious danger, and the intersection he now stood at could cost him his heart depending on which direction he chose.

Care about the woman's feelings?

Or take cover behind a mask of indifference?

He shifted on the barrel, embracing the sharp pangs in his back.

"Tatsu'hwa," he breathed out.

Her footsteps padded to the door. Of course she couldn't hear him whisper, not with the shush of the breeze rustling the leaves and waving the pine boughs. He could still tuck tail and run the other way. Pretend it didn't matter. Stiff-arm the empathy rankling him as much as his ruined flesh.

He sucked in a breath and called out. "Sit with me, wife."

Eleanor hesitated, one foot on the threshold. The sting of Samuel's rebuke still burned in her ears—yet it was a just anger. She deserved it, more than he deserved the whipping. He'd nearly been killed because of her.

"You heard me, woman."

She whirled, expecting to see him inches from her.

But he hadn't moved. He sat with his back to her. Deep red lines crisscrossed his back, the skin purple in some patches, yellow in others. Scabs covered most of the stripes—only one trickle of blood seeped from the widest gash.

Yet her stomach twisted. That had to hurt.

"You going to stand there gawking at my back or come join me?"

Drat the man! Of course he should be angry with her, but not for caring about him, not for tending him in every possible way to ease his pain. Why did he not berate her for bringing trouble to his own back? Why not censure her ignorance for housing a foreign horse in his stable? Why not simply send her from his home? Not one of her former masters would have taken such a beating in her place—then ask that she sit beside him.

Emotion clogged her throat as she retrieved a barrel from the other side of the porch and dragged it next to his. How could Samuel Heath tie all her guilt and humiliation into one big knot and cast it far afield, asking her to keep company with him instead of dismissing her from his life? He'd be better off with her gone. She sank onto the barrel, smoothing wrinkles from her skirt. A silly occupation, yet as soothing as the sun on her face. "You are very kind, sir."

"Kind?" A low chuckle rumbled in his chest. "I've been called many things. That's not one of them."

"Oh, but you are! You dote on your daughter. You put up with my cooking. You sleep on the floor, and you took a lashing that should have been mine. Beneath that gruff exterior, I think you are very—" She pressed her lips tight. Embarrassment burned up her neck and flushed across her cheeks. Would she never learn to hold her tongue?

"Careful now." He turned toward her. "You're starting to sound like my wife."

"I. . .I. . ." She what? How did one possibly reply to such a statement? Her fingers snagged on her skirt, creating a new crease instead of removing them.

He cocked a brow, humor flashing in his dark eyes.

She flailed for a new topic. Any topic. "I. . .uh, I could not help but notice the other marks on your back. Would those scars be the reason you know so much about bears?"

His gaze pierced, digging deep.

But a grin parted the dark stubble on his face. "I've had a run-in or two."

She glanced at the purplish-streaks reaching across the side of his rib cage, then shot her gaze back to his. "It appears the bear came out the winner."

He smirked. "I'm the one still breathing."

"Indeed." She studied the lines at the corners of his eyes, each a testament to a life lived on the edge of want and need. He belonged here in this rough and rugged land. He was part of it. "I perceive you are a survivor. . .of many things."

He looked away, gaze fixed on the tree line—though she very much doubted he saw it, not with the way a twitch throbbed at the apex of his jaw.

"Tell me your story." His voice drifted out soft, a plea. An invitation.

And quite possibly his own evasion tactic.

"Story? Me?" A bitter laugh quivered on her lips. "That would be a very short book, I am afraid."

"Even so, I would hear it."

Memories stole her breath. She spent most of her time denying the past. To voice it would breathe life into a dragon she'd rather not face. "There is not much to tell, really."

"It would take my mind off the hurt of my back."

La! He couldn't have trapped her more securely than by using one of his steel snares. She ran her hands from thigh to knee, pulling the fabric taut. "England was my home, though I have not any family left. My mother died birthing me. My father. . .well, some called him a gentleman."

His face shot to hers. "But not you."

Guilt sank in her chest. Was she not this very morning teaching Grace to give thanks in all things? "I am sorry to give that impression. Yes, my father was a gentleman, with land holdings in Devonshire. His position afforded me the privilege of attending one of the finest finishing schools and later a position as governess in several great households."

Furrows dug deep into his brow. "Why did you not simply live with your father until you married?"

"I said my father *was* a gentleman. He died when I was eighteen."

"If he had land, seems like there ought to have been enough money to provide for you, even after his passing. Why did you seek employment?"

This time she looked away—away from his questioning gaze, the question itself. . .and as far away as possible from examining the real reason she'd traded in her dreams of marriage for the lonely, set-apart life of a governess. She clenched her skirt and squeezed, creating as many wrinkles as her father had willfully cut into her life.

"I'm not the only one with scars, aye? Look at me, Tatsu'hwa."

His tone challenged, calm yet strong, the same voice he'd used when frightening off the bear, compelling her to turn his way.

His eyes glimmered with too much knowledge, like he could see the torn soul she kept buried deep. "Take it from someone who knows...Don't let the past fester inside. The sooner you move on, the sooner you'll heal. Sometimes you got to cut your losses."

"And what if that loss is your life?" She spewed out the words like cream gone bad, the barrel rocking beneath her. "My father lost his land, his dignity, *my* dignity. Tell me, for you are a father, what kind of man asks his own daughter to repay his gambling debts by trading her innocence for gold?"

Samuel's face hardened to flint. Fierce. Deadly. A savage look that chilled her to the marrow.

"I'll tell you what kind." His voice shook. "The kind that didn't deserve a daughter like you."

Then just as suddenly, the lines of his face softened, and he reached for her hand. "You were wronged, true. But we're all wronged some time or another. Even God. And that's the only reason you can let go of bitterness—because He did." He spread her fingers and turned her hand palm up, then let go.

She blinked, the truth of his words as stunning and raw as the stripes on his back. Her hand dropped to her lap, her thoughts to a brand-new pool of wonder. For the first time, she shrugged off the word *trollop* and examined it in the afternoon light, remembering the rage in her father's voice when she'd refused to yield to his request, the flare of his nostrils when he'd cast her out. The heavy weight of his rejection.

"It was not about you, child. It was always—ever—your father's wicked choices."

Her gaze shot to Samuel's mouth, but his lips were shut.

Gooseflesh lifted the skin on her arms.

She went back to smoothing her skirt, her eyes following the movement. What if this whole time she'd driven her life to combat a lie? What if her father's rejection had been nothing but his own desperation? A thrashing, miserable death of his dreams, murdered by his vice—not hers.

Her hands stilled. Peace blew over her, gentle and warm as the July breeze. She searched Samuel's face, marveling. The wild man in front of her could have no idea the gift he'd just handed her. "I did not realize you were a God-fearing man."

He tilted his head, his swath of dark hair hiding the scars on his face. "There's a lot you don't know."

Chapter 18

Samuel chucked the last log beneath the shelter of the new lean-to, then straightened with a grunt, swiping his brow with the back of his hand. Unyielding heat trickled sweat down his back, stinging the barely healed wounds. He stretched a snarl out of his sore muscles. Three weeks and still his body complained. So did he. Against Red Bird with all her smothering ideas of what he should and should not be doing. Against Ben Sutton, who had yet to send word about the expected negotiator. Against himself for the temper rising as hot as the last breath of July and as impossible to keep in check. Ahh, for a good rumble with Inoli, but his friend had not yet returned from Chota—though he should be back any day now.

He snagged his shirt off the top of the stack and shrugged it on, wincing as fabric scraped over his wounds. Painful, but could be worse. Thank God infection hadn't taken root.

Far off, a low rumble snagged his attention. Could be nothing, and most likely was, yet he lifted his head, blocking out the thrumming insects and chattering birdcalls, and. . .there. A layer beneath. Reverberation pounded at ground level, growing louder the longer he listened.

He grabbed his rifle from where he'd propped it against the lean-to wall and strode to the front of the house.

Six horses tore up the road and fanned out in front of him, McDivitt at the crux. Samuel shouldered the stock and aimed the muzzle at his chest, dead center.

Angus turned aside, a line of tobacco juice nailing the dirt. Sunlight glinted off a few drops clinging to his beard, dancing as he spoke. "Afternoon, Heath. I see your back is doing better."

Next to Angus, a jaunty bay trotted forward, sailing past the pack of men like an arrowhead. The flash of the rider's red coat stood stark against the drab colors of the others. Samuel stifled a groan. Major Andrew Rafferty. Death always seemed to accompany the man.

"Good day, Mr. Heath. As hospitable as ever, I see. But you might

135

as well put the weapon down." The redcoat moved like a phantom in the wind, whipping out a double-barreled pistol and firing off two rounds into the dirt at Samuel's feet. "You can't shoot us all."

Samuel stood stunned. Two shots without reloading? A double barrel? He'd heard such things were possible, but he'd never seen it. Where had Rafferty gotten such a weapon? Unease crept down his spine. If the major had one, how many others in the British military sported such?

Samuel kept his rifle trained on McDivitt but spoke to Rafferty. "Don't need to shoot you all. There's only one I aim to hurt."

"Humph," the major snorted. "I'm surprised 'tis not me."

Samuel swung the rifle, sighting the barrel on Rafferty. "Didn't say it wasn't."

Florid splotches bloomed on the major's clean-shaven face, glistening beneath a wash of sweat. His dung-colored hair clung to his brow, making a desperate attempt to escape the cockaded hat atop on his head. Fool. Even a trade shirt was too hot to wear on a day like this, yet the man kept his coat buttoned at the chest.

"Come now." A bead of perspiration rolled off the tip of Rafferty's nose. "You may live in the wild, but you do not have to behave as a beast."

This sweating pig had the guts to call him a beast? He fingered the trigger.

A movement caught the edge of his vision, and he slipped his gaze sideways. In the cabin's window, another flash of red appeared, framing porcelain skin and wide eyes. Hopefully by now Red Bird had gained enough frontier-sense to stay inside.

But all the same, he lowered his rifle, cradling it and setting the hammer to half-cock. To Rafferty's right, Jackson and Wills sat stone-faced atop their mounts. Beside McDivitt rode Stane and a fellow so thin, his bones looked as if they rallied to escape his skin.

Samuel turned to Rafferty. "What's this about?"

The major's horse shied a step, and he jerked the reins. "These are dangerous times, Mr. Heath. Men's loyalties are fickle at best. I'm on the hunt for a traitor."

His heart skipped a beat. Was this it? Had his Sons of Liberty affiliation been discovered? The gaze of the woman at the window hit him like a shot to the head. What would become of her? Not that she wasn't resourceful, he'd give her that, but she wouldn't last long in the backcountry without him. Nor would Grace. Defeat tasted sour, and he was tempted to turn aside and spit like McDivitt.

But he swallowed instead.

To You, God. I commit them to You.

He set his jaw and lifted his chin. "Then happy hunting. Take your fancy firearm and get off my land."

"I suspected as much." The major swung a long leg over his mount and slid to the ground. He rummaged in a pouch worn on a strap across his chest as he walked toward Samuel. "As I recall, our last venture required a little persuasion as well."

He held out a rolled-up piece of rag paper.

Samuel ignored it. "You gave me no time to bury my wife. I was supposed to be happy about that?"

"There wasn't anything left to bury." McDivitt's words flew through the air and rained hot coals on Samuel's head.

Samuel snatched the paper from Rafferty's hand and broke the seal. Each carefully penned word added stone upon stone, boxing him in.

Crushing the paper into a wad, he met Rafferty's pale blue stare, hating the English all over again. "Fine. I'll leave first light."

"No." Rafferty sniffed, sucking up the drips of sweat above his upper lip. "We leave within the hour."

"We?"

"The man I'm after is like no other. Violent. Cunning. Reminds me a lot of you, actually." A grin slashed across Rafferty's face. "At any rate, it will take the lot of us to bring him in."

Days, maybe weeks, with this man? And McDivitt? Samuel shook his head. "No. I go alone. With this many men tromping around in the woods, you might as well add some drummers and a fife. If the fellow you're after is as good as you say, we'll never find him that way."

Rafferty's shoulders lifted. "You're the tracker. That's your worry."

"You can't tie a man's legs together and expect him to run!"

"The crown expects loyalty, sir, not excuses." Rafferty's eyes narrowed to slits, releasing a fresh cloudburst of sweat-beads rolling down his temples. "Are you refusing to comply with your duty?"

Duty? He smirked. Duty to a capricious ruler who lived halfway around the world?

But the wad of paper in his hand weighed heavy, like a boulder, immovable and crushing. The document was more than a summons or a simple command.

It could very well be his death warrant.

A wasp buzzed near Eleanor's cheek, the sting of her last encounter still radiating pain on the back of her hand. Horrid creatures. She eased back from the window, far enough that the wasp lost interest and zigzagged away from the porch.

Outside, five men remained mounted on horses. She knew one—the brute, McDivitt. Only the British soldier stood on the ground, an arm's length in front of Samuel. Detecting their words was impossible, but she didn't need to. Samuel's shirt stretched taut across his shoulders—his I-will-not-be-moved stance, one she'd come to learn the hard way when asking for a visit to Molly and Biz.

The redcoat towered a head above Samuel, but only because of his ridiculous hat. Eleanor lifted a hand to the back of her neck and rubbed away a kink. Since when had she thought a British uniform ridiculous?

She approached the window again, comparing Samuel's plain, yet functional clothing to the proper military suit in front of him. The redcoat's smothering wool versus Samuel's loose-breathing linen. The audacious color rivaling Samuel's earthy tones. One tight and buttoned and regulated. The other homespun and practical and handsome.

Handsome? She stiffened. Surely she'd been out in the woods too long to think an overbearing, demanding ruffian pleasing to the eye.

Samuel ended the stalemate with a nod, then spun on his heel and stalked to the cabin. His back toward the redcoat, he couldn't see the sneer lifting the soldier's upper lip.

But Eleanor did. Whatever these men wanted, it couldn't be good.

She turned from the window as Samuel blew through the door like a brewing tempest. Grace looked up from her endless stacking of blocks but must have decided an annoyed father was less interesting than the crude pieces of wood. Her little fingers grabbed another block.

Samuel strode to a shelf of earthenware and pulled down the jar of the dried mixture he called pemmican, then proceeded to stuff a handful into a leather pouch. His muscles flexed and bulged with his jerky movements—a sure sign she ought fade into the background.

But morbid curiosity nudged her a step forward. "What is happening?"

He tied the pouch to his belt, then wheeled about and crossed to a chest near the bed. He snatched down a key from a peg on the wall, then bent to unlock the padlock, pausing to slip his gaze toward her before opening the lid. "I'll be gone for a while. Stay near the house."

This was new. Usually he simply disappeared into the woods and came back unannounced. Why the forewarning this time? She dared another step. "How long will you be gone?"

He turned to the chest, his long hair swinging against his collar, the ends bleached by the sun. He pulled out another tomahawk, a blade the size of a child's leg, and retrieved enough balls and powder to take down a brigade of dragoons.

Alarm clenched Eleanor's stomach. He never went into the woods like this.

He wore the tomahawks at each hip, ready to yank out and throw in tandem. He shoved the knife into a sheath he'd added to the strap crossing his chest. Retrieving his rifle, he swung it over his shoulder, then gasped when it rested against his back. He strode over to Grace and picked her up, holding her face-to-face so that her feet dangled midair, well away from the weapons. "Behave yourself, little one."

Then he set her down and stamped toward the door.

Clearly the man was avoiding her question. "Mr. Heath! When shall I expect your return?"

He turned toward her, a feral glimmer in his dark eyes. "Why? You going to miss me?"

The tips of her ears burned. Must he always tease in such a fashion? She fought the urge to go poke the big bully in the chest. "How long do you think Grace and I can survive on our own?"

The playfulness drained from his gaze—the loss of it like a sudden gust of cold air. "I'll be gone as long as it takes, not a moment more. That's all I can tell you."

"Those men, they are not. . ." She edged a step closer. "You are not in trouble, are you?"

"Woman, my whole life is a big ball of trouble." He huffed. "But no, as long as I do what they say, I'll be fine. As will you and Grace."

"What is it they want?"

He studied her for a moment, and she wondered if he'd answer or just turn and walk out the door.

Slowly, he retrieved a small wad of paper and tossed it to her.

Bits of wax fell to the floor as she smoothed the paper open. Precise penmanship scrolled at center:

July 12, 1770

*Mr. Samuel Heath is hereby notified of immediate service to
the Crown in the manner of tracking William Blacking—
known traitor—and bringing said criminal into the custody
of Major Andrew Rafferty.*

*On the orders of,
Major General George Patfield
Pvt. T. T. Downing, Sec.*

Eleanor read the missive twice. So. Not only did her husband trap animals, but apparently men as well. Was that how he'd earned that medal in the stable? It all flew in the face of the patriotic sentiments he sometimes let slip. She lifted her face and studied him instead of the letter. Who was this man?

His slouch hat cast his eyes in shadow, a day's growth of stubble shaded his jaw. Her gaze followed the angle of his rifle strap, crossing his chest and down to his hips, where the awful war-axes hung. Then lower, down the length of his deerskin leggings and on to the leather-wrapped hilt of another knife handle sticking out the top of his booted moccasins. God help the man he was tracking.

She bit her lip. *And, God, please, help Samuel.*

"Be careful." Her voice sounded tight, thin, tied to a whisper of fear. "Please."

He tipped his head, his swath of hair falling to one side. "I might almost get the impression that you care."

"Of course I care!"

"Do you, now?" He advanced toward her, the tomahawk handles bouncing against his thighs, the creak of the leather strap and swish of his breeches loud in the room. Even Grace watched him move.

Eleanor retreated to the wall.

He didn't stop until the tips of his boots touched the hem of her skirt. The gleam in his eyes shivered down her back and settled in her legs.

"Mr. Heath, please." She darted right.

He threw out his arm, resting his big palm against the wall and blocking her escape. "If I remember right, it was Samuel not too long ago."

Fire lit her face, and she dodged to the left.

His other arm shot up, trapping her between the two. His warm breath fanned against her lips. Surely burn marks would mar her cheeks.

His hand caught a loose curl of her hair. He tucked it behind her ear, so gentle, so light. Was she dreaming?

No. His fingers brushed along her earlobe, and she trembled—but not from fear. A strange, wholly new, wholly unsettling twinge tightened her belly.

"I promised you on our wedding day that I wouldn't touch you." His husky voice wrapped around her like a warm embrace, pulling her toward him. "Do you want that to change?"

A foreign desire ran along every nerve. She froze, unsure if she could speak or even breathe. Afraid if she did, everything would change. Forever.

"No," she forced the word past lips she was terrified to open.

"Because if you do"—he brushed his thumb along the curve of her neck, leaving a trail of fire—"all you need to do is ask, Tatsu'hwa."

His brown eyes held her in place, demanding she understand his meaning—and when she did, the implication stole her last bit of breath. Want and need charged the thin space between them, but whose? His or hers?

He turned so fast, a whoosh riffled against her face. He stalked to the door, then glanced over his shoulder. "Mind what I said. Stay close to the house."

She stood there for a moment, all heat and life and air sucked from the room—until she heard his horse tear out from the stable.

Shoving from the wall, she snatched up Grace on her way to the window. The little girl clung tight for the wild ride. Samuel led the men down the road, and Eleanor wasn't sure how to feel about that. Why care now whether the man stayed or didn't? He was hardly around much, anyway.

One horse lagged behind. McDivitt's. Once Samuel was out of sight, he turned, his gaze shooting to the window like a musket ball—and stared right at her.

Eleanor yanked the burlap shut and darted to the door, Grace squealing from the bouncy steps. She shot the latch, locking the entrance.

So many emotions roiled in her gut she set the girl down and pressed a hand to her stomach. This time there was no guarantee Samuel would come back.

Could she really manage without him?

Chapter 19

Samuel's gaze swept the forest floor. Wohali lagged behind on his tether. So did Samuel's thoughts. *Focus. Focus!* By now, an entire day after leaving home, he should've forgotten the feel of Red Bird's hair between his fingers, the softness of her skin, the vulnerability in eyes as blue as Marshall Creek at sunrise. English or not, the woman crossed all kinds of barriers he'd erected to hide behind. Walls he'd never expected to be breached. He should set a stronger guard around his heart.

His foot snapped a twig. Blast! He should also be engaging all his senses in the hunt. A scowl weighted his brow. His entire life was built on a shaky foundation of *should*s.

Behind him, maybe thirty yards eastward, a shot rang out from Barton's Hollow, the echo spreading like the ripples in a pond. Samuel stifled a growl. Fools. First the lighting of a fire last night. Now this? Unless the traitor was five or six miles out, he'd know they were closing in—which meant the man would either double back or set an ambush.

Taking care to avoid any more sticks—though at this point, did it really matter?—he plodded upward, traversing an old buffalo trace cut between towering pine and oak, scouring the ground as he went. If the man was bent on heading into Cherokee country—which is what he'd do in the same situation—this would be the most likely route.

Hold on.

He dropped into a squat. The sharp edges of a boot print, inches from a rock, cut into the dirt.

Setting his tongue against his teeth, he pushed out air in a whippoorwill call. Three times. Then took the time to pull out a piece of jerky from the pouch on his belt.

Soon a white shirt atop a black horse trotted up the trail. A day's growth of beard added a shadow to Rafferty's ruddy complexion. There was no stopping the scarlet splotches on the man's face, but at least he'd given in to reason and removed the red coat.

The major slid from the saddle. "What have you got?"

"Over here." He led Rafferty to the rock on the trail and crouched. "Boot print."

"Humph," Rafferty snorted. "Doesn't look like much to me."

Samuel pinched the bridge of his nose to keep from rolling his eyes. "Look closer. The edge is sharp on one side only because the man hit this rock with the left side of his foot, compensating on the right with his full weight. You won't find a full boot print, not after three days. You're lucky I saw this one, what with the critters roaming this wood. I'd say this is your man, Blacking. He's heading west, to Cherokee lands."

Rafferty stood, rubbing his knuckles over his chin. As he was ordinarily clean-shaven, the growth had to be itchy. A wicked grin tugged at Samuel's mouth. The man's discomfort ought not please him, but it did.

"Tell me, Mr. Heath, why would a man choose death by torture instead of an honorable hanging?"

Honorable? Samuel snorted as he straightened. "Don't matter how death comes. It's never dignified."

Rafferty shrugged. "I suppose I should expect no less from a traitor."

The word circled overhead, like a hawk to the kill. Samuel turned from Rafferty and strode to Wohali, feigning a search through a pack on the back of his saddle. Better to keep the major looking at anything but his face. Secrets had a way of surfacing if stared at long enough.

"You never told me what this traitor did," Samuel said.

"William Blacking would be better named blackguard." Rafferty's horse whickered, as if in agreement with his master. "He bedded the major-general's wife."

Samuel turned from Wohali, fire burning in his veins. "I was pulled away from my family for a grudge hunt?"

"It's more than that. During the...er...encounter, Blacking lifted some sensitive information and sold it to the bloody Patriots."

Samuel yanked out another piece of jerky and bit off a big chunk, hiding a smile. Maybe he ought not be looking so hard for Blacking.

Hooves pounded on the trail. A grey horse carrying a man with even greyer eyes halted in front of them. Stane's biceps bulged from holding back the animal. "McDivitt's found something."

Samuel clenched his jaw. The only thing McDivitt could find without help was another man's wife. Too bad Angus wasn't the traitor. That would be a hunt he'd relish.

Even so, he mounted Wohali, and he and Rafferty set off with Stane.

Half a mile down the trail, Stane's horse veered east. Barton Hollow wasn't far off. Was McDivitt to blame for the shot? Stane led them among a stand of ash, then reined in where Angus stood next to his horse.

Samuel dismounted and approached him. The man fairly reeked of gunpowder, and black stains darkened the forefinger on his right hand. But something else fouled the air. Metallic. Acrid.

Death.

Samuel scowled. "I thought I made it clear no one is to discharge their firearm without my say-so."

McDivitt's watery blue eyes narrowed. "You're not God, Heath. You don't make the rules."

Rafferty stepped between them. "Gentlemen, must I break up yet another skirmish?"

McDivitt eyed him, then spat, the brown liquid narrowly missing the major's boot.

Rafferty's face drained of its usual florid color—a sure sign something was about to blow.

Samuel sighed. The sooner they found this Blacking, the better for them all. "What have you got, McDivitt?"

Angus hitched his thumb over his shoulder. "Over there. Heard a tussle. Thought for sure we caught the man, so I pulled one off."

Samuel waded into a growth of pea vine so thick, it reached past his knees. Ten yards out, he noticed a mist of blackflies gathering in a swarm. Five yards, he sniffed the stink of warm blood and split guts. One more yard, and the vines flattened into a splattered mess.

A doe. Stomach ripped open. Entrails pulled out and left in a heap. His gaze followed the direction of the strewn innards, along the trampled undergrowth, and landed on an ash trunk, where the escape route turned south. Red smeared a stripe across the grey bark, hip level.

He tromped toward it. A small plug of black fur snagged on the tree. So, the killer he and Inoli had detected was still out here—and now paying a cost for it. Maybe McDivitt's blind shot got lucky, but more likely not. And a wounded fiend was an angry one.

Samuel turned and stalked back to the men.

McDivitt puffed out his chest. "Told you. That man, Blacking, must've just killed that doe and was gutting her when I happened by. I think I hit him, too, judging by the blood I saw on that tree trunk. . .unless you didn't catch that, Heath. We're close. I say we hightail it after him."

Samuel clenched his hands. Ahh, what a pleasure it would be to knock that smug look from Angus's face.

But now was not the time. He splayed his fingers. "That deer wasn't taken down by a man."

McDivitt spit out a curse like a stream of tobacco. "All hail the mighty tracker, Samuel Heath. You couldn't find your way through a wheat field on a July day."

Rafferty stepped forward. "You are certain, Mr. Heath?"

"I am."

"Then it seems that boot print to the west is the direction we ought to go." Rafferty turned on his heel, one hand fluttering up in the air toward the dead deer. "This is no concern of ours."

Samuel shook his head, hard pressed to decide if he ought to pity or scorn the major's lack of understanding. "We better make it a concern. A rogue bear is nothing to be trifled with, and if this one's wounded, it's all the more dangerous."

"Well, well. . .and you left your woman all alone?" Angus clicked his tongue. "Might be another wife to add to your kill count by the time you get back."

Rage simmered hot, turning the world red. He could think of a certain bushy-bearded man he'd like to add to his kill count.

But as quickly as the fury rose, it twisted.

Into fear.

Hopefully Red Bird heeded his warning and stayed near the house. There was no predicting this beast, except that it meant to maul anything in its path.

With each chuck of the shovel point into the hardened earth, a new whiff of dirt exploded into a reddish cloud. Eleanor paused, leaning heavily on the handle, breathing hard and sweating hard, too. Her lips curled into a smirk. Sweat, indeed. A lady merely perspired, but there was nothing ladylike about the drips raining down her brow, her neck, and dampening the hollow between her shoulder blades. In little over half a year, she'd traded her prim English governess costume for the dust-covered skirts of a backcountry Colonial. Even she didn't know who she was anymore. Or what she wanted.

What did she want?

She lifted her face, spying Grace across the lot. The girl played chase with a pretend kitty—nothing more than a few pinecones sewn into a scrap of cloth and tied to a string. Her fair hair streamed like a ray of the July sunshine, flashing white and gold, flying happy. Oh, to be a child again, with no worries and no aim except to enjoy life.

Arching her back, Eleanor gazed up at the sky. Thin ribbons of white wisped across the endless blue, prodded along by a hot breeze that hit the back of her neck. Would that God might tie those cloud ribbons into a bow and hand her the gift of wisdom.

"What am I to do with this life you've given me, Lord?" Her voice blended with the trill of a thrush. "In England, it was so clear. I knew where I was going and how to get there. But now. . .I am a wife, but not really. A mother to a child who is not mine. A foreigner unsure of my place. You have put me here, but why?"

Grace's laughter floated like dandelion fluff on the air.

Eleanor pursed her lips. "If it is to teach me to be joyful, then it is not working."

With a sigh, she gripped the shovel with both hands and turned over another piece of crusty soil. When she'd started digging this garden earlier in the day, it had seemed like a great idea. Now, with barely eight square feet loosened enough to maybe accept seeds, she wondered at the notion. Perhaps there was a reason Samuel had never planted a vegetable patch.

Samuel? She dug deep, throwing her whole body into the chore. The man's Christian name came too easy, the memory of his touch too vivid. She might belong to him by law, but that didn't mean her thoughts and feelings must be his as well.

Another waft of breeze curled over her shoulder, and she straightened, her nose twitching. A faint odor of something wicked lifted bumps on her arms. What?

She inhaled until her lungs begged her to leave off. Pine. Sweet. Tangy. Nothing more.

She blew out the breath and heaved the shovel into the dirt. If Samuel were going to be gone for days on end, it wouldn't do to live in fear the entire time.

The next waft, and the handle dropped from her grip. She froze, straining to smell, to hear, to breathe. The musky stench grew stronger, but there was no crashing of underbrush, no snapping of twigs. And thankfully, no clacking of sharp teeth.

Still. . .she drew in another deep breath. Undeniable. The same pungent stink she'd encountered that day at the creek—when Samuel came to her rescue. The reek of a bear.

Panic prickled from head to toe, magnifying with each of Grace's giggles. This time there would be no Samuel. Only her.

"Stand and take charge. . . Tell it to go away."

Samuel's instruction surfaced, and she grabbed on to it like a piece of flotsam bobbing on a sea of fear. She had to turn. Face this thing. Force back a scream and issue out a command. Her mind knew it. Her body, not so much.

She stiffened her shoulders and her resolve. If nothing else, she'd go down fighting. On the count of three, then.

One.

Two.

She whirled.

Samuel's instruction fell to the dirt, grinding beneath her heels as she backed away. He hadn't taught her how to deal with this.

A brown body emerged through the woods, naked except for a breechclout. Eyes honed on her. Fierce.

Frightening.

Eleanor gasped.

The man cleared the trees. A bow and quiver of arrows bounced on his back, the leather strap the only stitch of decency on his naked chest. A knife hung from one hip, a tomahawk the other. Blood covered his leg, a gash from knee to moccasin. No wonder the man didn't charge toward her.

But that didn't mean she wasn't his prey, not the way his dark gaze bore into hers.

She turned and bolted.

Grace looked up at the movement. The string fell from her fingers. Her face split wide with a grin as bright as the summer day. "Ee-no-lee!" She squealed and jumped in a happy dance.

Eleanor's blood turned cold. The little one could have no idea the danger they were in. She thought this was a game.

Eleanor grabbed Grace and swung back. The man was halfway across the yard now. Closing in. Near to the cabin. A line of blood stained the freshly dug dirt behind him. If she ran, hard, she could just about clear the porch and lock the door.

She sprinted.

Her heart pounded. So did her feet. Fire ants crawled over her scalp. She'd read of natives and their penchant for cutting off a trophy of hair.

Oh God, please.

Her foot hit a rock. The world tilted, ankle twisting sideways. If she fell, both she and Grace were dead.

Chapter 20

Pain shot up Eleanor's ankle as she raced away from the savage. Her knee gave way. She leaned hard right, holding tightly to Grace with one arm and flailing the other for balance. Compensating for the twist, she hopped twice on the other foot, giving her enough time to brace for the shock of putting her full weight on the wrenched ankle.

But not enough. Agony stabbed.

She cried out—yet didn't stop. She raced up the cabin stairs, biting back a scream. The savage was maybe five yards away. She wasn't sure, and she most definitely wasn't stopping to count.

Flying across the threshold, she whisked Grace to safety and slammed the door shut. She threw the wooden bar into the slot, locking it into place. A great crash smacked the door, rumbling the wood in the frame. Her hands shook as she lifted them to her face. She'd secured it, but barely in time.

Oh God, thank You.

She leaned against the wall, giving in to the horrific realization that she and Grace had nearly been taken by an Indian. If she listened hard enough, she'd hear the man's breathing on the other side of the door.

No, not breath.

She froze.

A voice. A deep one, placid yet commanding. *"Ipa."*

"Ee-no-lee," Grace sang back. The girl ran to the window and jumped up and down. The top of her little head only reached the sill, yet she bobbed in earnest hope that maybe the next jump would allow her a view.

Eleanor's heart skipped a beat. The window! How to lock that? Not that a man's body could fit through the opening—unless the man removed a tomahawk and hacked it into a larger hole.

"Tatsu'hwa! Ipa!"

Her jaw dropped. No! How? Only Samuel called her that. The name sounded harsh, wrong, blasphemous coming from anyone else. Had this man tortured the name from Samuel then killed him?

A hundred questions bombarded her, punching her backward, toward the table where her pistol sat. Her gaze bounced between window and door, window and door, as she reached back for her firearm.

"Grace." She coaxed an even tone to her voice. "Come here, love. Come to me."

The girl continued jumping, keeping time to her song. "Ee-no-lee!"

A brown face appeared in the open window. Blue dots stretched from one cheek to the other, spanning the bridge of his nose. His shiny black hair was pulled back, a feather hanging off one ear.

Eleanor clicked the hammer halfway. "Grace!"

The girl turned.

And the man shoved his arm through the window, baring the underside of his forearm for her to see.

Eleanor narrowed her eyes.

A scar violated his smooth, brown muscle. The skin puckered in a line, in exactly the same place and—yes—the same arm as Samuel's. First the name, now this? What did it mean?

He pulled back his arm and looked down at Grace. "Ipa."

The girl ran to the door.

"No!" Eleanor lowered the pistol and raced to pull the child away.

Too late.

Grace planted two chubby hands on the latch and jumped, forcing open the lock.

The door swung open. The man walked in. Grace wrapped her arms around the leg not covered in blood.

Eleanor pulled the cock wide.

The man shook his head, his voice a warning. *"Alewisdodi."*

She fingered the trigger. The pistol shook, or maybe she did. Shooting at trees was one thing. This was a man's life, a soul—

The pistol flew from her grasp, clattering onto the floor. Pain in her wrist matched that in her ankle. She drew back her hand, rubbing the offense. The man had struck so fast she never saw it coming.

He eyed her for a moment, then swept past her. Grace tagged after him.

Nothing made sense. Not the way he rummaged through things as if he knew what the containers held. Not the way he snatched up one of Samuel's shirts.

And especially not the way he bent and spoke with Grace, his words as gibberish as hers. The smile on the child's face faded. Her eyes widened, and a single, solemn nod swung her hair against her shoulders. He patted her head like a benediction, then without so much as another glance at Eleanor, strode from the cabin and shut the door behind him.

Eleanor dashed to relock the latch then darted to the window, expecting, hoping, desperate to see the man disappear into the forest.

But he sank onto the stairs and set his teeth to Samuel's shirt, tearing it into strips. Once finished, he stood and hobbled over to the water bucket near the door, dumping most of it in a waterfall over the wound on his leg. Returning to the stairs, he sat and reached into a pouch tied to his breechclout. He pulled out something white and fluffy, then packed it onto the wound. She couldn't see his face, but from the look of the slashed skin and muscle, it must hurt. Nevertheless, he made no noise, not even a grunt. He wrapped the fabric tight, from ankle to knee. Red seeped through. He applied another layer, until all of Samuel's shirt bound his leg.

Eleanor's clenched jaw loosened. Good. Now he could leave.

But he merely shifted, setting his back against one post and stretching out his long legs, blocking the only way out of the cabin.

Eleanor retreated from the window, chest tight. She and Grace were as trapped as a fox in one of Samuel's snares.

"What do we do now?"

Stane's question was as rough-edged as the man's voice, grating against Samuel's ears. He squatted in the dirt, running his finger along what might be a print of a boot heel—but most likely was just a remnant from a hoof of a buck on the run.

He stood and looked out at the rolling rises and dips of a land as determined to choose its own course as man. After three days of miserable heat and gnats and with no more sure signs of Blacking's escape route, Samuel knew the truth.

It would take a miracle to flush out the traitor because the man was long gone—and a bigger miracle was in order to make Major Rafferty accept that fact. He lifted his face to the green canopy, browned in ugly patches because of the drought.

You've shown me miracles before, Lord. Show me again.

He tugged down his hat brim, then retrieved Wohali's lead. Grabbing the saddle horn, he hoisted himself up. "We turn back."

Stane grunted. Not an argument. No debate. Just a grunt. Would that Rafferty might offer the same response.

With a click of his tongue and a yank on the reins, Samuel turned his mount and rode back down the old Ani'yunwiya trail. Stane followed. They didn't stop until they reached Canebrow Creek, at the rendezvous where a fallen log breached the water.

Jackson, Wills, and the thin man—who for some odd reason went by the name of Brick—draped themselves on the far bank, violating a patch of flattened cane grass. A flask passed from hand to hand. Samuel stifled a growl. He'd have had a better chance tracking the traitor if he'd been sent out hog-tied and blindfolded than to be crippled with this lot.

Wohali splashed across the creek bed. Samuel dismounted, then gave the horse lead enough to drink her fill. He swung off his water skin and quenched his own thirst. Swiping his hand across his mouth, he faced the men. "Any luck?"

Jackson snickered. Brick arched back his head and drained the flask, his enormous Adam's apple bobbing.

Wills smirked. "Aye. Lucky we brought rum."

Anger burned in his gut, but it would do no good to let it flare. He dropped onto the ground, laced his fingers behind his head, and lay back, staring up at the sky. Until Rafferty and McDivitt returned, there was no point in arguing with drunkards. He knew that all too well.

His anger fizzled into a smoldering coal of shame. Thank God for forgiveness.

Wohali's teeth sank into a hunk of grass, the ripping noise more pleasant than the men's ribald chatter. A year ago, he'd have joined them. But now. . .ahh, sweet mercy. He unhitched his thoughts and let them roam at will—though he knew exactly to which field they'd run.

To a woman with red hair and blue eyes.

Hopefully Red Bird remained close to the house. He'd found no more ripped carcasses, which could mean either McDivitt's shot had killed the bear, or the beast had turned back. And if a rogue crossed his wife's path, well. . .guilt, familiar and unwelcome, beat against him as harsh as the sun on his face. He was no stranger to leaving women in dangerous situations. Mariah had been at risk whenever he came home. But this time, worry about his new wife's safety pained him like a tooth gone bad. Always there. Low and throbbing. This time was different.

He closed his eyes, the sun lighting red rings in the darkness. Hours later, he opened them to hooves kicking up water. He stood as Rafferty and McDivitt dismounted.

McDivitt's breeches sported a new tear on the thigh. Scratches roughed up one of Rafferty's cheeks. Dirt and sweat etched lines on their faces and necks. They'd had quite the day.

"Find anything?" he asked.

McDivitt rummaged in a pocket, his fingers poking one way and another—and came out empty. He glowered. "Wild turkeys and wilder country. I got a feeling you sent us off on the most treacherous trail."

Samuel shrugged a shoulder. "You're the one who wanted to be the big hero."

"And you, Mr. Heath?" Rafferty pulled off his ridiculous hat and mopped a soiled handkerchief over his brow. "What did you uncover?"

"Nothing. Trail's cold. I'd say we're done."

"Some tracker you are." McDivitt wheeled about and stomped into the creek, dropping to drink like a dog.

Samuel fought the urge to tear after him and plant a solid kick in his upended rear.

Rafferty balled his cloth inside a fist. "Am I to understand you are refusing to comply with the major-general's order?"

"No." Samuel advanced, squaring his shoulders and setting his jaw. "Here's what you're to understand, Major. You came to me three days after you lost Blacking. Three days! And then you shackled me with this—" He swung out his arm to the men passed out on the banks. "Maybe—and I mean maybe—I might have found him alone. But there's no chance, now. Blacking could be anywhere."

He pivoted, Rafferty spearing his back with a foul curse. Fine. The man could bluster all he liked, but it wouldn't change the truth. He snagged Wohali's reins and swung up into the saddle.

Rafferty lifted a face stained the color of spilled wine. "Where are you going?"

"Home. I suggest you follow."

The major whipped out his fancy pistol, sighting the double-barrel straight at Samuel's chest. "I could shoot you for treason, here and now."

Samuel stared him down. "You really think you can get yourselves out of here in one piece without me?"

Chapter 21

Samuel reined in Wohali where the trail split into two. To the right, the long decline to Newcastle. The left, home. Ahh. The thought loosened the muscles in his shoulders. Wohali dipped her head, ears twitching. He leaned forward and patted the mare's neck. "Almost there, girl."

Behind him, the steady plod of hooves grew louder. He edged his mount off the trail, allowing the other horses to pass. Jackson, Wills, and Brick mumbled their goodbyes as they filed in front of him. He nodded his. Stane said nothing, as usual, just rode right on by.

Rafferty and McDivitt halted.

Samuel met the major's cold blue challenge with a piercing glare of his own. "This is where we part ways."

Rafferty sneered, skin pulling over cheekbones more prominent for having eaten little on the trail. "I cannot say it's been a pleasure, Mr. Heath."

Wohali blew out a snorty mist and sidestepped. Samuel didn't blame her.

"Neither can I, Major." He clicked his tongue—not that Wohali needed the encouragement. The mare strained onto the path leading home.

McDivitt's voice followed. "Told ya, he's as yellow as they come. If we'd have pressed on, I have no doubt we'd have wrangled up that traitor. Heath knew that. He didn't want the fight, and furthermore. . ."

The words faded. Samuel let them roll off—but the stripes on his back burned. Everyone had their thorn in the side. His just happened to sport a bushy beard.

The closer he drew to home, the faster Wohali dug in. Apparently the mare had tired of wild grass and wanted a pail of oats and soft bedding as much as he longed to stretch out on furs with a filled belly, even if it was Red Bird's cooking.

He cleared the woods and slid from the saddle, glad to bear weight on his feet instead of his behind. Grabbing the tether, he guided the horse across the yard.

Inoli emerged from the shadows on the porch like a specter from the grave. Face granite. And leg wrapped with a cloth stained brownish-red.

Samuel strode to meet him. "What has happened?"

Inoli's dark gaze bore into his. "A lone fox is no match for a blood-drinking bear."

His brother's meaning drove the air from his chest, and he sucked in a breath. "Yet you live."

"So does the bear."

Samuel swallowed a curse. In former days, he would've relished the expletive. Now, it sat like a stone in his gut. "Tell me."

Sunlight glinted off Inoli's black hair as he spoke. "I returned from Keowee with a mind to call on you. There is much to say on that matter later."

"No doubt." He cracked his neck one way, then the other, working out the tension—for naught. A nerve cinched all the tighter when he finished.

Inoli folded his arms, a favorite storytelling stance of his. This would be quite the tale, then. "Half-mile out, the rise near Hornrock Ridge, I caught the beast unaware."

"No wonder. You move like a spirit. Looks like you got yourself some new bear grease in those shiny locks of yours, too. Maybe Keowee wasn't all business, hmm?"

Inoli's lips twitched.

So, he'd hit home.

"There is more to hunting than animals and intelligence, my brother. Sometimes tracking a skirt is the most difficult hunt of all."

Samuel grinned. "As always, you speak truth."

"Unless a rogue bear is involved." Inoli's eyes burned like black coals. "My arrow sailed true, catching the animal between throat and chest. Yet it was not enough. The beast charged."

"How did you escape?"

"This one plays with its prey. The first charge was a bluff, so I ran."

Inoli's speed was renowned, but this Samuel could not believe. He shook his head. "Even you can't outrun a bear, my brother."

"I didn't." Inoli's gaze dropped to his wrapped calf. "I wedged into the crevice at Hornrock. The bear took many swipes before giving up. One of them caught my leg."

"Blast!" Samuel rubbed his jaw, fingers rasping against whiskers, mind scraping up the bits of information Inoli served. "How long ago?"

"Two days."

"Two? Hmm." The Barton's Hollow incident was what. . .three? He scuffed the dirt with his moccasin, replaying the past grueling days, then looked up at Inoli. "Your arrowhead may not be the only wound angering this one."

Inoli cocked his head. "How so?"

"McDivitt pulled off a shot that might've grazed him—or hit square on. Either way, there's a whole lot of rage bundled up out there in fur and fangs."

"And claws." Inoli grimaced.

The cabin door flew open. "Samuel?"

Red Bird stood in the doorway, grasping the frame as if she bore the weight of the entire cabin. Even so, worried or not, she was a sight more pleasant than the men he'd camped with.

Grace tore out, riffling the woman's skirts as she dashed past. Her little legs flew until she plowed into him. He swung her up high, her loose hair raining down on his face. Why was God so good to him? "How's my girl?"

"Edoda!" Grace squealed. "Papa's home!"

"Someone's learning new words, eh?" He nuzzled his whiskers atop her head until she squirmed, then set her down. The girl raced circles around him and Inoli.

He lifted his face to Red Bird. "Come out, Tatsu'hwa. There's someone I'd like you to meet."

Her eyes widened, and she hesitated. Slowly, her fingers moved from clutching the door frame to grabbing handfuls of her skirt as she picked her way across the porch. Descending the stairs, she bypassed Inoli and edged toward Samuel, keeping her gaze fixed on the native as if he might strike like a rattler.

Samuel stifled a grin. For all he knew, this was the first native she'd ever encountered. Truth be told, though, the way she sought his side for protection sent a rush of warmth to his gut. "He won't bite you, woman. This is my brother, Inoli. I trust him with my life—or yours and Grace's, for that matter."

"Ee-no-lee!" Grace marched around the man like a soldier on parade.

"But. . ." Red Bird's gaze followed Grace's dance; then her brow crumpled as she looked up at him. "But he trapped us inside the cabin!"

Trapped? He chuckled. "For your safety, no doubt. What were you doing when he came?"

"I thought to make a small garden, plant some herbs. . ." Her fingers fluttered out.

He followed the movement. On the far side of the yard, close to the edge of the woods, small mounds of red dirt dried in the sunshine like heaps of forgotten bones. What a strange woman he'd married.

"Why would you do that?" he asked. "There's enough vegetation out in the woods to fill your belly ten times over."

Her freckles faded, masked by the pink spreading over her cheeks. "Oh. I. . .I did not know."

"Speak with your woman later." Inoli unfolded his arms. "If we hope to end this rampage before dark, my brother, we need to go now."

Weariness crawled under his skin. He'd trade tracking a killer bear for a mug of ale and a crust of bread—but Red Bird didn't bake worth a holler, and the rogue's taste for blood increased the longer it lived.

He whistled between his teeth, short and sharp. Wohali trotted over, flicking her tail. He grabbed the lead and handed it to Inoli. "You're riding."

A storm brewed in the blackness of Inoli's eyes.

Samuel held up a hand. "I just spent four days with a pack of fools. I'm in no mood to argue with you. Either you ride, or I go alone."

A muscle on Inoli's neck stood out, but only for a moment. Without another word, he swung his injured leg up and over the mount's back, gaining the saddle.

Red Bird frowned. "What is going on?"

Samuel strode past her, taking the stairs in a long-legged leap. Swishing skirts trailed him. He toyed with the idea of informing her about the bear, but why? The woman was skittish enough without adding to her fears. No, she did not need to know the details of that beast.

"I need fresh supplies." He unlocked the wooden chest and pulled out a pouch of shot and more gunpowder.

"Do not tell me you are leaving again."

He slammed the lid shut, then went on to raid the crock of pemmican, grab some leftover johnnycake—stale and dry—and stalk to the door. "All right. I won't."

"Samuel!"

He wheeled about so quickly, his boots skidded on the porch's wooden slats. "Well, well. Glad to hear you've finally gotten around to using my proper name. Next thing you know, you'll be asking for that kiss."

Her face blanched, then flamed into life, nearly matching the fire of her hair.

A smile played on his lips. Why was it so satisfying to make the woman blush?

"Ya'nu, we go now."

Inoli's voice was a chill wind at his back, pulling him to the matter at hand. He cleared the stairs and swept up Grace. "You mind, you hear?"

Her little head bobbed. He set her on the steps and lifted his face to Red Bird. "And you stay in the cabin until I return, understand?"

Her shoulders pulled taut, like a sail in the wind—and an angry gale at that, judging by the ferocious scowl drawing her brow into a line. "I am not a dog to be ordered about, sir."

He snorted. "That sure didn't last long."

"What?"

"You calling me Samuel."

Her lips pinched tight, and if he cared to look, he just might see her fingers coiling into fists. But he spun on his heel and tramped across the yard.

Wohali's hooves clopped after him. "Your woman looks to kill. Maybe she ought come along."

He smirked over his shoulder. "I don't think the bear would be the one in danger."

Eleanor watched the two men disappear into the wild, staring until nothing but sunrays and shadows moved along the path they'd taken. Emotions chased one after the other, like a dog after its own tail. Relief that the fearsome Inoli was gone. Confusion that Samuel called the dark-skinned fellow his brother. Anger—accompanied by a small feeling of being valued—at Samuel's dismissive commands. And for some odd reason, a cold, hard terror lodging deep in her stomach. There was something Samuel wasn't telling her.

A frown twisted her mouth. There was always something he wasn't telling her.

"Drink, Ama?"

Grace's pet name for her turned Eleanor's face from the wild to the child. Grace squatted by the water bucket, peering up at her over the rim.

"You know how to use the dipper, little one. You may get your own drink."

The girl shook her head. "No drink."

Turning her back on the wilderness, she crossed over to Grace. Usually the girl loved to play in the water bucket, serving herself and make-believe companions so much water that it drenched her dress. Perhaps after seeing her papa for only a few minutes, Grace felt as out of sorts as she did.

She drew near to help—but the water bucket was empty.

"Drink?" Grace repeated.

La! What to do? Samuel had hardly been gone ten minutes. Should she disregard his wishes so soon? She could grab the bucket and refill it in a thrice with a quick trip to the creek. But what would he say if he returned for some forgotten item and found her gone?

She bit her lip. She knew exactly what he'd say, for his anger, when unleashed, left welts on her heart. He may have a fierce friend in Inoli, but the man was savage himself when crossed.

She held out her hand. "Come along, Grace. We shall find something to do inside until your papa returns home. Hopefully he will not be gone long."

But he was. The afternoon dragged. Grace alternated between crying for water and screaming for her papa. Eleanor preferred the crying. Surely the girl would collapse from the effort, pop her thumb into her mouth, and doze off. Where had the sweet-tempered child of only a few months ago gone? Eleanor calculated as she searched out the window for the hundredth time. If she'd arrived from England nine weeks ago or so, as near as she could tell—though maybe more like ten or eleven—and Grace had been a little over a year and a half at the time, then. . . She drummed her fingers on the rough wooden sill. Of course. The girl must be two years old now. Life was about to get very interesting—and tiring. She'd have to pick her battles with the care of an infantryman. Behind her, Grace wailed again. The day had been long, but a full night of weeping would be an eternity. It appeared this skirmish would go to the child.

Eleanor whirled from the window. "All right, little one. There is no telling if your papa will be home before dark, and the shadows are already knitting themselves together. I shall go get your drink."

Snatching her pistol off the shelf, she tucked it into her pocket, along with the powder horn. Then with a firm, "Stay here," to Grace, she slipped through the front door and retrieved the bucket.

The day's heat left a haze in the air. Perspiration dotted her forehead. Surely she could blame that on the heat, could she not? She crossed the yard unafraid, but as she drew nearer the creek, an old companion joined her, wrapping its arms tight around her chest. Fear. She dashed the rest of the way down the trail.

Keeping her gaze pinned on the opposite side of the bank, she bent and dipped the bucket into the water. If she stared hard enough, the shadows shifted into all manner of dragons and beasts. The wood of the bucket scraped against gravel as she scooped it up. If rain didn't break soon, even this supply would dry to rocks and silt.

The dirge of an owl floated overhead like an unmoored ghost, chasing her all the way back to the cabin. By the time she slammed the door shut behind her, her heart raced, her lungs burned, and she was pretty sure she'd spilled most of Grace's drink.

But why was there no fair-haired pixie sprinting to greet her?

Eleanor scanned from wall to wall. "Grace?"

No movement. No sound. Just crickets outside and a thudding heartbeat pounding in her ears. Eleanor set down the bucket and searched from crib, to bedstead, to behind the crates stacked like shelves. This time fear didn't just embrace her—it swallowed her whole.

Grace was gone.

Chapter 22

Samuel squatted and sniffed. The bear vanished. Just like that. No more broken twigs. No flattened brush. Not even any more piles of scat. He rolled his shoulders, surveying the forest floor. How could such a strong trail suddenly disappear? It was as if the hand of God reached down and lifted the bear into the heavens. Rising, he pivoted slowly, scanning from trunk to trunk.

"Ya'nu! Over here."

He jogged the few yards to Inoli, who stretched out an arm from his perch atop Wohali. Nearby, shreds of missing bark scarred a pine trunk. So, God hadn't reached down.

Apparently the bear had escaped on his own up to the heavens—or more like up a tree trunk.

Samuel lifted his face, a welcome change from reading the dirt. A beast that size would follow the lower branches, only those large enough to hold his weight, and only those reaching close enough to touch. Gaze fixed upward, he waded through the undergrowth, reconstructing the bear's most likely route. Cunning devil. Not many men would have owned the wits to try such an evasive action.

When the trees thinned, he slowed. There. More gashes. He lengthened his stride, circling the area, then let out a growl.

Inoli's voice closed in on him from behind. "This bear knows the great Ya'nu is on the hunt."

"And he's laughing at me all the way. The beast is headed south, right back the way we came. We must've passed it a quarter mile ago, judging by these tracks. At least we'll be upwind this time."

He tromped off, Inoli guiding Wohali beside him, keeping the horse's hooves from cracking sticks as much as possible.

Samuel spoke in a low tone. "Tell me of Keowee."

"Running Doe sends her regards." Inoli rarely laughed. He didn't have to. His voice smiled.

Samuel scowled, even though his brother couldn't see the glower. "You know that's not what I'm asking."

"I could tell you of my own conquests, but I think what you want to know is that the Beloved Man was not there this time. Word is he rode to Tamassee for a peace council."

"Peace!" He spit out the word, then winced. Upwind or not, the loud exclamation would tip off the bear of their presence. "I wager five to one he's rallying warriors."

Inoli reined his mount closer. "Which would be why he sent a dispatch to Dragging Canoe."

Interesting. Samuel worked over the piece of information as he swept his gaze back and forth over the ground. Everyone knew Dragging Canoe sided with the British, as did his father, Attakullakulla. The chief wouldn't have sent word to his son to determine his allegiance, but to muster it—or mayhap to send Dragging Canoe to gather more warriors, making Attakullakulla appear to be all harmony and goodwill toward the colonists. Samuel swiped a horsefly away from his cheek. The man—both, actually—were as wily as this bear.

"I suppose that's why I've not yet heard from Sutton about the negotiator," he thought out loud. "He's giving Attakullakulla time to figure out exactly what he can offer."

"There is more."

Samuel stopped. There was no smile in those words. He wheeled about and faced Inoli. "What?"

"Your name came up." Rage flashed in his brother's dark eyes, black upon black. "Some question your allegiance to the Ani'yunwiya."

"They have a right to. I am conflicted." He blew out a long breath. "Thanks to my ancestors, my heart is captive to both Cherokee and whites. I thought to live here in peace, give Grace what I never had—a real home. But. . .I don't think that's a possibility anymore."

His shoulders sank, though hard to tell whether from the strain of hunting the rogue bear—or from the realization that the coming war was inevitable.

Or maybe it was from the weight of Inoli's gaze.

"Did you ever stop to think, my brother, that maybe such a dream was not given you by God, but by your own unmet desire?" Inoli leaned forward in the saddle, his trademark feather skimming his shoulder with the movement. "Perhaps God is not calling you to live for peace, but rather to fight for it."

The words hit like a swift uppercut. He swung away from Inoli, working his jaw as he set off. Better to focus on the wild beast at hand than entertain such a monstrous suggestion.

Eleanor flung open the cabin's door and scanned the yard. In the setting sun, everything looked haunted.

"Grace!" she called, eyes willing a light-haired head and big smile to emerge from the coming night. Surely if the girl had followed her to the creek, she'd have heard her, or even run into her on her way back to the cabin if Grace had lagged behind.

Oh, sweet heavens. What if the child had blazed her own trail to the water?

Eleanor leapt down the stairs and tore across the yard, then studied the perimeter nearest the creek, step by step. She called the girl's name as she went, until it grazed out her throat.

"Grace!"

No flattened or bent weeds. No disturbed dirt kicked by little feet. Where had she gone?

A deep moan wailed at her back—too low to be a child. Too close to ignore. Had Samuel returned? Was he hurt? What would he say about his daughter going missing?

Straightening, she pivoted. "Samuel, I—"

The explanation died, cold and cruel on her tongue.

An enormous bear, black as mire, stood on all fours at the center of the yard—a solid barrier between her and the cabin. White fangs jutted. A terrible snap and clack of its jaws sounded like bones breaking. It did not rise up on its hind legs, but she had a terrible suspicion that if it did, it would be twice the size of the beast she'd faced at the creek.

She jabbed her hand into her pocket, but when her fingers met steel, Samuel's words barreled like a shot in her mind.

"If you come upon a bear, it is easier to stand and take charge. Tell it to go away. More often than not, it will."

Slowly, she eased her hand from her pocket. She could do this. She had to.

The bear's ears flattened back, like a mad dog's. The jaws snapped once again, followed by a spray from the beast's nose as it huffed. Then. . . nothing. The black eyes assessed her with a deadly calm.

Well, maybe this wouldn't be so bad after all. Maybe the silly thing would turn tail and run. Just because this bear was bigger didn't have to mean it was more dangerous.

Eleanor squared her shoulders and stepped forward.

"Shoo! Leave!" She whisked her hands, urging it to run away.

The bear lowered its head.

And charged.

Samuel and Inoli followed the bear's trail in silence. It was hard to pinpoint when the unease first settled in Samuel's gut. Might have been when the route stopped an ambling zigzag and straightened into a definite line. Or perhaps when the tracks deepened, the vines upended without thought to stealth. But there was no denying his alarm when he realized the killer headed straight toward the cabin. If Red Bird or Grace were outside. . . . He swung off his rifle and checked the security of the loaded ball with the ramrod.

Then froze.

"Shoo! Leave!" Red Bird's cries were an arrow to the heart.

Samuel broke into a dead run.

Wohali's hooves crashed behind.

He leapt over logs and dodged new pine and hemlock, all the while forcing his mind to remain blank. Don't think. Don't imagine. Just run like the wind. Become a beast himself. He gripped the stock of the rifle so tightly, it was a wonder the thing didn't crack in half.

Red Bird stood brave in the middle of the yard, her shoulders thrown back, just as he'd taught her. Facing her fear, exactly as he'd instructed. A beast of a bear charged at her.

Oh God.

His bowels turned to water. He'd sent her to her death.

Her forearms shot to her face at the last second before impact, protecting her head. Her skirt caught on the beast's front leg, ripping off like a piece of flesh as the bear tore past.

Samuel plummeted down the rise, Inoli and Wohali behind. If the bear circled back before he reached her. . . .

He bolted into the clearing as the beast pivoted and pawed the ground. There was no way to usher Red Bird to safety, and from this angle, no direct shot to kill the animal without putting his wife in danger.

The bear clacked its jaws, exposing fangs large enough to shatter bone with but a nip.

Think!

The beast tucked its head.

Breathe!

It shifted weight to its hind legs, ready to barrel ahead like a five-hundred-pound shot.

Act!

Samuel threw the rifle up to Inoli. Their eyes met. Inoli nodded, catching the firearm with one hand.

Samuel tore into the yard, a growl ripping out of his throat.

Red Bird whirled. "Samuel!"

Her cry was a magnet. The bear's nose lifted, re-sighting the woman.

Samuel surged ahead, waving his arms. "Hyah! Over here!"

The killer wagged its great head, snapping his jaw.

Samuel roared.

The bear hurtled straight at him.

He dropped to the dirt. The ground vibrated beneath his cheek, torn up by claws drawing closer—razors that would strip away his flesh in deep gouges.

A shot exploded.

The ball whizzed over his head.

A snort, rank and hot, raked over his ear. Black fur skidded past his nose, spraying his face with gravel. Air whooshed out. Then—

Nothing.

He rolled aside and stood.

The killer lay at his feet. The last few beats of the bear's heart shooting blood from a severed neck artery.

Samuel closed his eyes. That had been close. Way too close. *Thank You, God.*

Next to him, Inoli grunted. "I will see to this. Go."

His eyes shot open.

Evening shadows wrapped around Red Bird, still standing her ground, face white in the gathering darkness. Her overlarge eyes glistened. Trembling fingers bunched her skirts into big knots.

Samuel skirted the carcass, strode across the yard, and held his arms wide.

She plowed into him.

No tears soaked into his shirt. Or maybe they did. Hard to tell with the sweat sticking the fabric to his skin. She didn't seem to mind, though, not the way she nestled her cheek against his chest. No wonder. Staring death in the face had a way of reducing life to things that mattered—and things that didn't.

He rubbed his chin over the top of her hair—and a jolt shot straight through his chest. Somehow, completely unbidden, this proper Englishwoman had come to matter to him.

Very much.

He wrapped his arms tighter, fitting her against him like a wife ought to be. "Shh. It's over. You are safe."

"No," she mumbled into his shirt, then planted her hands against his chest and pushed away. "You do not understand."

Trouble swam in the big, blue pools gazing at him.

Her mouth twisted into a silent scream, but the quiet words that escaped her lips screeched like a banshee's wail.

"Grace is missing."

Facing the fierce-raging storm in Samuel's gaze was more frightening than staring down the bear. Eleanor shrank back a step. This was too much. All of it. The bear. The man. The fact that he'd nearly died protecting her. And how did she repay him? By losing his only daughter. Her heart beat loud in her ears. It was a miracle the thing yet pumped.

All she wanted was to go home, but—a sob choked her. Where would that be? What did home even mean anymore?

"What do you mean Grace is missing?" Samuel's question cut into her, sharp and jaggedy. All the gentleness and concern—every last measure of safety he'd offered mere moments ago—vanished. Just like that. Blown to the wind like a thousand milkweed seeds, and just as impossible to gather back.

Advancing, he grabbed her shoulders with his big hands. The way his fingers dug into her skin, she got the impression he'd like to shake her as a rag doll, until no stuffing remained.

He shoved his face into hers. "Tell me everything. When and where?"

She sucked in a shaky breath, averting her gaze to his chest. Better to focus on the wet stains she'd left on his shirt than bear the awful fire in his eyes. "You and your friend left so early this morn, and the water bucket was empty, and. . .Grace was relentless." Her voice faded along with her confidence. The excuse sounded pathetic even in her own ears. "She wept the better part of the day, crying for a drink."

"So you went to the creek to draw a bucket." He released her and wheeled about, yanking off his hat and slapping it against his leg. "Blast it, woman!"

Her shoulders slumped. He was right, of course. Not only had she nearly gotten him killed twice over—now she'd endangered little Grace's life as well.

Across the yard, crouched by the bear with a knife in hand, the man—Inoli—looked up. His eyes narrowed on her, more exposing than the ripped piece of skirt uncovering her leg.

She stepped closer to Samuel, reaching out a hand to his sleeve. "I am sorry. If you had told me about the bear, I never would have—"

He pivoted so fast, her fingers flew from his arm. "And if you'd do as I say, you wouldn't get yourself and my daughter into such predicaments."

She set her jaw. One thing she did not need right now was his condemnation—she could do a good enough job of that on her own. "We can either stand here and argue, Mr. Heath, or we can join forces and find Grace before it is too dark to see—"

Inoli's voice cut her off. He uttered something in his guttural language, and Samuel threw back his head and laughed.

Eleanor threw her arms wide. "How dare you laugh at a time like this?"

"Woman, you will be the death of me." A last chuckle rumbled in his throat as he pulled on his hat. "Look at the stable."

She spun on her heel. There, in the gaping door, a blond head appeared, straw sticking out like a fright. The girl rubbed her eyes, a big yawn stretching her mouth.

Eleanor's blood ran cold. If the child had left the shelter of the stable just five minutes earlier, when the bear charged—she slapped a hand to her mouth, stifling a scream.

Big hands rested on her shoulders. Hot breath ruffled the top of her head. Samuel's warmth wrapped around her from behind. "My guess is when you went to the creek, Grace made a break for the stable, straight to Wohali's water bucket. And after crying all day, likely curled up in the straw and dozed off. I'm surprised she woke up at all."

Repentance tasted sour in her mouth. The man had left his child in her care—and she'd almost gotten them both killed.

She turned in his grasp, facing him. "I never should have opened the door. At the very least, I should have taken her with me." Her words rushed, faster, crazier, forced out by rising guilt and shame. "I do not belong here. I may never belong. You and Grace would be better off without me."

The brown of Samuel's eyes deepened to a rich velvet. "You're my wife, Tatsu'hwa. There is no other place for you."

He probably meant to comfort. Yet the words were anything but. She tucked her chin to her chest, weighted by a sense of loneliness. She didn't belong anywhere—and never had, really. The ragged hem of her skirt, torn and ruined, was a tangible picture of her life. The longer she stared, the more she trembled. *Oh God, can You—will You—mend this life?*

A big knuckle wedged beneath her chin, and lifted, pulling her face to Samuel's. "Don't fret. All is well now."

Stunned, she blinked. Had she been wrong about this man all along? He was rugged, true. And often brusque or careless of manner. Indeed, he was many things, and likely even more than she'd discovered thus far. But for the first time, there with the sun bathing him in a last ruddy glow, she viewed him in an altogether new light—one that completely stole the breath from her lungs.

As her husband.

Chapter 23

Grace bounced on Eleanor's lap as the wagon bumped into town, her little hands reaching up and skewing Eleanor's hat. At times it seemed as if the girl possessed well more than two arms for the havoc she could wreak. Eleanor reset the hat and scanned the road for a chance glimpse of Biz or Molly. The buildings looked as she remembered them to be—but the guffaws of men, so many stamping horse hooves, and the hum of activity were completely different. Newcastle looked like a kicked anthill, people scurrying everywhere.

Eleanor peeked up at Samuel, who slowed the wagon in front of Greeley's. "Why are there so many people?"

"Whoa, now." He tugged on the reins without looking at her. "Go on and pick yourself out some fabric. Grace and I will be in when it's my turn at the dock." He nodded toward the couple of wagons in front of theirs, lined up and ready to be loaded.

Evasive as ever. She nibbled her lip for a moment, deciding if she should press the matter. . .but why? If the man didn't mind unleashing her for some shopping, then neither did she—especially if she might steal a few minutes with Molly. Eleanor set Grace on the seat next to her father, then climbed down over the side of the wagon.

Hefting her skirts to avoid a mound of horse droppings, she picked her way up the steps to the mercantile. The front door opened, and she paused to allow a trim lady in an indigo gown pass by.

But the woman didn't pass. She stopped, her brown eyes widening. "Elle Bell!"

Eleanor's jaw dropped. "Biz?"

The woman laughed and twirled, the swirl poofing out her skirt and petticoat. A sateen ribbon streamed from her bonnet, and the lace at her sleeves rippled. "Aye, 'tis me. Din't think to see me in a dress, did ya?" She leaned close, one hand aside her mouth. "Nor did I."

"Why. . .you are lovely! Absolutely lovely."

And she was. Biz's fair hair had grown longer and curled around her face in a comely fashion. The cut of her dress hugged curves that her former men's clothing had hidden. Cleaned up and dressed properly, Biz Hunter could turn the head of any man in town.

"Pish!" Biz blew off the compliment, but the pink on her cheeks belied the gruffness. In fact, her whole face glowed. Apparently she'd thrived these past several months.

Biz narrowed her eyes, studying Eleanor from head to toe, then stepped nearer. "Molly and I were gettin' worried, not having seen you for so long. We thought that. . ." She glanced over her shoulder, where Samuel waited in line. The jingle of harnesses floated on the air as one of the carts pulled away from the dock.

Turning back, Biz lowered her voice. "How's that man of yours? He treating you a'right?"

This was new. Biz caring for someone other than herself? Eleanor cocked a brow. "I own that Mr. Heath is not one to coddle, but yes, he treats me well. He is firm yet fair. I could ask for nothing more."

Biz ripped out a curse.

So, she hadn't changed that much.

"O' course you could!" The woman stepped nearer. Any closer and she'd be atop Eleanor's shoes. "And if you want me to help you run off, just say the word."

What on earth? She gaped. "But why would I want—"

"Eleanor!" Molly darted out the front door and parted her from Biz. She wrapped her in an embrace, her growing babe a swollen mound between them.

"Oh!" Molly's voice broke. "How happy I am to see you."

Eleanor squirmed away. Something was not right. She folded her arms, using her governess stance to shame them. "The two of you are acting as if you never expected to see me again."

Molly and Biz locked gazes.

Eleanor looked from one to the other. "There is something you are not telling me. What is it?"

With a glance at the door, Molly tugged on her arm, pulling her farther down the porch. Biz followed, and they huddled close to her.

"I've only a few moments before Mrs. Greeley discovers me missing, so pardon my abruptness." Molly reached a hand to Eleanor's cheek, her green eyes pools of sorrow. "Did you know you married a murderer?"

"What?" Eleanor batted her hand away. "Do not be silly."

Biz's mouth twisted as if she'd bit into a lemon. "Nothing silly about it. I knew something weren't right with that man the day he took you. Takes a bad seed to recognize another."

The words crawled in, shallow at first, the seeds Biz spoke about poking around for a place to root. Eleanor eyed them both. "I think you had better explain yourselves."

Molly licked her lips, angling her head ever so slightly across the road. "That burnt patch of ground over there, well, hard to tell now with the weeds all grown. But that used to be the house where Mr. Heath lived with his first wife, Mariah."

Biz tipped her chin to a rakish angle, making some kind of point.

But Eleanor had no idea what that point might be. She frowned. "Yes, I know he has been married and his wife's name was Mariah and that she died. That proves nothing. It does not mean he is a murderer."

"Shh!" Biz swiveled her head as if Samuel stood at her shoulder, then she pinned Eleanor with a burning stare. "But do you know *how* she died?"

Doubt dug in, roots sinking lower, reaching to her stomach. She had no idea, for Samuel had never spoken of the incident in detail. She'd assumed childbirth—but she didn't really know. She pursed her lips, giving a little shake to her head. "No. My husband is reluctant to speak of it, nor do I blame him. It cannot be easy losing someone you love."

Biz blew out a snort. "He didn't."

"Did not what?"

"Love her. The word is she married him because she had to." Biz wiggled her eyebrows, the insinuation made even more vulgar by the action.

Eleanor banished the thought. Samuel had ever been the gentleman in that respect the entire time she'd lived with him. Still. . . "That is hardly grounds for murder."

"Molly!" A voice harsh as a crow's hawked from an upstairs window. "Where are you?"

Molly laid a hand on Eleanor's sleeve. "I haven't much time, so listen. Please. The story is Mariah arrived in Newcastle with her father, a banker, who intended to make it rich in the fur trade. He did quite well until he died from the ague, leaving Mariah alone. Maybe if he'd lived, none of what followed would've happened."

Biz huffed, sharp and short. "She shoulda packed up and gone back to

Charles Towne. I woulda. Better prospects there."

Molly shot a glower at Biz. "Regardless, she didn't. She set her cap on Mr. Heath, the wealthiest man in the territory."

Eleanor sucked in a breath. None of this made any sense. "No. Impossible."

"Hah!" Biz laughed. "You din't know?"

Eleanor shook her head, hoping the movement would reassemble all the information from Biz and Molly into some sort of picture.

Molly patted her arm. "He was also quite the drunkard, as I understand."

"No!" Eleanor pulled away, her shoulder hitting the wooden slats of the mercantile's wall. "That is not true. I have never seen him take a drink."

"Molly!" This time the voice sailed out the front door, followed by the clack of heels.

"Eleanor, listen." Molly leaned closer. "You gave me advice once on how to care for Mrs. Greeley. I took it to heart, and it made my life easier. Grant that you'll do the same with my advice. Go stay with Biz and Reverend Parker. It is not safe for you to remain under Mr. Heath's roof, whether he's your husband or not."

"But I do not think I am in any danger—"

"Molly!" Mrs. Greeley's voice shrieked like an off-tune violin. "Come when you are summoned!"

Molly darted off, calling over her shoulder, "I must go. Do say you'll come tonight."

"Come where?"

But it was too late. Mrs. Greeley grabbed Molly's upper arm and swept her into the store. Eleanor had no choice but to turn back to Biz. "What is she talking about?"

"You look as bewildered as the first time I laid eyes on you back in Bristol. There's a—" Biz's face paled as she looked past Eleanor's shoulder. She lowered her voice. "Here comes yer man. I'll make this fast. You should know that Mariah went after your Heath. But someone named McDivitt wanted her for himself. There's bad blood between those two, so to spite him, Heath gave in to Mariah's wiles."

Grace's babble carried from the stairs.

Biz spoke faster. "But turns out the woman were after his money, so the marriage din't go well from the start. One night, after a drunken rage, yer man set fire to the house, burning her alive. Some say as he was remorseful though, being he ran back in and pulled out his daughter. But all say it were his fault."

"Then why did he not go to jail?" Eleanor whispered.

"He did. But they let him go. It was his word against a dead woman's—and the dead don't testify."

Wariness buzzed inside her heart like a swarm of bees, stinging and pricking and poisoning. How was she to understand any of this? The man who'd saved her life, twice over now, and never forced himself upon her was a schemer, a drunkard—a murderer? "I can hardly believe it," she murmured.

Footsteps thudded behind her. A low voice curled into her ear. "You pick out that fabric yet?"

She swallowed against the tightness in her throat and turned to face Samuel. "No, not yet. May I introduce you to Miss Hunter,"—she swept out a hand—"though you met her that first day when you collected me. Miss Hunter, Mr. Heath."

"Aye. I remember." Samuel tugged the brim of his hat. "Miss Hunter."

"Mr. Heath." Biz tossed her head like a saucy mare and faced Eleanor. "Say you'll come to the festival tonight."

Eleanor glanced up at Samuel, expecting him to say no immediately. He said nothing, just slid his gaze to hers. Who knew what went on behind those dark eyes of his?

She wetted her lips. "Biz and Molly have invited me to some sort of festivity this evening. Might I. . .er, I mean, may we stay?"

"Festivity?" Samuel's eyes shot to Biz. "Prettied up the name, did you?" Biz scowled.

Clearly they both knew something she didn't. The unwelcome feeling was becoming all too familiar and beginning to pinch. She studied Samuel's face for a clue. "Is there a festival or is there not?"

His lips twitched. Nothing more. "I've not heard it called such before. Some say it's a rendezvous. Others call it the Summer Outfit. I say it's an excuse for brawling and drinking."

Well, then. Apparently she had her answer. She reached out and squeezed one of Biz's hands. "I am sorry we cannot stay. Please give Molly my apology as well. I appreciate the invitation but—"

"We'll be there."

Eleanor whirled to face Samuel. "We will?"

Why would he want to stay for brawling and. . . *Oh, God.* Drinking?

Surely he would not, would he?

He flashed a smile at her and tipped his hat once more at Biz. Stooping, he swept up Grace, who'd held on to his leg, then strode across the porch and entered the mercantile.

Eleanor turned to Biz, trying hard to keep from gaping.

Biz arched a brow. "If I were you, I'd be careful."

Samuel threw the last pelt atop the stack beneath the canvas, a slapdash shelter which was tied to one side of the wagon and staked to the ground. Not a tent fit for royalty, but it would do for one night. He straightened and slipped his gaze to the west. Beyond the rise of blue hills, the sky stretched ever bluer, endless, pure, without blemish of cloud. Warm, but no threat of rain. Indeed. The shelter would do.

Pivoting, he strode the few yards to where Red Bird sat on a quilt spread beneath a hickory. Grace sprawled like a hound, head in the woman's lap, a chubby thumb popped in her mouth. The girl did not lift her head at his approach. Her eyes merely followed his movement. Red Bird's did not. She'd not met his gaze since earlier in the day.

He crouched on one corner of the blanket and nodded toward the improvised tent. "Grace can sleep over there for now, and you can both sleep there tonight."

The woman's lips flattened as she eyed the tent. "You seem rather well prepared. As if you'd intended we stay all along."

A sigh—more of a huff, really—whooshed out his mouth. The whole ride this morning she'd been nothing but smiles and curiosity, open and warm. Now she was a trap snapped shut. Cold. Steely. He frowned. "Something's eating at you, woman. What is it?"

"Nothing."

He scrubbed a hand over his face, whiskers rasping against his fingers. He knew exactly where this conversation was headed— nowhere. He'd learned long ago that when a woman said *nothing*, she meant she'd die a bloody death before divulging what she thought he should already know.

So he shot to his feet. "I got someone I need to talk to. I won't be gone long. You and Grace stay here."

"Of course." Red Bird tucked her chin, the crown of her head hidden by a straw hat, the meaning of her words every bit as concealed.

"What's got into you?"

"I do not know what you are talking about."

He stepped closer, making divots in the quilt where his boots fell, and didn't stop until he reached the hem of her skirt. "Look at me."

It took a moment, but eventually she lifted her face—yet her eyes never quite reached his, just focused somewhere on his chin.

"Tatsu'hwa."

Slowly, her blue gaze slid to meet his.

His chest tightened, and suddenly breathing required effort. He'd seen that look before. A lifetime ago. Just before his shot met its mark. It had always bothered him when trepidation registered in Mariah's eyes, but from Eleanor it was a kidney punch.

He sucked in a breath. "You look as if I'm about to strike at any moment."

"Ridiculous." She dipped her face again, this time smoothing her hand along Grace's loose hair.

A valiant effort at disguise—but one that didn't work. Not the way her fingers trembled. The woman feared him in a new way—but why? He sorted through the events of the day like rummaging through a haversack, picking out one memory after another, examining each, none of which. . . ahh. She'd spoken to that fair-haired vixen friend of hers at the mercantile. A fierce scowl pulled down his brow. That fear in his wife's eyes was put there by one thing.

Gossip.

He turned on his heel. The sooner they were out of this town, this bed of vipers, the better. "I won't be long."

He clomped off, digging each step more forcefully than needed. A reckless gesture—but satisfying in a small way. As he set foot on the road leading into Newcastle, the stench of manure, sweat, and clothing and bodies that hadn't been washed—maybe never—crawled in and festered in his gut. A hive of men swarmed around the trading post. Renner had to be grinning about that.

Beckett's outfitting shop had a line snaked clear out the door. He passed the length of men, keeping to the other side of the road. A few called his name. He merely lifted a hand in greeting and kept eating up ground with his boots.

The closer he drew to Grey's Tavern, the more determination it took to keep going. His step hitched only once. At the door. When the scent of rum reached out, taunting, tempting. Saliva rained at the back of his mouth. It would be easy to give in. Just one drink. Only one, and leave it at that. His jaw clenched. That was a lie he'd bought one too many times. Still. . .what made him think he was strong enough to resist this time?

Oh God, help me.

He swallowed and lurched through the door.

Though still daylight outside, night shadowed the room, windows so coated with soot and grease and the shame of men that light didn't stand a chance. Did he? He hadn't set foot in here since—his stomach clenched.

Ignoring the catcalls from a table of men seated in the corner, he stalked to the bar.

"Well, well, look what dragged in the front door. Never thought to see you in here again." Nehemiah Grey slammed a mug down on the counter in front of him. "What's it to be?"

Samuel worked his jaw. One word, and that mug would brim over with ale. Foamy. Tangy. He stared, long and hard.

Then shoved the mug away. He pinned Grey with a fierce glower. "Information."

Grey's lips parted. Teeth—what few remained—hung from his gums like crooked fence posts. "That's more expensive than my best rot gut. You buyin'?"

Reaching inside a pouch at his waist, he pulled out a leather sack. The coins inside jingled as it hit the counter.

Grey's arm struck like lightning, the pouch disappearing behind the counter before the last jingle faded. "What makes you think I know anything?"

Samuel widened his stance. "Secrets pour out with every bottle you serve. I just want to know if anyone's rode in from Charles Towne with a mind to go to Keowee."

Grey cursed so sharply Samuel feared one of the man's teeth might break loose and hit him like a shot.

The bartender's gaze narrowed. "You know as well as I do, Heath, that half the trappers out here pass by Keowee. I could name more'n a dozen men without even trying."

"Not talking about a trapper."

Grey sniffed, his brows rising with the action. "Why would anyone other than a trapper or a half-blood venture a trip out there?"

Samuel studied the man a moment more, then wheeled about. Grey didn't know anything. Sutton hadn't either. It appeared that perhaps the negotiator gave him the slip and wasn't coming through Newcastle.

He stalked out the tavern door, foul mood sinking into rancidity. Maybe his time would be better spent at Keowee. Better for him—but maybe not so much for Red Bird.

Chapter 24

Eleanor leaned her head against the hickory and closed her eyes, fanning herself with a handkerchief. She'd thought it warm at the cabin, but down here in the valley, heat took on a whole new meaning, like dragon's breath, all sticky and moist. Good thing Grace slept, or she'd be whining. Eleanor peeked open one eye, checking to make sure the girl yet curled beneath the shade of Samuel's canvas shelter. Light hair sprawled over a soft piece of buckskin, right where she'd laid her.

Good. She shut her eyes once more and went back to deciphering all the bits of information she'd learned of Samuel. Nothing added up, not satisfactorily. The beginnings of a headache throbbed in her temple. Could be from the heat, but more likely from the conflict between what she'd heard of Samuel—and what she knew of him from experience.

"Afternoon, Mrs. Heath."

Her eyes shot open. Angus McDivitt stared down at her, an arm's length away. How had he drawn so close without her hearing?

She rose, but he crouched, pulling her down to the quilt along with him. "Din't mean to disturb you. Is yer husband around?"

The pounding at her temple rolled out like a thunderstorm, the beat dangerous. Clearly the man could see that Samuel was absent. "I. . .I am certain he shall return soon."

A lump moved along the man's lower cheek, lodging toward the back of his jaw, then slowly a smile spread. Brown juice coated his teeth. "Shame he left you here alone. Unprotected. Course you ought to be used to that by now, eh?"

She remembered well what it'd felt like to be left alone with Samuel those first few days. Cold fear, always present, the wondering, the *what ifs*. But here, now, breathing in the sweaty, almost fishy odor of this man, his gaze boldly holding on to hers, the wretched twist in her belly drove her to the edge of the quilt. Where *was* Samuel?

McDivitt sank fully onto the blanket, stretching out his legs and leaning against the trunk she'd abandoned. "Maybe I'll just wait for him then."

Eleanor forced her breathing to remain even. This was awkward. Would the man just sit there and stare at her until Samuel magically appeared? And if he chose to, what could she do about it?

She crushed the handkerchief in her hand, weary of playing the victim. No. This man would not get the better of her.

Nor would Mr. Heath.

Tucking her legs beneath her, she sat straighter, higher, positioning herself to look down upon the man where he slouched. "Mr. McDivitt, I know that you and my husband have some differences. I am wondering, though, if you would tell me what they are?"

His eyes narrowed. "What's he told you?"

"Nothing."

The lump moved to his other cheek before he answered. "Not surprised, really. You married a snake in the grass, and snakes are silent killers."

She curved her lips into an encouraging smile, one she often used with young, frustrated charges. "I should like to hear what you have to say."

"Well, well. A lady who values truth." He eyed her with an entirely different gleam in his eyes. "Sure, missy, I'll tell you what happened, but once you know, you might not want to go back home with him. Ever. And if that's the case"—he leaned toward her—"I want you to know I'll protect you. I couldn't save Mariah, but you've still got a chance."

Her smile faded. "I am not asking for protection, sir. I am asking for facts, nothing more."

A drip of brown leaked out the corner of his mouth, and she willed it to disappear into his beard. To have it hang there, glistening with afternoon light, turned her stomach.

"All right," he said, finally. "I came to Newcastle long before Heath. Shoot, wasn't even known as Newcastle back then. Wasn't known as anything. It was the sweat of my brow, along with Stane and Renner, what built this town." At last his tongue darted out, and he licked away the horrid juice. "We fought off Injuns, sickness, a winter snow so deep it near buried the horses. You'd think with the prosperity I brought, the civilization, holding the ground against those savages, why, the government ought to grant a respectable citizen like me the rights to the acreage all around here."

He stared at her as if he'd made some kind of grand revelation.

She tucked a wayward strand of hair behind her ear. "I am sorry, Mr.

McDivitt, but what does the government have to do with you and Mr. Heath?"

He turned aside and spit out a thick wad the size and shape of a hairball. For one horrified moment, she feared he'd hit the quilt, until the thwack of juice met grass.

He swiped his mouth. Mud-colored liquid smeared across the back of his hand, and he wiped it on his thigh. "The governor awarded Heath the land for service in the French 'n' Indian Wars. It's your man what owns all the acreage from here to Keowee."

"But. . ." She shook her head, which didn't do much for her headache or her comprehension. "I thought that land belonged to the Cherokee? Why would those people agree to give it to Mr. Heath?"

He cocked his head. "You really don't know nothin', do ya? Yer man *is* part Injun. Lived with 'em the better part of his life."

The handkerchief fell from her hand. If she listened hard enough, she'd hear her father laughing at her all the way from the grave. She'd married a. . . a Cherokee? Allied herself to a savage when all her father had asked of her was that she take on a gentleman?

McDivitt laughed, grating, almost a chirrup, and ended with a hacking cough. "I ain't even told you the half of it yet."

She swallowed. Did she even want to hear more?

"Heath come to Newcastle back in '66, thinking to live out yonder like a heathen." He swung out his arm, stained fingers fluttering toward the blue hills behind him. "And he did, for a time. But that changed when he first laid eyes on Mariah."

The lines on McDivitt's brow hardened into deep ruts, and a foul curse ripped out of his throat. "Just like the land, she shoulda been mine, too. For always."

Then, like a spent spring tempest, his eyes brightened, the lines softened, and he looked past her, as if the woman stood right behind her shoulder. Something wasn't right about that gleam. Something wasn't right about this man.

The pounding in her head traveled to her chest, and her breath hitched.

"Ahh, Mariah. Battin' those eyelashes. Swaying those skirts. Hair fine and soft as a whisper." His gaze shot to her, sparking. "Heath stole her right out from under me. Forced himself on her. Made her marry him. You know what that's like, don't you?"

"I married Mr. Heath to care for Grace, nothing more." She stood and retreated off the quilt, the turn of the discussion not at all to her liking. "Thank you for the information, but this conversation is finished. I think you should wait elsewhere for my husband."

He shot to his feet and reached for her, hands clamping on her upper arms, fingers digging into the soft flesh beneath. "You don't think that's why Mariah married him, too? He's the one what got her with child. He ruined her life. He's a destroyer. A thief. Always taking. Taking! And he'll take you, too."

He shook her, and her teeth rattled from the force.

"Let me go!"

"I told her. . .I told you. . .Mariah, you got to listen." He shoved his face into hers, his breath condensing on her cheeks like a rash. "Don't go with him. Come away with me."

She wrenched and wriggled. The man was mad. "Mr. McDivitt, please!"

His arms wrapped around her, pulling her closer. "Shh, shh. He won't know. He never did, did he?"

He crushed her to his chest, mashing her cheek against his waistcoat, his heavy breathing loud in her ear—

But the sharp click of a cocked rifle was even louder behind him.

"You've got one warning, McDivitt, and that's a mercy." Samuel's voice was quiet, steady, and altogether chilling. "Get away from my wife."

Rage painted everything scarlet. The sky. The hickory. McDivitt. Samuel stood rock still, nothing but a faint puff of breeze shoving back the hair against his collar. Would this never end? His finger pressed against the trigger. Just a bit more pressure, a twitch. . .and he could finish it. But he couldn't take the risk of hitting Red Bird. Nor could he play God, sending McDivitt to an eternity he wouldn't wish on even him.

Angus reached his hands to the sky and pivoted.

Samuel narrowed his eyes. What was this? McDivitt never yielded, not on purpose.

Red Bird dashed to the wagon, away from Angus—and away from him. Keeping the muzzle trained on McDivitt's chest, Samuel sidestepped, gaining a view of Red Bird as well. "Did he hurt you?"

She shook her head. The imprint of one of McDivitt's buttons on her cheek and the way she gripped the side of the wagon for support belied her denial.

He slid his gaze to McDivitt. He could let fly a shot now and ask for forgiveness later. . .but that still didn't make it right.

Angus tsked. "You gonna shoot me in front of the woman? Won't that be a pretty picture for her to remember."

Ahh. So that was the man's game. Goading him into playing the beast. He took his finger off the trigger, tripped the hammer, and cradled the rifle. "My wife is no concern of yours. Now get out of here. You got no business with me."

Angus lowered his hands, folding his arms over his chest. "Now there yer wrong."

It was a fight, but he kept from rolling his eyes. Except for a pint or a loose skirt, there was nothing Angus liked better than to point out when Samuel was wrong—and it usually took him three ways until Sunday to expound on the matter. "Say your piece, man."

McDivitt rocked on his heels, clearly enjoying the thought that he might have something Samuel wanted. "A rider came in 'bout an hour ago. Needs a guide to Keowee come morning."

Samuel didn't bat an eye, just kept his gaze steady—but his thoughts took off like a wild stallion. Was this finally the negotiator he'd been waiting for? Made sense, to ride in when Newcastle was a hive of activity, use the trading and outfitting day as a camouflage.

Or. . .he peered at Red Bird from the corner of his eye. Was this simply a way for McDivitt to separate him from his wife?

He breathed in suspicion along with the stink of stale tobacco stained on Angus's shirt. "What's that got to do with me? There's plenty of men in town who can guide."

Angus smirked, the action rippling through his beard. "You think any of them will be conscious by sunrise?"

"Since when are you so accommodating?"

"I ain't never been nothin' but." He leaned sideways, eyes seeking out Red Bird like a hawk to a mouse. "Why, I'll even see yer wife and child get home safely, you wanna take that guide job."

Samuel reached for his tomahawk. He might not be able to take the man out with a shot, but he could make Angus wish for death with a few well-placed swipes.

McDivitt had no qualms about rolling his eyes. "Just let me know, Heath. I'm happy to oblige, and something tells me yer wife wouldn't mind at all, either."

Samuel choked a hold lower on the handle, primed for throwing.

Either McDivitt didn't notice or didn't think the threat was real. He merely unfolded his arms and fumbled around inside his waistcoat. A small pouch appeared, and he took out a fat pinch of tobacco, jamming it between gums and cheek. Smacking his lips, he stuffed the pouch away and strolled over to Red Bird.

"McDivitt! I'm warning you—"

"Shut yer gob, Heath. I'm going." But before Angus stalked off, he lowered his voice and said something to Red Bird.

She pressed shaky fingers to her lips.

Samuel swung back his arm, resetting the weight of the tomahawk in his fingers, the temptation to let the blade fly a sharp need in his bones. The gall of the man to poison her mind right in front of him!

"Samuel! Do not!"

Red Bird's plea sliced through him, and he sucked in a breath. What she must think of him.

McDivitt sauntered away, his whistling tune a burr in Samuel's ear.

He thrust the tomahawk back into his belt and strode to Red Bird. Her sweep of freckles stood stark against a face pale as a winter moon. She lifted her chin but did not meet his gaze.

McDivitt could have told her any number of lies, but if he'd told her the truth. . . Samuel swallowed the acid rising up his throat. "What'd he say? And don't tell me nothing, because we both know he did."

"He. . ." Two pearly teeth worked her lower lip. "He offered me protection."

"From what?"

A crow swooped overhead, landing in the hickory with a jagged caw. But Red Bird said nothing.

He grabbed her shoulders, forcing her face up to his. "He offered you protection from what?"

Her mouth twisted, and a blue flame flared in her eyes. "You!"

He staggered, immediately splaying his fingers. *Oh God. Forgive me.* In the past five minutes, he'd proven McDivitt right by everything he'd said, thought, done. What was wrong with him?

He stared at her, his gut clenching, hating the questions in her gaze, but mostly hating himself. "I'm sorry, Tatsu'hwa. I shouldn't have. . ." He sighed, frustrated with himself, with McDivitt, with life in general. "I shouldn't have brought you here. The things you'll hear. . .and probably already have. . ."

Shaking his head, he wheeled about. What more was there to say?

A hand on his sleeve stopped him.

"You are right. I have heard much—but not from you." Brittle grass crackled beneath her feet. She circled, stopping in front of him. "You asked me once to tell you my story."

Her eyes finally met his—and his blood drained. A world of hurt shone in that sea of blue. Her lips thinned for a moment.

And her next words hit him broadside. "I would hear yours."

She could have no idea what she asked of him. Blood rushed through his veins, pumping in his ears like white water. He spent most of his time forgetting. Ignoring. And now she wanted to rip the scab off his barely healed past and probe around in the wound?

Her fingers once more rested on his sleeve, her touch gentle, her gaze fierce. "Please, Samuel."

His nostrils flared. He could feel it. There was no other option, the way he inhaled until his lungs burned.

A single, stunning realization pierced his heart like an arrowhead shot true. If he wanted a real relationship with this woman, one he'd never experienced before—not even with Mariah—then he needed to tell her the truth.

Was that what he wanted? To know and be known by this slip of a woman? And an English one at that? He clenched his jaw, fighting against the answer.

God help him, he did. But how on earth could he dredge up the past without breaking?

Chapter 25

The late afternoon sun hovered low in the sky, trying to decide if it should hold its position or give in and sink. Going backward was not an option—for the sun or for Eleanor. What had possessed her to ask Samuel about his past? She ought not care about a thief, a destroyer, and possibly a murderer, not if everything she'd heard from Biz, Molly, and McDivitt was true. But after living with this man and seeing his integrity, how was she to believe such things?

She studied Samuel's face, looking for answers. The thumbnail scar near the bridge of his nose, the half of his cheek hidden behind a curtain of loose hair, the strength in the muscles on his neck alone all labeled him capable of the accusations. He could be violent. She'd seen it.

But she'd also seen him love his daughter with a fierce kind of tenderness, passionate and authentic. He'd quietly taken a whipping in Eleanor's stead, faced a bear—not once, but twice—and provided for her every need. She pursed her lips. Yes, she did want to hear of his past from his own mouth, and more than that, she owed it to him.

He stood silent for so long, though, that she doubted he'd answer at all.

Behind them, Grace murmured in her sleep. The girl would wake soon, and the thought of losing this moment of truth tasted like loss in her mouth. Eleanor swallowed and gave it one last shot. "Samuel?"

His face jerked aside as if she'd slapped him. He stalked away and dropped onto the blanket, rumpled by McDivitt's hasty departure. Drawing up his knees, he rested his forearms atop them. For a moment, he looked like a little boy, sullen yet ready to give an account to his mother for stealing a biscuit. "What do you want to know?"

She sifted through questions as she chose a spot on the quilt to best see his face, close enough to hear every nuance of his voice yet far enough to flee if she must. Lowering to the ground, she gave thanks for the solid earth beneath her. At least something was constant. Dependable. Not like the crazy churning in her stomach. She'd never been so forthright, so intimate in conversation with a man, and judging by the way he pressed his lips together, this might be new for him, as well.

She smoothed her skirts, then met his stare. "I think a good place to start would be with your first wife, Mariah. She is Grace's mother, after all, and if I am to help you raise her child, then I think you are indebted to all of us to honor her memory."

"Honor?" The word flew from his mouth like a musket shot. "There was no honor in that woman."

Bitterness colored his tone. Apparently he had some sort of motivation to have killed her.

"She wronged you?"

The scar on his nose whitened against the black scowl twisting the rest of his face. "You could say that." Then it cleared. Just like that. The hard lines smoothed. No, not just evened out, but drew into a jagged, painful grimace. "And I wronged her right back."

She lost him then. She knew it. Could see it in the way his gaze floated past her, stared into the distance and straight into the past. His jaw tensed. The brown of his eyes hardened into a blank void. What kind of abyss did he plummet into?

"Mariah," he said at length. "She was a dragonfly on a summer day, flitting here and there, and when she landed. . . Well, half the time I wondered why such a beauty would notice a wretch like me."

Eleanor leaned forward, fearing the way his voice trailed off that he'd say no more. "And the other half?"

His gaze shot to hers. "The other half I was too drunk to care."

She gasped.

He worked his forefinger and thumb, rubbing them together for a time, then his fingers curled inward. "Up until a year ago, the bottle was my god."

"What happened then?"

"The real one showed up."

She sank back, unsure what to think, what to feel. . .and especially what to say. "So, you do not drink anymore?"

He shook his head, his swath of hair brushing his collar in emphasis. "By the grace of God, no. The man you married is not the same one as wed Mariah. And that's a mercy for you."

She bit her lip. She could end it here, on a positive note—but she might never grasp another chance to discover the truth. Her teeth scraped across her lip as she released the pressure. "Mr. McDivitt said you had to marry. That Mariah was with child. . .and the child was yours. Is that true?"

He didn't need to answer. The downward curve of his shoulders said it all.

"Aye. To my great shame, she was." His head dipped, the brim of his hat hiding the naked emotion in his voice. The man could face charging bears and lashing whips without a flinch, but the way he crumpled now in front of her broke her heart. Scooting closer, she rested her hand on his leg. "A wise man once told me not to allow the past to fester inside. That you must let it go."

Slowly, his face lifted to hers, a faint gleam lightening his gaze. "So. . . you do listen to me, hmm?"

She smirked and released her hold. "I do, and I should like to hear more."

"You are a dog with a bone, Tatsu'hwa." He sighed as if disgusted, but a half smile lifted the corners of his mouth—then faded as he continued. "I came to town about the time Mariah's father died. Funny, though, now I think on it. . .grief never did slow her down. The woman simply knew what she wanted and went after it."

"And that was you?"

"No. It was my money."

"So it is true?" She folded her hands in her lap, puzzling over his answer. She'd served in fine homes. The best, really. And they all had a certain smell, a unique feel of privilege and arrogance that permeated the walls. This man's simple cabin and simpler lifestyle slapped that construct right in the face. "You are wealthy?"

"That depends on what you count as treasure." He scrubbed his fingers across his chin, studying her, dissecting how she'd react.

She didn't blame him. If his first wife snared him for money alone, no wonder he hid in a no-account log home in the woods. She peered up at him. "I have learned that money is easily lost and just as easily steals the souls of those who value it."

"Would that Mariah had been as wise as you." He closed his eyes, his nostrils flaring. Whatever demon he wrestled with pinned him without mercy.

"Did you. . ." She paused, not wanting to breathe life into the question that nagged her, but the swelling inside her heart forced the words free. "Did you love her?"

"I thought I did." His eyes snapped open, seeking hers, stealing her breath with the exposed sentiment he allowed her to see. And it was an allowance, for he could as easily shutter his feelings as he always did.

"I had no idea what real love was." His voice lowered, husky around the edges. "Not then."

The warmth of his gaze lit a fire in her belly, and she pressed her fingers against her stomach. Oh my, but she could fall for this man, fall and never reach the bottom of the love she read in his eyes. The veracity of it pulled her forward—and pushed her back at the same time. How could she give herself to a man who might be a murderer?

"I must know. . . . What happened the night Mariah died?"

Like the rolling up of a parchment, sealed with wax and just as unreadable, his eyes darkened, closing her peek into his heart.

"What have you heard?" His voice was flat, the warmth cooled, almost icy.

She shook her head. "It does not matter what I have heard. It matters what you tell me, for I expect you will tell me the truth."

"What makes you think you can trust me?" He stiffened, like a bowstring about to snap. Whatever she said next would either loosen that tension—or break him.

But did she really trust him to tell her the truth?

She searched his eyes. This time he remained hidden, somewhere deep inside, forcing her to answer based on what she already knew of him. "Granted, you have not given me much information, but I believe all you have spoken thus far is reliable. Mr. McDivitt has shown he is not of sound mind. And Biz and Molly, well. . .they were not there that night, were they?"

The lines of his brow crumpled, and he leaned forward. Reaching out, he brushed his knuckles along her cheek. "You are a curious woman, Tatsu'hwa."

Temptation to nuzzle into that touch burned with each stroke. Yet she held firm.

"All right." He dropped his hand. "Make of this what you will. It was a year ago now. I'd been out drinking all day, knowing I'd have to leave the next. Major Rafferty—that soldier you met—needed a tracker, and there's no drinking on the trail. So I aimed to fill myself with so much rum it would last for days. I got home late that night and stumbled through the front door. Angus tore out the back."

A thundercloud swept across his face. "Mariah didn't deny it, didn't even have the decency to care that Grace was in her cradle the whole time. That was the worst—and last—quarrel we ever had."

"Did you...did you kill your wife?" She held her breath.

Color rose up his neck, flushing his face to the almost purple shade of a bruise. The fabric of his shirt stretched tight against his chest as he sucked in a breath.

Then slowly, almost imperceptibly, he nodded.

The movement hit her like a rock through glass. Thousands of shards poking and needling and drawing blood. Shattering her perceptions, all she'd hoped for and wanted to believe about him. All she thought she knew of him. Her jaw dropped, as unhinged as her feelings, and she shrank back on the quilt. Biz and Molly had been right. So had McDivitt. She stared at him, horrified.

"That's right. Look at me like I'm a fiend." His voice was throaty and raw. "Because I am one."

"I can hardly believe it." The words came out shivery. Funny they came out at all.

"I said things no man should, God help me." He pinched the bridge of his nose and rubbed, up and down, up and down. "Some say liquor talks. I say it's the soul showing its true colors. Those words...they hurt her bad. Real bad. I don't remember much of what Mariah said to me, but I do remember her grabbing all my jugs and smashing them, one by one against the wall, alcohol drenching everything. Grace crying. Me being a coward and running away."

The words swirled like autumn leaves caught in an eddy of cold wind. Around and around. Gathering them took an awful lot of scurrying, but she sorted each one and laid them out in a row. Pressing her fingers against her temples, she massaged as she tried to make sense of what he'd said compared to what she'd heard from others.

"Wait a minute . . ." She lowered her hands, clarity dawning bright as a July morn. "You ran away? And Mariah was still alive?"

"She was more than alive. She was a cannonball, pitching dishes and pots and pans at me out the door. I know now that I shouldn't have left. I should've stood there and taken it like a man. If I had. . ." His voice broke. "Oh God, if only I had."

He shot to his feet.

She shot to hers, grabbing his sleeve. "What happened? How did she die?"

He wrenched from her grasp, wheeling about.

"Do not run away this time!" She gasped, as much out of shock at her own boldness as from the glassy gaze he turned on her.

In two strides, he stood nose to nose with her, his words thundering against her cheeks. "You want to know the kind of man you're living with? Do you! I collapsed out near the back of the trading post that night, dead drunk. If it weren't for half the town yelling, 'Fire!' I doubt I'd have wakened. When I staggered to the house, the flames. . .the screams. . ."

He retreated a step, shaking his head, the sorrow on his face enough to drive her to her knees. "I ran in, but part of the roof had already caved, the timbers crushing Mariah's legs. There was no time to think, even if I were sober. I grabbed Grace from her cradle and got her to safety. And when I tried to go back in for Mariah . . ."

His throat bobbed. His lips twitched.

But no more words came out.

She folded her arms, the only shield she'd have from the answer to her last question. "Did you start that fire before you ran off?"

Hanged. Drawn. Quartered. Death by any means of torture would hurt less than the suspicion written in the creases of Red Bird's brows. Samuel ground his teeth against the searing loss of her trust—for surely having asked such a question, doubt must be gnawing a hole in her gut. Of course he'd grieved Mariah's death, but this? This time he'd lost something he cherished.

He reached for her, but inches from contact pulled back. He didn't have the right. Not anymore.

"No, Tatsu'hwa. . . ." His voice crackled, and he cleared his throat. "Mariah and I had our differences, but I would never have started that fire, not even drunk."

"Then. . ." A tide of confusion darkened the blue of her eyes. She blinked, saying nothing. Slowly, she unfolded her arms and spread her hands. "That explains why you were released from jail. But if you did not kill your wife, why do you bear the guilt?"

He studied her face. Was she mocking him?

A clear gaze, pure as the August sky, stared back. Sweet, underserved mercy! The woman seriously did not realize the depth of his treachery.

He closed the distance between them and rested his hands on her shoulders, as if by sheer touch he might make her understand. "Don't you see? If that house hadn't been filled with my drink, it wouldn't have gone up so fast, not like that."

"But Samuel, you said yourself you did not start that fire."

He shook his head. "If I hadn't been a drunkard, if I hadn't left when I did, if I hadn't—"

Her hand shot up, stopping his mouth, her fingertips an ember against his lips. "And if Christ had not given His life on the cross, then you would be guilty. But in your own words, you are a different man because of that grace. Samuel." Her eyes filled, shimmery and heartbreakingly beautiful. "You need to forgive yourself."

He clenched every muscle, afraid to breathe, to hope, to maybe believe that she was right. He could turn and run. Flee to the woods and work off the guilt and shame—but wasn't that exactly what he'd done by moving to the wild, holing up in a cabin with Grace, accepting God's forgiveness but condemning himself?

As if reading his mind, Red Bird slid her hand away from his lips, trailing her fingertips upward. Fire tingled on his skin where she touched. Her fingers slipped beneath his swath of long hair, lifting, exposing, resting like a whisper on his ruined cheek.

His breath hitched—audibly.

She smiled, her beauty unmatched by all the angels in heaven. "Forgive yourself, Samuel. The scars will remain, but you will be healed on the inside."

He turned that thought over, like a warm stone in his hand, enjoying the feel of it until he could bear it no longer. He covered his fingers over hers and nuzzled his face against her palm. How could she offer such unconditional comfort when her life had been anything but comfortable—especially the past several months?

"Papa?" Sleep thickened Grace's voice from the tent. Moments later, arms wrapped around his leg.

Despite all the pain, the loss, the tragedy that followed him around life like a hound of hell, he chuckled. "Woman, I do not deserve you or Grace. Why is God so good to me?"

Red Bird pulled back, disentangling her hand from his. "Because He *is* good. It is His nature. Nothing more—and nothing less."

Silence stretched between them, filled with cricket song and the far-off whoops of traders and trappers—and broken only when Grace tugged at his leg. "Hungry, Papa."

"Well, now." He bent and tossed her into the air until she giggled, her braids flying golden in the early evening light. Satisfied, he tucked her in one arm and offered the other to Red Bird. "Would you like to go to that, er, festival and get a bite of supper, Mrs. Heath?"

"I would." She beamed at him and rested her hand in the crook of his arm.

He'd walked into Newcastle before. He'd ridden. Driven. And one time even rolled in on a loosened load of barrels broken free from the back of a wagon. But he'd never flown in, steps as light as an eagle on the wing. Telling Red Bird everything about his horrific past hadn't weighed him down in shame. It had freed him—even when he passed in front of the charred reminder of his former home. His steps slowed, and he looked closer at the ruins. Sure, a few scorched patches remained, but mostly weeds and grass spread over the lot. New growth. He peered down at Red Bird to find her gaze upon him.

He winked. "You know, I think I just might sell that piece of land to McDivitt."

She swatted his arm. "You, sir, are a scoundrel."

He grinned. "Ahh, but I'm your scoundrel, and there's not much you can do about that now, is there?"

A blush to shame the fairest June rose blazed across her face—and warmed his heart. He stifled a chuckle. If Inoli knew how soft he was becoming, the teasing would be endless.

At the far end of Newcastle, near the road leading to Charles Towne, a square of land had been cleared. Tents ringed the area. Tables of all sorts, constructed from planks and logs, clustered on one side. The smoky aroma of roasted venison and pork wafted on a cloud hovering above the gathering. Musicians plucked warm-up notes on fiddles and flutes. Even a drum rat-a-tat-tatted.

Samuel scanned the assembly, wondering which man needed guiding to Keowee. The thought of having to ask McDivitt for an introduction galled him, but how else would he discover the negotiator's identity?

Grace bounced against his shoulder, pulling him back to the reality of her hunger. He purchased three meat pies from a vendor, then seated his family at a corner table, keeping his eye on those nearest—and keeping his wife far away from those two friends of hers who might poison her mind further against him.

Torches flamed to life as they ate, dancing atop thick posts driven into the ground, adding to the festive feel. Grace shoved the rest of her pie toward him and hopped off her barrel.

"Grace!" Red Bird rose.

He reached across the table and tugged her sleeve. "Watch."

The girl darted ten paces off, joining with a group of girls spinning in circles to the music.

Red Bird faced him, a frown marring her brow. "But what if she—"

"The girl slept half the day away. Let her dance."

The setting sun lit streaks of fire in a loose curl brushing against Red Bird's neck. The urge to loosen all that hair, watch it tumble over her shoulders, run his hands through it until he wept, drew him to his feet. He rounded the table. Her gaze followed his every movement.

He caught the strand between forefinger and thumb, the silkiness of it shooting heat up his arm. He tucked it behind her ear, whispering into it. "And what about you, Tatsu'hwa? Would you like to dance?"

She retreated a step, eyes wide. "I. . .I am not familiar with the steps."

"Why, woman, all you got to do is follow." He held out his hand.

Her gaze bounced between his open palm and his face. Then slowly, like a rabbit creeping out from a stand of grass, she lifted her hand.

Before she could change her mind, he entwined his fingers with hers and guided her to where a line of skirts swirled and bobbed between an opposite line of men. When he pulled her to take their places at the end of the rows, a jolt shot from his heart to his belly. What was he doing? For a moment, he stood, stock-still, the laughs and chatter of dancers around them fading so that all he heard was the rapid beat of his heart.

"Samuel?" She wrinkled her nose, her funny, endearing way of asking what on earth was wrong with him.

But no, for this one grand and glorious moment, nothing was wrong. Not. One. Thing. He smiled in full. "This is a fast one. Follow my lead."

They looped and dipped and circled their way down the line and up again, both their chests heaving by the end of the reel. Red Bird's cheeks flushed to a breath-stealing hue, her eyes gleaming like a spring pond warmed by the sun. True, Mariah had been a stunning beauty, but the sincere loveliness of Red Bird, innocent and genuine, unmarred by greed and manipulation, stoked a hunger inside him that could not be denied much longer.

Without thinking, he grabbed her hand and tugged her past the dancers, beyond the torches, all the way to a break between tents and forest. Her steps kept pace with his, showing no sign of hesitation. The rising moon shamelessly tagged along.

He stopped and wrapped his arms around her waist, pulling her close. Desire shook along every nerve, sending a warm ache through his body. He lowered his forehead and rested his brow against hers.

"Tatsu'hwa," he whispered.

A funny sound garbled in her throat, and she leaned against him. The heat of her body burned through his shirt. The sudden realization that she wanted him heightened all his senses, and he inhaled her sweetness.

"Are you asking?" The question came out too husky, too revealing, but he couldn't stop it.

She lifted her face, her nose bumping against his, her lips less than a breath away. It would take no effort—none—to press his mouth to hers, taste her, know her. Claim her for his own.

But that would destroy the tenuous trust she'd placed in him.

Oh God, help me stay strong.

Her eyes, too dark to discern the color, held on to his. Her lips parted. The tension between them a shiver in the night. One word, just one word from her, and he'd make her his wife in more than name only.

She mumbled something about Grace, then wrenched away, darting back to the torches.

He watched her disappear into the throng, a smile stretching across his face.

She hadn't asked for that kiss yet—but she also hadn't flatly refused him.

His grin grew.

Progress.

Chapter 26

Eleanor dashed toward the crowd, tall grass snagging her dress though she bunched the fabric nearly as high as her shins. Highly inappropriate—yet necessary. Night air slid up between skirt and stockings, the temperature having dropped some since sunset, but she burned. White hot fire blazed from her cheeks to the pit of her stomach. Samuel watched her. She knew it. Could feel the weight of his smoldering gaze embracing her from where he yet stood at the edge of the woods. Her body begged to revisit the keen feelings he stirred, maybe even turn back and find out what it would feel like to have his lips one with hers, his body one. . .

Oh God, forgive me.

Who was this brazen woman inside who'd almost asked for a kiss? Who'd maybe have asked for more if given a chance? She pumped her legs faster. She didn't even know herself anymore.

Darting between two tents, she entered the fray of merrymakers—then pitched forward, the toe of one shoe caught on a rope tied to a stake in the ground. She flailed.

But a wiry arm caught her fall. "Slow down there, missy."

"Thank you," she breathed out, winded from the race and her thoughts of Samuel. Straightening, she drew back and smoothed her skirts.

Torchlight flickered over the face of the man in front of her, highlighting a large nose and completely skipping a cavern where an eye should've been. A grotesque sight—and one altogether familiar, for she'd gazed upon it over a campfire many a time.

"Mr. Beebright." She smiled. "Such a surprise. Good evening."

His single eye widened, one grey brow arching to the night sky. "Well, well, ain't seen you in a spell, and look at ya." He cocked his head, studying her down to the tips of her boots. "I knew living with Heath would change yer ways. Got the straitlaced starch beat right out o' you, eh? Why yer a regular upcountry wildcat now, I reckon."

Her fingers flew to her hair. La, she must look a fright—not a topic she wished to explore, especially with a man.

"I trust you are well?" she asked.

He laughed. "Likely faring better than you. Least yer still standing."

She pursed her lips. What was she to say to that? "I am sorry; I do not understand."

Beebright sucked in air between the gap in his front teeth. "Heath's first wife didn't last a year afore he got rid o' her. I was kind of hoping you wouldn't meet with the same lick of bad luck, though I didn't want to tell you that up front."

The words were a slap in the face. Had anyone in this town taken the time to find out the truth from Samuel? She lifted her chin and stared him down. "My husband had nothing whatsoever to do with that tragedy."

Beebright rocked back on his heels, howling, his slanted shoulders riding the crest of the laughter like a fisherman's bobber in the water. "Got to you, did he? That Heath, he do have a way with women. I 'spect you'll be popping out a babe in no time."

"Mr. Beebright!" she hissed, then darted past him, unwilling to listen to any more wicked conjecture. His laughter followed for a time until it blended into the backdrop of music and other revelers.

Skirting the dancers, she searched for Grace. The little blond head yet bobbed with a circle of other girls, right where she'd left her.

Eleanor bent, calling for the child. "Grace, shall we get a drink?"

The girl broke from the circle and ran to her. "Thirsty!"

"I thought so." She smiled and held out her hand, her grin growing as little fingers wrapped around hers. Somehow, Grace always managed to set her world right.

Weaving past tables, Eleanor ignored a few lewd comments from trappers who'd clearly drunk enough to loosen their lips. The tang of homemade liquor stung her nose. This was no place for her and Grace on their own. Maybe she should have waited for Samuel to catch up.

But as she neared a sideboard loaded with crocks of cider and ale, the tension in her jaw slackened. Molly and Biz huddled together in front of it, jabbering away.

She led Grace to where they stood. "Good evening, ladies."

Molly spun, beaming. "Eleanor! So happy you made it tonight." She stooped and tugged one of Grace's braids. "You, too, Miss Grace."

The girl giggled, burying her face against Eleanor's skirt.

"Where's yer man?" Biz craned her neck, scanning the area, then blinked her feline eyes at Eleanor. "So, you run off, aye? Smart choice. I'm sure I can get Parker to take you and the girl in. He's got a kind streak wide enough to drive a cart through. Maybe two. God's truth, cuz I been using that to my advantage."

For some odd reason, Biz's wink and trademark smirk annoyed her, and she sighed. "No, Biz, I did nothing of the sort. And I want both you and Molly to know that what you told me about Mr. Heath this morning is patently untrue. He explained everything this afternoon. He is not to be blamed, leastwise not for his wife's demise."

"Demise?" Biz spit out the word as if tasting a lemon for the first time.

"Death," Eleanor explained.

Molly looked from the child to Eleanor. "How can you be certain? The terrible things I've heard—"

"Are exactly that, Molly. Hearsay." Eleanor shot her a pointed stare, driving home her point. "It is nothing but gossip and lies, and I will thank you to not repeat it anymore."

"Hold on here a minute." Biz elbowed her way between her and Molly. Her blue gaze dissected her like a butterfly pinned to a display board. "Why. . .yer as sweet on him as Molly is on Ben Sutton."

"I am not!" Eleanor's rebuttal shot out with Molly's, both as jarring as the sudden tattoo of a drum, rat-a-tat-tatting on the night air.

Biz laughed. "You can say otherwise, Elle Bell, but look at yer cheeks. They're a-flamin' like a gypsy's torch. Oh, you got it bad, luv. Din't think to see that happen, you all bookish and mannerly and whatnot—and him no better than a cock fighter back at Old Nichol."

"Do not be ridiculous. We have an understanding, Mr. Heath and I, and I assure you it is all very proper." She tugged Grace sideways, bypassing Biz and snatching a cup of cider from the table.

Biz elbowed her as she passed. "I think yer a-wishin' that would change though, aye?"

Snubbing Biz's rudeness—and the traitorous agreement fluttering in her own belly—Eleanor bent and handed the cup to Grace.

"Stop it, Biz," Molly scolded. "Don't drive Eleanor away when we have such precious little time with her as is. Besides, I haven't told either of you yet about the new arrival. She's quite scandalous, really."

Eleanor straightened, glad for the change of subject.

"Oh?" Biz jutted her chin. "Bit of competition for me, eh?"

Molly shrugged. "I shouldn't think so. The woman is a missionary."

A curse spewed out of Biz. She slapped her hand over her mouth and slipped a wild glance around. Apparently living with a pastor was affecting her in some small way. "What's so scandalous about that?"

Molly leaned toward them both. "She rode into town alone."

Grace banged the cup against Eleanor's leg, and she took it from the child, setting it back on the board. All the while, she mulled over Molly's information. Women simply did not ride alone in the wild, especially not an upstanding one. She faced Molly. "A lone woman traveling this backcountry. . .is that not a bit odd?"

Molly nodded. "To be fair, she does have a Negro manservant with her, and her situation could not be helped. The poor thing lost her uncle, you see—the reverend she'd traveled with from Charles Towne. He suffered some kind of fit a few days back, never to recover. They had to bury him. Oh, Miss Browndell is so brave! She reminds me of you, Eleanor. She pressed on and made it to Newcastle on her own. Can you imagine?" The whites of Molly's eyes glowed in the torchlight. "I'd be so frightened."

"Yes, very brave," Eleanor murmured as she thought back on the past three months, faced with bears and Indians and all manner of harshness. A frown pulled at her lips. If it weren't for Samuel, she'd not have known how to deal with any of it. And if it weren't for herself, he'd not have risked his life so many times. Her heart squeezed.

"Eleanor?"

She jerked out of her morbid thoughts and offered a half smile to Molly. "Indeed. Miss Browndell must be very intelligent to have survived in the wilderness after the loss of her uncle."

"She is!" Molly clasped her hands in front of her, almost a stance of worship. "Not that I've had the chance for much conversation with her, mind you, but listening to her discussions with Mrs. Greeley is quite exciting."

"Pish!" Biz's face screwed into a disagreeable mask. "Can't imagine she'd have anything to say I'd want to hear. I get an earful enough at home with 'scripture says this' and 'scripture says that.'"

Eleanor quirked a brow. Clearly the woman had not heard enough to mend her ungodly ways.

Molly stepped closer. "But here's the most interesting thing. The woman, Miss Browndell," she indicated with a nod of her head toward a petite lady not far from them, talking with the plump Mrs. Greeley, "says she plans to continue on with her uncle's mission—clear into Cherokee lands, with naught but her manservant to accompany her. Why, 'tis positively outrageous!"

Biz narrowed her eyes. "Either this fine miss is askin' for a scalpin'. . .or there's more to her story than preachin' to some heathens."

Grace yanked on Eleanor's hand, and she swung the girl up into her arms. For once, Eleanor realized, she agreed with Biz.

"Come on, girls." Biz charged forward, glancing over her shoulder. "God fearin' or not, I'd like to meet this scandalous woman."

Molly bit her lip. "I don't know, Biz. Mrs. Greeley might not like us barging in."

Biz turned around, walking backward, a wicked wiggle to her eyebrows. "Don't worry. Elle Bell there will use her pretty manners to make it all right."

Molly shot her a pleading look as Biz scooted over to where Mrs. Greeley and Miss Browndell stood at the far end of the refreshment table.

Eleanor held Grace all the tighter. As excited as she had been to reunite with her friends, she suddenly wished for the seclusion of Samuel's log cabin. A single rogue bear was less dangerous than a curious Biz—or a newcomer with mixed morals.

Samuel stalked past the outer ring of torches and stepped over the body of a longhunter who'd already hit the dirt from too much rattle-skull. Three steps later, he turned back. That passed-out sot could've been him—no—that *was* him, in years past. Stooping, he grabbed the man beneath the armpits and hauled him off to the side, dropping him next to the canvas of someone's tent. At least there the fellow wouldn't get a boot to the ribs or kick in the head and could sleep off his stupor in peace.

He wheeled about and shouldered past two traders leaning against each other for ballast. Time he found McDivitt, asked about the man seeking a guide, then got Red Bird and Grace out of here.

"Heath!"

The silhouette of a broad-shouldered man loomed black in front of a torch, five paces off. Sutton. After a rank-smelling trapper stumbled past, Samuel veered toward him, following where Sutton had disappeared behind the tent line. He caught up with him where he crouched in the grass, away from the festivities.

Samuel squatted as well. "What have you got?"

Even at this distance, the line of torches lit the whites of Sutton's eyes in the darkness. "Newcomer rode in today, asking for a guide to the Lower Town."

He chewed the inside of his cheek. Sutton's words added credence to what he'd already learned from McDivitt. . .but Sutton wouldn't have pulled him aside if there weren't more to it. "You think it's the negotiator?"

Sutton shrugged. "I can hardly square it. It's for you to determine. All I can do is supply you with information."

"Such as?"

"It's a woman and her manservant what's seeking passage. A Negro."

Samuel rubbed the back of his neck, thinking hard. McDivitt hadn't said anything about if it was a man or a woman.

"There's more." Sutton's low voice cut into his thoughts. "She's trying real hard to cover a Yorkshire accent, and doing a fair job of it, mind you. But now and then she slips, ever so slightly, and I can tell, my mam being from that part of the country."

Samuel shook his head, a vain attempt to line up the strange nuggets of intelligence. "Why would a woman, an English one no less, want passage to Keowee?"

"Says she's carrying out her uncle's dying wishes."

Woman. Unchaperoned, save for a servant. English. Bent on a promise to a dead man. How was he to track that trail? Which way did it lead? He blew out a long breath. "Either this woman is a naive fool, or she's got grit. Unless it's the manservant who's using her for cover. Suppose I need to figure out which."

The twitch at the corner of Sutton's lips confirmed he'd already come to the same conclusion.

Samuel stood. "All right. Time I met this woman. Where is she?"

Sutton rose, staying him with a hand to the shoulder. "One more thing you should know, unrelated."

Samuel shot him a sideways glance. "I'm listening."

A fierce scowl carved into Sutton's face, flickering torchlight intensifying his rage. "McDivitt. Watch your back."

Samuel frowned. "That's nothing new. He's always had it in for me." He cocked his head, searching Sutton's eyes for an underlying message. "But you know that."

"It's different this time." Sparks flamed in Sutton's brown gaze—and not from the torches. "It's not just you anymore. The man is unhinged. Even grabbed Greeley by the collar the other day, claiming he'd been shortchanged. He threatened Greeley with a strip-down beating right there on the loading dock if he didn't get his money back. Didn't care that God and half the town was watchin'."

Samuel scrubbed his jaw. This was new. "What did Greeley do?"

"Said he'd bring in the law from Charles Towne and see McDivitt's reign of terror over Newcastle was done."

He snorted, wishing he'd been there to see Angus's face. "That didn't set well, I imagine."

"Aye. McDivitt told him where to go, and it wasn't to Charles Towne." Half a smile lifted his mouth, then faded, a grim set to his jaw replacing any humor. "Something bad's going to happen; I feel it in my gut. Greed's eating the man alive. There's no telling what McDivitt will do."

"There never is." The memory of McDivitt's hands on Red Bird shook through him from head to toe. He stalked toward the tent line.

Sutton trailed him, his words a tomahawk between the shoulders. "If I were you, Heath, I wouldn't just watch my own back. I'd keep an eye on my wife."

He searched past the heads of men, drawn to a flash of red hair peeking out beneath a straw hat across the way. His wife huddled with her two friends near the drink table—friends every bit as dangerous as McDivitt.

He glanced back at Sutton. "Mind your own back as well, my friend."

Weaving through those still standing, he set off to collect Red Bird— then find this lone woman with the gall of a man.

Chapter 27

Eleanor and Molly tried to trail Biz, but the woman dashed off with the skill of a pickpocket bent on a mark. Perhaps she truly had been the finest cutpurse in the Old Nichol rookery. To be fair, though, a toddler didn't cling to her neck, slowing her steps. Eleanor shifted Grace on her hip and quickened her pace, Molly at her side.

They'd nearly joined the small group of women when Biz stepped up to Mrs. Greeley and Miss Browndell, her words as brash as her volume.

"Evening, Mrs. Greeley. Don't think I've met yer new friend here yet. Seems I ought let the reverend know when there's a new sheep to be fleeced, I mean, a sheep in his flock, or something like that. I'm Biz. Biz Hunter. And you are?" Biz grabbed Miss Browndell's hand, pumping so that the smaller woman's entire arm jerked with the movement. She paused for a moment and lifted the woman's fingers eye-level, letting out a low whistle at a gleaming, silver ring. "Say, that's a real beauty. Must have set you back a few coins, eh?"

"Really!" Mrs. Greeley's face pinched to an unbecoming shade of red. Her head swiveled toward Molly, a spasm cinching one eye nearly closed. "Molly! Bid your friend goodnight."

Before Molly could form any words—or even open her mouth—Mrs. Greeley turned to her guest. "My apologies, Miss Browndell. You'll find that manners are scarce in this part of the country. It's been a great trial for me, but I suppose one cannot expect a pig to behave as a butterfly."

She skewered Biz with a steely gaze.

Judging by the cocky set of Biz's jaw, she was about to unleash a few words that would burn a sailor's ears. Molly shot Eleanor a pleading look.

Oh, la! Samuel's cabin in the woods sounded better with each passing moment. Eleanor unwrapped Grace and set her down, tethering her with a firm grip on her hand, then faced Mrs. Greeley. "I beg your pardon, Mrs. Greeley, but I have been admiring your fichu all evening. Is that Hampton lace, the finest from Nantatter's of London? My former employer, Duchess Brougham, simply adored their work. I can see your taste runs rather aristocratic."

Mrs. Greeley's fingers fluttered up to her bodice. Her lips opened and closed like a landed codfish. "Why...er...thank you, Mrs. Heath."

"Heath?" Miss Browndell aimed a perfectly arched brow at Eleanor. Her auburn hair was pulled back into a knot, set beneath a snappy riding cap of green felt. She smiled with lips the color of warmed sherry, the rest of her skin surprisingly white in spite of her long trek from Charles Towne. The woman was a faerie. Ethereal. Artists would drop to their knees, begging to paint her portrait. Her tiny frame would make any man feel virile and protective of such a beautiful, porcelain treasure.

Towering a full handspan above the woman, Eleanor felt like an ogre.

"Oh, yes. Forgive me." Mrs. Greeley's head bobbed, the single feather atop her cap scolding her own slip in manners. "Miss Browndell, this is Mrs. Heath. Her husband is the fellow I was telling you about."

Why was she surprised when Miss Browndell's lips parted, revealing pearly teeth all lined up in a row? Of course she'd have a pure smile. Everything about this woman, from her beauty to her holy quest to spread God's Word, was flawless.

Eleanor's fingers itched to reach out and yank a curl out of place from her impeccably coiffed head. She gripped Grace's hand tighter and masked a grimace. She wasn't just an ogre, she was a wicked one at that.

"So pleased to meet you." Miss Browndell's voice was the resonant tone of angel song. "And I hope soon to meet your renowned husband."

Little hairs stood at attention on the nape of Eleanor's neck. An irrational urge rose to find Samuel, grab him, and run far and fast. She shifted her feet yet returned the woman's smile, forcing a light tone to her voice. "Oh?"

"Miss Browndell is in need of a guide to the Cherokee Lower Town. Naturally, I thought of your husband as he is"—Mrs. Greeley sniffed as if she'd stepped in a pile of horse droppings—"very familiar with such a route."

Grace tugged at her skirt, and she patted the girl's head, hopefully pacifying her for a few moments more. The woman in front of her simply must have a defect—and she determined, here and now, to find out what that might be.

"If I may be so bold, Miss Browndell," she lowered her voice, mixing just the right amount of curiosity and revere to her tone, "why would you risk travel to such a remote place?"

"I own it is a perilous mission, but you see, I owe it to my uncle's honor." A little sigh escaped her—much too fleeting to be serious grief. Either the woman belonged on a Drury Lane stage, or the impact of losing a loved one hadn't quite hit home.

A tiny quiver rippled across Miss Browndell's lower lip. "You see, it was my uncle's dying wish to bring the Word of God to the heathens."

"What makes you think they don't already have it?"

Samuel's deep voice wrapped around her from behind, the heat of his body warming her back as he stepped close. If she retreated, just an inch or so, would his strength calm her whirlwind thoughts—or ignite them into the wildfire she'd experienced in his arms?

Reverend Parker drew up behind Biz as well, a good-natured twinkle in his eyes. "Surely that's a moot point, Mr. Heath. Can one ever have enough of the Word of God?"

"Well said!" Though Miss Browndell spoke to the reverend, her brown eyes gazed past Eleanor—and devoured Samuel. "So happy to finally meet you, Mr. Heath. I hear you are the best guide in the area."

"That so?" Samuel's breath warmed her ear as he spoke.

"I'm told there's none better." The woman beamed up at him with a flutter to her eyelashes. "I'd like to hire your services, sir." She leaned forward with a little bounce to her toes, clapping her hands together as if the world were a party and she the guest of honor. "And I should like to set out come morning. Do say you'll take me?"

"Oh!" Mrs. Greeley's exclamation piggybacked on a screechy note from the fiddle. "Miss Browndell, I object. It wouldn't be seemly for a single young woman like yourself to travel unaccompanied with a man, even a married one. And most especially out in the wild."

"Ahh, but you forget, Mrs. Greeley. My manservant, Mingo, attends me." With a flicker of her fingers, she indicated a large black man standing with folded arms, ten paces off.

Eleanor bit her lip. Oh, how she wanted to spin about, study Samuel's face, and see if he seriously entertained the notion of guiding this woman and her servant to Keowee by himself. But she settled for listening with all her might, picking apart the inflection, volume, and timbre of his voice.

"It's a hard trail." His tone was flat. Emotionless. As matter-of-fact as if he merely instructed how to load a flintlock. "Nothing like the road you just traveled from Charles Towne."

"I assure you, Mr. Heath, I have excellent horsemanship—among other talents." Her smile changed, almost unnoticeable, but Eleanor didn't miss the predatory slant to her lips. "If you're half the guide I've heard about, then I trust you'll let no harm come my way."

Eleanor stiffened. This was no missionary, not the way her brown gaze fixed on Samuel. Too bold. Too daring. Why did no one else notice the woman was a fake? Didn't Samuel see through her facade?

Or had Miss Browndell's flattery entrapped him every bit as much as his former wife's?

In front of him, the fabric of Red Bird's dress stretched taut across her shoulders. Samuel stifled a smile. He couldn't see her face, but he imagined a tight pull to her brow and a frowning dimple deep-set on one cheek. The more Miss Browndell praised him, the more his wife stilled. He'd never seen her react so strongly to another woman. And—God's truth—he hadn't been this amused since the time Inoli slipped on a moss-covered rock and landed face-first in the creek. What sport it would be to fan that tiny ember of Red Bird's jealousy—if it was such—and see what kind of flame would erupt.

But playing with fire was dangerous, and this was no trifling situation, not if the woman asking him for passage to Keowee was the negotiator. He ground his teeth. Blast the British beasts! A good cover, but sending a woman out on such a dangerous mission? Had they no souls?

Grace let go of Red Bird's hand and grabbed on to his fingers instead. Miss Browndell's gaze flicked down to the child, hardened ever so slightly, then softened as she lifted her face back to his.

Something was definitely not right—or righteous—about this woman. He met Miss Browndell's gaze. "Why are you bent on leaving in the morning? Did you not just arrive this afternoon?"

She tilted her head—any more and her halo might slip. "Time is of the essence when it comes to saving souls, sir."

"Bravo, Miss Browndell." On the other side of Red Bird, standing directly behind her firebrand of a friend, the Reverend Parker grinned. A few new creases lined his face. What other marks had that hellcat Biz left behind? God surely had a sense of humor putting that one in the reverend's household.

"You've set your heart on a noble quest," Parker continued. "But Mrs. Greeley brings up a good point. It would not be proper to travel alone with naught but Mr. Heath and your manservant. No quarter should ever be given to impropriety. Mrs. Heath should be in attendance as well."

"Why, yes! A brilliant idea." Miss Browndell reached out and grabbed Red Bird's hands, clasping them in hers. "I should be delighted to have you as my companion. We shall become the dearest friends, I just know it."

Red Bird didn't yank back her hands—but neither did she speak.

Behind Samuel, the songs grew bawdier, the music as discordant as the suggestion. "If I agree—*if*—you should know what's ahead of you, miss. With my wife and child along, it'll take six days or more to reach Keowee. The trail is narrow, treacherous, and we pack our horses only. No wagon. No comforts."

"So long?" The woman dropped Red Bird's hands and lifted a pout his way. "Surely a man of your prowess could get us there sooner."

His earlier amusement fled. Her manipulation wrapped around his throat like a noose, altogether too familiar. This snip of a dress was a sight smaller than Mariah had been, but head to head, the two could've raced a fair match.

"I can do it in three days if pressed, but not with two women." He bent and scooped up Grace. "And especially not with a child."

"Hmm." Miss Browndell tapped a finger to her mouth, likely fully cognizant that the action pulled everyone's attention to her lips. One tap, two, three, then she turned her charms to Parker. "The souls, Reverend. An entire field ready to harvest. Just think of it. Surely you could take in the child while we travel to do God's work. Why, in a sense, you'd be part of bringing salvation to a dark, dark place."

Samuel's gut clenched. Keowee was light and air compared to the calculating black soul batting her eyelashes at the reverend.

"I hadn't thought of that, but yes. Of course." Parker glanced at him. "Miss Hunter and I would be delighted to look after little Grace in your absence."

Biz spun, poking a finger into Parker's chest. "Are you out of your God-fearing mind?"

"Perfect!" Miss Browndell clapped her hands once again. "It's settled, then, is it not?"

The woman leaned forward and blinked up at him, forgetting that her new "dearest friend" stood between them.

A ramrod couldn't have been straighter than Red Bird's spine. She didn't turn. Didn't seek his face. Didn't anything.

Samuel rubbed the back of his neck, muscles tight. God knew he didn't want to take Red Bird into Running Doe's lair. But neither could he leave her behind as easy prey for McDivitt. Rock. Hard place. Must that thin space always be where he lived?

"Mr. Heath?"

He lowered his hand. Four sets of eyes waited on his answer—but not the blue gaze he most wished to see. Either Red Bird's mind was far off and she'd not heard the question, or she chose not to influence his decision.

"Fine. We leave in the morning." He steeled himself for a finger to his own chest.

But Red Bird didn't turn and accuse the way Biz had. She didn't need to. The slight flinch jerking her shoulders was a more direct blow to his heart.

God, help me.

Chapter 28

An orange line thickened on the horizon, chasing away dawn's grey light and painting a healthy glow on Miss Browndell's cheeks. The woman was a portrait. Eleanor rubbed her knuckles across her own cheeks. She probably looked a sight, having slept on a blanket on the ground with Grace, while Miss Browndell had enjoyed a feather bed as a guest of Mrs. Greeley.

A frown creased Eleanor's brow. She probably looked as weathered as the log walls of the livery they stood in front of, waiting for Samuel. Wohali flicked her tail where she waited as well, tethered near the door.

"Oh! This is so exciting." Next to her, Miss Browndell beamed, her eyes as bright as her merry voice. "I've dreamed of sharing God's Word since I was a little girl."

Eleanor tugged on her sleeve hem, annoyed. How could the woman be so enthusiastic this early in the day? Or for that matter, at all? "I own I am more nervous than excited to travel into Cherokee lands, yet I have a husband to look after me. You are alone. It must be very difficult for you, having lost your uncle."

A shadow darkened her face—some kind of raincloud from the inside, for the sun broke true in a flawless sky. "Yes, my heart does ache, but I know my uncle would want me to continue."

Shame tasted as bitter as the coffee Samuel made before they'd broken camp that morning. La, she was becoming as rude as Biz. "I am sorry. I should not have mentioned your loss."

"All's forgiven." Miss Browndell leaned over and patted her arm. "Besides, I'm not alone anymore. I have Mr. Heath and you."

The woman's gaze shot to the open door of the stable where Samuel and her manservant, Mingo, emerged. Mingo led a mount laden with packs. Samuel held a firm grasp on a tether attached to a high-stepping horse and. . .Eleanor narrowed her eyes. That was no sidesaddle.

"This one's yours." He handed the reins to Miss Browndell, a smirk lifting half his mouth as the horse shied violently away from her.

Miss Browndell pulled the mount under control without so much as wrinkling her skirt. "Not that I don't appreciate the effort you've put into tacking up this horse for me, but where is the mount I rode in on?"

"That one would never make it. Not on the trail we'll be traveling." Samuel reset his hat and stared down at the petite woman. Either he credited her with proficiency or was making some kind of point. "If you can't manage this, say so now. I'll not have your broken neck on my conscience."

Eleanor held her breath. Would the journey end before it began? Yes! Hopefully. *Please, Lord?*

Miss Browndell arched her perfect little brow at Samuel, then urged the horse forward. She swung herself up and over the saddle, settling her skirts astride as if she rode like a man every day of her life. But hardly before her small backside stilled, the horse took off like buckshot.

"Samuel!" Eleanor's hands flew to her chest. "She will be hurt."

He stood, immovable, his eyes following the flight of the horse and rider—until Miss Browndell eventually trotted back, her cheeks all the rosier for the exertion.

"I think I shall enjoy this horse very much." She smiled down at him. "Intuitive choice, Mr. Heath."

A muscle jumped on Samuel's jaw, but he said nothing. He merely wheeled about and untethered Wohali. He swung one long leg up and over, indicated Mingo should do the same with his mount, then trotted over to Eleanor. Bending, he offered her a hand. "Up you go, Tatsu'hwa."

"You cannot be serious." She frowned up at him. "Where is my mount?"

"You ride with me."

Her lips pulled into a pout to rival one of Grace's, yet there was nothing to be done for it.

"I can manage a horse as well as Miss Browndell." She clamped her mouth shut. Did that petulant voice really belong to her?

"I'm not taking the risk." His dark eyes bore into hers, void of humor. Even the brim of his hat frowned at her. "Grab my hand and hike your foot up on mine. I'll do the rest."

Rage crawled like ants beneath her skin. She was being treated no better than a child. Was that what he thought of her? She grabbed his hand and hauled herself up, straddling the horse behind him like a common hussy. Altogether horrified, she yanked her hand from his.

He cut a sharp look over his shoulder, the sweep of his long hair brushing against her cheek. "You can hold on to your anger all you like, but you better grab hold of me, as well. I'm not exaggerating when I say this will be a hard ride."

If you're that concerned, perhaps you ought strap me to your back like Grace. The retort bristled on the end of her tongue, and she clenched her teeth. What was wrong with her?

"Is there a problem?" Miss Browndell angled her mount to line up with them. Behind her, Mingo's horse snorted.

"No." Eleanor lifted her chin. "No problem at all."

Twisting slightly, she slipped her arms around Samuel's waist in a slack hold. Solid muscle warmed through her sleeves, heating her skin. . .and her cheeks. This was obscene. No lady should have to be treated so—

"Hyah!"

Wohali took off before she was ready. Eleanor jerked backward, nearly tumbling off, but one of Samuel's hands grabbed her forearm before she slipped loose. She threw her body against his back and clenched handfuls of his shirt. Sweet heavens! This was going to be a long trip.

Shifting, she dared a peek over her shoulder. Mingo brought up the rear. Miss Browndell rode safeguarded in the middle, her eyes gleaming and hardly a hair out of place beneath her jaunty riding cap.

This was going to be a very long trip indeed.

The day wore on with few stops—only for water and necessary breaks, and once to retrieve bread and dried venison for them each. Miss Browndell chattered during their stops, mostly to Samuel, but her manservant never said a word. He remained at the fringe of their company, compliant to whatever Miss Browndell or Samuel asked of him, but completely silent.

Slowly, the grandeur of the Carolina woods chipped away at Eleanor's animosity. There was simply no way to remain out of sorts in the midst of such scenery. Noble pines, ash, and oaks towered around them, a canopy of green. Birdsong and squirrel chatter sang what might be praises, for surely how could it not be? The warmth of the afternoon sun on her back and the heat of her husband at her front lulled her into a trance.

Sleepy, she leaned her head against Samuel's shirt, the move of his muscles riding against her cheek. She felt brazen and free and for once didn't give a fig what anyone thought of it. She loved this land more than the stifling manor homes in England. And more than any man she'd ever known, she loved. . . .

She bolted upright, heart racing, unwilling to finish that thought.

Samuel glanced back, a lift to his brow, yet he said nothing.

Neither did she. Nor did she relax against him again.

An hour or so later, Samuel guided Wohali off the trail, onto a flattened area sheltered on one side by a great boulder wall and on the other by an uprooted tree. He reined in the horse and turned in the saddle. "You can slide off here."

Her legs tingled when her feet hit the ground. Her rear tingled even more. She arched, stretching the small of her back as Samuel swung off Wohali.

Miss Browndell and Mingo caught up, but neither dismounted. "Don't tell me we're stopping for the night." The lady's tone accused.

Samuel rolled his shoulders, saying nothing. So, it'd been a long ride for him as well? For some wicked reason, the notion pleased Eleanor.

"But it's not sunset yet." Miss Browndell huffed. "Surely we could cover a bit more ground?"

Samuel scrubbed his hand along his jaw, three days' growth rasping against his fingers. "You've proved yourself on that horse in daylight. Night's different. It falls fast and hard."

"But I—"

"But nothing. My wife is wearied, and we camp here."

Eleanor stared at him, mortified. *She* was tired? Wasn't he the one just rolling the kinks out of his shoulders?

"I'll gather some wood, and your man there can do the same." He nodded at Mingo, then wheeled about and stalked off, calling over his shoulder. "You women unpack the blankets and set up camp."

Behind her, Miss Browndell dismounted, her feet hardly a light tap as she landed. "It must be very difficult for you."

Eleanor turned, facing her. "What do you mean?"

"He's so. . .demanding." She fluttered her fingertips to where Samuel disappeared into the woods. "Seems a bit rugged for a woman such as yourself."

Was that a slight against Samuel or her? Either way, it rankled. "And what kind would that be?"

A feline smile lifted her lips. "Oh, nothing."

Insufferable. The woman reminded her of the housekeeper at the first home she'd served in. That woman had never liked her—and dropped innuendos into her mistress's ear so often that she'd had to defend herself constantly.

"Mingo, see to the wood." Miss Browndell marched past Eleanor, dusted off the top of a large rock, and sat.

Eleanor frowned. Clearly the woman had no intention of helping. She whirled and crossed to Wohali, working to unbuckle and remove the saddle. As she whumped the leather to the ground, her fingernail caught and tore off to the quick. She lifted her finger to her lips, tears stinging her eyes—but not from the pain. Who was this woman she'd become, manhandling a saddle, about to sleep another night on the ground? What of the English miss, accustomed to warm counterpanes and meals served on porcelain? The fabric of her life had been picked apart, thread by thread, leaving nothing but a heap of strings.

Miss Browndell watched her from her perch. "Tell me, Mrs. Heath, how did you meet and marry Mr. Heath? Such an unusual match."

She snatched a blanket off Wohali's back and shook it open with a sharp snap. How was she to answer that with any dignity? Kicking aside a few stones, she laid the wool flat on the ground, stalling while her mind whirled.

"Of course, if you'd rather not answer. . ." The woman's voice taunted from where she sat, as of yet, still not lifting a finger to help.

"No, I do not mind." It wasn't a lie, not really. Though it would prick to tell the full story, she'd finally settled on a version not quite as damaging to her pride. She retrieved one more blanket, speaking without facing the woman. "Samuel and I met when I arrived from England. He asked me to marry him straightaway. That is all there is to it."

"Hmm. Charming."

She smoothed the blankets and straightened, the knowing gleam in Miss Browndell's eyes an indictment. Nosy, prodding woman.

"I think I shall need a moment to myself. But I'm unsure of where to go." The woman's gaze darted about the immediate area and finally settled back on Eleanor. "Would you be so kind as to find a necessary place for us, being that you're used to such, er, harsh conditions?"

Eleanor clenched her teeth. The woman could manage a horse but not find a suitable place to do her business? She let out a long, low breath. In truth, she could use a break herself—especially from the conversation of Miss Browndell. She wheeled about and tromped back onto the trail, retracing the route to a side shoot she'd spied earlier.

She arrived back at camp the same time the sun slipped below the horizon, raising shadows from the dead. Samuel crouched in front of a pile of kindling, tinderbox in hand.

Miss Browndell huddled close to his side. "So glad you approve of the camp I made. Really, this trail is a bit much for your wife. Poor thing."

Poor thing! Eleanor's fingers dug into her palms. She was the one who'd set up the area. She stamped forward and dropped onto one of the blankets. Sparks caught the kindling and grew. Fire flared, painting everything red—exactly how she felt.

Samuel tucked away his flint and looked over at her. "You faring all right?"

"I am…" How to answer? Did he want truth or peace? And what about her? She gnawed the inside of her cheek as she considered which one she desired before finally answering. "I am well. Do not concern yourself."

He narrowed his eyes.

She yanked off her hat, a snag of hair falling down from the violent attack. With more force than necessary, she curled the wayward piece behind her ear, then set her battered straw hat in her lap and stared at it, unwilling to meet Samuel's gaze. She'd been wrong about this trip. Entirely wrong.

This journey would be never-ending.

Samuel dangled his hands between his knees where he squatted, studying Red Bird. Refusing to look at him, she sat like a toad on a log, trying hard not to be noticed—quite the opposite of the woman perched on a rock next to him. That one was a peacock in a skirt.

He rose and crossed over to his wife, extending a hand. "Let's walk."

She lifted her eyes to his fingers, but no farther.

Neither did she grab hold.

"Tatsu'hwa," he whispered.

"Oh, don't worry on my account." Miss Browndell called behind him. "I'll be fine right here by the fire. No doubt Mingo will return soon with more wood and we'll have quite a merry blaze going before you return."

Red Bird shoved out her hand and wrapped her fingers in his. He pulled her to her feet, and when she tried to yank away, he held tight. Guiding her back onto the trail, the last of day's light shading everything to monotone, he strode until they were beyond earshot of Miss Browndell.

He cut her a sideways glance. "You feeling poorly? I need to know if you are. There's no shame in illness."

Catching him off-guard, she wrenched her hand from his. "I told you I am well."

He hid a grin. Her behaviour said anything but. Clasping her shoulders, he forced her to face him. "You got something to say?"

"No. Nothing." Her bottom lip quivered more than when he refused Grace a sweetmeat from Greeley's.

"You've been a trap about to snap ever since you crossed paths with that woman." He leaned closer. More than words spoke truth. The tic of an eye. The barest twitch of a jaw. He studied every nuance. "Why? What's gotten into you?"

She jerked her face aside.

He grasped her chin and drew it back, resistance warm against his fingers. "I asked you a question."

The blue of her eyes changed to purple-black—the threat before a storm. "How can you be so taken in by her? She is a fake! A sham. I do not know why Miss Browndell wants passage to Keowee, but I doubt very much it has anything to do with God."

Blast it all! Did she not credit him with any sense whatsoever? He counted to ten before answering. "You think I don't know that?"

"Then why are you guiding her?" She blinked up at him, her brow a confusing mix of lines—lines that straightened as her eyes narrowed. "Oh. I see."

Those three words changed everything. The freckles on the bridge of her nose darkened—no. Her entire countenance blackened to a sharp piece of obsidian. She twisted from his hold and sidestepped him.

He caught her arm and pulled her back. Staring hard into her eyes, he read her soul, and the jealousy he saw there sank to his gut, as satisfying as a bowl of bison stew on a winter's day. His mouth curved into a smile. "Go on. You might as well admit it, for you're doing a poor job of hiding your feelings."

Fire flamed on Red Bird's cheeks, matching the color of her hair. "What are you accusing me of, Mr. Heath?"

"You know. . . ." He reached out slowly, provocatively, and ran his fingertips soft up the curve of her neck, brushed a whisper over her earlobe, and nestled a wayward curl up with the rest.

Her nostrils flared. So did her blush.

His grin grew, and he tapped her on the nose. "You're mighty pretty when those cheeks turn all pink like."

She whirled and marched off.

He chuckled. It was entirely too much fun to tease her. But as he followed and they drew near to camp, his smile faded. If Red Bird was this vexed by the slight flirtations of Miss Browndell, the attentions of Running Doe might kill her—leastwise her spirit.

Miss Browndell glanced up at their approach. "Sort everything out?"

Behind her, Mingo stood like a dark sentinel. The whites of his eyes gleamed in the firelight, but he said nothing. He couldn't. His tongue had been cut out long ago. Samuel doubted Red Bird had figured that out— nor would he tell her unless she asked.

Dropping to the blanket, Red Bird pulled another cover atop her and turned her back to them all. For a moment, nothing but the click and whir of insects broke the silence.

Miss Browndell tipped her face to his. The campfire cast shadows on the boulder wall to the north. An eerie sight. Like bats swooping out of a cave.

"Bed down." His gaze slipped from Miss Browndell to Mingo. "Both of you. I'll see to the horses and take first watch. You can take second."

He turned—and footsteps crackled the forest floor behind.

Miss Browndell caught up to him by the time he reached for Wohali's tether. "I do hope I've not caused any strife between you and your wife. Lord knows there's enough discontent in this land." Her small hand rested on his sleeve. "I wonder, Mr. Heath. . .are you discontent?"

He met her bold stare. "Not anymore."

Her mouth twisted. "What a curious answer. You are a puzzle, sir." Then she lowered her voice, quiet enough that only he could hear. "One I intend to figure out."

Chapter 29

Green. Brown. Up. Down. Horse and leather and Samuel's back. The days wore into a routine on the trail, one that Eleanor might almost embrace if not for the continual burr of Miss Browndell's company. God could not possibly have found a better way to test her charity, for the woman pushed her to the limits of civility—and beyond.

On the fourth day, early afternoon, they crested a wooded bluff, and Samuel reined Wohali to a halt. "We walk the rest of the way."

He helped Eleanor dismount with a strong arm. Mingo slid from his seat, but Miss Browndell remained astride.

The woman quirked a brow. "Would it not be faster to ride?"

Lifting his hands to his mouth, Samuel cupped them and blew out a bird sound. Eleanor couldn't guess what kind—but the ethereal call would haunt her dreams, so unearthly did it float through the woods.

Then he pierced Miss Browndell with a dark-eyed gaze. "We enter as one of the people, not as conquerors."

Three brown-skinned men, clad only in breechclouts and deerskin leggings, materialized from the woods, as solid as the tree trunks from which they emerged. Only a leather strap crossed their bare chests, bows and arrows slung across their backs. Each wore a tomahawk on one hip and a knife on the other—just like her husband. But unlike Samuel, their hair draped down their back in long tails, black as pitch.

The largest of the three strode over to Samuel and they clasped forearms, speaking some kind of greeting. The warrior cut a dark glance at Mingo, uttering foreign words, then flashed a smile at Samuel, who threw back his head, laughing.

Miss Browndell slipped from her horse and drew near. "Apparently your husband doesn't know only these woods—he knows the people."

They followed two of the men down the trail, Samuel leading Wohali with Eleanor at his side, and Miss Browndell and Mingo guiding their respective mounts behind them. The other native stayed behind on the crest.

Through the trees, Eleanor spied a vast settlement down in a valley, stretched along a wide river. Squares of tilled land dotted the outer edges. Cone-shaped huts squatted next to rectangular dwellings, smoke curling out the tops. At the center was a large open space, grass brown and flattened. People scattered like bunches of sheep—leastwise that was the nearest image Eleanor could pull from her experience. It was hard to make sense of this settlement. The closer they drew, the more her heart pounded. The people were fearsome, night to day compared to those in an English village—especially the bare-chested men.

The path opened into the clearing, and she huddled closer to Samuel. "How long will we stay here?"

"A few days." He glanced down at her, and a deliberate smile stretched across his face—the kind that sifted and measured and stirred up more feelings than she wanted to admit.

Mouth suddenly dry, she licked her lips. "Why do you look at me that way?"

"You're as twitchy as a wren." Though his hair covered one eye, no doubt both glimmered. "What are you nervous about?"

How could he do that? Dive right into her thoughts uninvited? She scowled. "Noth—"

"Don't tell me nothing, Tatsu'hwa."

She sighed. Sometimes he was as insufferable as Miss Browndell. "It is all so. . .foreign. I hardly know what to expect."

"Do you think I would lead you into danger? There's nothing to fear here."

The tightness in her stomach lessened. Of course not. This man had stood in harm's way on her behalf time and time again. What had she been thinking? She offered a small smile. "No, you would not."

He winked. "Then don't fret."

The man ahead of them stopped. Samuel handed him Wohali's lead and with a nod of his head indicated Miss Browndell should hand hers over to Mingo. "Your man and Rides Like Wind will see to the horses. You come with us."

Eleanor huddled closer to Samuel, thankful he knew exactly what to do and say. Without him, she'd be at a loss—and they both knew it. She peeked up at him. "What will become of Miss Browndell now that she is here?"

"I suppose that's up to her."

"What do you mean?"

He peered over the top of her head, to Miss Browndell, then wheeled about and strode toward the center of the village. Children trotted toward him. So did others nearby.

She dashed after him, gaining his side before private conversation would be impossible. "Samuel? Will she be in danger?"

"No." A glower darkened his face. "She *is* the danger."

Eleanor blinked, astounded, as much from Samuel's blunt statement as from the foreign sights and smells. Though she desired to press Samuel further on the subject, now was not the time. Their threesome was quickly becoming the center of attention. She'd read of curious natives surrounding whites, pawing at their garments, touching their faces. Sucking in a breath, she steeled herself for the violation.

But oddly, the people gathered around Samuel, not her or Miss Browndell. In fact, the only ones who showed any interest in her were a few children.

Samuel chatted easily with all—and everyone seemed to have something to tell him, though she couldn't understand a word anyone said. This went on for quite some time until a tall man, all sinews and brawn, cut a path straight to Samuel. A silver gorget gleamed on his chest, and engraved armbands adorned each brawny bicep. He laid a hand on Samuel's shoulder, and Samuel returned the gesture, connecting them in a way that Eleanor suspected went further than touch.

Afternoon sunlight glinted almost bluish streaks in the native's black braids. After more words, he released Samuel, and his dark gaze shot to her. A line of blue dots ran over his nose, extending from cheek to cheek. Near his temple, a black feather dangled at one side—and she gasped. This is what Inoli would look like in twenty years. Was this man his father?

Miss Browndell leaned toward her. "I didn't realize your husband spoke Cherokee so fluently."

She nibbled her lip. She knew he spoke the language, but so well? And how would Miss Browndell fare when Samuel left for home? "Miss Browndell, are you sure you want to—"

"Excuse me." Miss Browndell darted around a few women who'd approached, blocking their line of sight to Samuel.

Eleanor was about to follow when something tugged her skirt. She looked down, into eyes the deep hue of drinking chocolate, black hair running free and wild around a child's smudged face. Her heart lurched.

Lighten the coloring, and she might almost be gazing at Grace. Oh, how she missed that little sprite.

Stooping, she smiled at the girl. "Hello."

Tiny white teeth flashed. The girl reached out and yanked Eleanor's hair, then giggled and ran off.

Eleanor rubbed the sting with her fingertips. Sprite indeed. That one and Grace would be a force to be reckoned with should they ever meet.

She straightened—then froze.

Eyes much darker, set deep into a face weathered to leather, stared at her the same unsettling way Samuel did. Lines at the corners of the woman's mouth puckered like fabric bunched too tightly, as if she couldn't make up her mind whether Eleanor were friend or foe. The top of her head barely reached Eleanor's chin, but with the way her shoulders pinned back and her jaw jutted to a regal tilt, she might be royalty.

"Umm, hello," Eleanor murmured. What else could she do? Samuel should have at least taught her a greeting, for the woman stared at her expectantly.

But it worked. The woman smiled, looking like a jack-o-lantern, so few were her teeth. When she spoke, her words whistled, a musical accompaniment to the singsong language.

With surprising speed, the woman shot out her hand and grabbed Eleanor's, then pressed Eleanor's fingers against her bony chest and bowed her head over it.

Eleanor fought the urge to jerk away. What kind of custom was this? She didn't want to offend, but neither did she want to touch the woman in such an intimate fashion. Beneath the woman's soft buckskin, her chest rose and fell. Eleanor stared at the zigzaggy part in her hair, unsure what to do or think.

An eternity later, Samuel's deep voice rumbled next to her, and the woman released her hand.

Eleanor grabbed handfuls of her skirts, unwilling to let anyone else repeat the procedure.

The woman grinned up at Samuel, eyes bright and watery. Some kind of emotion thickened her voice, and so many words flew between them Eleanor wondered if they even took time to listen to each other.

Eventually, Samuel burst out laughing. He'd laughed more here in the past half hour than in all the months she'd lived with him.

Eleanor frowned. "What is she saying?"

Samuel cocked a brow at her. "She asks if I am your warrior."

Her breath caught in her throat. If these people thought that she and him were. . .that they belonged together as man and wife. . .what other kind of customs would be expected? "What did you tell her?"

He brushed his thumb along her cheek and smirked. "Maybe you ought to learn the language."

Usually she liked it when he winked at her. This time she did not.

The woman garbled out more words, all the while lifting a rawhide thong from around her neck. A single claw was tethered to it. She approached Eleanor and settled the necklace over her head, straightening it at her collarbone, then retreated and beamed at Samuel.

Eleanor fingered the black claw. It curved smooth against her touch, the point long since worn down. The woman nodded at her, clearly expecting some kind of reply.

Samuel bent and whispered in her ear. "Say *wado*. It means thank you."

"Wah-doh." Her tongue ran over her teeth, tangling on the word, and she tried once more a bit louder. "Wado."

The woman bowed, then turned and disappeared into the remaining onlookers.

Eleanor peered up at Samuel. "Why did she give me a gift?"

A huge grin split his face. "It's not for you. Come."

He strode past a gaggle of children, and Eleanor stifled a growl. Judging by his tone and determined step, she'd get no more information from him.

Miss Browndell linked arms with her, propelling her forward. "I can tell you what the woman said."

Eleanor cut her a sideways glance. "You speak Cherokee?"

"Of course, dearest." Miss Browndell's fingers patted her arm. "How else would I impart the Word of God, hmm?"

Eleanor's earlier meal of blackened fish turned over in her stomach. She hadn't quite yet figured out what exactly Miss Browndell was up to, but she'd wager high stakes it didn't have anything to do with spreading the Gospel. Any apprehension she'd entertained for the woman's safety here at Keowee disappeared.

Ahead, Samuel stopped near one of the cone-shaped dwellings.

"It seems odd that I was singled out with this." She lifted the bear claw, hating to ask Miss Browndell but hating even more not to. "Why did I get a necklace?"

"As your husband said, it is not for you." The woman flashed a wicked smile at her. "The old lady said it is for your son."

Eleanor shook her head, doubting very much whether Miss Browndell spoke Cherokee as she claimed. "But I do not have a son."

The woman's grin grew. "Apparently you will."

Samuel tugged the brim of his hat, shadowing his eyes to watch the approach of his wife. The bear claw bounced against her bodice as she walked. Grandmother's prophecy burned a trail to his gut—and lower. If Red Bird knew the significance of the bauble, her prim senses would be mortified enough to swim all the way back to England.

He folded his arms and leaned against the side of the lodge where he waited, toying with the idea of telling her. Such sparks, such an explosion that would be—and God help him, he'd rather that passion be spent in fulfilling Grandmother's prediction instead of rousing his wife to anger.

Though the smaller of the two, Miss Browndell pulled Red Bird along, their arms linked. Whatever she said caused his wife's head to shake with a violent dismissal. His former warmth chilled. Miss Browndell's smirk and the arrogant lift of her shoulder set his teeth on edge. The sooner they shed this snakeskin, the better.

Red Bird disentangled herself from the woman.

He stepped from the wall and faced Miss Browndell. "This is the guest lodge. I suggest you rest, for you've been granted privilege to speak at the council this evening. I suspect it will run late. No doubt you'll have a lot to say. . .and I'm guessing you won't need a translator."

"I daresay you could provide the service though, hmm?" She lifted her face to his. The sun had pinked Red Bird's cheeks, but not this woman's. Her skin remained porcelain, as icy and cool as her stare. "You are much more than a guide, are you not?"

He bent and spoke for her ear alone. "I think we're both more than what we admit to."

Then he grabbed his wife's hand and stalked off before the woman could say anything further.

Red Bird's feet skipped double time to his. "Should I not accompany her?"

"No, you don't stay there." He nodded a greeting to old White Owl as they passed. The elder sat on a woven mat near his lodge. His eyes, milky with age, followed their movement.

"Did you not say that was the guest lodge?" Red Bird's step hitched as she looked over her shoulder, back to where Miss Browndell had hopefully taken his advice and rested—instead of stirring up trouble, as she no doubt would.

"You are not a guest." He squeezed Red Bird's fingers. "You are my wife."

"But where are we going?"

"To my family's lodge."

Her fingers wrenched from his, and she stopped smack center of the village. "You may play word games with Miss Browndell all you like, but I will not have it. Who are you? Really?"

Nearby, the steady grind of corn being pounded for bread and the shushing noise of arrowheads being sharpened stopped. Two boys ran past, giggling, but the laughter of three women quieted, their gazes questioning Red Bird's display. If he didn't get her moving, soon and quietly, all the aunts would pour from their lodges and circle them like vultures.

He reached for his wife's hand, a trickle of sweat inching between his shoulder blades. He must maneuver her to move along willingly or more tongues would be wagging tonight than Miss Browndell's. "Do not shame me. Come. I will tell you all you want to know."

Her blue eyes narrowed, but she wrapped her fingers in his. "Very well."

He blew out a long, low breath. Relating his past wouldn't be easy—but at least since she followed him, it wouldn't be public. He steered her toward his grandmother's lodge. How to recount years of loss and confusion in such a short distance?

"Samuel?" she prodded.

If nothing else, he'd married a persistent woman. He peered at her from the corner of his eye. "I may be wealthy now, but I didn't grow up that way. My father worked the shipyards in Charles Towne, scrapping for every bit of coin he could. And he was a scrapper—Scots-Irish blood in his veins. Thankfully, though, my mother and I were the only mouths he had to feed."

"But if you grew up in Charles Towne, how can this be your home?"

Late afternoon sun beat against his shoulders. He tried to hold on to the warmth of it, the softness of Red Bird's fingers entwined with his, the smoky waft of home fires and damp scent of the river. But it vanished. All. How could a man remember so vividly the blood and loss of a boy almost twenty years later?

"I was a lad of seven when I lost them." The words tasted sour, and he was unsure if he should spit more out or swallow them all. He'd never told any of this to Mariah. He'd never told anyone.

"How?"

He'd have to answer, for she'd not be put off. But he allowed Red Bird's question to float around until they drew nearer his grandmother's lodge.

"My father was pressed into service by the British Royal Navy—supposedly the finest fleet in all the seas." His throat tightened, and he cleared it. "Nothing fine about it, though. He was dead before his ship set sail, caught dockside, the life flogged from him for desertion."

He shook his head. Even now the brutality still made no sense. "All he wanted to do was say goodbye."

Red Bird's eyes shimmered up into his. "I am so sorry."

"Don't be. I'm long past pity." He stopped in front of the open door of Grandmother's summer lodge. The familiar smell of juniper, sage, and dried hickory nuts greeted him, removing the sting of memories better left buried.

Behind him, grass flattened beneath leather, and a low voice followed. "Ya'nu, a word."

He stifled a snort. He'd expected Standing Raven to seek him out, but this soon? He'd not been here an hour yet. He swept out his hand toward Grandmother's lodge before turning to face the man. "Go in and rest Tatsu'hwa. As I told Miss Browndell, it will be a long night. We will speak more later."

"But. . .what of you?" The little dimple on her cheek frowned at him. "Will you not come in with me?"

Did she want him at her side simply because she wanted to hear the rest of his story? Or because she was anxious? Or. . .dare he hope. . .that she wanted to be with him? He reached and tucked back the same rogue curl that always managed to escape from her hairpins, fighting the desire to brush his knuckle along her smooth cheek. "I will come back for you. Grandmother is inside, and she will be more than happy to care for your needs."

Red Bird's nose bunched. "Grandmother?"

He lifted the bear claw at her neck, holding it up for emphasis. "The one who gave you this."

Her brows shot skyward. "She is your grand—"

"Ya'nu!" Standing Raven called from behind. "Come."

With a sigh, he turned from Red Bird, ignoring her protests as he strode to Standing Raven. The man didn't speak another word. His long legs simply ate up ground as he wove past summer and winter lodges. He stopped at the riverbank, folded his arms, and gazed out at the water.

Samuel followed. There was nothing more to be done. One could poke a stick at Standing Raven all he liked, but the man would not be moved until he was ready.

Finally, Standing Raven spoke, without varying his gaze from the horizon. "The Beloved Man has heard of your arrival—and of your white wife."

Samuel bent, scooping up some pebbles. One by one he skipped them across the water. Two could play at the waiting game. When the last of the ripples dissipated, he turned to Standing Raven. "And?"

"He sends me." The man looked down his crooked nose, broken several times over—once by Samuel. "He says it is time for you to choose."

Samuel threw his arms wide. "It is time for everyone to choose. You know the people are not one. Some back the British, believing their lies to stop the stealing of land. Others side with the colonists, for they are many with their firearms and promises."

Standing Raven lifted his chin. "That is not an answer."

"Well I don't have one."

A scowl pulled the man's face, the bump on his nose more prominent from the action. "You are as divided as your blood."

"Do I not speak truth?" He huffed. How to make him understand? "You know the people are not one on this matter, bloodline or not."

Standing Raven's jaw hardened. Water rippled, lapping at the banks. A host of sparrows swooped overhead. But the man said nothing, just stared, a study of stillness.

Samuel widened his stance, preparing for the long haul.

He wasn't disappointed.

The sun shifted lower on Standing Raven's shoulders before he spoke again. "I have thought these things myself. . .how to turn my back on brothers I would die for. Yet I stand with whatever the Beloved Man decides."

"I respect that—but I will not commit." Not out loud—and especially not to the Beloved Man's earpiece.

"You cannot straddle a river for long, Ya'nu, and expect to remain standing."

He grunted. He knew that, all too well. . .which is why he'd already made his choice.

But if Attakullakulla knew his stance, the man would have him shunned as anathema for some trumped-up reason—and Grandmother, his only living ancestor, would be lost to him forever.

He pivoted and stalked away on silent feet. It didn't matter the color of skin. McDivitt. Attakullakulla. Black hearts beat in them both.

Chapter 30

Samuel ducked into the large council lodge, trading fresh night air for the heat of many bodies packed into the meeting space. All were here—except those confined to their sleeping mats—even children, though the little ones were relegated to the back edges. And that's where Miss Browndell's manservant Mingo squatted. Always in the shadows. Keeping watch over his mistress. His intent was as hard to figure out as a shaman's dream. The man's loyalty lay with Miss Browndell, but why?

Beside him, Red Bird gripped his hand tighter. He'd intended to explain what would happen during this council, but she'd slept away the daylight hours. Whatever Grandmother had put in her tea still coaxed a yawn from her. Thankfully his clan sat nearest the door, and he bade her and Miss Browndell to remain near to him. Grandmother nodded her head in greeting as they sat.

Directly across from them, Attakullakulla rose, standing at the edge of the cleared center. Samuel schooled his face to remain blank, but inside his breath caught. How the Beloved Man had aged since he'd last seen him. New creases carved lines at the sides of his mouth and eyes. His head remained shaved, except for a long scalplock, which was now laced through with white strands. Golden rings pulled his earlobes to his shoulders, but likely not from the weight. More like the drooping skin of an elder, matching the flap at his chin.

The Beloved Man lifted his hand, and chatter ceased. "My family, it is an omen the white woman comes the night before I leave for Chota. It was meant."

Grunts and whispers traveled the circle. Samuel resisted cutting Miss Browndell a sideways glance. No wonder she'd been so insistent on getting here. If she'd missed this opportunity, she'd have had to wait until next year.

"We will hear what the English have to say, and then we will talk." The Beloved Man retreated to his mat on the floor. "Speak, woman."

Samuel glanced at Miss Browndell, wondering if she'd understood. More often than not, his instincts proved true. Would they this time?

She met his stare. . .then slowly rose and advanced.

"Brothers and sisters." She pivoted as she spoke, ensuring all might hear. "I come with an offer from your family across the big water. The great ones see your land is being taken, that you are pushed from your hunting grounds. And they are in agreement—it is not right."

Many heads bobbed. But not all. Samuel mentally tallied those who showed no eagerness, then shot to where Inoli's father sat. The man could be a champion card player should he ever wish to enter the white man's world. Not surprising. Samuel gave up gaming with Inoli years ago because he always won.

Miss Browndell reached into her pocket and pulled out a single gold coin the size of her palm, along with a folded piece of rag paper. Torchlight gleamed off the scarlet seal affixed to the document, looking like a pool of blood. The image lifted bumps on Samuel's arms.

"Once you and your son, Dragging Canoe, pledge your warriors, this treaty ensures peace between our people." She handed the money and the paper to Attakullakulla.

The Beloved Man turned the coin over, the flash of gold gleaming in his eyes. He tucked it inside the opening of his white trade shirt, then pulled out a knife. With a quick jerk, he slit the seal, the movement eerily like slashing a throat. His black eyes traveled the length of the paper, then he passed it off to Standing Raven, who sat at his right hand.

Miss Browndell stood firm, without a ripple to her skirt.

A baby wailed in the interim, and once the suckling smack of lips replaced the crying, Attakullakulla spoke. "Peace will not be had by words and gold alone, woman."

Next to him, Red Bird shifted, scooting closer to his side. His stomach clenched—even without looking to see what bothered her. Ten to one if he glanced two clans to his right, he'd spy Running Doe giving his wife the evil eye. He knew it would happen. Could see it coming like a far-off storm billowing on the horizon. Likely it was a good thing Red Bird had remained hidden in Grandmother's lodge all day.

"What you say is true, Great Chief." Miss Browndell's confident tone drew every eye toward her. "And this is why, once you and Dragging Canoe sign that treaty, wagonloads of firearms and ammunition await you at an undisclosed cache."

Samuel stiffened, listening with his whole body. This was why he'd been sent. The single purpose to enduring Miss Browndell's abrasive personality the past five days. Men would die for this information.

Hopefully he wouldn't be one of them.

The Beloved Man rose, towering above Miss Browndell's small frame. Yet she did not flinch.

"Why should I believe you, white woman? Where is your proof?" He grabbed her jaw and held fast. With the snap of his arm, he could break her neck.

Near the door, Mingo shot to his feet—but as quickly two warriors arose on each side of him, both lifting a knife to his neck.

Miss Browndell stood tall. "Release me." Her words came out garbled.

Tension thickened, as strong as the smell of bear grease. Attakullakulla narrowed his eyes to slits, then released her.

Miss Browndell slipped her hand inside a side-slit in her skirt to access her pocket and pulled out a shiny, new, double-barreled breech-loading pistol—the same type of deadly firearm Major Rafferty carried.

Samuel eyed the woman with a new understanding. No wonder she'd not been the least bit nervous to travel those few days to Newcastle with naught but a Negro. With Mingo and that pistol, she could kill a pack of wolves in a heartbeat.

She offered the pistol on an outstretched palm. "Just a sample."

The Beloved Man snatched the pistol, sighted along the barrel, then aimed it directly at the woman's forehead.

Silence sealed the lips of every clan member. Red Bird slapped her hand over her mouth. Behind him, Mingo's breaths came heavy and fast.

A smile split a gash in the Beloved Man's face. He lowered the pistol and tossed it to Standing Raven, then untucked the talking stick from his waistband. His black eyes sought Samuel's. "Ya'nu, take the woman back to the lodge."

"But. . ." The word died on Miss Browndell's lips, so fiercely did Attakullakulla turn on her, shoving the carved piece of hickory in her face.

"The talking stick is in my hand, woman. Not yours. You go now."

Samuel stood, pulling Red Bird up alongside. Normally he'd mind leaving a council meeting mid-discussion, but not tonight—not if it meant he could somehow wrangle the munitions information out of Miss Browndell.

And he had to—or a killing spree would bloody this land, the likes of which these colonies had never seen.

Eleanor fixed her gaze on the awful sight of Miss Browndell toe to toe with the most fearsome warrior she'd ever seen. The man shoved a stick in her face, yet she didn't cower. Steel girded the woman's bones—and for a single, curious moment, Eleanor wished she might be as brave as Miss Browndell, for it certainly captured the attention of her husband. He'd not pulled his eyes from her since this council began. He'd never studied her, his own wife, that intently, and for some odd reason, that irked her. Though it oughtn't. . .should it?

She lowered her face, refusing to watch the confusing scene—or sort through her even more confusing emotions. Surely such unrest must be blamed upon the strange-tasting tea Samuel's grandmother had urged on her this afternoon. Or maybe she'd simply become oversentimental after hearing about the death of his parents. Whatever the reason, no good would come of forgetting that Samuel Heath owned her, nothing more.

Pinching a loose thread on her sleeve between forefinger and thumb, she rolled it back and forth, trying to ignore the hard-edged stare of a native woman who sat farther down the circle. Eleanor had made the mistake of glancing at her when she'd entered the lodge, and that brief flash of contact had lifted tiny bumps on her arms. She'd seen that look before—the night she'd refused her father's proposal to keep company with one of his debt holders. Rage came in many colors, of course, but she'd identified a new shade that night—hellfire red.

Why would a native woman take such an instant dislike to her? Had whites been responsible for some tragedy in her young life? For she was young. Maybe a few years less than herself. The woman's skin was the lovely color of burnt cream, fresh from the oven, and her deerskin dress hugged shapely curves. Surely she didn't see Eleanor as competition for one of the other men here?

Silence fell on the council, but it came as a sweet reprieve. The twisted language made no sense whatsoever, and in truth, she was tired of hearing it. Why had Samuel brought her?

His big hand wrapped around her arm, lifting her to her feet. She peered at him, but his face was unreadable in the dimly lit lodge. He led her to the door without a word.

The urge to stamp her foot at his crass treatment nearly caused her to stumble out into the night air. She knew exactly how Grace must feel—for he wouldn't have treated her any differently. Shuffled here. Put there. Stay in this lodge. No, go to that one. Eleanor pulled from his grasp as soon as they cleared the council hut. "Why did Miss Browndell give that man money and a firearm? What did they say? Surely this had nothing to do with God."

Samuel retrieved one of the many unlit vigil torches leaned against the lodge wall and touched it to a larger flame that burned atop a beacon post. "None of your concern, wife."

"Stop treating me like a child!" This time she did stamp her foot—and immediately regretted it.

He lifted his hand to her face, humor twitching the corners of his mouth. "Then stop behaving like one. Now I'm going to cut you some slack because Lord knows what Grandmother gave you to drink today, but listen well. What's being said in there"—he jerked his head toward the lodge— "is dangerous for you to know. A danger I'm not willing to take. Understand?"

"No. I do not. If you would just—"

"Well, well." Miss Browndell's voice interrupted. "I hope I'm not intruding upon a tender moment."

Samuel dropped his hand, and Eleanor retreated a step as the woman fully emerged from the lodge. She advanced toward Samuel, stepping so close, her skirt swung out to touch his pants hem.

"I'd like a word with you, Mr. Heath." She slipped a catty glance at Eleanor. "Alone."

Eleanor looked deep inside, trying to find her own measure of steel, resolving to not care one way or another how Samuel answered. Even so, she leaned toward him to hear his answer.

He turned to her, away from Miss Browndell and her black knight, Mingo. The movement reset her world on its axis.

Then knocked it completely askew when he handed her the torch. "Do you remember your way back to Grandmother's lodge?"

She gripped the stick, burnt pitch acrid in her nose, his flat rejection of her every bit as acerbic. Not that she wanted him to spend the night with her, but surely he wouldn't while it away with Miss Browndell?

And why would she care if he did?

She gave a sharp, short nod.

Something flickered in Samuel's dark eyes—something more than firelight.

"You'll be fine, Tatsu'hwa." His voice softened, mellow as a late summer day. "There is no danger for you here."

Some of her resolve drained, but not all. Suddenly she was unsure which to hold on to—the tender tone he used with her alone, or anger that he was choosing Miss Browndell over her.

The decision was made for her. Miss Browndell stepped up to his side and ran a finger along his bicep. "Don't fret, Mrs. Heath. I'll return him in one piece."

Heat blazed up Eleanor's neck and spread across her cheeks. A more brazen woman would not be found walking the Wapping Wharves at night. Yet Samuel said nothing.

His jaw might have hardened, but Eleanor couldn't be sure, for she whirled so fast the torch spluttered. She stomped ahead, but the farther she drew from the council chamber and the bright beacon torches, the more blackness closed in on her little light. She swallowed. Maybe it hadn't been so bad being treated like Grace. At least she hadn't been alone.

An owl's mournful hoot echoed the emptiness in her heart. How had her life come to this? Pining like a schoolgirl for a man she'd pledged the rest of her life to.

She stopped dead in her tracks, stunned, the realization as bright as a noonday sun. She loved him—and had for quite some time if she were brutally honest. And it was brutal, this feeling, as if she walked upon glass and must be careful or all would shatter. For one crazed eternity, she considered turning back, running full force into Samuel's arms, and telling him everything. How she wanted him. How he'd become her world. How she needed his touch, his kiss. . . .

Miss Browndell's giggle carried on the night air, stabbing her in the back. Sucking in a lungful of cool air, Eleanor packed up all her tender feelings and stowed them away. Far. Deep. Better to hide them and forget—a lesson she'd learned all too well the day her father stopped loving her.

Grasping the torch tighter, she marched across the field, stars and crescent moon her only companions. So be it, then. She'd show Samuel Heath. She'd be the best, most compliant servant wife he could ever imagine—but he'd never coax another smile out of her. Let him savor Miss Browndell's lurid grins, if that's what he really wanted.

She fumed all the way to the darkened lodge, set close to the river.

A good sleep would smooth the jagged edges of her emotions. Maybe she might even find another cup of his grandmother's tea. She stopped before the door, allowing the nearby river sounds to wash over her ruffled feelings. Indeed. A sound sleep on soft furs. The whooshing rush of water over rocks.

And the sharp crack of a stick just behind her.

Chapter 31

Samuel watched Red Bird stalk off into the darkness, shoulders straight, steps determined, the sway of her hips denouncing him in ways he wasn't sure he understood. Something simmered under that lid of compliance. A slow fuse burned. When and where she'd explode concerned him. What kind of damage, how much hurt, and why worried him more.

"Such an odd little wife you've chosen, Mr. Heath." Miss Browndell's voice curled into his ear. "Which makes you all the more an enigma. I rather like that."

He spun and grabbed her by the throat, pressure not enough to choke her, just the right amount to make a point. Behind her, Mingo advanced—until Samuel lifted a killing stare at him.

He lowered his gaze back to the woman. "You're no more interested in me than you are in any man. Drop the charade."

"We all know you won't harm me." Her voice vibrated beneath his palm. "We are two players on the same team, you and I."

The idea of being yoked with her for anything left a rancid taste in his mouth. He dropped his hand and retreated a step. "I'm listening."

A skeleton couldn't have grinned with more eerie finesse. "Major Rafferty said you hold your cards tight to your chest. He wasn't jesting."

His mind rifled through every conversation he'd had with the woman the past five days. She'd never once mentioned the major. Either this was a trap. . .or a confirmation that she believed him loyal to the crown. But which?

He slipped his gaze past her to the open door of the council, where the low drone of discussion wafted out, then snapped his stare back to her. "These are dangerous times. I had to be sure of you and your manservant."

She tipped her face to a seductive tilt. "And are you?"

Absolutely. This woman was death in a skirt. He folded his arms instead of voicing his conviction. "Certainty is a currency I rarely trade in."

"Have I not shown my true colors?" Torchlight danced in her eyes, the

241

flames reflecting a soul as lost as Hades.

Fatigue weighed heavy on his shoulders. This night, this entire journey sapped the life from him. He walked a razor-thin line between showing too much eagerness in conversation or not enough. Slipping one way or the other would keep the information inside her locked tight.

He unfolded his arms and lowered his voice, speaking as he might to a friend—though the act chipped away at his dignity. "Like I said, Miss Browndell, the charade is over, and for that I am grateful. What do you want to know?"

She glanced over her shoulder at the lodge, then lifted her face back to him. For the first time, doubt flickered at the corners of her mouth when she spoke. "What will they decide in there? What will be the outcome? You're one of them. You would know."

He rubbed a thumb along his jawline, stalling. How to steer this conversation through the white water of her quick mind? "My guess is Attakullakulla will prevail here—but at Chota?" He shook his head. "Dragging Canoe will not easily be convinced."

A frown marred her face. "What will it take?"

"The Ani'yunwiya are tired of white lies. It will take more than the flash of a shiny new pistol to sway their minds."

Her lips flattened, and she started pacing. Three steps one way, three back. Good. Let her come to her own conclusions before asking him. Finally, she stopped and faced him. "What do you suggest?"

"As I said, nothing is certain." He shrugged. "But if you let one of them confirm the firearms exist, at least they'd know it's not an empty promise."

"No. Absolutely not." Her voice turned to a freshly sharpened axe blade. "If that location gets into the wrong hands, there will be no mercy for me, though I am a woman."

Planting seeds was always about timing. Waiting for the soil to warm. The fall of spring rains. Unearthing the dirt to just the right depth. Samuel counted the seconds, as if his mind were working to solve the dilemma for her, when all along his words were ready to sow.

"What if . . ." He rubbed the back of his neck, adding to the effect. "I suppose you could change the location once it's confirmed. That way, Dragging Canoe will be satisfied the firearms are set aside for him, and you'd be assured the munitions are tucked away somewhere else. Even if by some chance the word got out, it would not matter."

The bait was set. The hook sharp. Nothing more to be done but allow the woman to decide if she would bite.

Except for prayer. *Your will, Lord. Your will.*

An angry voice shot from the lodge door, sharp as an arrow. Attakullakulla roared like a bear in response. Apparently the Beloved Man met with unwelcome opposition.

Samuel grabbed another vigil torch and lit the flame. "It will not bode well if we are found lurking at this door. I'll see you to the guest lodge, Miss Browndell."

The woman remained as silent as Mingo, who followed behind. Even when Samuel stopped at the lodge door and handed her the torch, she said nothing.

Holding hands with failure was never one of his favorite sensations. It needled. It chilled. But pressing her any further would be a dead giveaway—and he'd be the carcass. At the very least, he could inform his contacts that there was a shipment of firearms ready to deliver. Somewhere.

He pivoted. "Goodnight, Miss Browndell."

"Wait."

Her voice turned him back around. Torchlight licked over her face, creating harsh shadows beneath her eyes. "The timing of it could work, I suppose. How long will it take me to travel to Chota?"

"You?" He hadn't expected that—and he didn't like to be caught off guard. Stepping closer, he looked for signs of deceit. "What makes you think Attakullakulla will take you and your manservant along?"

"I have my ways, Mr. Heath." Her returning confidence gleamed in the white of her smile.

"A few weeks, maybe." His words came out slow, but his thoughts galloped. What did the woman have brewing in that sharp-toothed trap of a mind?

"Perfect!" Her feral grin grew.

"For what?"

Fumbling with the torch, she pulled a ring from her pinky finger and handed it to him. "This is your ticket into Fort McCaffrey. A man like you ought to be able to make it there and get to Chota by the time we arrive, hmm?"

Oh, how he longed to yank back on the line and set the hook deeper into her pert little jaw. But timing, whether hunting for deer or answers, required patience and resolve. He refused to wrap his fingers around the silver band. Not yet. Not too soon.

He looked from the ring to the brown of her gaze. "What makes you think you can trust me, Miss Browndell?"

She threw back her shoulders like a general about to go into battle with an unflinching determination to win. "Because, Mr. Heath, unlike you, I pride myself on certainty."

He allowed a half smile, just the right amount to please her, and tucked the ring away inside a pouch at his waist. Though it galled him, let her think he was standing side by side with her in principal. *Pride goeth before destruction, and an haughty spirit before a fall*—and he sure wouldn't mind seeing that pretty face hit the dirt.

A stick cracked behind Eleanor. Dried grass rustled beneath a footstep. Eleanor fumed. Now? Samuel came to escort her now that she'd already walked alone in the dark to a hut as foreign to her as a manor home would be to him? Words sat like thistles on the tip of her tongue, to tell him to run back to Miss Browndell. That she didn't care a fig where he spent his night. She'd be fine without him.

She whirled. Then stiffened.

The native woman from the council meeting stood a breath away. Though the moon lent spare light and the torch nearly flickered out, this close, her beauty mesmerized. Skin rich as honey heated over a flame. Eyes large and wide and keenly intelligent. Lips full. Cheeks high. Sculptors from artists' row back in Shoreditch would bloody knuckles for the chance to immortalize this exquisite woman in Italian marble.

Their gazes locked, and Eleanor swallowed. What did the woman want from her? What was she to say? What *could* she say?

Slowly, the woman circled. Eleanor bristled, for surely this was what it felt like to be a mouse in a cat's paw.

"You?" The woman's voice was resonant as chamber music, her English accented but understandable. She finished her circle and spread her arms. "You are what Ya'nu has nearly lost his life over? Who he chooses to cover with his blanket?"

For a second, the name *Ya'nu* swirled in Eleanor's mind, and finally landed when she realized it was what Inoli called Samuel. But then the rest of the woman's words hit home. Heat flared on her cheeks, the blunt insinuation shocking.

"Ahh." The woman leaned closer, gaze poking, prodding, delving into parts of Eleanor that ought not be exposed, especially by a stranger. A smirk twitched her lips. "You have not known him yet. You are frigid as a January moon."

The accusation slapped, sharp and loud. Eleanor fought to remain frozen as charged, for to recoil would lend credence to the woman's allegation.

"And where is the child? The one you were to mother?" The woman peered past Eleanor's shoulder, searching the darkened lodge behind, then shot back to her. "You fail at that, too, I think."

The torch spluttered out. Something deep inside her fizzled as well. In nothing but a few murmured sentiments, this woman—a complete stranger—bludgeoned Eleanor's resolve to be the finest mother to Grace and most efficient wife to Samuel.

The woman narrowed her eyes. "You do not speak?"

Enough. More than enough, actually. Eleanor drew herself up, posture perfect, and looked down her nose at the woman, a stance she'd mastered when facing the duke himself. "Of course I do. How absurd."

Then she wilted a little. She sounded absurd, even to herself.

And wilted further when the woman sneered, clearly not impressed. "You will not please him. You cannot." The woman shoved her face into hers, voice lowering. "You will be the death of him. For Ya'nu's sake, go back to your people, white woman, and leave him to me."

Chapter 32

Samuel sauntered across the field, steps as light as when he'd taken down his first buffalo on a long hunt. Timing might be tricky, but if he and Red Bird left tomorrow and rode hard, he could leave her at Newcastle and bust a trail to Charles Towne, inform his contacts of the munitions, then hightail it to Chota. Good weather, clear paths, and Miss Browndell would be none the wiser that he'd ridden anywhere other than Fort McCaffrey. Why, he might even beat them to the Cherokee Middle Town.

And once the promised firearms and ammo moved out the gates of the fort, an ambush would already be in place.

He lifted his face to the night sky, thankful for God's handiwork on display in the heavens—and right here at Keowee.

But his stride faltered as Grandmother rose like a specter from where she sat outside her lodge door. Her old bones loved a soft fur and a long sleep—neither of which were traded without good reason.

He rushed forward. "*Elisi?* What has happened?"

Her face lifted to his, lines creasing her brow. "Red Bird is sick."

"Sick?" How was he to understand that? She'd been fine. . .wait. . .she hadn't. Her cheeks had burned earlier, and she'd been fatigued all evening. He sucked in a breath and strode toward the door. "Has she a fever?"

"No, my son." Grandmother's arm shot out, catching him in the belly and stopping him flat. The strength of her hold belied her sixty winters. "Your wife is sick of heart, not body."

He turned to her, a scowl begging to be released—but such impertinence might very well still earn him a swat. "Speak plain, Grandmother."

"Running Doe left the council meeting early. She passed me on my return. Your woman weeps inside."

His hands clenched, as did his stomach. He knew this was coming— but he still shouldn't have let it happen. "What did Running Doe tell her?"

"I do not know." Grandmother's head wagged. "But words are not needed to know what ails your wife. When a woman hides her tears, the pain is unspeakable."

Yanking off his hat, he ran a hand through his hair. Blast! Jealousy ran thick in Running Doe's blood. He should've known she'd take this opportunity to spear Red Bird like a carp on a pike. What kind of man did not protect his own wife from an expected attack? He jammed his hat back on. Suddenly his victory with Miss Browndell lost all its sweetness.

"Tell me, Ya'nu." Grandmother peered up at him, starlight painting her eyes with a milky sheen. "Why do you not make your wife your own? Why do you wait? Had your woman been well loved, Running Doe's barbs would not have torn as deeply."

He swallowed, the bitterness of her words scraping his throat. He hated that even without being told, she knew exactly what was going on— but mostly he hated that she was right. His fists clenched tighter. There was nothing to be done for it now. "I will not force myself on a woman, not even my wife."

The lines on Grandmother's face folded into great sorrow. "One of you must bend, my son, or you will both break."

A sigh drained his anger, and he turned from her. Tossing aside the door flap, he crossed to the dark shape huddled on a woven mat and crouched next to it. Red Bird lay facing the wall, a thin piece of deerskin covering her body. She did not stir.

Waiting for his eyes to adjust to the darkness, he listened, keen to detect if she yet wept. No sniffles. No shaky breaths. No sound at all, really, besides the sizzle of Grandmother's torch outside, the shush of river beyond, and the muted voices of those returning from Council.

Beneath the covering, Red Bird's shoulders rose and fell as if she slept. Did she? Had Grandmother been mistaken?

He rocked forward on his toes, bending closer. Her breathing was too quiet. If she slumbered, he'd hear relaxed inhales and exhales, not forced silence.

"Tatsu'hwa, I know you do not sleep."

She didn't move.

"Come." He brushed his fingers down her arm. "We will talk."

Nothing. No shiver. No flinch. Not a word.

Standing, he rolled his shoulders, fighting the urge to sweep her up and give her a sound kissing. "You can leave this lodge on your own two feet or slung over my shoulder. Makes no matter to me."

The blanket hit his feet. Her small frame shot upward, fully dressed.

There was no way this woman had been sleeping, for she was tense as a riled polecat—and about to drop a raincloud of polite expletives over his head.

He tried not to smile.

Before she could launch an assault, he grabbed her hand and pulled her from the lodge. No doubt Grandmother's eyes lit with approval, but he moved past her so fast, he couldn't be sure. He led his wife beyond the last line of lodges, along a trail he knew so well he didn't need a torch to light his way. The stiffness of Red Bird's fingers censured his every step.

Ducking beneath a bower of sumac, he tugged her along until they entered a small clearing—a favorite haunt leftover from his days as a lad.

He stopped and turned, catching her other hand so that he held both in a firm grip. She glowered, her gaze stringing him up and hanging him high. What on earth had Running Doe said?

"What ails you?" he asked.

She ripped her hands from his. Whirling, she wrapped her arms around herself, her back a rigid shield, holding him at bay. "Why have you dragged me out here? I am well."

Well! *This* was well?

"That's a lie, and we both know it." His harsh tone boxed his own ears. He sighed, and tried again. "What did Running Doe say to you?"

Moonlight burned along the loose braid hanging down her back, matching the scorch of her words. "I do not know what you are talking about."

Women. Must it always be so difficult? The rustle of a small animal in the undergrowth at his back seemed to swish a *yes, yes, yes*. He sighed, unwilling to fight against nature, and stepped toward his wife.

She stepped forward, too.

A mad dance. One that needed to stop. "Do you deny a woman spoke to you at the lodge before Grandmother arrived?"

Her silence gave her away. He advanced too fast for her to escape, grabbing her arms and turning her back before she bolted. "Listen, if I'd wanted Running Doe as a wife, I'd have taken her. But I didn't. I took you."

"Do not!" She wrenched away like a cornered badger, all claws and bristle. "Do not pretend you chose me like some gallant knight in a faerie tale. You purchased me for the care of your daughter, nothing more."

"True. But things have changed."

Her brows rose, mocking him in a way that cut sharper than a tomahawk to the skull. "Do you want to break the contract?"

The question circled overhead then dove straight to his gut. He staggered back a step, the realization nearly driving him to his knees. *God, help me.* He didn't want absolution. He wanted consummation.

"No." The word came out tied to the thread of a ragged whisper.

She threw her arms wide. "Then what is it you want?"

His chest heaved as he stared at her. So innocent did her eyes shine. So vulnerable the quiver in her voice.

"You." His voice broke.

"Really?" She lifted her face and stared right back. "Have you tired of Running Doe and Miss Browndell?"

A growl rumbled in his chest, and in two steps, he grasped her shoulders. Was she really that blind? "Can't you see what's in front of your face, woman? Don't you understand?"

"Understand what? That I am nothing but a servant, bought with a price? Someone to be ordered about as a child? That you feel you own me, body and soul?"

"No!" The word echoed from tree to tree, stunning them both by its ferocious veracity.

She blinked, her face paling to match the soft wash of moonlight—and prosecuting him more thoroughly than a jury bent on conviction.

How could he be such a beast? To frighten a woman who'd left everything she'd ever known to live with a man harsher than the wild land they inhabited? "I'm sorry. I . . ."

His throat clogged, stopped up by words he never expected to rise from the depth of his heart. He tried to swallow them back, force them down, but the strong beat of his heart pushed them out. "I want you, Tatsu'hwa. I want you as a real wife."

She wrenched from his grasp. The sharp crack of her palm stung his cheek, jerking his face aside.

"Is that what you told Mariah as well?"

Blast it! He'd had enough. He snapped his gaze back to hers, ignoring the sting on his face and heart. "Never! I never loved Mariah. She was not a wife to me. She was my disgrace."

He dodged her and strode to the sumacs, finished with her, finished with all women. And definitely finished with the foolish inkling that love was a noble and good thing.

"Samuel!" Red Bird's teary voice shredded some of his resolve—but not all.

He charged ahead.

"Stop!"

Footsteps pounded the ground at his back. He shot forward.

Red Bird sobbed. "I am asking."

He froze. So did his lungs. His heart. The world. Surely he hadn't heard right. Wheeling about, he grabbed her wrist, for there'd be no turning back, not if he'd heard correctly.

Oh God, please. Let it be so.

He stood, still as a buck about to be slaughtered. "What did you say?"

Samuel's gaze burned into hers, feverish. Searching. Wrought with trepidation and hope. Her entire future with this man depended upon what came out of her mouth next—and they stood toe to toe together on the edge of that cliff, waiting. Daring. Terrified by the enormity of the tension, sizzling like a lightning strike. It had been easy to ask the first time, to his back, as he strode away and broke her heart with each step.

But now? Facing this living, unpredictable creature? Breathing in his heat and desire?

His fingers wrapped tighter around her wrist, hot and shaking with need.

She inhaled until her stays cut tight into her ribs then held her breath. All of nature did. Samuel stilled as well. Time stretched like the last note of a violin crescendo.

Then she lifted her chin.

"I am ask—"

His mouth came down hard. Hungry. Like a starved man, long deprived of a meal. He cupped the back of her head and pulled her closer, his other hand wrapping around her waist and making her one with his body.

A warm ache started in her belly and spread like wildfire. She leaned into him, aghast by her own appetite. The need that he birthed frightened and delighted, a confusion of sensations. He tasted of starlight, smelled of the woods, cedar and oak, strong and warm. His lips wandered along her jaw, down her neck. She trembled, out of control, her own body a wanton stranger.

"Tatsu'hwa." Samuel whispered the name against her skin, imprinting it into the curve of her collarbone—his name for her alone.

A thousand suns exploded. This was what it meant to be loved by a man? To burn and melt and quiver? She whimpered, so beautiful the act.

Samuel groaned—then pulled back, releasing her. No warning. No explanation.

Nothing.

Night air was a cold stranger between them. Her chest heaved. So did his. As if he'd run across the world to this clearing. To this moment.

She lifted her fingers to her lips. The skin burned, swollen—and wanting more. "Samuel?"

His eyes gleamed with a foreign shimmer, and she swallowed. She wasn't sure she knew the man anymore. Why had he pulled away?

Lowering her hand, she grabbed her skirt. "Do I...do I not please you?"

A shudder rippled across his shoulders. One big hand reached out and brushed back her hair. His fingers skimmed along her cheek and down to her neck, light as a summer breeze.

"You please me very much. Too much. More than I think you're ready for."

His voice was throaty, deep, and so quiet she drifted toward him, wishing to make a home there in his arms.

He grabbed her hand, entwining his strong fingers with hers, then set off at a long-legged pace away from the bower. Their bower—as it would always be, whether they returned here again or not.

He cut her a glance as they sped along the trail back to the village. "We've an early morning and some hard days of riding ahead."

Why the mad pace? Why the mad escape? That kiss had addled more than her body, for clearly she couldn't think straight. "What do you mean? We just arrived today."

"And we leave tomorrow," he said, matter of fact, as if the journey here had been naught but a fool's errand.

Why would a man given to leaving behind his daughter and undergoing a journey of no small effort suddenly want to turn back—or more like...flee?

She upped her pace, double time to his, wanting—craving—to read his face. "Is it because of Miss Browndell or Running Doe?"

He kept his gaze fixed forward.

"What is it?"

The trail opened onto the edge of the village clearing. A few torches yet bobbed here and there. Samuel said nothing, just made a straight shot toward his grandmother's lodge.

His hand gripped hers in a way altogether familiar, yet foreign. She'd discovered much about this man tonight, but not all. Apparently he still held on to some secrets, and she wasn't sure how to feel about that.

But would he be the same man if he didn't? Was that mystique not a part of him she'd come to admire—an assurance that once she shared her inner self with him, he'd not reveal it to anyone else? Ever. What belonged to him, belonged to him alone. Exclusively. And God help her, that's exactly what she wanted.

His grandmother sat outside her lodge door on a log. Odd. Why had the old woman not gone to bed?

Samuel must have wondered the same, for his voice lifted in a question. Whatever she said did not sit well with him, for his fingers let go of Eleanor's. Some kind of debate followed, with a few gestures.

Then the old lady rose and moved toward Eleanor. She lifted her hands and rested both palms against Eleanor's cheeks. The last bit of torchlight and a leftover glow from the moon highlighted the lines spidering out from the old woman's eyes. How many years had she known? How many loves? How much wisdom? For surely those were some kind of sage words she bestowed on Eleanor like a blessing.

Eleanor swallowed, unsure what to say or do, and merely watched as the woman retrieved her torch and shuffled off to the next lodge over. "Where is she going?"

Samuel swept open the door flap, saying nothing.

But when Eleanor crossed the threshold, she knew exactly what grandmother and grandson had argued about. Low lights burned at intervals. The sweet scent of rosemary and sage perfumed the air. A thick bed of furs spread soft in invitation.

Eleanor's heart beat hard. A rushing noise whooshed in her ears. Yes, she'd asked for a kiss. . .but was she ready for this? She pressed her hands to her stomach, a vain attempt to still the strange twinge inside.

Warm breath feathered against the nape of her neck, and she whirled. One look into the bright gleam in Samuel's eyes, and she didn't know if she should run from here—or nestle her face against his chest.

He bent, his lips resting light as a faerie's wings against her brow. A tremble shivered down her back and settled into her knees, leaving behind a wobbly and warm sensation.

Then he bypassed her and snatched the top fur off the pile. Without a word, he stalked to the door. The more distance increased between them, the more panic chilled her to the bone. She didn't want him to leave—but did she really want him to stay, knowing what would happen?

"Samuel?"

He paused at the opening, looking over his shoulder. "Goodnight, Tatsu'hwa. Sleep well. We leave before first light."

Loss tasted sour, chasing away the memory of his sweet kiss. "But where are you going?"

A slow smile, full of danger and seduction, slid across his face. "Far, for your own safety."

Safety? Her brow tightened. "But you have told me I am safe here."

His smile grew. "Not from me. Not tonight."

Chapter 33

Samuel's head drooped, and when chin met chest, he snapped his face back up and urged Wohali on with a heel to the belly. Stifling a yawn, he worked his jaw. He hadn't felt this woozy since recovering from that jug of bad grog back in '65. Better half-asleep, though, than fully awake and aware of Red Bird's softness pressed against his back. He'd driven them both to such distraction the past four days that she dozed behind him.

Four days. Good time. Amazing time, actually, thanks to the drought—and his own need to run far and fast from the kiss he'd shared with Red Bird at Keowee. After tasting of his wife's lips, it was a flat-out miracle he'd held back from doing it again. . .or more. He'd learned long ago that he couldn't stop at one sip of rum. He'd not be able to stop at a simple kiss next time, either.

So they rode hard, pausing only when necessary or darkness covered the trail. The first night had been the most difficult. He'd lain awake, listening to Red Bird breathe. Counting each murmur in her sleep. Counting his own ragged heartbeats and the reasons why he should not take her in his arms and do as Grandmother suggested.

Oh, but he'd wavered, at one point slipping over to where his wife curled up on a blanket. The silver brush of moonlight on her cheek was nearly his undoing. The throb in the hollow of her throat, his temptation. A thin blanket rode the peaks and valleys of her body, an enticement of the most exquisite pain. It had taken every bit of strength he owned to turn from her and walk it off that night—and he had a ripped sleeve and ugly bruise on his shin to prove it.

Thankfully, she hadn't asked him about it, and the following evenings he'd been too tired to think straight. The day would come when such measures would not be needed, but not yet. Even with Grandmother's blessing, it wasn't right, not when he'd be gone for the better part of the next few months. But when he returned from Chota, sweet mercy, what a homecoming that would be!

"Samuel?"

He stiffened. If Red Bird knew the path his thoughts wandered on, she'd be mortified. The urge to tell her welled, to watch the blush spread up her neck and fan over her cheeks like a summer sunrise. He cleared his throat. Wicked. He was wicked. "Aye?"

"How did your grandmother get to be your grandmother?" She shifted against his back, her cheek warm between his shoulder blades.

"I thought you were sleeping."

"Mm-hmm. I am." A yawn punctuated her words. "But I still want to know."

Wohali descended a sharp cut on the trail, one that curved at the same time, and it took a bit of concentration to keep them upright. It was also a fine excuse not to answer. Dredging up the past always stung, even now, years later. He clucked his tongue, steering the horse away from the edge of a ravine drop-off.

"Samuel?"

Her sleep-thickened voice melted through his shirt. She would not be put off, and he was hard pressed to decide if her persistence annoyed him or made him proud of her. But if he did give in and tell her the story, at least it would take his mind off the way she fit so perfectly against him.

When the trail evened out, he began. "After my father died, there was no money. No food. My mother gave all she had for me...even her life. She died of a fever. I lived on the streets then, alone."

"How sad, living on your own." Genuine sympathy, not scornful pity, warmed her voice—then faded. "But you said you lived in Keowee."

"And so I did, after fending for myself for nearly a year." He tugged at his collar, ugly memories as choking as the late August air. The starvation he'd endured, the swollen belly and cramps sharp as a long knife. Sleeping in alleys. Meeting time and again with the jagged end of a drunk's bottle. He rubbed a thumb absently at the scar near his eye. No young lad should have to suffer such indignities. "I nearly didn't make it. Were it not for Inoli's father, come to Charles Towne with Attakullakulla to meet with an agent, I'd surely have perished."

Red Bird pulled away from him, clearly awake now. "How did he find you?"

He snorted. "He didn't. I found him. I tried to steal a blanket off his horse when I thought he wasn't looking."

"Oh," she gasped. "Were you captured?"

"I suppose you could call it that. I went willingly, though. I figured perishing in an Indian village couldn't be any worse than dying in a Charles Towne alley. Besides, they had something I wanted."

"What?"

"Food."

She swatted his shoulder, and though she couldn't see it, he grinned. He could get used to this banter, to this woman. His grin morphed into a smirk. Who was he kidding? He already had. She'd grown to become part of him—the softer part, as Inoli might say, and no doubt would say when he asked his friend to watch over her and Grace while he rode to Chota.

She nestled her head against him once more. "You still have not answered me."

"About what?"

"Your grandmother."

The woman was as dogged a tracker as himself. He eased Wohali over a log, remembering the first time he'd traveled this same trail on the back of an Indian horse. If he closed his eyes, would the same apprehension and excitement rush through his veins? "When I arrived at Keowee, I had two surprising encounters. First, Inoli knocked me flat, angry with his father for bringing me into their home."

"But you are friends," she murmured against his shirt.

"Not so at the beginning. Not until I saved his sorry backside from a bear."

"Oh? No wonder you learned to manage those beasts." Her grip tightened around his waist. Was she perhaps remembering her own scrapes?

He grunted. "Aye, but I didn't fare so well that time."

For a while they rode in silence, well past Breakpass Thicket. Tedious colors of brown and withered green dulled the eyes. The movement of Wohali's sure steps hypnotized as well—until the horse skittered sideways from an unexpected partridge darting onto the trail.

Red Bird jerked up her head. Another yawn cooed from her, and she stretched. "You never finished your story. Your other encounter?"

A smile twitched his lips. He'd chosen a perfect mother for Grace in this one—thanks to God alone. His daughter wouldn't get away with much under Red Bird's care. The woman didn't forget a thing.

With a click of his tongue, he urged Wohali past a rare patch of broadleafs—frowning at the scarcity of them. This time of year the greenery ought be abundant, not dried and shriveled.

Pulling his thoughts from useless worry—for truly, he could do naught about a drought—he turned Wohali onto a shortcut toward Newcastle. "Grandmother helped care for me after that bear attack. With my shirt stripped off, she saw the claw necklace, the one you wear now. My mother gave it to me. It was given to her by her mother—my grandmother. The same old woman you met."

"So, your mother was a native. . .but your father was Scots-Irish. How on earth did they meet?"

He glanced back, and as he suspected, fine, white teeth nibbled her lower lip. She could think all she liked, but she'd never guess the truth.

Chuckling, he faced forward. "My mother met Abraham Heath down at the Charles Towne docks, where he worked. She was part of a sending party, blessing her father as he crossed the great water."

"Her father traveled on a ship? My . . ." Red Bird's voice trailed off, then grew as she strung together all his words. "But he must've been very important."

"He is."

"Is?" She leaned forward, as eager as Grace bent on a discovery. "He's still alive then?"

"Aye." Once more he turned in the saddle, not wanting to miss the flash of understanding when she added all his information into a tidy sum. "You know him as Attakullakulla."

"You mean . . ." Eleanor leaned back and studied Samuel's brown eyes. Dark, yes. Dangerous? Sometimes. But no unbridled bloodlust gleamed in his like she'd witnessed in that man Miss Browndell had confronted at the council.

Her gaze roamed over his face as it bobbed with the horse's gait. Samuel's cheekbones were not as high. His nose not as wide. The hair, lighter, the height and breadth of him larger than the fellow she'd seen at that meeting. No, she must be wrong. Like the fanning of pages in a book, she riffled through memories of the men she'd met in her short time at Keowee. None looked like Samuel.

"Which man was he?" she asked.

"The one who led the council."

That man. . .that leader. . .that fearsome, scarred warrior was Samuel's grandfather? She gasped, stunned, then chided herself for such a silly response. She should've known. Samuel wore authority like a second skin. She'd seen men bend to his will without a word.

"What?" He cocked a rogue brow. "You don't think I resemble him?" Humor lifted his lips.

The movement dared her to gaze at that mouth, to remember how it felt to have it pressed against hers, but she turned her face aside and focused on the passing pine and ash. Clearly he'd forgotten the incident, for he'd not made a move to claim another kiss in the four days since. That not only irked her, it wrapped around her like an unbearable grief.

She frowned. Better to keep her mind on the topic at hand. "You look nothing like the man."

"True." He shrugged. "I am the image of my father."

"Yet you command attention every bit as much as your grandfather."

His brow raised, as did a flush of heat up her neck. Thankfully he said no more and faced forward again. La! How loose her tongue had become.

A bee buzzed past her cheek, and she reared back, grabbing hold of Samuel's waist to keep from falling. It was a familiar hold, the ride of his solid muscles moving beneath her fingers, one she enjoyed—maybe too much. But even more intimate were the glimpses of his past. He didn't always answer her questions, but when he did, it painted him—his life—in colors that captivated.

She had no idea if he'd share further, but she was hungry to hear more. "Why did you not stay at Keowee?"

With a cluck of his tongue, he urged Wohali onward. By now she was certain the callouses on her behind had grown callouses. Walking might never be the same after this trip.

"I wanted a home. A real home. Living on the streets, well . . ." His voice blended with the steady beat of the horse's hooves, and she leaned closer, loathe to miss a word. "It changes you. Not that I wasn't grateful for my grandmother's lodge, but I needed a place to call my own, as selfish as that sounds."

"No. . .it does not."

And surprisingly, it didn't. His words breathed life into the recent portion of scripture she'd read the night they'd left Grace behind with Biz and the reverend. She thought aloud, trying to make sense of it.

"I think there is a reason Jesus said He went to prepare a place for us, that His Father's house has many mansions. Not that we were not created to fellowship with others, for we are, but perhaps the desire to have a space of one's own is but a shadow of what is to come, what we will experience in eternity. A place just for us, created by the Creator. Some, like you, feel it more keenly."

He reined Wohali to a halt and turned in the saddle. The shadowed look on his face was impossible to read. Was he angry at her candid speech? Annoyed with her impertinence? What had gotten into her, anyway?

His big hand brushed along the curve of her cheek. "You always surprise me, Tatsu'hwa."

Her heart beat hard against her ribs. The last time he'd touched her like that, looked at her with that heated gleam. . .she leaned toward him.

He turned and cracked the reins. "Hyah!"

Grabbing his waist to keep from tumbling off, she held tight as the horse sped along the trail, weaving between trees. Thankfully the larger foothills were at their back. She'd expected some kind of reaction from him—but not this.

Eventually they slowed to a less breakneck speed. Her eyelids drooped as she thought on the events of the past few weeks. It seemed like an eternity since she'd tickled little Grace and listened to her giggle. How had the child fared with Biz? Or how had Biz fared with Grace? No doubt they'd both be changed.

The claw necklace poked against her chest, and she twisted it around behind her neck. She could take it off, she supposed, but for some odd reason, that felt disrespectful to the old woman who gave it to her.

She frowned. "Samuel, your grandmother. . .what will happen to her when she is too old to care for herself? Will you take her in?"

"No." He shook his head, his long hair brushing against her cheek. "Attakullakulla is many things—stubborn, proud, impetuous—but he will see that she is cared for. As long as he is able."

The tone of his voice sent a shiver across her shoulders despite the afternoon heat. "That sounds rather ominous."

"Times are changing." His words weren't just a prophecy—they were some kind of accusation.

"What do you mean?"

A sigh rippled the fabric across his back. "Years ago, there was war between the French and English, a fight for this land. I saw no good in siding with either, but the Ani'yunwiya backed the English, leastwise at the beginning. I fought for them, for Attakullakulla. It did not end well."

The memory of a golden medal in a dirt hole flashed bright as the summer sun, as incongruous an image as the man in front of her. How must it feel to be rewarded by the very ones who'd killed his father? Was that why he kept it tucked away? Emotion clogged her throat. Her heart broke for his loss, what he'd been obliged to do for the sake of integrity. "It must have been hard for you, fighting with those who took your father's life."

A muscle on the side of his neck stood out, but his calm voice belied the tension. "Honor always comes at a price, else it would be worthless."

Honor, indeed. Of all the wealthy and noble men she'd served, not one matched the virtue in this man, clothed in a simple linen shirt, smelling of gunpowder and strength.

The path descended along a now-familiar route. She eased back and squinted past his shoulder. Yes, there was an expected bend in the trail and the large rock she'd nearly banged her foot against when they'd traveled this way a little more than a fortnight ago. The closer they drew to Newcastle, the more anticipation pulled her from her groggy state.

She bounced, more from eagerness than the sideways step of Wohali.

Samuel shot his arm back, holding her in place. "Don't fall off now. We're near to home."

"I am anxious to see Grace," she admitted. "I have missed her."

He chuckled. "Me, too."

But his humor faded, and he glanced over his shoulder, a grave twist to his mouth. "I'll miss you as well, Tatsu'hwa."

Fear tasted brassy at the back of her throat, and she swallowed. "What are you talking about?"

He tugged his hat lower, the brim hiding his eyes. "As soon as I see you and Grace home, I'm leaving."

Chapter 34

The final rays of sunlight bled away, the day dying like a great beast. Darkness rushed out from the woods like a band of demons, lifting the flesh on Eleanor's arms. She scooted closer to Samuel on the wagon seat, seeking his protection from nothing but a silly thought.

Surprisingly, Grace didn't stir. The girl lay limp in her arms, dead to the world. A week and a half with Biz had worn her out. A small smile tugged Eleanor's lips as she brushed her fingers along the girl's cheek, following the curve of dark shadows beneath her eyes. Surely it was mercy alone that supplied the reverend with patience to put up with Biz.

Eleanor's smile faded as the night shadows wrapped around them, especially when she peeked up at the grim set of Samuel's jaw. Trying to decipher what went on inside that mind of his was impossible, especially with the way he hid his eyes beneath his hat brim and long curtain of hair. For the better part of the last few hours, she'd tried to discover where and why he'd be going on the morrow, but the man simply would not answer.

A sigh slipped past her lips. Why had God made men such mule-headed creatures?

"Six." His voice rumbled with the wagon wheels.

She frowned up at him. "Sorry?"

"That's the sixth time you've sighed in the past mile." He glanced down at her. "At that rate, there'll be no air left in you by the time we turn into the yard."

"Well." She squared her shoulders. "Perhaps if you told me—"

"The less you know, the less likely you are to get hurt."

She jerked her face aside, unable to quell a sudden wave of petulance. "As if that matters."

"It does."

She snapped her gaze back to him, but he said nothing more. He slapped the reins, urging Wohali onward, eating up the last stretch of road to home.

When they pulled into the yard, Grace stirred on her lap. A lantern glowed inside the cabin, reaching out the front window like a yellow warning. Eleanor turned to Samuel, about to ask who he thought might be inside, but his big finger rested on her lips, cutting her off. With his other hand, he pulled out his rifle.

Alarm prickled at the nape of her neck—until a grin split Samuel's face, and he hopped off the seat.

Eleanor peered back at the cabin. The silhouette of a warrior blackened the open door.

"Ee-no-lee!" Grace awoke with a cry and squirmed out of Eleanor's grasp, clambering off the wagon and tagging her father's heels.

Eleanor grabbed her skirts and followed. How had the man known they'd return home this night? What kind of otherworldly connection did he and Samuel share?

The men clasped arms at the top of the stairs, exchanging words. Eleanor paused, imprinting the scene on her mind and heart. This cozy cabin. The tall pines hugging the yard in a protective embrace. The warmth of light shining inside and the loamy fragrance on the early evening air. This was more than a little slice of heaven. For a single, breath-stealing moment, it felt like home. What a queer feeling, one she wanted to own, but she suspected that if she reached out, it would slip from her fingers.

Samuel's growl and subsequent slap of his hat against his thigh grabbed her attention. Whatever Inoli told him was not sitting well. She picked her way up the steps as he ran his hand through his hair.

"Samuel?" She drew close to his side, giving the native a wide berth. Inoli may be a trusted friend, but his solemn-eyed stare and coiled muscles still unnerved her. "Why is Mr. Inoli here?"

The two men exchanged glances. Without a word, Inoli vanished through the cabin door on soundless feet.

Samuel shoved his hat back on his head, lightning flashing in his eyes as he faced her. "Seems McDivitt's been raising a ruckus while we've been gone. Calling in debts. Shooting threats around like buckshot. Inoli feared the man would burn down my house to match the lot in town I wouldn't sell him."

"I see." And she did. She remembered the look in McDivitt's eyes, crazed and wild. As if Satan himself peered out from the inside. She'd seen a stallion put down once for a gleam of far less madness.

But what if McDivitt decided to carry out his threat while Samuel was gone? She lifted her face to his, trying to hold back the fear from quivering in her voice. "Does that mean you will stay here, or will you still leave tomorrow?"

For a moment, he stood there. Granite. The calm before a terrible squall. A muscle jumped on his jaw.

Pivoting, he tramped to the door and disappeared inside.

Eleanor wrapped her arms around herself, warding off the early evening chill—but it did nothing to stop the coldness seizing her heart at the thought of Samuel's absence.

Samuel stared out at the blackness from where he sat on the porch. Something wasn't right about this night. The crickets were too loud. The cicadas, too buzzing. Everything was brittle. Sharp. Like walking on a thin piece of ice, knowing the hairline cracks were about to give way and frigid water would swallow him whole.

Judging by the way Inoli stood on the edge of the front porch, arms folded and alert, he felt it, too. Even Grace had cried herself to sleep, a wailing cry, the eerie keen of something more than fatigue.

"The air is not right." Inoli spoke without turning around. "You should not go to Charles Towne. Not yet."

"You sound like Grandmother." Samuel grunted. "And if I don't make haste and return to Chota as if I've done nothing more than make a run to Fort McCaffrey, then Miss Browndell and Attakullakulla will know I've been up to something more. I would be exposed for what I am."

"And what is that, Ya'nu?" Inoli's black gaze drifted over his shoulder and pinned him in place.

He shook his head. "Sometimes I wonder."

"You are an honorable man. At times, too honorable."

"What's that supposed to mean?"

Inoli faced the yard again, his back rigid. He stared into the night as though he could see what evil awaited them. "You cannot right all the wrongs in this world. You will die in the trying."

The crickets stopped. So did the cicadas, replaced by a low rumble in the distance. Samuel shot to his feet, snatching up his rifle as he went. Lights like fireflies flickered in the east, growing larger. The pounding did, too. He and Inoli stood ready, waiting, silent. No words were needed. They'd hunted together for so many summers, they moved as one.

Five horses thundered up the road, each rider carrying a torch. Stane led the pack. Foam gathered at the corners of his mount's mouth, and the horse reared when yanked to a stop. Men and horses spread out in front of the porch, Stane at center.

Blood rushed in Samuel's ears. Something big must've happened to warrant a ride in the dark way out here.

"We need you, Heath." Deep breaths poked holes in Stane's words. "Mercantile vault's been robbed. Cleaned out."

Samuel cradled his rifle. "What's that to do with me?"

Torchlight danced over Stane's grim jawline, the shadows making him more ghoul than human. "Sutton's lying near to dead because of it."

Every muscle in him clenched. Ben Sutton had been the only man who'd never looked askance at him, not once lifted an accusing brow or whispered what Samuel's part might've been in Mariah's death.

Samuel forced words past his tight throat. "Who did it?"

"Two men. One, a stranger, rode in during the Summer Outfit. The other"—Stane's horse shied sideways, and he reined him in—"McDivitt."

The name pierced like a well-aimed arrow, and he widened his stance to keep from staggering. McDivitt had taken it too far this time. Crossed the line. This wasn't just about robbing a vault. Taking down Sutton was a direct strike against Samuel. His hands shook on the rifle stock.

"How long ago?" he asked.

"Few hours. Will you lead us?"

One man—Pickens—tipped his hat. The rest sat stony-faced, torchlight licking their faces like the flames of hell.

Blast! What to do? If he went after McDivitt, could he still make it to Charles Towne and back to Chota in time?

Stane spit out a curse. "Time's wasting, man. What do you say?"

Samuel glanced at Inoli, who nodded almost imperceptibly. He cut his gaze back to Stane. "Go on home. All of you. I ride with Inoli alone."

Stane roared. "You can't—"

"You challenging me?" Samuel stared him down. "I'm the best hope you've got if you want them brought in. Remember what happened with Blacking."

The torches sizzled. One horse snorted. Another pawed the ground. No one spoke.

Finally Stane shook his head. "Every man here had money in that vault."

Rage tasted bitter, traveling down his throat to his gut. "I got more than money riding on this. Sutton's my friend."

Stane's gaze seared into his. Then he gave a stiff nod and jerked his mount around. "Come on, boys."

The horses rumbled off—yet the crickets did not resume their song.

Inoli said nothing as Samuel stalked into the house. Shadows filled the tiny cabin, but he didn't need any light. Anger burned bright enough inside him.

Red Bird stood at the window. He breezed by her toward his storage chest.

"Samuel, please tell me what is happening."

Her words hovered in the night air, as unnerving a sound as Grace's choppy breathing. He ignored both and rummaged in the chest, pulling out bags of shot, his spare powder horn, and an additional knife for his other boot.

Footsteps padded behind him. "You are frightening me. Please, tell me what happened."

He reached inside his hip pouch and pulled out Miss Browndell's ring. No sense losing that on the trail—for no doubt this would be quite a ride. The metal heated his skin, and he squeezed the life from it before splaying his fingers. The ring landed silently inside his storage chest, a small act, setting a course he would not be able to turn from.

"Samuel?"

He slammed the lid shut, slid the knife into his boot, and swung the extra powder horn and hunting bag over his shoulder. Then he stood and faced his wife.

Everything in him screamed to pull her into his arms, kiss away the fear on her face, whisper endearments that would redden her cheeks. But it wasn't time. Blast! It was never time. And what if...*Oh God*...Closing his eyes, he swallowed, throat tight. What if it never would be time for them?

Then better he withdraw. Here and now. Not start something he didn't know if God would give him grace enough to finish.

His eyes shot open, and he branded her image into his mind, for this could very well be the last time he saw her.

When he walked out the door and hunted down McDivitt, it was kill or be killed.

Chapter 35

Two days of stifling heat, increased winds, and now this. *Doomed.* Samuel picked up the word as he might a pebble in his shoe, then as forcefully flicked it away while he squatted and studied the forest floor. Thundering remnants of an earlier cloudburst rolled in the distance, the rumble mimicking his frustration. Not enough rain had fallen to quench the drought-ravaged land, but the right amount to wash away McDivitt's tracks. Standing, he kicked a stick with the toe of his moccasin. *Now?* Three months with no rain and a thunderstorm had to break now?

He wheeled about and stalked back to where Inoli held Wohali's lead. Snatching the leather strap, he frowned up at his friend. "Nothing."

Inoli simply stared at him.

Growling, Samuel swung into the saddle and yanked his horse around. "Whoever McDivitt's tangled himself up with is good. Almost too good."

Inoli drew next to him. "Yet you do not turn back."

"No. I'm not giving up." He scrubbed his face with one hand, thinking hard. "They have the advantage of the elements, but we know this land. Where would you go if you were being hunted?"

"West. North and south are too peopled."

"No, that's too general a guess." Loosing his hold, he allowed Wohali to ramble on while he followed a trail in his mind. Of course they'd head west—as were he and Inoli. But how, specifically? What route? McDivitt would take the path of least resistance. Always had. But the other man surprised him with his twists and turns. He'd taken the bottom of a ravine when Samuel would've chosen higher ground. Picked along a rocky crag when splashing through what was left of a river would've been easier. So, what was the most unlikely course from here?

He scanned the forest, this time looking for an impossible passage westward instead of logical. Not far off, his gaze landed on a deer trace that cut northerly. The wrong direction, but one that would eventually curve back and pass near a salt lick next to Stoneclad Falls. Stoneclad?

He reined in Wohali. Stoneclad sported a jagged drop of sheer cliff.

The waterfall was terrible. The swirling expanse above it too risky to cross. The river at the bottom was cursedly wide, though much shallower—if one could navigate down the treacherous landscape to reach it. But once there and safely across, the country flattened. There'd be no stopping them.

His gut tightened. That was it.

He glanced over his shoulder at Inoli. "Stoneclad Falls. That's where they are."

"How do you know?"

"Just do." He kicked Wohali into action and shot forward on the deer trace, pressing the horse as fast as he dared on such a narrow track. They rode for the better part of two hours. Now and then the ground dipped, and he adjusted speed, slowing their progress. It wouldn't do to turn Wohali's ankle, not when he felt sure they were finally on the right track.

Farther on, Wohali pinned back her ears and slowed to a trot. Samuel scanned from tree to tree. What did his mount sense that escaped him?

There. A deep impression in the dirt. Some kind of skirmish, maybe?

Samuel tugged on the reins and jumped off, Wohali nickering a complaint. Five paces from the trail, a horse lay on its side. Samuel circled the carcass as Inoli dismounted. The front foreleg of the poor beast was bent at an ugly angle near the ankle, bone breaking through the skin. Glassy eyes stared at the sky, an entrance wound near the temple—and another accompanied by an exit hole through the neck. Samuel crouched, examining the torn flesh. Either one would've been sufficient. Why two?

"What say you, Ya'nu?" Inoli's quiet voice was a rustle of leaves, nothing more.

Samuel stood, rubbing his jaw. "Horse went lame. That's clear enough. Put down recently, since the body is not yet stiff and scavengers haven't eaten their fill. But I can't account for why they'd waste two shots. That doesn't make any sense." He met his friend's gaze. "Still, this slows them. We have the advantage."

They rode in silence the rest of the way. Sure enough, the closer they drew to Stoneclad, the more signs he picked up even from atop his mount. A half-curve of a hoof print. Droppings. And as the rush of the waterfall grew louder, so did men's voices.

Angry ones.

He slid from his horse and tethered Wohali to a tree. Inoli did the same. Slipping out his rifle from the side holster on his mount, he checked to see the ball was still tightly snugged down in the barrel.

Inoli removed the bow from his back and carried it loose-fingered, arrow fitted, ready to snap into action. Their gazes met, a thousand words traveling between them, then Samuel set off toward the falls on silent feet, Inoli flanking him ten yards to his left. At the edge of the tree line, before growth gave way to a flattened strip of rocky land running along the river, Samuel held up his hand. They both froze.

Ahead, Angus McDivitt and a squat excuse of a man faced off, each holding a pistol, cocked and ready to fire at the other's chest. A lathered horse stood closer to Inoli than to Samuel, loaded with bags and head hanging. If they didn't give that horse a rest soon, he'd meet the same fate as his partner back there on the trail.

"Shut up, McDivitt!" The shorter man cursed. "I've had more than enough of your mewlin'."

"You've near to killed me at least five times today, but that's yer plan, ain't it? No! I'm not going down that cliff's edge, and neither are you. We backtrack and cross the river up higher, where it's safe."

Rage twisted Angus's voice. The man was dangerously close to pulling the trigger. Good. Let the two of them finish each other off.

Samuel glanced over at Inoli and blew a sparrow call. When his brother's dark eyes slid to his, he lifted a finger and pointed to the horse bearing the stolen money bags. Inoli gave a slight nod. Bow and arrow still at the ready in one hand, he crept out from his hiding place. He held out his other hand in a gesture of peace to the animal, who'd lifted its head, already catching the man's scent.

Samuel lifted his rifle, quietly cocking the hammer wide open. He trained the barrel on the fighting men, in case one of them spotted Inoli. Once the horse was out of the way and secured, he and Inoli would each wound a criminal and haul in their sorry backsides for justice.

A ghost of a smile eased the tightness of his lips. Angus McDivitt facing the law instead of brandishing it. *Oh God, make it so.*

From the corner of one eye, he saw Inoli stalk forward, an animal on the hunt. Closer. Five, maybe six more steps and—

The horse shied from him with a whinny. Two rifle barrels immediately swung toward Inoli.

Curious how time slowed in the last moments before death arrived. The thing was, though, that one never knew who would receive the calling card first.

Inoli spoke to the men in Cherokee, but his words were for Samuel. "I take Angus. You take the other. On my mark. One. Two—"

He never made it to three. A shot cracked loud. The ball grazed Inoli's shoulder.

But that didn't stop him. Inoli yanked up his bow and pulled back on the string. His arrow sliced into McDivitt's chest, the force knocking him backward.

Samuel trained his muzzle at the other man's heart, held a breath to steady his aim, then squeezed his trigger. A brilliant blaze sparked—and the gunpowder flashed in the pan. Blast! He grabbed his powder horn and poured out more black danger.

Too late.

The next shot tore into his flesh. Pain exploded just below his collarbone.

Eleanor scooped her bucket into the creek, dredging up silt along with the water and not caring a bit. Leaden clouds hung low, as gloomy and dark as her mood. And why not? After two never-ending days without Samuel, everything wore a grey pallor. Even Grace was naughtier than usual—though that could be attributed to her time spent with Biz. But the girl did seem clingier lately, almost edgy. Like she knew her father wouldn't be coming back.

Sighing, Eleanor hoisted her bucket and shook off the melancholy. This was ridiculous. Of course Samuel would be back.

She trudged up the bank, water sloshing over the bucket's rim. Thunder rolled in the distance and had been all morning. If it were going to be a regular thunderstorm, then why did the heavens not simply burst and be done with it?

But this was different. Something wasn't right, and it was more than just Samuel being gone. No birds chattered. No squirrels romped. No whirrs, no clicks, no buzzing of insects. The air tasted coppery and smelled of. . .what? She sniffed as she hiked the path toward the cabin, trying to pick out the underlying odor. Her nose wrinkled when she figured it out. Singed hair, that's what. The same stink as when a loose lock drifted too near a candle flame.

Setting down the bucket in the middle of the yard, she turned a slow circle, scanning from road to trees to cabin. All familiar. Nothing different, except that dusky shadows choked the life from the day—and it was hardly past noon. A queer desire to pack up Grace and trek the long trail into town rallied stronger with each breath.

And what would Samuel think of that, were he to return home to find them gone? La! What a skittish colt she'd become.

She snatched up the bucket and tromped to the house. Perhaps this was simply how storms went here, giving a warning to seek shelter, unlike the sudden downpours of London.

Giggles leached out the cabin door and she sped her steps, depositing the water supply on the front porch. She froze in the open doorway, eyes widening. "Oh Grace!"

Samuel's storage chest lay on its side, contents spilled. Grace had pulled out everything and flung it around the entire cabin. Eleanor slapped her hand to her chest, eyes darting from wall to wall to make sure no gunpowder or other dangers posed a threat to the child. A chair wore Samuel's extra hunting shirt. The ripped pair of breeches she'd meant to sew for him hung off the table like a brown waterfall. At the center of the room, Grace grinned at her, wrapped in Samuel's fur coat, the bulk of which trailed her as if an animal snuck up from behind. A knife with a broken handle lay inches from the girl's feet, a chunk of lead to be melted for balls next to it. Other than that, though, no more weapons or ammunition. Samuel must've cleaned the chest out well when he'd left the other night.

Relief loosened the tightness in her jaw—until anger clenched it back up. What a mess.

"Grace Abigail Heath!" She growled as she strode to the girl and yanked her arms from the coat a little more forcefully than necessary. Grace wailed, but that didn't stop Eleanor from grabbing the girl's hand and marching her to the corner. "You will stand here, little miss, until I say otherwise."

Eleanor popped her hands onto her hips, daring Grace to move before she turned back to clean up the strewn belongings. Maybe it was a good thing Samuel wasn't here to see the wildcat Grace had become. And maybe...Eleanor's fists uncurled, and her shoulders drooped. Maybe Grace's bad behaviour wasn't from Biz's influence at all, but bought and paid for from her own lack as a caregiver. A crack of lightning jolted outside, as jarring as the sudden realization. Who was she fooling? Grace needed a mother, not a governess, and she was neither. Not anymore.

Her throat closed, and she stomped to the chest, righting the thing, wishing with all her heart she could as easily right her life. Retrieving Samuel's fur, she carried the coat to the bed, then shook it out to fold it.

Metal plinked against wood. What in the world?

She bent and scooped up a piece of silver. A ring. Much too small and dainty to fit on any of Samuel's fingers. Come to think of it, he didn't wear any jewelry. Narrowing her eyes, she studied the band. Had this been Mariah's or his mother's? No stones. Just an engraving on the front—a swirly letter B.

Recognition stole her breath, and she dropped the ring. Air. She needed air. And lots of it.

Dashing to the door, she ignored the cry of Grace as another bolt crackled across the sky. She stumbled onto the porch and leaned one hand against a post. Why would Samuel have Miss Browndell's ring in his possession? Either he'd stolen it—though with his wealth he needn't have—or she'd given it to him, but for what purpose?

White lit the yard. An instant blink, followed by an ear-splitting bang. And still no rain. The heavens roared without a hint of satisfaction, as untamed and harsh as Eleanor's thoughts. Clearly Miss Browndell had made some kind of bargain with him, wielded some kind of power. . .or attraction.

Samuel's words barreled back, reverberating in her chest as real as the thunder. *"The less you know, the less likely you are to get hurt."*

Too late. Her heart twisted, truth cutting deep and drawing blood. All the flirtations on Miss Browndell's part, the feigned rebuffs from Samuel. Of course. What was to stop him from returning to Keowee to claim Miss Browndell. . .other than his integrity, for he was a man of conviction, was he not? A fierce battle raged in her heart, between her own insecurity and what she'd seen of his character in the past several months.

Another crack of thunder, and Grace bawled from inside. Defeated, Eleanor wrapped her arm around the post and pressed her cheek against the rough wood. She should run to Grace, comfort her with a hug, but her feet wouldn't move. She wasn't even a good nanny.

She closed her eyes. *What good am I, Lord?*

Everything she set her hand to failed. Her posts in England. Losing her reference for a position in a fine Charles Towne home. Harboring a horse that earned Samuel a whipping. Grace's horrific conduct. Fail. Fail. Fail. A sob welled in her throat, and she pressed her hand against her lips, stifling the cry. Her mouth trembled against her fingertips, as hot and quivery as when Samuel had kissed her. Obviously she'd failed at that as well, for he'd never so much as hinted at kissing her again.

"You will not please him. You cannot. You will be the death of him."

The words struck her afresh, spoken by the almond-eyed beauty who knew Samuel long before she did. The woman was right, of course—and she'd been a fool to ever think otherwise.

The next pop of lightning lifted the tiny hairs at the back of her neck. White flashed, lighting the yard as starkly as what she knew she must do. Then blackness. Grace shrieked, and Eleanor pulled from the post.

She didn't know how or where, but when Samuel returned, she was leaving. He—and Grace—would be better off without her.

Chapter 36

Wounded animals always roared. Samuel was no different. The groan tearing out his throat sounded wickedly primal even to his own ears. The punch of the ball knocked him off balance—and he used the momentum to reach with his good arm for the tomahawk on his opposite hip. He yanked it out, sucked in a breath, then pivoted and let loose. The blade flew.

The man who'd shot him, desperately reloading his rifle to stop Inoli, didn't see it coming. Samuel's tomahawk split clean through his trousers, laid open the flesh on his thigh, nicked into bone, then dropped to the ground.

A heartbeat later, Inoli's arrow took the man in the side of the gut—and stuck there. A banshee's scream couldn't have been louder. The man fell backward, grabbing his leg and side.

Samuel dropped to his knees, yielding to the fire between chest and shoulder. He pressed his hand against the wound, a pathetic attempt to stay the blood. Sticky wetness oozed through his shirt and between his fingers. He was alive, though. That was enough. For now, anyway.

"Ya'nu!" Inoli broke into a dead run toward him, alarm darkening his eyes.

The crack of a rifle violated the air.

Inoli stumbled. A dark stain spread on his chest.

"Nooo!" Samuel jumped to his feet, running hard, breathing harder.

Like a downed buck, his brother pitched forward, hitting the ground chin first.

Behind Inoli's fallen body, McDivitt charged forward, throwing his rifle to the ground. He yanked a knife from a sheath at his belt. Blood grew on his shirt like a cancer, darkest where Inoli's arrow had pierced through bone and flesh.

Inoli!

Samuel stumbled. But there was no time to mourn. To think. Just to act. Move. Kill—or be killed.

So be it.

Samuel's war whoop rang from tree to tree. He grabbed the knife at his waist, cleared the trees, then crouched, waiting for McDivitt's advance.

They circled. A macabre dance. Madness brightened McDivitt's eyes to an unnatural sheen. He slashed forward.

Samuel twisted, then followed-through on the arc, coming full circle to slice McDivitt's upper arm. Not a killing slash. Just enough to goad the man into a frenzy—for an angry man fought slipshod.

"Filthy cur!" Angus howled, beads of spit foaming on his beard. "Good-for-nothing half-breed."

Rage bubbled up from Samuel's gut, coloring everything red. Hot red. Everything in him wanted to slit McDivitt's throat, end him here as he'd taken down Inoli. But then he'd be no better than the killer in front of him. He readjusted his grip on the hilt of his knife—and let Angus strike. Repeatedly. Learning his pattern. Memorizing his footwork. Until he knew. Could predict.

Then he roared. "Murderer!"

Samuel jabbed one way, expecting an opposite diagonal slash from Angus—one he could exploit to drive his own blade into McDivitt's stomach.

But Angus turned and ran.

What?

Samuel tore after him.

Angus dipped, picking up a rock at the riverbank's edge, then whipped around and let it fly.

The crack to Samuel's skull juddered from head to toe. He staggered, dazed.

Long enough for Angus to skirt him, reversing positions. Now Samuel's back faced the rushing water. Two paces, just two, and he'd be sucked under to a murky, choking death.

McDivitt's teeth punctured his beard. "I been waitin' a long time for this, Heath." His grin smeared into a smirk. "Too long."

McDivitt lifted his blade.

Samuel watched Angus's eyes instead of the knife. *Wait for it. Wait.* And there. The flash of pride. Of victory. The overconfidence of a man who thought he'd vanquished his enemy.

Samuel shot out his arm, blocking the strike. Stepping forward, he jammed his foot against Angus's boot. Then twisted. Pulled. Shoved.

Knocked off balance, Angus pitched forward, sailing headfirst into the swirl of white water.

Samuel snapped into action, racing along the bank toward the waterfall. He followed McDivitt's red head, bobbing along, surfacing and going under in a sick rhythm. As much as he'd like to be finished with the man, his job wasn't over yet, not until he heard the clang of iron against iron with Angus on the other side of a jail's bars.

All waterfalls had their cache of deadwood, snagged at the edges, caught in eddies that wouldn't let go. And McDivitt was headed right toward a heap of hickory logs on Samuel's side of the river.

Samuel planted his feet and lifted his hands to his mouth, shouting to be heard. "Grab the wood, Angus!"

An arm shot out of the water, clawing for a hold on a jutting limb and finding it. Barely. The rushing water pulled Angus's legs toward the drop-off.

But he held.

Samuel's chest heaved. Did he have enough strength remaining to haul the man up to safety without being pulled in himself? He sucked in a breath. He'd have to, God help him. *God help us both.* "Hang on, McDivitt!"

He glanced wildly around for a piece of wood he could extend as a lifeline. The pain in his collarbone burned like wildfire.

"Ain't goin' to!"

Angus's voice yanked his face back toward the river. "Hang on, man!"

McDivitt's head bobbed under, and he came up spitting a mouthful of water. "I ain't going with you."

"Just stay put!" There, shoved up near the water's edge not far from Angus, lay a half-submerged limb. Samuel lunged for it.

"I'm going with Mariah," Angus yelled, his voice noticeably weaker. "This one's on you, Heath!"

"Angus, no! Just wait—"

McDivitt let go.

The water grabbed him, jerking his body sideways before slamming him over the edge.

Samuel stood. Panting. Bleeding. Looking inside for some measure of satisfaction—and finding none. He was numb. Cold. Empty.

Drained.

Eleanor awoke with a start, groggy and disoriented. Grace's hot body pressed against hers, a strand of her hair sticking to Eleanor's cheek. She picked it away and lifted her head, gazing around the cabin. Everything looked ghostly, like a fog hovering above a moor. Shifting Grace from her lap to the mattress, Eleanor pushed herself up on the bed. A dull roar droned in her ears. She yawned, then stretched. That had been some nap. Hopefully now they'd both be in a better frame of mind.

But as consciousness seeped in, the haze did not dissipate. She stood, then coughed. Why was it so hot in here? *Oh, please. Not a fever. Not now.* Pressing her hand against her forehead, she stilled. Warm skin met her touch, not burning. But her eyes stung. She rubbed them with her fingertips, then blinked away the last of her nap.

A cloud levitated shoulder-height and above, thickening up near the rafters. Fear prickled down her arms, from shoulders to fingertips. This was no fog. This was—

Oh God, have mercy.

She dashed to the door, her heart racing as fast as her feet. Flinging it open, she gasped, then staggered onto the porch.

Hell approached from the other side of the creek. Black smoke capped shooting flames of orange and red. Grasping the edge of her apron, she covered her nose and mouth, then darted down the stairs and across the yard. She stopped at the trees, held back by heat and terror.

Peering down the path to the creek, she gaped into the jaws of a living inferno, eating everything in its path. On the opposite bank, tree trunks glowed like the sun. Crackling. Snapping. Popping. Thus far only smoke and hot air cloaked this side of the land. Having lived in a country of perpetual dampness, she didn't know much about forest fires, but surely a riverbed would stop the monster from advancing. Wasn't water a natural barricade? Of course it was. It *had* to be.

Please, God, make it so.

She whirled from the sight, throat raw, eyes streaming. She'd snatch up Grace and they'd run down the road, away from the horrid fire. But before she took a step, an awful crack, then another, and another spun her back around. Trees fell, crossing the river like flaming bridges, spreading the destruction to her side of the creek.

Move! She sprinted to the cabin, taking the stairs in one big leap, then stumbled as her toe caught the hem of her skirt. Flailing, she pressed on, lungs burning, eyes watering. Praying.

My precious Lord;

My only hope;

My Saviour, how I need You now.

Grace lay exactly where she'd left her, dead to the world. Eleanor shuddered from the thought.

"Grace! Wake up, little one." She lifted the girl off the bed. "Wrap your arms around my neck and hold on."

Thankfully Grace complied, whether from obedience, fatigue, or maybe even from having breathed in so much smoke, Eleanor didn't know. Nor did she care. The only thing that mattered was escape.

She sped out the door, ran down the stairs, then stopped mid-stride. A barricade of shooting flames cut off the road.

Now what? This fire could not be outrun, especially not with a toddler in her arms.

Panic was no stranger. She'd met him once or twice. Footsteps behind hers in a London alley. The sensual stare of a man undressing her with his eyes. The day she'd faced a bear. But this time panic outdid itself. It climbed beneath her skin, stealing her breath, her heartbeat, her soul.

Grace clutched her neck, burying her face in Eleanor's bodice. The child's life depended on her clear thinking, but who could think when caught dead center in a blazing underworld? Was this it, then? Her last breaths? Grace's last breaths? Darkness edged in from the periphery. It was too hard to think anymore. To live anymore.

"Face your fear. I've got you."

The voice was quiet, low, more bass than the roar of the fire. She spun, choking, coughing out hope. "Samuel? Samuel!"

No broad-shouldered man staggered through the smoke. No strong arms appeared to steal them away to safety. Nothing but sparks, heat, flames. Ruin. Just her and Grace and destruction.

And God.

She stiffened. God, here? In fire and certain death? But. . .of course. Had He not only encountered death, but experienced it—and endured Hades itself for the sake of all men?

"Face your fear, little one."

Reality barreled back, and slowly she turned. A blast of acrid air singed her eyebrows, coming from the creek. That's where the worst of the fire burned. Where hell breathed and lived and moved. Face that? She gasped, rasping for breath.

"I've got you."

Against all reason, she bolted, crouch-running into the inferno. The flames hadn't crossed the path yet, but her skin burned nonetheless. To her left, a blazing wall raced to cut her off from the water. The closer to the creek, the more intense the burning. She skidded down the bank, ripping her gown. Pulling her hair. Scraping and bruising. No matter. Even breathing didn't matter anymore. She couldn't, anyway.

She splashed into the water and cast them both down, nothing but their heads exposed. Thank God the creek was low or they'd both drown for sure—but was it enough to protect them from the fire?

Chapter 37

Death wore many costumes. This one was ragged and black, and Eleanor loathed the ghastly shroud, wanting to look away but unable to do so. It was as if a giant hand had slit the world's throat, bleeding out all color and life. She lay in the shallows of the creek, staring up at the sky. Grace lay atop her, head on her chest, arms wrapped tight around her waist as if she might disappear at any moment. And who knew? Maybe she would. The very forest, more stalwart and unshakeable than her, had vanished.

At the top of each bank, trees stood naked, crooked, like so many tombstones in an aged graveyard, leaning upon one another for support. A breeze rattled the branches, the sound of bones knocking against a door. Every now and then a sharp crack exploded as another limb plummeted to its death.

She no longer measured time by minutes, but by breaths. Using that scale, an eternity had passed. Night was not far off—and a creek was no place for a child to sleep.

"Time to move, little one," she croaked out.

Grace lifted her head and stared. She didn't blame her. Did that gruff voice really come out of her mouth?

She stood and hoisted Grace to her hip. Water poured off her back and down her skirts. Grace was still wet, but not as soaked as her. They both shivered. Grace whimpered. Slogging up the bank took the last of Eleanor's strength, and she paused at the top, chest heaving, lungs burning. The bruises and scrapes on her arms and legs still hurt. But the pain in her body faded as she stared at the destruction around her. There was no more path, no shrubbery or growth blocking her view to the cabin—and there was definitely no more cabin. There was nothing. She might as well be standing on a barren moor, with smoke smoldering up in wafts instead of mist and fog.

She stumbled forward, picking a trail over fallen timber to the yard, careful to avoid the hot patches yet smoldering. Ash coated the world like hoarfrost. A faint orange glow of embers speckled the collapsed timbers of Samuel's home. The stable, a blackened heap, sent up spirals of white smoke, thin ghosts trying to escape. Grace buried her face in her neck, and a sob clogged Eleanor's throat.

Oh God, whose neck shall I hide against?

A steady pounding grew louder. At first, she attributed the noise to the thudding of her heart—but it came from the direction of the road, not her chest.

"Mrs. Heath!"

Two men guided their horses over the maze of downed wood. Scarves hid the bottom half of their faces. Their hats rode low. Hard to tell who they were, but neither sported the rock-solid shape of Samuel.

She stood, waiting. Shivering. What more was there to do?

The first man rode the perimeter of the yard, surveying the damage. The other approached her and swung down from his saddle. He yanked off his kerchief, revealing a band of clean skin from nose to chin and identifying him as Reverend Parker. Soot blackened the creases at the edges of his eyes as he peered at her. "Thank God! Are you and the child all right?"

An insane urge to laugh shook through her. All right? She stood in the middle of Sheol, and he asked if she were all right?

"You're trembling. Here." He shrugged out of his coat and draped it over her shoulders. "We came as soon as we saw the smoke. Though it grieves me to see you in such a state, it is a mercy you and Grace survived. And we can all thank the good Lord the fire moved uphill, away from Newcastle, sparing more lives than your own. It's a shame about Samuel's house, though."

She let him ramble on. Honestly, what was there for her to say?

The other horse trotted up, and the reverend turned to the man atop. "Mr. Stane, help me get them mounted, if you please."

Without a word, the man slid from his horse, and they both worked to get her and Grace atop the reverend's horse. It would've been better to separate them, making for a much easier ride into town, but Grace cried, clinging all the tighter to Eleanor's neck and refusing to let go. By the time they reached the reverend's house, darkness cloaked the world, and Grace slept against her.

Biz tore out the front door as Reverend Parker dismounted and held his arms up for the sleeping child.

"Oh, caw! What a sight!"

Eleanor reached for Biz's outstretched hand, grateful for the help. When her feet hit the ground, her legs shook. Maybe from the ride. Or maybe just from this horrible, never-ending nightmare of a life.

"Thank you," she rasped, throat still tender. Oh, for a cup of chamomile.

Biz ushered her inside and shoved her down into a chair. "Wait here."

She was left alone with silence and despair. Of all the rooms for Biz to deposit her in, it had to be this one? A memory she'd rather forget lived here, real enough she could reach out and touch it. Should she?

She rose on legs wobbly as a newborn foal's and crossed the rug, stopping in front of the mantle. Absently, she traced her finger along the wood. She'd stood here, this very spot, and exchanged vows with a man she hadn't known. Her gaze followed the movement of her fingertip, back and forth, for if she closed her eyes, no doubt she'd remember the feel of her hand wrapped in his. See the stubble on his cheek as he moved his jaw to say, "I do." Hear the deep resonance of his voice. She hadn't wanted to be his that day. Now there was nothing she wanted more.

But what kind of wife was she? She stifled a cry. One who nearly got him killed, several times over.

It was too much. All of it. Clutching the mantle, she pressed her forehead against the wood and sobbed.

Footsteps rushed into the room. Hands gripped her shoulders, but she refused to turn, to accept comfort of any kind. There was a time for grief—this was it.

Stoneclad Falls swallowed McDivitt's body in a swirl of foamy water. Samuel stared, numbness giving way to horror. McDivitt was dead, and it was his fault. Such a fate was what *he* deserved, what every man deserved, unless redeemed by God's grace.

Sucking in air, he closed his eyes. *God, forgive me. Again and again and again.*

He pivoted and sprinted back to Inoli. A charcoal line split the horizon, low, dividing leaden clouds from a thin strip of cleared sky. The last of day bled out its life there, deep red. Blood red. Samuel pumped his legs faster. *Hold on, my brother.* His toe caught on a rock and he stumbled, but pressed on, the need to reach Inoli pounding strength into every step. Perhaps it wasn't too late. Maybe McDivitt's shot hadn't been mortal. Samuel would remove the ball, stanch the flow, and all would be right.

The other man, McDivitt's accomplice, lay on the ground exactly where he'd fallen, still clutching his leg. He howled for help, and would need it soon, especially with an arrow shaft yet sticking out of his gut, but Samuel bypassed him and dashed ahead.

His steps slowed as he neared the place Inoli had fallen.

His brother was gone.

A trail of clawed earth led to the woods. There, Inoli sat propped against a pine. Eyes wide open. Hands folded in his lap. Long legs sprawled out in front of him. Like he waited for nothing more than for Samuel to make a campfire and swap tales of their boyhood long into the evening.

"Inoli?" Samuel skidded to a stop next to him and dropped to his knees, wincing as pain radiated out from his own wounds. "Brother?"

Inoli didn't answer. Didn't even turn his face. His chest, shirt fabric ripped where the ball had exited, did not rise or fall. There wasn't much blood—not as much as there should be. Not if a heart still pumped inside.

Samuel reached out a hand, shaky as an elder's, and placed two fingers on his brother's neck. Cold skin. No pulse. The shaking crawled up his arm, skimmed over his shoulders, and settled deep inside, until his very soul shook.

"Noo!" Anguish tore out his throat. How could this be? This man, this warrior, gone? Just like that?

He pulled Inoli into his arms and rocked back and forth. Back and forth. The same motion he used to put Grace to sleep. He might be sobbing. Hard to tell. He didn't hear anything but a rushing noise in his ears and the thudding of his heart. No more would he and his brother run through the woods, hunting for deer and turkey. There'd be no more exchange of knowing glances, speaking of life and God, of what was to come or what had been.

There'd be no more anything.

By the time Samuel pulled away, night shadows crept from the woods. He laid his brother back against the tree trunk. Blood from the wound on his own chest had soaked into Inoli's shirt and blended with his brother's. He pressed his palm against it and stared at his fingers.

"Goodbye, my friend." The ragged voice didn't sound like his—nor was it, for he'd never be the same again. Why should he expect to sound as before?

The night was long. The next day never ending. He moved as through a thick fog, stumbling about in a grey mist of grief and pain. He patched up himself and Barton—the other man's name, he learned—as good as could be expected. Good enough to travel on horseback, anyway. He'd forced Barton to help him bury Inoli. . .of sorts. With no shovel, nor the strength to dig even if one were available, they stacked rocks atop his body. Samuel fashioned a crude cross of wood and staked it at the head of the pile. Not a usual Cherokee ceremony, but there'd never been anything usual about Inoli to begin with. He was a man unlike any other.

By the time Samuel retrieved the horses, tied Barton to Inoli's mount, and tracked down the runaway horse with the money, the day was well spent. But Samuel drove them onward despite the lack of light, putting as much distance between him and the awful hurt behind.

More than anything, he just wanted to go home.

Chapter 38

Eleanor pinned up her hair by the weak light of a newborn day seeping in through the window. Already dressed in one of Biz's borrowed gowns, all that was left was to slip on her shoes. Today was a new chapter. A whole new story. One she didn't want to read but determined to plow through anyway. Fitting, really, that she'd walk out the door of this chamber, the one she'd shared with Biz when she first came to Newcastle, into a different life.

"Yer up early." Biz's sleepy voice drifted behind her.

"I intend an early start." She turned from the window as Biz unwrapped herself from the bed sheets. "Thank you for the gown and, well, for everything. I owe you."

Covering a yawn, Biz eyed her from across the room, then left the sleeping Grace behind to stare up into her face. "You ain't fooling me, Elle Bell. I know that look. Seen it before on bawdy house girls."

"What look?"

Biz lifted her chin. "Yer running away."

She frowned. With Biz's uncanny discernment, she'd have made a fine gypsy fortuneteller. "I would not call it such, but since you have brought it up, yes. I am leaving. And I need your help in securing a horse."

"A horse?" Biz cocked her head. "Where do you think yer going?"

"Charles Towne."

Biz snorted. "Of all the hare-brained ideas. What the nippity-skippet for? You won't last a day on yer own."

"Maybe so, but I cannot stay here." She folded her arms, turning from Biz's direct gaze. "Not anymore."

Biz would have none of it. She scooted around Eleanor, stopping right in front of her. "Why you leaving?"

The question hit her broadside. There were many reasons, some ridiculous—such as her jealously over Miss Browndell—but others were more valid. She gazed into Biz's eyes, weighing, measuring. How much should she tell her?

A sigh deflated her chest. She owed Biz an explanation, especially after her tearful display in the sitting room the previous evening.

"The truth is that I am not meant for this frontier life. I am not strong like you. Not courageous, despite what Molly says. I am a liability. Do you know how many times Samuel nearly died because of me? It is better for him that I should leave. I will not put his life at risk again."

"Pah!" Biz spit the word out like a plug of tobacco. "Yer crazy. Seems to me that man can fend for himself."

Of course he could, but he needn't fend for her as well, not when her ignorance had nearly cost them all their lives. Her stomach twisted. For a moment, she opened the lid on her sorrow, just for a peek, then slammed the cover shut with a shudder. No, better to carry out her plan and deal with the grief later.

She met Biz's hard stare. "I wondered if you would care for Grace until Mr. Heath returns? And, as I have said, help me secure a horse for my journey."

Biz cursed as she paced to the other side of the room and back, the movement stirring Grace in her sleep.

"Take a care, Biz. You will wake Grace."

"Look, Elle Bell, I don't know what you got in that delicate little mind of yours, but you have no idea the dangers out there for a woman alone. You can't ride to Charles Towne by yerself. You'll never make it. Caw! You'd not last one night on the road without getting into bad trouble."

Eleanor set her jaw. Of course she'd assessed the dangers, and decided that the odds were nearly impossible. But had she not learned God was the master of impossibility? "I know. Yet it is a risk I am willing to take for Samuel and Grace's sake. I am in God's hands. I firmly believe that."

Biz's face screwed up, her mouth twitching one way and another, then as suddenly cleared. "It's more than them, ain't it. You got something deeper gnawing at you."

Eleanor jerked her face aside, choosing instead to gaze out at the dawn's grey light than the dogged pursuit gleaming in Biz's eyes. "I do not know what you are talking about."

"Yes, you do."

She sucked in a shaky breath. How could such a former gutter rat know her so well?

"Get it out. All of it. Confession's good for the soul, or so Parker tells me." Biz's steps drew near behind her, and a hand rested on her shoulder.

"Eleanor, please."

Her throat tightened. Of all the times for Biz to turn soft, she chose this one? She pressed her forehead to the glass, cool against her skin. "I. . . I feel I need to succeed at something, *anything*, or I shall die on the inside. I have failed here. Dismally. Grace deserves a better mother than me. Samuel, a better wife. A real one. It was a sham, all of this, despite my efforts to make it work. My father predicted I would not amount to much. I guess. . . ." Her voice faltered, the last of her words coming out on a breath. "He was right."

She fought back a cry and spun to face Biz. "There is nothing more for me here! I am going to Charles Towne, and I will not be turned from it. If I am accosted along the way, then so be it."

A growl rumbled in Biz's throat. She whirled, her nightshift swirling around her legs. Storming to a chest at the foot of the bed, she rummaged through the contents. She retrieved something small enough to fit in one hand, then closed the lid and marched back. "Then yer going to need this."

She placed a crumpled piece of paper into Eleanor's hands and retreated a step, a defiant light in her gaze.

"What is it?" Eleanor unfolded the paper, heavy with coins inside. Why would Biz give her money? Where had she gotten it from? But. . .wait. The embellishment of writing on the paper, fine, strong strokes, looked familiar. She tilted the paper to catch the pale light diffused by the poor window glass, and her stomach clenched.

"Where did you get this?" she whispered.

"I stole it, that's what. On the passage over. I took it right out of yer gown, when you were asleep on the ship."

Eleanor jerked her face back to Biz, horrified.

"You know what kind of woman I am." A scowl darkened Biz's brow.

"But. . ." Eleanor gaped. If only she'd had this before, how different life would've been. No log cabin. No bears. The only danger a broken fingernail or perhaps a torn hem. She'd have lived in a fine Charles Towne home, educating children in mathematics and French, not chasing after a fair-haired toddler through dirt and brush.

Her shoulders sagged. She'd also have been working for a man and woman far removed from her company. Alone once the children were abed. Banished to an upper room of solitude instead of sharing evenings on a porch with a man she loved. She blew out a long, low breath, a vain attempt at dispelling the pervasive sorrow wrapping around her like a shroud.

"I'm sorry, Elle Bell. Truly. Living with the reverend, well, it's rubbing off I suppose. I done a lot of wrong. I know that now." The woman's head lowered, contrite, repentant—and as out of character as Eleanor's outburst the previous evening. "Only half the money is there. I spent some."

Without waiting for a response, Biz lifted her face. "But I didn't read yer letter. Whatever it says is yer secret alone. I. . .I can't read."

She ought be angry. She ought at least denounce the woman in some way. But Eleanor's heart broke at the quiver on Biz's chin. She opened her arms and pulled her friend into an embrace. This was no friend she'd have chosen, but Biz was an unconventional gift nonetheless.

Biz hugged her back, hard. "You ain't cross?"

"How could I be?" Eleanor released her then grabbed Biz's hands. "You have just given me a ticket to my future."

"I did?"

"Indeed. This paper is my reference to an employer in Charles Towne. I shall have a place to stay, a job to do." She smiled. "You have given me a chance to start over."

"Start over. I like the sound of that. I hate to see you go, but I understand the need. Why, I'll take the best care of Grace I can till yer man comes for her, so you needn't worry on that account." She squeezed Eleanor's fingers, then turned and rushed to the door, snatching a wrap off a peg and tying it around her waist. "I best get about finding you an escort. Parker will know if anyone's planning a ride in to Charles Towne, or maybe even take you himself."

"But Biz! You are not even dressed yet."

The woman stopped at the threshold, casting a glance over her shoulder. "Pah! Never stopped me before."

Unconventional, indeed. Eleanor's heart swelled. She'd miss this woman, more than Biz could ever imagine. "Thank you. You have turned into a fine woman, as I knew you would."

An unladylike word flew out of Biz's mouth, squelching the sweet moment. "I ain't that fine."

Once the door closed, Eleanor rushed to the table and pulled out a piece of rag paper from the drawer. Poor quality, but better than nothing. She carved a fresh tip on a quill with a penknife and dipped the tip into a bottle of ink. How did one write a goodbye to a man she didn't really want to leave? A husband, if only by word and threat alone? It took a few tries, some blotted words, and not just a tear stain but several before she composed a suitable letter:

Dear Samuel,
Forgive me for the familiar greeting, but it seems odd to call
you Mr. Heath after having shared so much with you. I am
deeply sorry about your home and hope you will not think too
ill of me for salvaging nothing. I am a poor colonist, I fear,
unsuited to such a foreign lifestyle.

Enclosed you will find a small down payment for what I
owe you. I intend to return in full all the money you paid for
my passage, but I ask for your patience in that respect. I shall
send more as I am able until such a sum is reached, which
ought serve to nullify the marriage agreement. Please do not
be angry if this takes me some time, for I don't imagine my
wages will be large.

I trust you will find a proper mother for Grace. She is a
dear little one, far too dear to be entrusted solely to me, espe-
cially at such a young age. She will likely not remember me as
she grows, but I shall never forget her. Nor you.

Thank you for your care. I learned a lot in our time
together. I leave here a different woman than when I first
came, changed in so many ways. I owe that to you. I owe so
much to you.

Yours,

~~Eleanor~~ Tatsuwa
(forgive the improper spelling)

Setting down the quill, she stared at the words. They weren't enough, of course. There was so much more to say. But if she gave in and wrote all that was on her heart, she'd never leave here—and even in the leaving, part of her heart would remain.

She lifted her hand to her throat and pulled out the bear claw. All she had left of their time together was this. Wrapping her fingers around the talisman, she debated, long and hard. She ought leave this. A family heirloom should remain with the family. But her stomach turned and nausea rose at the thought of never having a piece of Samuel to take with her for the long, cold nights ahead. She pulled on the tether until it cut into the back of her neck.

But she couldn't do it. Couldn't yank it off completely. Could not sever this last tie.

She buried the necklace beneath her bodice and instead slid all but one coin atop the letter to Samuel. She'd need something for the journey to Charles Towne, if only a paltry sum.

She stood on legs that didn't want to move, not really, and crossed over to Grace. Tangled in the counterpane, the girl slept, curled on her side. Golden hair fanned onto the pillow like rays of sunshine. Eleanor reached out yet refrained from touching the child. It would be hard enough to leave her without the girl watching her walk out of her life. Tears would undo her. Of course she'd loved children before and experienced difficult departures, but this was different. Part of her heart would remain in the tiny fist pressed against the girl's cheek.

Holding back a sob, Eleanor whispered, "I shall always love you, little one."

Her throat closed, and she sped to the door. Grace would be better off without her. So would Samuel. She had to believe that, wrap her hands around that boulder, and let it sink deep into her belly. Believing otherwise would crush her.

"Heath!"

Samuel jerked up his face and sucked in a breath. A blur of green and brown slowly sharpened into trees, trail, canopy, and ground. Wohali blew out a snort and bobbed her head, his mount as annoyed by Barton's voice as he was.

Sweat beaded on Samuel's forehead, and he swiped it with the back of his hand, skewing his hat. For the first part of September, it surely felt like midsummer—except for the recurring chills that shook him from head to toe.

"We going in circles?" Barton accused from behind.

Samuel ignored him, forcing his eyes to remain open—hard to do when, with each of Wohali's steps, he wanted to wince. The wound on his chest burned like hellfire. Oh, for a bottle of rum right about now...but he didn't drink anymore. Did he?

Swallowing the old desire, he slipped his gaze from a jut of granite, to a forked scarlet oak, and on to a southward bend in the trail. All of it familiar. Too familiar. Full consciousness punched him in the gut. Barton was right. They'd been here. Yesterday. And maybe even the day before that. Inoli would have a good laugh about that when he heard—Samuel's heart seized. No, he wouldn't. His brother would never laugh at him again.

He pulled back on the reins with his good arm and voiced a low "whoa" to the two horses strung behind. He had to get his bearings—and not let on that he'd lost them in the first place. Not that Barton was in much better shape than him. The man's leg, wrapped and tied, was on the mend, but the arrow wound in his gut festered. If they didn't reach Newcastle by sundown, neither of them would see another day.

Barton hacked up a wad and spat it to the ground. "Yer lost, ain't ya?"

"Shut your mouth, Barton. You talk too much." Wide awake and wishing he weren't, Samuel sniffed. Then sniffed again, trepidation growing with each inhale. How had he missed the smoky stench in the air?

He twisted in the saddle. Pain seared the entire left side of his torso, and he grunted. The breeze carried a burnt stink from the east, up toward a rise of pine and hickory. The direction of his house.

Oh God. No.

"Hyah!" He dug his heels into Wohali's belly. The mount took off like a well-placed musket shot.

"What in the—"

"Shut up, Barton!" Samuel yelled. Half a mile later, an old buffalo trail intersected their path. He steered his mount onto it. All three horses slowed on the incline.

"Ain't Newcastle south? I need me a doc. I can't take this much longer."

The man's whining burned into Samuel's back like a hot poker. Or was that from the fever he could no longer deny? Either way, he understood why McDivitt had wanted to shoot the man. Four—or was it five?—days in Barton's company could drive anyone to the act.

One more mile, and Samuel's heart started beating hard. Acrid air hit the back of his throat, rubbing it raw. A half hour later, and his heart stopped. So did Wohali. The other horses whinnied. All three halted at the line where growth and greenery gave way to charred ground and blackened timber. Ahead, trees sprawled like dead men. Only a few brave survivors stood tall and blistered.

Behind, Barton cursed.

Samuel leaned forward, whispering to Wohali. "Home, girl. Take us home."

A great shiver ran the length of his mount's neck; then Wohali trotted onward, stepping high over logs. Samuel gasped, clutching the reins so tight his fingers ached. Better to focus on that pain than passing out—or on the horror that he might find when his homestead came within sight.

With every step closer, he couldn't help but wonder if Red Bird and Grace had made it out alive. Had they plenty of warning? Had his wife known what to do? His blood ran cold, and he trembled. Uncontrollably. Had they met with the same end as Mariah?

He should've been here for them—he should've been there for Mariah.

Loosening the reins, he gave Wohali plenty of lead to pick her way down the creek bank then up the other side. When they cleared the rise, the ruined area of black land punched him in the lungs, stealing his breath. Samuel slid from the horse and ran to what should've been his yard, his stable, his home. His life.

Nothing but charred heaps of rubble remained. Not even any smoke curled out. Like life had loaded up its mount and moved on.

How much loss could a man take and still stand? Not this much. Not him. He dropped to his knees. Gravel dug into his flesh, poking through the fabric of his breeches. Good. Dig and cut and shred. Why not? He'd lost it all. His brother, his daughter, the only woman he'd ever loved.

A cry started deep, plowing up heart and soul and yanking them along as it tore out his throat. The wail swelled up to heaven. It had to. There was no other place for it to go.

Spent, he pitched forward and lay prone, rock and dirt mashing into his cheek. Eventually, his eyes closed. Maybe forever. If God smiled on him, he'd never open them again.

Chapter 39

Charles Towne
November 1770

Snap! The piece of chalk broke in Eleanor's fingers, the sharp crack filling the schoolroom like the breaking of a bone. Seated in front of her, ten-year-old William Taggerton glanced up from his sketchpad. She smiled down at her young charge with the feigned look of pleasantry she'd mastered in the past three months. "Give me a moment more, William."

The boy shrugged and went back to sketching out a likeness of a ship with a charcoal stick. He wouldn't care if she ever finished.

Eleanor drew in a deep breath, then pocketed the broken half of chalk and went back to writing sums with the leftover stub on a small slate. What was wrong with her today? A grimace tightened her jaw, and for the space of a heartbeat, she nearly gave in to the truth of what ailed her every day. Sorrow. A grief so acquainted it had no qualms about climbing into bed with her each night so that she woke in the morning to a pillow dampened by tears.

Oh, Samuel, would that things had been different.

"Miss Morgan, look!" Susan's cheerfulness squealed from the girl in a pitch that set Eleanor's teeth on edge. Across the table from William, his younger sister grinned up. A stack of buttons wobbled in front of her, like a castle tower about to tumble under siege.

"Very nice, Susan. How about you sort them now, by color perhaps?" She forced a lightness into her tone that she didn't feel. Couldn't feel. Not when every time she looked at the girl, all she longed to see was Grace's pixie face. What a horrid quirk of fate that her new charge also had golden hair.

"Miss Morgan?" A woman's voice called to her from behind.

Eleanor stashed away the rest of the chalk into her pocket. "See if you can do these sums for me, William." Handing the slate to the boy, she whirled to answer the housekeeper's summons. "Yes, Betty?"

The woman stood framed in the schoolroom doorway, looking like a spooked horse, nostrils flaring, the whites of her dark eyes large. "It's Mr. Taggerton, miss. He be askin' for you in the study."

Eleanor pressed a hand to her stomach. In all her time as governess in this home, she'd never once been called to the study. In truth, after the first week here, she'd hardly seen or spoken to either the master or the mistress. "Me? Now?"

"Yes'm." The woman bobbed her head, the white kerchief on her hair in stark contrast to her ebony skin. Casting a wide-eyed look over her shoulder, as if perhaps a hound of hell tagged her heels, she scurried into the room and lowered her voice, for Eleanor alone to hear. "And miss? You ought to know. . .he ain't smilin'. He be in a foul mood, so mind yer step."

"Very well." Eleanor smoothed her clammy hands along her skirt. It must be bad if Betty were this riled. "Thank you. I shall be down directly."

Betty whooshed out the door, apron strings flying. Eleanor watched her disappear, unease creeping down to her stomach and tightening into a knot. Why would the master call her midday when he ought be out attending to more important matters of business?

Mulling the possibilities, she crossed the rug to a bookcase and pulled off a picture book. Running her hand farther down the shelf, she grabbed a reader, then returned to the table and set them down. "When you are finished with your tasks, children, I would like you to do some reading. I shall be back shortly."

"Yes, Miss Morgan," their voices joined together, Susan's lisp adding a hissing quality.

Eleanor frowned as she hurried out the door and down the corridor. As she sped along, she contemplated what to try next to get Susan to annunciate more clearly—a vain attempt to keep from thinking about why Mr. Taggerton had summoned her.

She descended the grand stairway, turned left, and stopped in front of the study. Pausing, she fingered her hair and tucked up any stray wisps. Necessary, yet also a stalling tactic, giving her enough time to compose the rapid beat of her heart. Surely she'd not committed some grievous error? If she were relieved of this post—no. Better not to think it, or she'd undo her last-minute primping and enter the room all teary-eyed and forlorn.

She lifted her knuckles and rapped on the mahogany, the echo bouncing in the small corridor.

"Enter." The command, though muffled, was stern.

My precious Lord;

My only hope;

My Saviour, how I need You now.

Holding tightly to the prayer, she shoved open the door and met with cigar smoke and tension thick on the air. Mr. Taggerton stood behind his desk, arms folded, blue eyes trained upon her. A severe line creased his brow. Without a word, his censure boxed her ears.

She stopped just inside the threshold, unable to make her feet travel any farther. Apprehension moistened her palms, and she folded her hands in front of her, giving no quarter for them to rub along her skirt and expose her nervousness. She'd not seen the master of the house look so austere in her entire time here. Swallowing for courage, she was about to greet him when a movement from the other side of the room attracted her gaze.

There, near the corner, another man stood at the window, back to her. He lowered his hand, and the sheer curtain he'd been holding back fell into place. Sunlight silhouetted him, light against shadow. A figure of darkness and strength. Her heart skipped a beat.

The man's hair was the shade of roasted chestnuts left too long in the fire, just like Samuel's, but it was pulled neatly back and tied with a ribbon. His shoulders were broad, with a fine, strong back that narrowed at the waist, but the tailored suit did not bulge out at the hip where a tomahawk ought to rest. Farther down, past legs wrapped in exquisite fawn-colored wool, leather shoes reflected a sunbeam from the window. Moccasin boots wouldn't do that—and that's all Samuel ever wore.

Eleanor swallowed a sour taste. Curdled milk would've been sweeter. La! Would she never be free of the man?

"Miss Morgan?"

"Yes, sir." She snapped her face back to Mr. Taggerton and dropped a curtsey. "I came as quickly as I could, sir."

He crossed to the front of the desk, looking down his nose at her the entire time. "I have just heard quite a tale. A fantastic one, really, though one I'm inclined to believe unless you say otherwise."

Biting her lip, she looked from one man to the other. The fellow at the window stood as granite, his back an unmovable mountain.

Mr. Taggerton's steely gaze was every bit as inflexible as he drew up in front of her. "When you first came here, Miss Morgan, you told me of your past, but I wonder if you told me all of it?"

"I. . ." She pressed her lips shut. What had he heard? Who knew anything about her? Had the duke somehow found out her location from his wife and was even now ruining her in a new land? Panic fluttered in her chest. "What is it you want to know?"

His gaze bore into hers, terrible and piercing. "Are you married, Miss Morgan?"

"No!" Without thought, her hand slapped against her chest, the bear claw beneath her bodice a sharp accusation as it dug into her skin. The tangible truth scorched her conscience, and she wilted back a step. God's wrath burned hot against deceivers such as herself. "I mean. . .I suppose I am, until I can pay off my contract. But I swear to you, sir, I never knew the man as a husband. In that respect I am blameless."

"Breaking a contract—either indenture or marriage—is a serious offense." Mr. Taggerton's eyes narrowed. "I could have you arrested. Imprisoned. Or worse."

"Me?" Panic choked her, and she gasped. "Please, no. I had no choice in the matter. I only did what I had to. You do not understand!"

Her voice broke, a ragged cry fraying her words to shreds—and like a hawk to a mouse, the noise drew the other man from the window.

Across the room, dark eyes found hers—and stared straight into her soul. "Then tell him everything, Tatsu'hwa."

The floor pitched, like the canting of the ship that'd first brought her to this land. She staggered to a nearby chair and grabbed on to the back of it.

Clean-shaven, dressed in the garb of a gentleman, and every bit as imposing as a Grosvenor Square aristocrat, Samuel advanced. This could hardly be the same backcountry savage she'd known. But there, the puckered scar near his cheek. The full lips that'd once pressed against hers. The muscular arms that'd held her and saved her and comforted her time and again.

Mr. Taggerton cocked his head at the scene, studying her in particular, but there was no way to hide the rush of emotions inside her begging release, whether he watched her or not. She squeezed the leather high-back, gripping tight to keep from tipping over.

"Samuel?" His name came out a shiver. A hope. A dream she'd long ago killed and buried and mourned.

"Well, well." Mr. Taggerton looked from her to Samuel. "It seems I owe you an apology, Mr. Heath. Forgive my doubt, for clearly you spoke true." Samuel shook his head, a familiar smile lifting half his mouth—the curve of which she longed to reach out and trace a finger along just to make sure he was real.

Oh God, please let this be real.

"No offense taken, Mr. Taggerton." Samuel nodded once, the powerful affirmation that he had everything under control. "My offer still stands. The compensation remains the same."

"Very generous of you, sir." Mr. Taggerton leaned back and snuffed out his unattended cigar, then strode to the door. "I shall give you a few moments."

The doorknob turned. The latch clicked. Eleanor flinched, not from the jarring sound but the sudden turn of events. For three never-ending months she'd tried to banish memories of this man standing flesh and blood in front of her. To deny she'd ever felt anything for him. To forget about his direct stare and the way he filled a room with security and strength simply by being in it. Yet now that he stood but a few breaths away, parts of her she thought she'd crucified rose to life.

She retreated a step as Samuel drew near. If he came any closer, she'd break. She must be careful. She was glass. Too many fragile sentiments surfaced, pooling just beneath her skin. He'd see, and she'd be undone, shattering to millions of pieces—unable to ever be put back to rights. She lifted her chin and forced herself to meet his gaze. Of course he'd not come for romantic reasons, but monetary. Nothing more. Had he not spoken so to Mr. Taggerton?

"Your face is white as a first snow." Without shadow of stubble or beard, a deep dimple highlighted the lift of his mouth. "You look as if I'm a ghost."

"You . . ." Sudden shyness thickened her tongue. Who was this stranger, this mighty man of suave power that wore a faint mask of Samuel? She cleared her throat and tried again. "You look so different."

"You think Mr. Taggerton would admit a savage into his home?" His grin grew.

She sucked in a breath at the sight, inhaling more than just his sandalwood shaving tonic. There, a layer beneath the freshly scrubbed skin and tied-back hair, gunpowder and wood smoke yet clung to him. If he opened his arms and pulled her against his chest, she'd smell all his familiar scents. Her legs quivered from the thought.

He angled his head and studied her. "You tremble. Are you well?"

How was she to think, let alone put words together, when he stood there so masculine and appealing? She licked her lips, hoping the action would grease the way for words to flow, and prayed for a voice that wouldn't break. "I am."

Liar. *Oh God, forgive me. I am weak. Be my strength.* She clenched her hands into fists, the cut of her nails against her palms stinging her back to reality. "How did you find me?" Good. Her voice didn't quaver a bit that time.

"I'm a tracker. It's what I do. Though you didn't really think the reverend would keep your whereabouts from me, did you?" He stepped closer and lifted her chin, looking deep into her eyes. "I'd have arrived sooner if not for a fever. Recovery took longer than I expected. Getting old, I guess."

His gaze burned into hers, and her stomach clenched. She knew he wasn't a patient man. Had experienced his lack many times over the course of the summer. She'd been a fool to ever think the small sum she'd left behind for him would've satisfied. "I am sorry to hear you were not well. And I am sorry I have not been able to send you a payment as of yet. Mr. Taggerton has not given me a quarterly stipend, but I swear, I shall pay back every penny I owe you."

Samuel shook his head. No long hair brushed his collar. Why did that feel like such a loss?

"I don't want your money. I've enough of my own." He stepped closer, the heat of his body beckoning, taunting, wrapping around her like a heady embrace. "Why did you leave?"

It was a quiet question. Hardly more than a whisper. But the pain riding the crest of it washed over her, drowning her so that she choked. "How can you ask that? I failed you in every possible way! You and Grace. I nearly got you both killed time and time again. Why did you come here if not for recompense?"

"Is that not obvious? I came for you, Tatsu'hwa." His big fingers slid down her arms, grabbing her hands as he slipped to one knee.

Her jaw dropped. She'd seen him prostrated such as this only one time before—when tied to a tree, his back torn open by a lash in her stead.

"I want you as my wife. My true wife." His husky tone left no doubt about his meaning. "But this time I'm giving you a choice, a *real* choice, with no coercion. Will you have me, Eleanor Morgan, as your husband, or do you want your freedom? Speak what is on your heart, and you shall have it."

Samuel stared hard up at Eleanor's lips, waiting for one word. Just one.

But waiting never came easy. Never had. Waiting for the grief of Inoli's death to pass—but that was a battle he yet fought every day. Waiting for the festering gunshot wound to heal so he could be on the move again. Waiting to find out if Stane successfully carried out the mission Samuel couldn't by bringing the munitions intelligence to the Sons of Liberty. One never knew with a mercenary. But apparently Stane had been amply compensated not only by Samuel but by the Sons, for Stane had made the trip to Charles Towne. Because of his information, an ambush waylaid those double-barreled firearms. For now, at least, the threat of violence from Attakullakulla and his ilk had been put on hold.

Still, the worst wait of all was the current slow bleed draining the life from him as he waited for Red Bird to answer.

He set his jaw, clenching his teeth until a crack sounded in his ear. He would wait, by God's grace. He would wait. There'd be no pressure this time, not from him. He'd have all of her freely—or none at all.

Staring up at her, he memorized the curve of her cheek. The outrageous red curl that refused to be tamed at her temple. How her eyes changed color from placid ocean to stormy sea.

"What about Miss Browndell?"

The question hit him like an arrow through the gut. He gaped. Of all the possible responses he'd concocted in his mind, of how Red Bird might accept or refuse his offer of troth, even during his feverish recovery he'd not thought of this one.

"Miss Browndell?" He couldn't help but repeat the name, hoping it might lend some kind of credence to the inquiry. It didn't. "What has she to do with anything?"

Tears shimmered in Red Bird's eyes. "I found her ring, Samuel, amongst your belongings."

Surely she didn't think. . .he and Miss Browndell? He'd laugh, but even a boor such as himself knew that would be the end of this conversation. "Woman, please don't tell me that's why you left."

Clipped steps sounded outside the door, and she glanced over her shoulder. By the time the sound faded and she looked back at him, the sheen in her eyes nearly spilled over. "I own I mainly left for your well-being. I put you and Grace into danger through my ignorance more than once. But yes, truth be known, Miss Browndell was also part of the reason."

Women. Who could understand their logic? Slowly, he rose, let go of her fingers, and cupped her face with both hands. Logic be hanged. He didn't need to understand this woman to love her—but clearly she needed to understand him.

"First off, stop blaming yourself for Grace's safety. I can't thank you enough for saving her from that fire. It was you, your quick thinking, that—" His voice broke. He'd almost lost his daughter once again to fire, were it not for this trembling woman in front of him.

He sucked in a breath and started again, staring deep into Red Bird's eyes. "Secondly, my well-being isn't your responsibility. It's not you who numbers my days but God. If He grants I die in saving you because of your ignorance—as you call it—I can think of no greater honor. And lastly, as for Miss Browndell, well…let's just say she was a means to an end, nothing more. She gave me information I passed on to. . . ." He paused. Who knew if these walls had ears or where Taggerton's political sentiments lay? Maybe someday he'd tell Red Bird of his involvement with the Sons of Liberty, but not now.

He shook his head. "I don't expect to ever see Miss Browndell again."

Red Bird's gaze fixed on his. "You did not care for her?"

He snorted, rude for such a tender moment, but completely unstoppable. "Did you? Did anyone?"

Little crinkles creased her nose, making her freckles dance. "No. I did not."

He leaned his forehead against hers, breathing deeply of her familiar scent, like sunlight warming a June afternoon. If he had to walk away from this room without her at his side, the sorrow would be unbearable. He ran his thumbs over her cheeks, and trembled from the soft skin beneath.

Closing his eyes, he poured out his heart. "You're the one I love, Tatsu'hwa. Not Browndell. Not Running Doe. Not even Mariah. I've never spoken those words to any woman, because I never meant them. But I do now. With you. Only you. So…what is it to be?"

Her fingers ran up his back, lodged behind his head, and pulled his mouth down to hers.

"You." Her word was a kiss. Her breaths thick and intoxicating against his skin. "Always. Only. You."

A tremor shook through him. Desire. Hunger. He kissed her with all the passion so long denied, and he didn't pull away until he'd backed her against the study wall. Horrified, he released her and retreated a step. Animal. He belonged in the woods. What must she think of him? "Forgive me. I'm not usually so unrestrained but—"

She reached out and placed a finger on his lips, so reminiscent of the times he'd done the same to her that his breath hitched.

"You forget, sir, that I know what a wild man you can be."

Her other hand fumbled at her neck and pulled out the bear claw necklace. A feverish gleam lit her eyes, one he'd never seen—and shot a jolt to his belly.

She lifted a defiant chin. "Yet I will have you anyway. For you see, I love you with as much abandon. Besides, we have your grandmother's prophecy to fulfill, do we not?"

He kissed her finger, and she pulled it away with a smile.

"Then come home with me, Mrs. Heath. I can't promise you a cabin in the woods, not until next year, but I know a certain little girl who can't wait to leap into your arms." He reached for her hand and pulled her close. "Nor can I."

Chapter 40

Spring 1771

"Grace?" Eleanor darted down the corridor, peeking into empty rooms, hoping to catch a glimpse of golden hair. The only answer was the tap of her own shoes, clicking against the barren wood floors as she dashed along. Outside the townhome, jingling tack and whickering horses sped her steps. Of all the times for the girl to go missing, it had to be this morning?

"It is time to leave! Where have you gone off to?" She mounted the stairway to the second floor, fingers running along the cool bannister—the only thing cool on this humid morn. Winded, she halted at the top of the landing, then set off down the hall. "Grace?"

A squeak of a voice came from the end of the passage. "Here, Mama."

Eleanor advanced toward the room she'd shared with Samuel these past five months. Why would Grace be in an empty bedchamber instead of out pestering her papa, especially on such an exciting day as this? She clipped through the door. "Why are you in here?"

Pausing, she studied the three-year-old who huddled in a corner, picking at a floorboard. Sunlight streamed through the window, Grace adding more dust motes to the rays with all her hard work. What on earth was she up to?

"What are you doing, little miss?"

With nary so much as a glance over her shoulder, the girl yanked on a board, and a six-inch section of wood gave way. Grace whumped onto her bottom, the thud reverberating the oaken planks. That had to hurt.

"Grace!" Eleanor darted to the child, but by the time she reached her side, the pixie stood and held up a small, wooden toy.

"My top!" Grace grinned, as pleased as if she'd pulled a plum from a Yuletide pie.

Eleanor planted her hands on her hips. Except for the yellow hair peeking from beneath the child's cap, Grace was the image of her father—and even more like him in her behaviours. Had not Samuel hidden his medal of honor in much the same fashion?

What to do, though? There was no separating an inborn bent. Eleanor sighed. Neither would it do any good to scold the girl about the hole in the floor, for that would only cause tears and delay their departure even more.

She bent, eye-level, and slipped a glance at the toy. The top had been a favorite, carved by Samuel and given to Grace on Christmas morn. She'd slept with the thing. Dragged it around from room to room on a string. Even insisted on keeping it in her lap during meals. But now that Eleanor thought on it, the top had been curiously absent the past month. She stared into Grace's brown gaze. "You love that toy. Why did you hide it?"

The girl pursed her lips, looking at her as if she were a recent escapee from Bedlam asylum. "I'm saving it for my brother."

Despite the girl's condescending tone, the earnest words spread warmth from Eleanor's heart to her tummy. "Grace, my sweet." She shook her head. "You cannot know that the babe will be a brother. It might also be a sister."

Her little shoulders shrugged, smart and dismissing and altogether adorable. "Papa said it's a boy."

Eleanor grinned and couldn't help but tweak the girl's nose. "Well Papa is not always right."

"Am I not?" A deep voice wrapped around her from behind.

Grace giggled.

Eleanor straightened and whirled. The heat of her husband's eyes assessing her curves weakened her knees. Such a look always did. Nevertheless, she threw back her shoulders. "No, sir, you are not infallible."

His eyes twinkled, and a half smile twitched his lips, lighting his face. Why had she ever thought him dark and brooding?

"Then tell me what I've been wrong about, woman."

She opened her mouth to reply, but in four long strides, he pulled her against him and kissed her. Again and again. His mouth warm as the spring morning, bold as the sunlight that peeked into their window. He tasted and consumed until her legs trembled. And she tasted right back, savoring his passion.

"You know I cannot think when you do this," she breathed out the words as his lips drifted down her neck.

He pulled away, a triumphant slant to his jaw. "Then I shall answer for you, for I concede there is but one thing I've misjudged."

"Oh?"

"How much I love you." His tone softened, as did the gleam of victory in his eyes. "I didn't think it possible, but I love you more every day, *uwoduhi atsiyehi.*"

She reached up and rubbed her palm along his smooth cheek. She'd never tire of the feel of his warm skin or the huskiness in his voice when he spoke his heart. "I shall miss this romantic side of you. You are a different man living in the city."

"Yes. . .and no." He caught her wrist and pressed a kiss into her palm. "I am a different man, but Charles Towne has nothing to do with it. It's you, Tatsu'hwa. Living with you has changed me. Inoli saw that after our first week together."

A shadow darkened his clear, brown gaze, breaking Eleanor's heart. He still mourned his friend—and likely always would.

As changeful as a March breeze, the look passed, and he released her hand. Sidestepping her, he swept up Grace, then wheeled about. "The horses are ready, as is the wagon. Are you certain you want to leave all this city life behind?"

Her gaze skipped past him, darting from wall to wall, remembering the winter they'd shared here as husband and wife. The cozy hearth that warmed them on their first night together. The glass windows keeping stormy weather at bay while they snuggled beneath a down counterpane. Was she really ready to give up all this comfort? Trade it in for a cabin not yet built in a wild backcountry filled with danger?

She stared at her husband, picturing him in his trade shirt, loosened at the neck, exposing muscle and flesh instead of the buttoned waistcoat hiding his chest. Him swinging his axe in the open air, not skulking around with businessmen or Indian agents. Grace running free in the wind, golden hair streaming behind. Eleanor's hand rested absently on the tiny swell of her belly. Their son, growing into the same kind of man as his father, friend to the Cherokee, one with the land—a land that held her heart captive.

She reached for Samuel's hand. His bare palm pressed against hers, the strength and warmth entwining her fingers still able to send a jolt up her arm. She peeked up at him, a grin growing with each of her words.

"I have never been more certain of anything in my life. Take me home, Samuel. Take us all home."

Glossary of Cherokee words and phrases

Alewisdodi – Stop
Anesta – Stickball, a major Cherokee sport
Ani'yunwiya – The Cherokee, literally the Principle People
Doh-nah-dah-goh-hun-I – Until we meet again
Edoda – Father
Eligwu – That's enough
Elisi – Grandmother
Etsi – Mother
Gawonisgv – Talk
Gilisi – English
Ha – Now
Inoli – Black fox
Ipa – Open
sa'gwali digu 'lanahi'ta – Mule
Tatsu'hwa – Red Bird
Un'ega – White people
Uwoduhi atsiyehi – Beautiful wife
Wado – Thank you
Wohali – Eagle
Ya'nu – Bear

Historical Note

Regulators

Outlaw gangs and criminals roamed the Carolina backcountry in the 1760s. Citizens organized to "regulate" government affairs and establish some kind of law and order. These regulators operated of their own volition, tracking down outlaws and thieves and enforcing their version of justice. Some of the leaders became corrupt and attacked innocent settlers for personal gain. Eventually the governor realized the legitimacy of the colonists' plight and established courts even in the far reaches of the area. By 1771 the movement was ended.

Attakullakulla *(At-a-kula-kula)*

Attakullakulla was a Supreme Chief of the Cherokee who held the highly honorary position of Beloved Man. He helped negotiate numerous treaties and agreements with the English. Because of this, the Cherokee lost much of their land in the Southeast. He and his son, Dragging Canoe, differed in opinions and eventually split ways during the Cherokee-American wars.

Bibliography

There is a wealth of information on Colonial Carolina, but here are some of my favorites:

Edgar, Walter. *South Carolina: A History*. Columbia, SC: University of South Carolina Press, 1998.

LaCrosse, Richard B., Jr. *The Frontier Rifleman: His Arms, Clothing and Equipment During the Era of the American Revolution, 1760–1800*. Union City, TN: Pioneer Press, 1989.

Logan, John H. *A History of the Upper Country of South Carolina*. Charleston, SC: S. G. Courtenay & Co., 1859.

Moore, Peter N. *World of Toil and Strife: Community Transformation in*

Backcountry South Carolina, 1750–1805. Columbia, SC: University of South Carolina Press, 2007.

Woodmason, Charles. *The Carolina Backcountry on the Eve of the Revolution: The Journal and Writings of Charles Woodmason, Anglican Itinerant.* Chapel Hill, NC: University of North Carolina Press, 1953.

Discussion Questions

1. In chapter 1 and throughout the story, **Eleanor Morgan** resorts to a prayer she teaches her young charges: *My precious Lord; My only hope; My Saviour how I need You now.* Do you have a prayer or portion of scripture that you bring to mind regularly?

2. In chapter 2, **Molly Brooks** tells Eleanor that she'd married because her husband's "words filled me clear up with hope." Is there anyone who encourages you in such a way? How can you be an encourager like that? Who is one person you could encourage today?

3. In chapter 25, **Samuel Heath** finally realizes he's accepted God's forgiveness but has continued to condemn himself. Has there been a time in your life when you've had that same kind of battle? Why is it so hard to forgive ourselves?

4. In Chapter 29, **Standing Raven** tells Samuel he cannot straddle a river for long and expect to remain standing. Read what the Bible has to say about indecision in Matthew 6:24. When have you had a hard time making a decision between two things?

5. In chapter 38, Eleanor describes **Biz Hunter** as, "no friend she would have chosen, but Biz was an unconventional gift nonetheless." Is there a person God has placed in your life that you wouldn't have chosen to associate with yet you are now glad you know? Think about taking time to write that person a note of gratitude.

6. Colonial life in the backcountry of South Carolina involved lots of struggles. What kinds of struggles are you facing today? There is hope for those struggles, no matter how devastating. Read Nahum 1:7.

Acknowledgments

A book is written by a single person but crafted by many. My heartfelt thanks go out to my faithful critique partners: Ane Mulligan, Lisa Ludwig, Shannon McNear, Kelly Klepfer, MaryLu Tyndall, Julie Klassen, Chawna Shroeder, and Yvonne Anderson. I couldn't do this without y'all.

Writing is a solitary profession but impacted by many. I am grateful for: Annie Tipton, the editor who made this book possible; Becky Durost Fish, grammar queen extraordinaire; Laura Frantz, for Colonial insights; Darrie and Maria Nelson for the writing retreat; Donald Smith, for teaching me the mechanics of a flintlock; Hugh Lambert, Cherokee historian with super amounts of patience for questions; Luther Lyle, director and curator for the Museum of the Cherokee; Aaron Griep, my fight scene guru; Kimberli Buffaloe, for South Carolina flora and fauna wisdom; and Stephanie Gustafson, who encourages unfailingly.

And a huge shout out to all my readers. You make this crazy journey all worthwhile.

About the Author

Michelle Griep has been writing since she first discovered blank wall space and Crayolas. She seeks to glorify God in all that she writes—except for that graffiti phase she went through as a teenager. She resides in the frozen tundra of Minnesota, where she teaches history and writing classes for a local high school co-op. An Anglophile at heart, she runs off to England every chance she gets under the guise of research. Really, though, she's eating excessive amounts of scones and rambling through some castle. Keep up with her adventures at her award-winning blog "Writer Off the Leash" or visit michellegriep.com. She loves to hear from readers, so go ahead and rattle her cage.

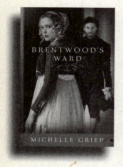

 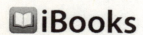